A Midnight Puzzle

Also by Gigi Pandian

A Midnight Puzzle

A Secret Staircase Mystery

Gigi Pandian

MINOTAUR BOOKS
NEW YORK

First published in the United States by Minotaur Books, an imprint of St. Martin's Publishing Group.

A MIDNIGHT PUZZLE. Copyright ©2024 by Gigi Pandian. All rights reserved. Printed in the United States of America. For information, address St. Martin's Publishing Group, 120 Broadway, New York, NY 10271.

www.minotaurbooks.com

Designed by Gabriel Guma

The Library of Congress Cataloging-in-Publication Data is available upon request.

ISBN 978-1-250-88020-8 (hardcover)
ISBN 978-1-250-88021-5 (e-book)

Our books may be purchased in bulk for promotional, educational, or business use. Please contact your local bookseller or the Macmillan Corporate and Premium Sales Department at 1-800-221-7945, extension 5442, or by email at MacmillanSpecialMarkets@macmillan.com.

First Edition: 2024

1 3 5 7 9 10 8 6 4 2

For Madeline Houpt. Thank you for being my partner in crime in turning the shadow of an idea into a worthy puzzle.

not all booby traps are created equal.

To be fair, the mechanics behind the first accident high in the hills of Hidden Creek couldn't be considered a proper booby trap. It was simply a shrewd trap disguised as an accident.

On the night a woman tumbled down the floating circular staircase, had someone deliberately damaged the penultimate step in an act of malice? At close inspection, the welded steel edge was ruptured just enough to split apart under the weight of the petite woman who had placed the ball of her foot on the red oak tread of the step.

Or was it shoddy construction by the Secret Staircase Construction crew, as the victim's husband claimed? While doctors fought to save his wife's life, he couldn't be found in the hospital's waiting room. He was busy talking to his lawyers, finding out how quickly they could draw up the paperwork to sue the small family-owned business who'd designed, built, and installed the winding staircase.

There were also whispers that the woman may have been helped on her way down with a push. Anyone who knew her husband wouldn't have been surprised to learn that was the case. Yes, he was superficially charming. But in his unguarded moments, you could see the ruthlessness that simmered just below the surface, waiting to erupt. Conveniently, he wasn't at home when the "accident" occurred. The woman now lay in a coma, so even if she knew what had caused her fall, it wasn't as if she could reveal what had happened.

But the second booby trap?

That was the one nobody saw coming.

The one resulting in murder.

The one not a soul could deny was both intentional and devious.

The one that threatened to destroy Tempest Raj's life—before it gave her the last piece of the puzzle she needed to solve the mystery that had defined her entire adult life.

PART I

☠ ☠ ☠

Midnight

Chapter 1

midnight," said Ivy. "That's it. We need to be out of here by then."

In the beads of light cast by the chandelier hanging from the gable high above, Tempest observed her friend's chipped pink nail polish, puffy pink vest, and pink work boots. The outfit was Ivy's way of remaining herself while working construction.

"We can probably finish everything if we stay until one o'clock." Tempest straightened the rumpled cloth tarp with her ruby red sneaker. "What do you say? I promise to buy you any amount of extra coffee you need tomorrow."

"I'm serious, Tempest. This job is cursed enough. I don't plan on being inside this creepy house at midnight."

"That's why you want to be out of here before then? You can't really believe this house is cursed." Tempest's long black hair swayed in the breeze that was sneaking into the room from the window they'd cracked open, and she was momentarily distracted by a shadow resembling a gnarled claw. Ivy wasn't wrong about the creepiness of being alone in the mansion on this deserted hillside street as it approached midnight.

Ivy said nothing. Her face was turned toward the section of the high ceiling they hadn't yet finished painting.

They were standing in the attic of the Whispering House, Secret Staircase Construction's current jobsite. The project at a Gothic Revival mansion built by a famed local architect had been cause for excitement at first—constructing a hidden staircase leading from the foyer to the oversize attic, restoring once-grand woodwork details that had been destroyed by termites and decades of neglect, and even building an architectural puzzle into the walls of the attic.

The mechanics of this puzzle room they were standing inside had been Tempest's biggest contribution, and one she found herself immensely proud of. The sliding puzzle panels of the attic's wainscoting would reveal a hidden door once you'd solved the puzzle. She reached out and touched the paper they'd taped in place to protect the wooden panels from dribbles of paint. With this job, Tempest felt she was finally an equal member of the team. She'd successfully transferred her skills in creating illusions to the family business.

But now? Not only were they running behind schedule because of the strange items they'd found when they'd opened up the walls, but the specter of losing the family business altogether was never far from their minds.

All because of Julian Rhodes.

The man was a bully, but he'd picked a fight with the wrong family. There was no way Tempest was going to let him ruin the small business her parents had lovingly built from nothing into a home renovation company that built magic into people's homes through architectural elements like a built-in bookcase that slid open to reveal a secret library, a reading nook accessed by stepping through a door hidden behind a portrait, or a faux fireplace that led to a playroom when you pressed bricks in the right order.

Tempest was now filling her mom's shoes as the member of the crew who thought up the most magical elements and the stories to go along with them, but she didn't yet have enough experience to know that you could—and should—say no to taking on some clients. Julian had been a difficult client from the start, but they never imagined how bad things would get. He owned the home across the street from the Whispering House and had hired Secret Staircase Construction when he learned his neighbor would be working with them. He pushed through his project plans so that his renovation at the Rhodeses' home could be completed first.

"It's creepy being in this old house after dark," Ivy said, when she finally spoke. "I know I'm supposed to think it's majestic or something, but we're right across the street from where Julian pushed Paloma down the stairs. Do you realize that was the same day we made that horrid discovery inside the walls—"

"You mean the rat's nest?" Tempest asked.

Ivy nodded. "Between that bad omen and Julian's actions, I feel like this whole dead-end street is cursed."

Tempest attempted to shake off all thoughts of the horrid man, which was difficult to do since Julian's house was the only other home on this narrow street high in the Hidden Creek hillside.

She wasn't supposed to be here tonight. Her mentor was in town from Scotland along with his assistant Brodie, but jet lag had gotten the better of him. They'd agreed to catch up tomorrow, so here she was.

She and Ivy had come to the Whispering House tonight to paint the interior walls of the upper floors of the home they were nearly done renovating. The secret staircase was complete, as were the puzzle panels and trim that hid its existence. Since coming to work for her dad's home renovation company, Tempest had learned that the proper term for a camouflaged door was a "jib" door. But the bland word stole the magic of a hidden door leading to a secret room, so she pretended not to have learned the official remodeling term. To Tempest, it would always be a hidden door, and she was sticking to it.

"I thought you didn't want to stay too late because you had to be up early," Tempest continued. "Don't tell me the fearless Ivy Youngblood has turned superstitious."

"Maybe a little bit of both?" Ivy refreshed her paint roller and stepped back onto the ladder.

A strip of painter's tape had come undone in the corner. The ribbonlike curl of blue tape swayed in the wind, causing a shadow resembling a claw. Tape. Just tape. Tempest pressed it back onto the wood. It wouldn't do to have her dad's delicate carpentry marred by frosted white paint.

Her dad didn't know they were there that night. The remaining members of the small crew didn't either. Tempest and Ivy had taken it upon themselves to finish the time-consuming cosmetic touches to lighten the load for the others. Stonemason Gideon was barely sleeping as he had his first art show to set up, but he was too responsible to take time off work until this job was done. And Darius, the owner of Secret Staircase Construction and Tempest's dad, was frazzled nearly to the breaking point by the lawsuit Julian Rhodes had filed and the mess of bad press surrounding Paloma Rhodes's unfortunate accident.

Unlike the others, Tempest and Ivy had always been night owls, so it was the least they could do to finish painting the rooms that were otherwise completed. If they hadn't been here at the Whispering House, they most likely would have been at Ivy's place watching a classic mystery movie projected onto the wall, eating freshly popped popcorn, and arguing about who was the best fictional detective from the 1930s.

Tempest and Ivy had been inseparable when they were kids before a tragedy got in the way. They had bonded over their shared love of mysteries, from Encyclopedia Brown and the

Three Investigators to Nancy Drew and Trixie Belden, and as preteens they graduated to the golden age of detective fiction. They had begun to read their way through the classic fair-play puzzle plot mystery novels of authors including Agatha Christie, Ellery Queen, and John Dickson Carr, until Tempest's Aunt Elspeth died live on stage in Edinburgh. At the age of sixteen, Tempest's happy life in an ever-changing fun house was torn apart. As was their friendship.

Tempest left for Scotland and ended up staying with her grandparents and finishing school in Edinburgh. She didn't realize Ivy was dealing with a difficult home-life situation and felt abandoned when Tempest left her for a life an ocean away. As a coping mechanism, Ivy disappeared into books. That's why a decade later, when Tempest returned home from the wreckage of her career as a stage illusionist in Las Vegas, Ivy was the most well-read person Tempest knew. But what was more important to Tempest was that they were approaching their childhood level of friendship once again.

"Could you get the window?" Ivy asked from the ladder.

Tempest stepped across the tarp to the dormer opening in the steep, sloped ceiling and pulled the wooden window frame upward.

"I meant to close it," Ivy added as the cool night air flowed into the room. "This paint is nontoxic. But the whispers of the wind are getting to me."

The house was named not for the whispers of the hillside wind but for an architectural feature on the first floor that carried sound through the length of the house. The same architect had built the town's Whispering Creek Theater, a theater that looked like a miniature cathedral that Tempest had rented for a single performance she was preparing. You had to give him credit for going all in with this Gothic style of architecture even though it was long past being popular.

The wind wasn't having the same effect on Tempest—until she turned back to the window. Before she could close it, a flash of headlights came into view. This was a dead-end street. The homeowner wasn't living here during the renovations, and Julian Rhodes had moved out of his house across the street after his wife's accident.

Who was coming to the Whispering House at midnight?

Chapter 2

A tall man with wild salt-and-pepper hair stepped out of the car. A man Tempest knew well. And one she thought was fast asleep in a guest room back at Fiddler's Folly. Nicodemus the Necromancer.

That was only his stage name, of course. Nicodemus was not actually someone who could command the dead. He was a Scottish actor who'd built a career performing a classic style of stage magic for the past fifty years and was now getting ready to retire after one last tour, which would begin in a few days. With his pointed goatee and mercurial gaze, he did rather resemble a devil, or at least a stylish demon. Tempest had known him since she was a child, but she couldn't seem to remember him looking any other way.

Ivy assured Tempest she could finish the last bit of the attic on her own, so Tempest headed down the two flights of stairs to meet Nicodemus at the front door.

"Couldn't sleep?" Tempest closed the heavy wooden door behind him.

"I could ask the same thing. I thought you slept the hours of the civilized world now."

Tempest shrugged. "These are the hours I've kept my entire adult life. It's hard to change."

"You're in your twenties, lass. There's plenty of time for you to change into anything you want to."

He wasn't wrong. She was simply stuck. Whenever she felt like she was moving forward, something held her back from fully embracing the change. From embracing *life*. She knew what it was. And what she needed to do. But she didn't know how to get there. "I didn't mean to abandon you at the house. You said you were tired and going to bed."

"I'm knackered, so I tried to sleep. Unfortunately, my body insists it's morning." He stroked his goatee. "Why are your arms covered in white paint? Are you a performance artist now?"

"Very funny." Tempest was well aware that she was perhaps the world's worst house painter. That didn't bother her. Her strengths lay elsewhere. Ivy had done 90 percent of the work tonight but had managed to remain paint-free aside from a few streaks on her fingers. Tempest was only on site to help as needed. "How'd you know where to find me, anyway?"

"I knew you and your da were behind schedule renovating the Whispering House. It's not difficult to find the address of a house that has its own name. It's far more challenging to find a restaurant or even a pub that's open at this hour in Hidden Creek, but I finally found one not far from here. Can I treat you and Ivy to a midnight snack? I'm desperately in need of breakfast and would love some company."

"I can do even better than that," said Tempest, turning toward the kitchen. "Follow me. Ivy is just wrapping up painting the attic, but our client Lenore insisted we help ourselves to the food she left in the fridge while we're finishing the house. She's been stealthily restocking while we're not here. What can I fix you? Looks like we've got the ingredients for French toast." She held a loaf of fresh sourdough bread in her hand that definitely hadn't been there the previous day.

"If you're cooking, I'll stick to toast." He plucked a bottle of strawberry preserves from the door of the fridge.

"I choose not to be offended by that comment." She *wasn't* insulted. She didn't actually know how to make French toast, but how hard could it be? She'd spent the last decade honing her skills to become one of the world's greatest illusionists at the expense of pretty much everything else. Even though things hadn't turned out as she'd expected, she wouldn't trade the skills she'd gained both creating and seeing through misdirection to know how to cook a midnight snack.

Tempest had moved back home after her career as a stage illusionist in Las Vegas had crashed and burned the previous summer. Tempest Raj. Twenty-six years old and living in her childhood bedroom while she was learning the ropes at her dad's company. It was solely his now that Tempest's mom was gone. Even though she'd lost the career she *thought* she wanted, she was surprised by how much she loved her new job. Creating architectural misdirection wasn't so different from crafting stage illusions. Her bedroom even came with its own secret staircase.

Like her mom before her, Tempest had an eye for how to elevate mundane objects into magical experiences. Her dad was a good general contractor and a brilliant carpenter, but his wooden creations were best when he executed other people's visions. Tempest was skilled at imagining what *could* be. Her new life creating architectural magic wasn't the job she'd envisioned for herself, but it was quickly becoming more perfect than she ever imagined.

Tempest sliced two lopsided pieces of bread and popped them into the toaster. You'd think with how precisely she could shuffle a deck of cards that she could cut a decent slice of bread. You'd be wrong.

Nicodemus twirled what looked like a folded greeting card of thick kraft paper in his fingertips. He pulled it open, revealing an intricate pop-up of a Gothic cathedral, its paper spires so detailed that vaulted windows appeared in the pinnacles. A top hat made of black cardstock paper sat in the open space of an arched main door. This wasn't a cathedral. It was the Whispering Creek Theater.

"My theater." Tempest took the card and wondered how long it had taken him to cut, fold, and glue. This wasn't one of his most ornate paper designs, even considering the delicate spires, and the edges weren't as crisp as she remembered some of his old pop-ups, but it did the trick to make her smile. Paper people and sets had more freedom than real ones, Nicodemus had always said, and pop-up paper art creations created their own magic.

"I wish you wouldn't think of it like that."

"You still don't approve of me renting it?"

"It's an exquisite building. Since you're taking me there tomorrow, this is what came to mind when I couldn't sleep. Though I still don't think it's a good idea to rent the theater where Emma—"

"Don't." Tempest slammed the card shut and her smile vanished. She squeezed the card even harder in her hands, but it popped back open, this time revealing the stage *inside* the Gothic exterior. She blinked at the paper theater in her hands—a double pop-up, with this layer hidden beneath the last. Red paper curtains were drawn back, revealing a stage, and a row of metallic silver stage lights swayed above the main attraction: two paper people center stage.

A sleight and a misdirect. Just like a magic trick. It was his specialty, and he'd expressed his disapproval just enough to get her to activate the magical theater he wanted her to see.

She looked more closely at the deceptive pop-up card. One of the paper people on the stage had long wavy hair that flowed almost to her waist, and she was posed with her muscular arms outstretched, as if about to begin spinning like her stage persona, The Tempest. What she hadn't noticed right away was that the flat paper shadows of the two people weren't mirror images. In Tempest's shadow, her hair billowed wildly as if caught in a fierce storm, and in the man's shadow, a top hat on the stage's trapdoor rested squarely on the shadow's head. Their shadow selves.

"Are you going to do more with your paper art in your retirement?" Tempest asked.

He snorted. "The whole point of retirement is to relax. These paper creations help me imagine the possibilities of what I can create on stage. But being on the stage is what's relaxing."

Tempest loved what the stage could do and the joy it could bring so many people, but she'd never call it *relaxing*. It was both exhilarating and exhausting. Never easy. "Then why are you even retiring? Why—"

He snatched the card from her fingertips just as the bread popped up from the toaster, only slightly burnt, and Ivy stepped into the kitchen.

"Good to see you, Nicodemus," Ivy said hastily, "but pleasantries will have to wait. I'm off. Tempest, the attic is done and the can of paint is sealed, but I didn't move the tarp. It can stay where it is. I'll get it in the morning when I paint the last room. Bye!"

Ivy barely took a breath during her speedy monologue, and she was out the door before either Tempest or Nicodemus could react.

"I don't remember your friend being so jittery," said Nicodemus as Tempest's phone began ringing.

Strange. Who would be calling her at midnight? Twelve o'clock wasn't remotely late for the performer's schedule she was used to, but it wasn't a time she usually received unannounced calls. She didn't recognize the number, so she should have let the midnight caller go to voice mail. But curiosity got the better of her, as it often did.

"Where *are* you?" demanded the angry male voice.

She would have hung up on instinct because of the vitriol in the voice, but she recognized it.

"Julian?" She was so surprised that she forgot to call him Mr. Rhodes. She'd been attempting to be deferential to placate the man who could easily ruin her life, but clearly, she was failing. It wasn't in her nature to bow down to bullies.

"Who else would it be?" he snapped.

Julian Rhodes. The man who could easily destroy Secret Staircase Construction. It was more than a nuisance lawsuit brought by an unhappy customer. The false accusation was big enough that if Julian won, the family business would be ruined.

They couldn't catch a break. After the murder at the housewarming party at a previous jobsite, they'd barely had time to regroup after Tempest caught the killer. They'd been excited about two new jobs at local historic homes—until Julian Rhodes attempted to kill his wife. After purposely breaking one of the top steps of the circular stairs, he was trying to blame his misdeed on the supposedly shoddy workmanship of the Secret Staircase crew. It wasn't true, but Julian Rhodes was the type of man who got away with his lies.

"It's two minutes past midnight." Julian spat out the words. "You said you wouldn't leave me waiting. Well, you did."

"I'm not supposed to be talking to—"

"Obviously. I don't like using our cell phones either. Oh." His voice shifted. It wasn't exactly friendly, but it was at least civil. "The door. Are you already inside the theater?"

"The theater?"

"I didn't see your car, so I assumed you weren't here. That was smart not to leave your car visible."

"I'm not—"

"Fine. I'll wait inside for you to get here."

"Julian. Listen to me." Tempest meant to sound calm yet forceful, but the words came out more frantic than she'd intended. Something odd was going on, and she didn't like it one bit. "Don't you dare go inside my theater. I don't know what you think—"

The line went dead. She stared at the phone.

"What was that about?" Nicodemus asked.

"I don't know." Tempest was already reaching for the sweater she'd left on a stool next to the kitchen island. She pulled it over her white T-shirt, not worrying about her paint-stained arms, and extricated her hair. "But I have a feeling it's something very bad."

"Where are you going?"

"To the theater."

"Tempest. It's midnight."

"I know." Tempest swallowed hard. Nothing good happened at the Whispering Creek Theater at midnight.

"That's where . . ." He let his words trail off.

Tempest raised an eyebrow. "Don't tell me you're superstitious, like Ivy."

He smiled. It was not a sweet smile. Her septuagenarian mentor was incapable of being "sweet." Macabre. Mysterious. Mischievous. Yes to all three. That's why he was far better as Nicodemus the Necromancer than playing bit parts for the BBC, which was how he got his start. He'd perfected his ghoulish stage smile performing with his first magician's assistant, the Cat of Nine Lives, who he raised from the dead each night. But right now, there was genuine concern in that smile, and Tempest couldn't stand it. She didn't need to be pitied for the past he was alluding to, or protected in the present.

Sensing that the piteous smile was too much, Nicodemus cleared his throat and moved on. "You said the name Julian.

Please don't tell me that was Julian Rhodes. The man is a *murderer*. Or at least an attempted one."

"One who's messing with my theater." Tempest grabbed her car key. "Are you coming?"

"I really don't think you should—"

"I'm going with or without you. If he's broken into the theater and messed with my notebooks or props, we can use that against him and his lawsuit."

Tempest didn't consider herself superstitious. But as she felt the key press into her palm and glanced at her bracelet filled with silver charms related to stage magic and folklore, one thought ran through her mind. The last time the Whispering Creek Theater had held a midnight show, someone Tempest loved dearly had vanished, never to be seen again.

Chapter 3

J ulian knows my family history," Tempest said as she and Nicodemus got into her jeep. "He's probably trying to mess with my head, show that we're unstable in the dirt he's gathering to strengthen his lawsuit against Secret Staircase Construction. He knows the Whispering Creek Theater is where my mom vanished. I'm sure he also knows about its supposedly haunted history. I need to show him he can't rattle me." She started the engine and glared at the empty house across the street where Julian had sabotaged the stairs.

Her silver charm bracelet, the only piece of jewelry she wore, slipped down her wrist as she turned the steering wheel on the steep, dead-end street.

"You're *certain* the voice was that of the man who's suing your dad?" Nicodemus asked.

Tempest took her eyes off the dark road for half a second to see what his expression was. "You're serious? You think it was someone else, like a deranged fan who's luring me to a fate worse than death?"

"We both know better than to assume anything."

The headlights shone on a steep hillside curve and she gripped the steering wheel tightly. "It was him."

"Asking you to meet him at the haunted theater where Emma vanished, at midnight. Julian Rhodes was making a business decision to sue you. But this? This seems so . . . personal. Why-ever that wretched man is luring you to the theater, it's *nae* good. It's not too late to turn 'round."

"I'm afraid you've played the part of Nicodemus the Necro-mancer for so long that you talk like a spooky character even when you're not on stage." It didn't help that it was midnight in a sleepy city that was deserted at this time of night.

He barked a laugh, but it sounded forced. "I've seen many things in my long and unusual—"

"In your long and unusual life? I've heard you give that speech before. On stage."

"Tempest, I'm serious. I don't like this. You don't know what that man is up to. But you *do* know what he's capable of. His murderous intentions—"

"Paloma Rhodes isn't dead, so he's not that clever." Tempest felt for Paloma, who'd ended up in a coma, and hated that her own family had been pulled into Julian's murderous plan.

It was easy to see what Julian had attempted to do. He had wanted to get rid of his wife *and* get a large cash settlement. He wouldn't be able to prove that Secret Staircase Construc-tion had produced a shoddy step, because it wasn't true, but the small family business didn't have enough money to de-fend such a huge case. They were insured, but that insurance didn't pay for a lawyer nearly as skilled—or as ruthless—as the team Julian had hired. Tempest's dad was already considering a settlement, which could be less costly than court fees. That was what they suspected was the real purpose behind Julian Rhodes's lawsuits: by hiring an intimidating team of lawyers and assuring the defendants that they'd dig up embarrassing personal information, Julian could strong-arm a payout up front. He'd already begun poking into their private lives to give them a taste of what he was capable of.

"I've already acknowledged he's a would-be murderer," Nicodemus granted. "But it really is splitting hairs. He meant to kill her. That's what counts."

"And he had enough presence of mind while his wife lay unconscious at the bottom of the staircase to make it look as if the step had snapped from our improper work before calling an ambulance."

"I assumed he thought she was already dead," Nicodemus said.

"How can you be so calm?" It was all Tempest could do to stay focused on the road. Her pulse and breathing were both steady when she was on stage. Real life was far more challenging.

"Why do you suspect I'm calm?" Nicodemus ran a hand through his wild gray hair. "I'm sure my blood pressure is double what it should be right now."

A stone cathedral-like structure came into view. The signage had been removed years ago after being destroyed by a rainstorm, so if you didn't know this was the Whispering Creek Theater, you'd think it was an abandoned church. The stone structure was built in the Gothic tradition with spires, pinnacles, and an oversize vaulted wooden door as the main entrance. It wasn't as impressive as having a miniature Notre Dame cathedral on the outskirts of town, as there were no stained-glass windows and no ornately carved stone saints or kings on the façade, but it did boast two gargoyle drain spouts.

The old theater had existed for more than a century of Hidden Creek history before closing several years ago. Because of an accidental death not long after its opening, there had always been rumors that it was haunted. Then after Emma Raj disappeared under suspicious circumstances, the theater was shuttered for a short time during the investigation. An ill-fated reopening followed, with theater casts reporting inexplicable ghostly sightings. A more modern theater in a bigger city nearby featured more comfortable seats, additional bathrooms, and a bigger lobby bar, so for the past few years, the theater had sat empty—until Tempest rented it.

Tempest pulled into the nearly empty lot. Tonight, there was something ominous about the familiar theater, as if it was hiding something.

"There's his car." Tempest parked near Julian's car and hopped out of the jeep. When her feet touched the ground, Nicodemus was already at her side. "You're freaking me out, Nicky."

"Tempest." His voice was a whisper. "Something is very wrong here."

"I know. There should be two of those old-fashioned streetlamps for light. Only one of them is on." That's what had given her the impression that the Gothic building was hiding. She tried to remember if it had been broken the last time she'd been there in the evening. She hadn't been there at all for a couple of days while she had been busy preparing for Nicodemus's visit and helping finish the renovation.

"I wonder . . ." Nicodemus stroked his goatee, looking even more devilish in the dim light.

"It's just me, Nicky. You're not on stage. You don't have to trail off with the hint of a creepy question to entice your audience."

"You said the theater was in perfect working order when you rented it."

"They did a safety check and fixed anything broken as a condition of the lease."

"Why, then," said Nicodemus in a stage whisper, "is that light broken?"

In polite company, Tempest was always the most dramatic one. In her circle of friends, though, she didn't take that top honor. "Let's just see what Julian is doing here."

Halfway across the parking lot, she realized Nicodemus hadn't been dramatic *enough*. She'd seen that tall, arched door in the Gothic tradition hundreds of times, but never as it was right now. Julian Rhodes stood at the door with his back to them, shrouded in shadows. His posture was all wrong. Unnatural. His body was slumped, yet he hadn't fallen.

"Impossible," Nicodemus whispered. "How on earth . . . ?"

That's when Tempest saw it. A gleam of metal shone in the dim light. A thick blade was sticking out of the door—and through Julian's chest.

"Julian?" Tempest called out. "Mr. Rhodes?"

He didn't answer. He didn't move. He couldn't. This was no longer a living, breathing, angry Julian Rhodes. It was his dead body, held upright by the sword's blade.

Chapter 4

This can't be real." Tempest took two deep breaths to steady her nerves, then stepped closer with Nicodemus by her side. "Julian is messing with me. It's got to be a dummy."

"That's no dummy," Nicodemus whispered. "It's a real body."

A body. Of a man she knew. Who died in the twenty-first century by being run through with a sword? And where had the hilt of the sword gone? It was only the tip of a metal blade that showed. Had it broken off with the force of pinning him to the door?

As she looked away, something else on the door caught her eye. A piece of masking tape at eye level, holding a ripped scrap of paper. The rest of whatever had been there was missing.

Tempest's hands shook as she called 9-1-1. Julian Rhodes had been a nasty man, but that didn't mean she was happy about finding his dead body.

"What are you doing?" Nicodemus pulled her phone from her hands before she could complete the call.

"Calling the police." Tempest glared at him and reached for the phone, which he kept out of reach. "At least I was until you took my phone."

"We need to leave."

"What are you talking about?" She gave a start at a sound in the distance. A car. Was the murderer fleeing?

"He's dead, Tempest. There's nothing you can do for him."

"We can't leave a crime scene."

"We shouldn't be here in the first place. Especially you. He's *suing* you. Do you have any idea how this will look?" He handed the phone back to her.

The faint sound of a car wasn't fading away. It was growing louder. Headlights flashed across the front of the theater, and a police car came to a stop a few yards away from them. A uniformed officer stepped out. Tempest relaxed at the sight of him. She knew the tall, gangly junior officer. She also remembered he hadn't reacted well the first time he'd seen a dead body.

"Tempest Raj?"

"Officer Quinn."

"We got a call about someone screaming." Quinn's Adam's apple bobbed up and down prominently in the stark shadows of light and dark from the one lamp. "I'm glad it's just you and a prop. Might be best for you to keep the loud parts of your rehearsal indoors at this time of night." He gave her a nervous smile she didn't return.

Officer Quinn couldn't have been much older than Tempest. Definitely still in his twenties. She couldn't blame him for not being world-weary and jaded yet.

"It's real," Tempest said, feeling like her voice was outside of herself. She had to hold it together. "I think. We just got here and found him like this. With that sword sticking out of his chest. I was starting to call 9-1-1 when you pulled up."

The smile fell away. Officer Quinn's gaze swept over the whole scene in a matter of seconds. He might have been new enough to hold false optimism, but he was competent. More than competent, she realized. In less than a minute, he'd checked the body for vitals, moved Tempest and Nicodemus away from the crime scene, instructed them not to move from where they stood next to his police car, and made an urgent call on his walkie-talkie.

"Backup will be here in a minute," Quinn said, pointing his flashlight around the perimeter of the dark lot. A nocturnal animal fled as the beam of light hit the hillside trees beyond the lot. "What do I need to know right now?"

Tempest was grateful he hadn't immediately ushered the two of them into handcuffs and the back seat of the patrol car. What *did* she know? Julian had been about to open the door of the theater when he'd disconnected their call, so he must have been killed soon after he hung up.

"The person who killed him is long gone," she said. "Julian Rhodes called me a few minutes after midnight from right there, and it took me nearly ten minutes to drive here, so the person who killed him had plenty of time to flee."

Quinn's shoulders relaxed, then immediately tensed again. "Rhodes. Isn't that the name of the man suing your dad? This isn't an actor?" For the first time since he had arrived, his voice had an edge to it.

Here it was. *Suspicion.*

"You two didn't touch anything, did you?"

"We did not," Nicodemus answered.

"Your name?"

"Nicodemus. Just Nicodemus." He handed the officer a business card with his contact information. She hoped it was the card where the ink would still be visible the next day.

"A relation of Ms. Raj?"

Tempest didn't think Officer Quinn had met her Scottish grandmother during the previous investigation, but of course he knew about her familial connection to Scotland. Just like she knew of his reputation for having a poor choice in girlfriends, the last of whom had wrecked his new car. It was a small town. Plus, her grandfather was an unabashed busybody.

"An old friend of the family," said Nicodemus. "I was with Tempest the entire time. I can vouch for her. Provide an alibi I believe is the correct term."

"She doesn't need—I meant to say, a team including a detective will be here shortly. Any second now." Quinn shone his powerful flashlight toward the theater's low, ornamental towers. "I know about this place. I used to come to shows here during high school. I was away in college when your mom disappeared here. By the time I came back a few years ago, it was shut down for good. But that led to other problems . . ." He continued to shine his flashlight around nervously. "Students would dare each other to break inside and leave a ghost light burning." His Adam's apple bounced up and down. "Do you know what that is?"

Tempest nodded. "The tradition of leaving a single light burning in a theater so its ghosts won't be left all alone in the dark."

She wasn't surprised. She hadn't heard about break-ins at the Whispering Creek Theater while it was abandoned, but it made sense. It was an old Gothic building on the outskirts of town that resembled a mini cathedral and had a macabre history of tragic deaths and disappearances. It was practically a flashing neon sign beckoning bored teenagers to take a look inside. At least the miniature towers were only as high as the attic of the Whispering House, and the ornamental windows weren't big enough for a person to fit through, so it wasn't like they could dare each other to do anything too dangerous.

Had Julian found some kids inside tonight? She could easily imagine them kicking his condescending face or defending themselves with pepper spray, but stabbing him with a sword?

Sirens screamed, and an ambulance came into view a moment later, pulling up beside them. Tempest and Officer Quinn didn't have to do much to explain the situation, and two men hurried toward the body to confirm the victim was beyond saving.

Besides the sound of their shoes shuffling on the asphalt and the frogs in the nearby hidden creek, all was silent, which was how Tempest was able to hear what happened next.

She knew that sound. She'd created many illusions that relied on the same principle. The snap of a metal brace and the coil of a metal spring, previously under pressure, *releasing.*

"Get away from the door!" Tempest shouted as she ran forward.

But it was too late.

A blade sprang from within the wooden beams of the door.

"What the—" The larger of the two paramedics stumbled backward from Julian's body as a sharp blade sliced into his shoulder.

That's why they hadn't seen the hilt of the sword that had killed Julian Rhodes. It hadn't broken off. *It was never there in the first place.* The blade had sprung from the thick wooden door itself. And now there was a *second* one.

"A booby trap," Tempest whispered. "A booby trap killed Julian Rhodes."

Chapter 5

The unwounded paramedic pulled his injured partner away from the booby-trapped vaulted door. The second blade wasn't as big as the sword that had killed Julian, and luckily it had only nicked the side of his shoulder.

There was something about that knife that triggered a memory, but everything was happening so quickly that it was all Tempest could do to focus on what people were shouting in the semidarkness.

"Get back!" the injured paramedic yelled. "I can't see where they're hiding. It's too dark."

"Suspect at the Whispering Creek Theater is at large," Quinn's shaking voice shouted into his radio as he motioned for Tempest and Nicodemus to get back to her jeep. "Armed with knives. When is that backup getting here?" He turned to Tempest. "How many back and side doors? And didn't I tell you to stay back?"

"One back door and an emergency exit on the right, but they're not still here. It's a—"

"Did you get that?" Quinn said to whomever he was speaking to. "Two doors besides the main entrance I'm looking at."

"It's a—" Tempest tried again to explain that it was a booby trap. And not a good one. She'd heard the mechanism activate. But Quinn wouldn't let her finish her thought.

"Suspect is inside the theater with two doors besides the one I can see." Quinn spoke over her into his walkie-talkie before turning to Tempest. "You have the keys?"

Tempest slipped the keys off her key chain and handed them to him. "Here, but—"

"Now get back. Lock yourself inside your car. Go."

"We're going." Nicodemus took Tempest's hand and pulled her back toward the car.

"You don't believe me either about it being a booby trap?" Tempest planted her sneakers firmly on the ground and refused to be dragged away.

"Oh, I do. I simply think a booby trap doesn't in itself mean the killer isn't still here." His hand shook in hers. "Please, Tempest. I *dinnae* like what's going on here one bit."

He was right. Now Tempest was the one who rushed them away from the theater.

A patrol car raced into the parking lot, followed by an unmarked car. From the relative safety of the locked jeep, Tempest and Nicodemus watched as the man from the unmarked car quickly conferred with Quinn and the two other officers who'd arrived, and the uniformed officers moved quickly to circle the exterior of the theater. Tempest didn't know the two officers who'd just arrived, but she recognized the plainclothes detective. Detective Rinehart. She'd last seen him when he'd arrested someone close to her earlier that year.

Dread knotted her stomach as his gaze turned from the theater to Tempest, but he didn't approach. Instead, he joined his team to search for the suspect they believed to be inside.

"I should tell them to watch out for more booby traps." Tempest reached for the door handle, but Nicodemus stopped her.

"They're trained. They're expecting knives to be thrust at them through doors now. They can handle it."

"I should at least tell them about the Shadow Stage." She left her hand on the door handle. "That would be a good place for someone to hide if the person who set the booby traps is still here. The door is hidden."

"Tempest. I know you hate sitting on the sidelines. Let them do their job. They can handle the Shadow Stage."

The old theater's second stage got its eerie nickname long before Tempest was born, but its nickname had been mostly forgotten until five years ago. The Shadow Stage was the name of the secret stage that had been rediscovered behind the main theater. A full duplicate of the stage, hidden *behind* it and built on the back of a revolving platform.

The hidden stage had remained a secret because of some clever architectural misdirection. Everyone who visited the theater knew about its "hallway-to-nowhere"—a twisting hall along the side of the lobby angled like a labyrinth—as a quirky feature of the lobby during the intermission. It's architecture was part of the performance. But when the authorities ripped apart much of the theater interior in their search for the woman who'd vanished on stage five years ago, they found that it was far more than a quirky architectural anomaly—they discovered a cleverly hidden door in the wall. A door that led to the Shadow Stage.

The Shadow Stage was a badly kept secret during the initial days of the Whispering Creek Theater. The whole stage, including both sides of the stage, rotated like a lazy Susan, enabling incredibly intricate set changes. It worked well until a stagehand was crushed to death by the gears that rotated the stage. That's when the first rumors of a haunted theater began. The Shadow Stage was no longer used after that tragedy, nearly a century ago.

The entrance to the Shadow Stage was hidden so that only the cast and crew could find it, but it was boarded over after the tragedy and had gone unused for so long that everyone had forgotten about it—until Tempest's mom used the theater for her final performance.

From the back of the parking lot, Tempest focused on the theater façade as the police continued to search for the killer she was convinced was long gone. Moonlight mixed with the light from the sole streetlamp cast an eerie glow over the old stone building. A fox hovered on the edge of the parking lot where it met the lush greenery of the steep hills, not quite setting foot on the asphalt, but clearly intrigued by the strange people on his hillside.

She stole a glance at Nicodemus. He'd removed a few sheets of cardstock paper and a pair of delicate scissors from his inner jacket pocket.

"Need something to calm my nerves," he said, not looking up from the thick black paper he was snipping. Though the movements were confident, Tempest caught the slight tremor in his hands. He wasn't handling the situation any better than she was.

The shadows of the recessed areas of the stones grew more ominous as the search stretched on. Tempest was usually good at keeping time, but she lost all sense of it as they waited for the full search of the area to conclude. The police didn't drag anyone from the theater or surrounding area, and when the crime scene team arrived and cordoned off the area around Julian's body, a weary Rinehart asked them to accompany him to the station to give witness statements.

Hidden Creek police station wasn't like the kind you see on television shows. Even in the dead of night, it had a cozy charm.

Which made sense given that it was located in an old Victorian-era house. All the buildings in the civic center were like that. Periodically, there was talk of modernizing the buildings, but the complex had such charm that the city council never approved the ideas.

Nicodemus went with Officer Quinn to give his statement and Tempest stayed with Detective Rinehart. Before giving him a statement, she insisted on knowing what they'd found.

"You know that's not how this works," Rinehart said. He was dressed smartly in a tailored charcoal-gray suit, and his dark eyes were as attentive as ever. "But you already know more than you should, since we had to act in the moment to conduct our search." He paused and rubbed his eyes. "The back door was crudely forced. That's how they got inside without Mr. Rhodes noticing anything was amiss. Preliminary estimates put the time of death before you and Officer Quinn arrived on the scene. The perpetrator had time to get away before anyone arrived. That doesn't explain how they were able to stab Mr. Mason."

"The paramedic? I tried to explain to him and Officer Quinn. It was a booby trap. That's why none of us saw anyone come out of that theater. And why you didn't find anyone on your search."

His chair squeaked as he sat back and appraised her. That was the thing Tempest remembered most about him. Those intense, birdlike eyes. His clothing told her he was a man who cared about appearances, but his eyes told her he observed more than you thought.

"Why do you say that?" he asked.

She could have asked why they hadn't listened to her when she tried to explain this hours ago. But she didn't. She wasn't being treated as a suspect, so she could have explained how, as a former stage magician, she knew all about creating mechanical devices, including what they sounded like when they sprang. But it wasn't herself she was worried about. She wasn't the only one who knew about building mechanical devices that could be considered booby traps. It was knowledge possessed by her dad, her grandfather, Nicodemus, and the whole Secret Staircase Construction crew—in other words, nearly everyone important in her life. Only her artist grandmother didn't know how to build mechanical devices. If you didn't count the complexities of easels that could withstand painting outdoors in inclement Scottish weather.

"I thought I heard the sound of a metal spring," she said instead. "Like a jack-in-the-box."

He nodded and scribbled a note. "We'll look into it. Now let's go through what happened tonight once more."

She went over everything she'd seen as quickly as she could, so she could stop reliving it. Her thoughts kept returning to her mom, since the murder had taken place at the theater where her mom had vanished.

"We're just about done with your statement," Rinehart said after asking her to repeat it a second time. "There's just one thing I don't understand. Why did you ask Mr. Rhodes to meet you here?"

Tempest tensed. Was this more than a witness statement? Should she call Vanessa right then? But if she called an attorney, there would be even more legal bills. And she really didn't have anything to hide. She hadn't called Julian. There would be records that showed that.

"He said that on the phone when he called me," she said, "but I didn't call him. The phone records will show that. I didn't—"

"I'm not talking about the phone. You left him a note on the door to come inside." He held up a note and read the three words. "*Come inside, Tempest.*"

She stared at the note. *It was her handwriting.*

There was no mistaking her combination of looped and blocky handwriting. Her writing was neater than that of many of her peers, and distinctive. Half cursive, which her mom had insisted she learn, and half block letters, because her dad thought cursive was a foolish pursuit and that people should write in a way that was clear to everyone.

Come inside, Tempest.

It could be read as an invitation. That's why Julian had tried to go inside the theater. *Her words had been used to lure him to his death.*

"The left and bottom edges are ripped," she said with a quiver in her voice. "Where did you get this?"

"It's your handwriting?"

"Yes, but I didn't write it for him. The cream paper. The torn edges. This must be from one of my notebooks."

"You write invitations inside your notebooks?"

"It's not an invitation. It's part of a script or stage direction."

Rinehart frowned as a sharp rap sounded on the door. "I'll be right back."

"Can I see—"

"No." He turned and left the room, taking the note with him.

Tempest had driven to the police station in her own jeep. Detective Rinehart couldn't really think she was a suspect or he wouldn't have allowed that. Right? She stood and stretched her legs, but there wasn't space in the small room to do much more than that. She wasn't claustrophobic in the least, but she preferred larger spaces where she had room to move her body. Especially when presented with a note that was used to lure a man to his death.

Rinehart returned five minutes later, looking simultaneously less angry but more worried. "You can go home," he said simply.

"That's it?"

"We know who we're looking for now."

"You do? Who—?"

"I'm sorry you had to see that tonight." He pinched the bridge of his nose, looking tired. "Go home. Get some rest. Mr. Nicodemus is in the waiting room already."

It was clear he wasn't going to say any more. But who did he think had killed Julian Rhodes?

Chapter 6

Back at Fiddler's Folly, Tempest and Nicodemus made sure not to wake anyone as they walked from the driveway to the main house. Her dad and Nicodemus's assistant were asleep in the house, her grandparents were in the tree house in-law unit farther up the hillside, and her lop-eared rabbit Abra, who was more than capable of making a racket with his large feet if disturbed, was in his hutch in the half-built tower with the words Secret Fort etched into the stone.

Fiddler's Folly was far less grand than you'd expect from its regal-sounding name. This was no ancestral home, but a hodgepodge of whimsical rooms built by Secret Staircase Construction, the home renovation company founded by Tempest's carpenter dad and stage magician mom. The idea was never to compete with larger companies but rather to fill a niche that appealed to both of them. Starting nearly three decades ago, Tempest's parents, Darius and Emma, began experimenting on their own home, expanding the small, single-story bungalow on a steep hillside of Hidden Creek, California, into a maze of secret staircases and disguised rooms that weren't what you'd guess from the outside. They gave their quirky home a name to match.

Darius got his general contractor's license when he and his wife formed Secret Staircase Construction. He was never a good businessperson, as he prioritized people over profits. Ivy, Gideon, and Tempest were all part-time employees, and none of them had skills that were an exact fit for what would have made sense for a home renovation company. Ivy was a welder who was studying to become a librarian. Gideon was a stonemason who hoped to become a sculptor. There was also part-time employee Victor Castillo. Victor had worked as a structural engineer at a high-pressure job at an architectural firm. After reaching burnout, he retired early to focus on building his dream home, and worked only at the start of big Secret Staircase Construction jobs. The connecting thread was creativity, and all of them had learned more general skills. Nobody was above doing any job, however mundane, and everyone worked together to make each Secret Staircase Construction project unique for their clients. They were a hodgepodge of people who got along like family, so despite their patchwork skills, it worked.

Dawn would break shortly, but in the darkness, security lights had clicked on as soon as they drove through the front gate. Tempest thought it was overkill to install the lights, but her dad had insisted on them after everything that had happened.

Tempest unlocked the front door to the main house and promptly crashed into a rail-thin man with cavernous features. Not the type of person who was fun to run into while her heart was already racing from the night she'd had.

"What are you lot up to?" Brodie's deep-set gray eyes bore into her. Nicodemus's right-hand man was staying in the smaller of the two guest rooms in the main house. There was nothing odd about him being awake before dawn—he had jet lag like Nicodemus—but why was he on his way outside at this hour?

Impossibly tall and thin, Englishman Brodie Frost was the kind of tall that made a person stoop when they walked through a door, and so lean he resembled a stalk of wheat that might blow over in a gust of wind. His distinctive physical features inspired a director to cast him as Ichabod Crane in a theatrical production of *The Legend of Sleepy Hollow* many years ago, after which other "character actor" roles followed. That's how he and Nicodemus first met, when Nicodemus still took the odd acting job to finance new illusions he was experimenting with but not yet using.

"Unexpected night," Nicodemus answered. "Do you think it's too late for a pint?"

"Just what kind of night did you two have?" Brodie scratched the stubble on his sunken cheek. His spiky hair, perfect for the roles he played on stage, stood on end.

"Let's make coffee," Tempest suggested. It would be bad coffee (she didn't know how to make any other kind), but she desperately needed a cup. Or four.

"That's where I'm off to," Brodie said. "Sun's nearly up. Your grandfather saw my light on from the tree house deck. Said he'd been up for hours and that he had both coffee and breakfast ready. I take it this has something to do with why Darius left during the night as well?"

"My dad's not here?" She was so frazzled that she hadn't even noticed her dad's truck was gone. She'd planned on telling her dad and grandparents everything once she arrived home, but Rinehart must have called them. She both loved and hated having returned to a small town. "We'll explain everything just as soon as we have coffee."

Brodie gave a single nod, ducked his head to pass through the front door, and glided onto the path leading up the hillside to the tree house. He didn't make a sound, even on the uneven flagstone that always crunched when it tilted underfoot. If it hadn't been for the murder, Tempest would have known it was simply that Brodie had worked in the theater for so long that his footfalls were graceful and silent. But right then, Tempest was not amused. She could have sworn he was floating like a ghost. Brodie gave them a backward glance before continuing up the hillside.

☠ ☠ ☠

"I can't believe that horrible man is dead." Grandpa Ash set a hearty platter of food on the tree house deck's dining table.

"And killed by a booby trap." Tempest shifted to move into a narrow ray of early morning sunshine on the deck.

"The authorities got inside the back door quickly to search for their invisible killer," Nicodemus added. "But they didn't find anyone."

Tempest had never seen Nicodemus looking so wretched. He avoided looking at the breakfast spread of food Tempest's grandfather had cooked for them to restore their energy after their harrowing night. She wondered if it was the first time Nicodemus had seen a dead body. He'd built his act on a Halloween-style fantasy of a conjuror who could control the dead, but it was a PG-rated type of horror.

The dawn sunlight filtered through the hillside trees, shining more brightly on the pastries on the outdoor dining table nestled next to an oak tree. Ash must've been up most of the night baking after he heard what had happened. There were blackberry scones, fluffy rice idli, and chocolate-filled empanadas—a mix of all the cultural traditions of the inhabitants of the house. The bounty made Tempest smile—until the light hitting the metallic platter made her tense. It reminded her of the blade she'd seen at the theater shortly after midnight.

"Eat," said Ash. Tempest's grandfather would never let anyone go hungry. Ashok Raj had been born in South India eighty years ago into a culture that took communal food very seriously. He adjusted the fedora resting on his bald head as he frowned at the people sitting at his dining table but not eating.

"Well, if none of you lot are digging in." Brodie shrugged and helped himself to a plate with a sampling of everything, temporarily averting the possibility of Grandpa Ash's head exploding at the sight of untouched food.

"Where did my dad take off to?" Tempest had expected him to be there waiting to hear how she was, like her grandparents were.

"He woke up the lawyer in the Julian Rhodes civil case," Morag said.

Tempest glanced toward the rising sun. "It's barely six o'clock in the morning."

"When has that ever stopped your headstrong father?" Morag smiled through her rose-tinted lips. No matter the time of day or the circumstance, Tempest's Scottish grandmother looked as glamorous as if she'd stepped off a movie set from the golden age of Hollywood filmmaking. "Even in death, Julian Rhodes could be our downfall."

Ash clicked his tongue. "Don't say that. Darius is simply being cautious. Preparing for whatever might come next." He fiddled with the brim of his fedora. It was stiffer than the rest of his hats. It must have been a new one. Tempest wasn't sure which was larger, Morag's collection of scarves or Ash's collection of hats.

"What could possibly come next?" she asked.

The downstairs door squeaked open and footsteps sounded on the stairs leading up to the kitchen. Tempest knew those footsteps well. A moment later, her dad was on the deck.

Darius Mendez was a man with presence. Tempest had gotten her height and propensity for muscles from him, and she used to think she'd gotten her stage presence from her mom, but now she wasn't so sure. While her papa's size turned heads, it was his calm, baritone voice and the gentle way he carried himself, even with arms like tree trunks, that kept their attention. People from eighteen to eighty looked dreamily at him on a regular basis, but he'd never shown any interest in another woman since his wife vanished.

Darius ran a calloused hand across his face. His gaze fell to Tempest. "How concerned do I need to be about this note they have?"

"You didn't go see the lawyer like you said you were going to?" Morag added. "You've been investigating?"

Darius tensed his jaw and answered his parents-in-law. "I did wake the lawyer. Then I went to see Detective Rinehart. Tempest, you should have called Vanessa when he told you about the note they found."

"What note?" Ash and Morag asked at the same time.

"It read, *Come in, Tempest*," Darius explained.

Grandpa Ash frowned. "That sounds like Tempest was the one being invited inside."

"It was in her handwriting," Darius added.

"I already told Detective Rinehart I didn't write a note to Julian Rhodes," said Tempest. "Obviously, it must have been taken from one of my notebooks where I plan my ideas for shows. A bunch of them are in the theater."

"So your fingerprints would be on it," said Darius.

"If I could get inside the theater to see if my notebooks of show notes are there, I can find where it was pulled from. But they wouldn't let me inside. If I can get my notebooks back, I can prove—"

"You can't be serious, Tempest." It was Nicodemus who spoke. He'd been uncharacteristically silent through the exchange, but Tempest was pleased to see he was looking slightly less like he was about to be sick over the railing of the deck. "The theater is a crime scene."

Tempest dangled a ring of keys in her hand. She'd been given two sets of keys when she rented the theater.

"Not happening," her dad said to her. "You don't need to butt in. You're lucky you're not a suspect. That they think—" He broke off when the buzzer from the front gate sounded.

"*Och!*" Morag cried as she leapt up. "That'll be Trina and Tansy."

"This early?" Tempest asked. She knew her grandparents got up early, and she was adjusting to the schedule of construction work, but six o'clock in the morning still seemed ridiculously early for guests.

"We made plans to paint the sunrise light through the trees, but with everything going on I forgot," Morag said from the doorway. "I'll greet them at the gate and tell them we need to reschedule."

The gate wasn't visible from the tree house deck, but Tempest was pretty sure she remembered Tansy, a contemporary of her gran who was a fellow ex-pat Scot. But in general, she couldn't keep up with her grandparents' myriad friends. They'd only moved from Edinburgh to Hidden Creek a few years ago, but Ash's friendly bedside manner from his years as a doctor and Morag's connection to the local art community meant that they had a far more active social life than Tempest did these days.

Someone's phone trilled, and Darius lifted his phone from his pocket. "Hey—She's fine. Arrested? No, why did you think Tempest had been arrested? She's not answering your messages?" Darius raised an eyebrow at his daughter. "She's right here. You want to talk to her? Uh-huh. Yeah, I'll let her know." Darius clicked off and turned to his daughter. "Check your phone. Puppy Dog has left you a bunch of messages."

Sanjay would be mortified if he knew her dad referred to

him like that. Performing as The Hindi Houdini, he was a successful enough stage magician to have a fan club (The Hindi Houdini Heartbreakers) and headline medium-size venues all over the world. Tempest had once been more famous, but her fall from grace had squished her flat. Sanjay was one of her few magician friends who'd stood by her, even when all the evidence incorrectly pointed to Tempest as the one responsible for the fire that ruined her career. His huge ego was balanced out by his enduring loyalty, and the fact that he was gorgeous and fun made it all the more confusing to know what to do with him now that they were both back in Northern California. Though he was currently out of town for a show.

"Puppy dog?" Ash repeated. "You're getting a dog? Nobody tells me anything around here. I don't think Abra will be very happy about that."

Ten-pound, lop-eared rabbit Abracadabra was surly, but also a softy. The fact that Tempest was a similar mix of contrasts wasn't lost on her. Abra was the perfect pet, and one she almost hadn't kept. Abracadabra had been a gift as a bit of a joke because she was a magician. Although she fought against magician stereotypes in her life and didn't use animals in her acts, Abra wasn't remotely like a bunny you'd see in a magic show. He was far too big. He also turned out to be an excellent judge of character. As soon as he'd bitten an annoying woman Sanjay had been dating at the time, Tempest knew Abra was a keeper.

She checked her phone. While talking to her family, she had indeed missed a string of text messages from Sanjay.

u ok?

where are u?

Tempest, seriously, we talked about this. HOW COULD U TURN OFF UR PHONE???

where are u????

can't focus. where are u?

dying. srsly. don't leave me hanging.

"I should call him back," she said. "I don't want to ruin his rehearsal. But first, Papa, why are you so sure I'm not a suspect?"

"They didn't tell you? They already have their main suspect. Julian's wife, Paloma Rhodes."

Tempest gaped at him. "I know I'm the one who said it was a booby trap, but how could Paloma have *set* the booby traps that killed her husband? She couldn't have set the booby traps before he tried to kill her and she ended up in a coma. I've been inside the theater since then. There were no booby traps. She couldn't have—"

"Paloma Rhodes," her dad said, "is no longer in a coma."

Tempest nearly dropped her phone.

"She woke up late in the day yesterday," Darius continued. "She checked herself out of the hospital, against medical advice. They can't find her anywhere."

"She could be sicker than she thought." Ash frowned. "Did someone check her home? She could have fallen and be unable to answer the phone."

"But that's not what the police think," said Tempest. "They think Paloma Rhodes committed murder and is on the run."

Chapter 7

Tempest cut the engine as she pulled up in front of the Whispering House. The old Gothic Revival mansion built more than a century ago looked completely different in the bright daylight than it had the night before. It no longer resembled a haunted house, even though it still had all the trimmings. Was she really doing this? Yes. She had to.

Tempest had come to the Whispering House jobsite not because she was expected after what she'd been through last night but because she needed to make sure that once the police figured out Paloma wasn't guilty, they wouldn't turn to Tempest or anyone else in her family.

The police weren't convinced about her booby-trap theory, so they were focusing on the wrong suspect. Surely the crime scene team would examine the booby-trap mechanisms and realize their mistake. The note from Tempest's notebook would turn their attention to her once they realized they were wrong.

She needed her best friend's help. And this was where she'd find her.

The sun was directly overhead as Tempest stepped out of her jeep. This style of home, with its steeply pitched roof, decorative gables, and arched windows, had fallen out of fashion by the 1880s when the house was constructed, but local architect Chester Hill had loved the past. All the buildings he'd designed were known for their Gothic elements, even as late as 1900. This was the house he had been living in when he died, and it was now owned by their client, retired architect Lenore Woods, who was one of Chester Hill's descendants. Lenore was restoring the house to bring many of its original elements back to life, and she was hoping to get a historic home designation from the city. Nearly 150 years didn't sound especially old to Tempest for a building, but Chester Hill had built several Hidden Creek landmarks. And hey, this was California, so 140-odd years was still pretty historical.

Julian and Paloma Rhodes's house sat across the street, slightly lower on the hillside. It wasn't a coincidence that the houses were directly across from each other. Julian had hired Secret Staircase Construction precisely because his neighbor had. He wasn't the type of guy who would let his neighbors have something better than him. He even rushed his plans through so that Secret Staircase Construction could fit him in first. His wife, Paloma, had been apologetic for her husband's behavior. Despite Paloma's behavior when she checked herself out of the hospital yesterday, Tempest didn't think she was a killer. At least not one who'd kill her husband with an elaborate booby trap at Whispering Creek Theater.

A face peeked out from behind the curtains inside Julian's house. For a fraction of a second, Tempest wondered if it was Paloma Rhodes. But no. As the person pulled the curtain shut, she caught a glimpse of their sleeve. This person wasn't wearing white, as Paloma always did. This was a uniformed police officer. They must have been staking out the place to see if Paloma would return.

Why had Paloma left the hospital—against medical advice—without having her husband come get her? Was it because she planned on killing him? But why bring him to the Whispering Creek Theater? And why use a note from Tempest's notebook? How had Paloma even known to look for it? Tempest didn't buy it. She glanced again at the house across the street. The officer was no longer visible.

Tempest needed another coffee. And then probably another. Since she'd been up all night and caffeine alone wasn't enough to make it through the day, after breakfast at the tree house, she'd pulled her curtains shut and fallen into a restless sleep. She'd woken up shortly before noon, tired but functional. She'd pulled on a fitted T-shirt, jeans, and her ruby red sneakers, which was pretty much her uniform these days now that she didn't have multiple closets filled with costumes. And now here she was, across the street from the house that might destroy Secret Staircase Construction.

Ivy's pink moped was directly in front of her. Her dad's truck and Gideon's baby blue Renault were parked farther down the street, but she didn't spot anyone or hear the sound of any power tools or hammering.

"It's about time," a voice called from above. "I'll be right down."

Tempest looked up and spotted Ivy leaning out of the attic's open window. Ivy's bob of red hair was visible beneath a pink baseball cap, and she was wearing rose-colored overalls and holding a respirator mask in her hand.

"You're not with your creepy mentor." Ivy set down a handled cotton bag as she reached the front porch. It clanged as it hit the wooden slats.

Tempest *did* want to spend more time with Nicodemus before his tour began in a few days. Especially since she could tell he was shaken. But Nicodemus and Brodie were already out for the day meeting a magic builder regarding a broken prop they needed for the tour. They were staying at Fiddler's Folly for two more nights and then flying to Los Angeles, where they'd meet up with the rest of the crew, three days before Nicodemus's tour kicked off.

"Just because he pretends to control the dead," said Tempest, "doesn't mean he's creepy."

"I rest my case." Ivy, with her head-to-toe pink attire and friendly smile, was the anti-Nicodemus. "Are you okay? I mean, after what happened last night after I left?"

Tempest glanced across the street. On the sloping hillside, the houses weren't too close to each other, but Tempest lowered her voice anyway. "How much do you know?"

"Your dad told us why you weren't here this morning. That Julian called you and asked you to meet him at the theater, and when you got there he was dead. Impaled on a blade on the theater door." It was a warm spring day, but Ivy shivered. "I would have texted you this morning, but he said you needed to get some sleep. Since you're not a suspect, I sacrificed my burning need to know."

"My dad told you that, too?"

"Everyone knows that much." Ivy pulled up a page on her phone and read, *"Paloma Rhodes, a person of interest in the death of her husband, Julian Rhodes, is missing."* She set the phone aside. "A 'person of interest' means the prime suspect."

"I'm pretty sure that's only the overly dramatic meaning in TV shows. But yeah, in this case, it's true."

The scent of toasted cumin seeds and fresh chili peppers wafted across the breeze. Grandpa Ash had brought lunch as usual.

"*Should* I be worried about you?" Ivy asked.

"I don't know." Tempest ran a hand through her hair and looked up at the decorative gable trim of the porch. "What I *do* know is that I don't believe Paloma could have killed Julian, but you're right that she's the main suspect. It doesn't make sense on so many levels. The killer involved me by picking the theater as the site of Julian's murder. Was the location just to get Julian to an out-of-the-way place or did they mean to implicate me? Was that why they used a booby trap? Not only that, but there was a note in my handwriting taped to the door—something the killer found in my notebooks to make it look like I was personally inviting Julian to open the door that killed him."

Ivy gaped at her. "I thought your dad told us everything, but . . . a booby trap?"

"That's why I need your help to find out what's really going on." There was something she didn't say out loud to Ivy. It wasn't only her own notebooks that were in the theater. There were also a few of the journals with magic show notes that her mom had left her. She couldn't bear the thought of losing those.

Instead of replying, Ivy opened the bag at her feet and handed Tempest a stainless-steel tiffin of warm food.

"No comment?" Tempest accepted the fragrant stacked containers. "You don't accept my challenge?"

"Oh, I accept. But if we're going to solve the mystery, we need some sustenance first. You can tell me the rest of the details while we eat."

"You've been hanging out with my grandfather for too long."

Tempest's grandfather Ashok Raj had christened himself the personal chef and *dabbawalla* to the Secret Staircase Construction crew. *Dabbawallas* help the city of Mumbai in India run smoothly by delivering home-cooked lunches to workers across the city. They pick up tiffin lunch boxes at homes, stack the circular stainless-steel containers on their bikes, and travel by road and train to offices so that workers can have a lovingly prepared home-cooked lunch. After his long career as a medical doctor in Edinburgh, Ash took up his passion for cooking, so when he moved into the tree house in Hidden Creek, he insisted on cooking lunch for his son-in-law's crew.

Ash's deliveries were always a hit and were known to be a perk of working for Secret Staircase Construction. Whenever the team subcontracted portions of a job, Ash was sure to cook enough extra lunches for them. He claimed that riding his bike across the Bay Area helped him stay in shape, which was technically true, but Tempest knew the real reason he loved it. He loved people. When you're an eighty-year-old man with a smile on your face and a bicycle stacked high with silver lunch box tins emanating delicious fragrances, it's easy to strike up conversations with people. He always brought extra cookies for just that occasion. He'd collected hundreds of business cards from the people he had met, which he kept in a Rolodex and referred to frequently. Tempest didn't know how he kept it organized, but her grandfather had always been magical.

"Do we need to worry about being overheard?" Tempest wasn't referring to their client Lenore Woods. Lenore owned two houses, so she wasn't staying at the Whispering House while the construction work took place.

"You mean your dad? He and Gideon are out back, half eating and half checking the masonry. I wasn't hungry, so I grabbed both our lunches and thought I'd wait and see if you showed up."

Tempest unlatched the lids of the interlocking containers. The first contained chunky salsa and guacamole kept fresh with lime juice. In the second was a fat burrito wrapped in parchment paper and homemade tortilla chips. When she noticed Ivy just watching her, not eating, she put the burrito back and closed the lid. "Now it's you that's holding back. What are you trying not to say?"

Ivy pursed her pink lips. "How do you do that?"

"What? Read your mind?"

"Obviously."

Tempest grinned. "Magic?"

"I can't help thinking about the bizarre booby traps . . . Doesn't it sound like *Moriarty?*"

Tempest wished Ivy was referring to the fictional character written by Arthur Conan Doyle in his Sherlock Holmes stories. She didn't know the true name of the real-life man they referred to as Moriarty. Ivy had dubbed him Moriarty because he was kinda sorta Tempest's nemesis. He was more an enigma than a nemesis. But he was definitely bad news.

"I know." Tempest kicked aside her lunch box. "I haven't heard from him since Corbin Colt's killer was arrested." Corbin Colt was a supernatural thriller writer who'd been researching Tempest's mom's disappearance for a book, and the man they knew only as Moriarty had played a small part in helping them find out the truth about Corbin's mysterious murder.

"So you think it could be him?"

"I don't know." Tempest shook her head as she stood up. She made sure she had space for her arms, then twirled into a pirouette. It was an easy movement from her stage show that she could do anywhere. Blurring out the world around her and focusing on that one motion calmed her, enabling her to think. After three spins, she came to a stop in front of Ivy. "He's killed before, but not like this. But there is one thing . . ."

"What?"

"Moriarty is my self-declared guardian angel."

"And Julian Rhodes," Ivy whispered, "was trying to destroy your family's business."

It was true that it gave Moriarty a motive, but it didn't feel right. "If Moriarty wanted to get rid of Julian, he would have done it in a way that didn't potentially hurt me. He wouldn't have made it look like I was somehow involved. In that sense, Paloma is more likely."

Ivy scowled. "You're the one who said you didn't think she was guilty. And we got to know her when we renovated her house. Now you've changed your mind and think someone that nice could be a murderer?"

Tempest fought an urge to roll her eyes. "You're biased because she used to be a librarian. For someone who loves deviously plotted classic mystery novels, how can you say that being *nice* means someone isn't a killer?"

"Fair. But you're the one telling me she's not guilty, so we're in agreement. Sit down and eat your grandfather's lunch and finish telling me what else you know."

Tempest obliged. "Paloma *is* the main suspect, as far as I can tell. But Julian was killed at the Whispering Creek Theater; he was actively attempting to destroy my family, and . . . Wait—"

"What?"

"I know that a note in my handwriting was on the theater door that killed him when he tried to open it, but how did he get a message in the first place telling him to go to the theater? Why did he think—" Tempest's words were interrupted by her phone.

Brodie's gaunt face appeared on the screen. Tempest shivered. She probably should have selected a different picture for Nicodemus's assistant.

Besides helping backstage, Brodie sometimes appeared *on* stage in one of Nicodemus's shows as a puppet, with Nicodemus as the puppeteer. Tempest had always loved how Brodie's long limbs kept perfect time with the jerks of Nicodemus's hands on imaginary strings and the truly magical effect of the magic lantern shadows of paper puppets on the wall behind them. His cadaverous face took little stage makeup to appear creepy, so she didn't love seeing that ghostly face fill her phone screen.

"I need to ask Nicodemus a question about our tour," Brodie said. "Could you put him on the line?"

"He's not with you? I thought you two had to plan some tour logistics today."

Brodie swore. "Bastard. He lied about where he was going."

"Why would he lie?"

"Because," said Brodie, "he's gone to protect you."

"What do you mean, *protect me?*" Tempest's skin prickled. Whatever was going on, this was bad.

"He knows you want to get inside the theater to get your bloody notebooks. He doesn't believe it's safe for you. Not with all the booby traps."

Tempest held her breath for four seconds as she processed the information, then ran to her car.

She tried calling Nicodemus as she started the ignition, but he didn't answer. She barely missed hitting a parked car as she rounded a corner on her way to the theater. The Whispering House and the theater were at opposite sides of Hidden Creek and several winding roads away from each other. It would take her at least ten minutes to get there.

Ten minutes later, stuck behind a moving van attempting to maneuver the small road, Tempest called Nicodemus's number again. He didn't answer, so she tried Brodie once more.

"I've gone after him." Brodie's voice was half obscured by the sound of a car door closing. "A hired car dropped me off at the theater. I see him." He paused. "Nic, come away from that bleeding door! The blade—!"

Nicodemus howled in agony. The phone line went dead.

No . . .

No, no, no!

It was happening again. Her nightmare from five years before was repeating. The theater had claimed the life of someone else Tempest loved.

Y ou should make it scarier," Tempest says the first time she meets Nicodemus the Necromancer.

She is ten years old and already taller than all the other girls her age. Braver, too.

"You want a truly frightening trick then, do ye, lass?" His mischievous smile rivals that of a child Tempest's age.

"Do your best," she says with a straight face. She doesn't yet know how to raise a single eyebrow for effect, but he can tell she'll get there soon.

"I *wouldnae* want to disappoint a child now, would I?"

Nicodemus lifts both his hands into the air, then presses his thumbs and index fingers together and gently pulls upward, as if he's tugging strands of invisible string.

"Let me tell you a story," he begins. As he spins a tale of friendship and betrayal, he manipulates the invisible string, bringing to life paper animals that cast eerie shadows on the wall of his magic workshop on the outskirts of town.

The wolf is the most frightening to Tempest, Nicodemus can tell. Her eyes widen as she follows its sharp teeth and a jaw that opens and snaps shut, and she wonders how a paper cutout can come to life so vividly. But as the story progresses, it is unexpectedly the wolf who saves the baby rabbit from the clutches of a hawk. Before Tempest can even blink, the paper animals have disappeared, leaving only the shadow of the outstretched wings of a hawk on the wall. When Tempest looks from the shadow to where Nicodemus was standing, he too is gone.

This is the summer Tempest realizes the power of magic. Her parents are building two secret libraries and an art workshop with sixty secret compartments for a wealthy client's sixtieth birthday. The house is isolated and near a dangerous cliff, so they've sent Tempest to Edinburgh to spend two months of the summer with her grandparents and her Aunt Elspeth.

Two weeks after Tempest is introduced to Nicodemus by Elspeth, Tempest appears on stage during one of his performances at the Edinburgh Fringe Festival. That first afternoon at Bedlam Theatre, Nicodemus can tell she is hooked on the feeling the stage gives her. Not the adrenaline rush of being the center of attention, which is what Nicodemus loves, but something else. Tempest is focused on the audience. She loves watching their faces. Seeing their eyes light up. She performs *for them*.

On stage, Tempest is a dancing shadow up until the finale, when Nicodemus hands a top hat to her. On accepting the hat, her shadow form becomes real.

Nicodemus disappears, but his shadow—his memory—remains with Tempest.

Chapter 8

THE HAUNTED WHISPERING CREEK THEATER HAS
CLAIMED ANOTHER LIFE

That was the headline that greeted Tempest when she checked her phone at the hospital. Someone had leaked news that Nicodemus was a victim of the booby trap, but thankfully, they didn't have all the facts. The knife's blade had stabbed Nicodemus—but he was alive.

Nicodemus's reflexes were quick enough to have saved his life—but not his *hand*.

Tempest's relief was immense. She'd lost both her mom and her aunt on theater stages. To lose someone else she cared about would have been bad enough, but to have it happen at a theater once again would have made her feel truly cursed.

Her relief was tempered by a stark truth. Nicodemus might not have truly escaped death. To a magician, a hand injury meant the death of a career he'd spent decades perfecting.

If he'd been younger, Nicodemus might have recovered with surgery and physical therapy. But the injury happening right before his last tour meant there would likely be no farewell tour. Tempest hated to think of his current state of mind.

She'd arrived at the theater just as the ambulance pulled out of the parking lot. Her dad came to the hospital as soon as Tempest let him know what was going on, but once it was clear both that Nicodemus was alive and that nobody would be able to see him while his serious hand injury was being treated, Tempest insisted her dad get back to the jobsite. They were on a tight deadline to finish Lenore's renovations, and she was fine waiting with Brodie. It was mostly true. It was fine at first, but as time stretched on, she grew more nervous. What was taking so long?

"Can't you stop that fidgeting?" Brodie scowled at her from across the waiting room.

An unkind thought crossed her mind, but she didn't say it out loud. Everyone deals with stress differently. "I'm going on a walk. Text me if there's any news."

When she got back to the waiting room twenty minutes later, feeling slightly better for having speed-walked around the hospital complex four times, Brodie was no longer in sight. She glowered at her phone, which showed zero new messages.

She found Brodie standing at the window of Nicodemus's hospital room. Nicodemus was awake and sitting up in a raised hospital bed, a hospital gown hanging loosely on his shoulders, and a large bandage wound around his left hand. With his right hand, he tugged at the edge of the sheet. The blinds were closed, but pinpricks of sunlight still seeped into the room.

"You're all right." Tempest didn't speak the words as a question. Even though she knew he'd survived, it was a relief to see him awake and fussing with his surroundings.

"If you consider losing the use of my hand all right." Nicodemus gave her a wan smile. "Severed nerve. I don't remember the last time I felt so damn helpless. No, that's not true. I do. It's a feeling I don't care for one bit."

"Huggable?"

He pointed to the mass of bandages on his left hand, which was elevated on a metal stand. "Avoid my left arm and you're golden."

Tempest wanted to squeeze him with all her strength, but she settled for a half hug.

"I swear I was cautious approaching the door," he whispered into her hair. "I don't know how—"

"Tour's off." Brodie was glaring at Tempest as she let go of Nicodemus.

The less generous part of her expected he was angry that he'd be out of a job. But she knew that wasn't true. He'd worked for Nicodemus for more than a decade. Nobody would have put up with Nicky's eccentricities for so long if they didn't care for him.

"Be a good lad and find me some coffee, Brodie?" Nicodemus asked.

Brodie shot Tempest a glance that would definitely qualify as daggers, then gave a nod to Nicodemus before departing.

"I'm sorry." Tempest wished, as she had many times before, that she could turn back the clock and have a do-over.

"At least it's my left hand. I can still feed myself properly."

"What were you *thinking* going back there?"

The look he gave her made her feel even worse. *He'd done it to protect her.* He knew what she was planning to do. And he'd been right.

"It's not your fault," he said, which only made it worse. "It was my decision. I could tell you wanted those notebooks back desperately. I know you, Tempest. I could tell you wanted them for personal reasons, not just because you wanted to prove the note left for Julian Rhodes was torn from one of your notebooks."

Tempest's heart thudded. Did he know she was looking into

her mom's and aunt's murders? She hadn't exactly kept it from him, but it's not the kind of thing that comes up easily in conversation. *How was your flight? Oh, by the way, I've been investigating my aunt's supposedly accidental death on stage, and I think my mom was killed because she found out who did it. Want to grab coffee?* She'd played it out in her mind and decided against it. She'd have come clean if he'd asked, but instead she'd opted to let him focus on his tour. Which was now irrelevant.

Nicodemus spoke even more gently now. "I know how much you care about those notebooks. They're one of the few things you have left of your mother. You don't want them held as evidence in a court case that could last for years."

"Nicky, I—"

"Tempest. Stop."

"You don't even know what I was going to say."

"I've known you since you were a child. You're headstrong, physically strong, and clever. But also remarkably capable of guilt for things that aren't your responsibility or your fault. You're welcome to bring me some of your grandfather's home cooking, or a performance of whatever new act you're working on, but *not* your pity."

"You practice that speech?"

His dry lips ticked into a smile. "Only once before. Being a seasoned performer has its benefits."

"And its drawbacks." Tempest sighed. The moment was gone. She wasn't going to worry him with her investigation. "That was a perfectly theatrical stunt. You didn't have to nearly kill yourself to stop me from going back to the theater. Why did you try to get inside through *that* door?"

"I'm a foolish old man. The police knew how to secure the other two doors of the theater, but I expect they were still wary of the main door. They'd already taken away the two blades, so only tarp and crime scene tape blocked it off, and only one officer was stationed on site. I simply waited for him to take a short break. I presume it was only to use the loo, since he was back in time to find me right after . . ." He shook off the memory of the blade that severed the nerve in his hand. The blade that had effectively taken his life.

"Looking at all three doors," he continued, "the main one appeared to be the easier option. I was *so certain* I understood what was going on with that booby trap. There has to be a pressure point to trigger it. I understand the principles of mechanisms better than anyone."

He wasn't exaggerating. Nicodemus built most of his own effects. He'd collected automata his entire life, often snatching up broken ones he'd fix himself. The precursor to modern robots, the clockwork precision of an automaton allowed magicians from centuries past to create spectacles that truly looked like magic, such as Jean-Eugène Robert-Houdin's famous orange tree, which grew from seed to tree live on stage—including real oranges. It was a style Nicodemus preferred over modern magic. He'd brought back to life the two fortune-teller automata in his studio in Leith on the outskirts of Edinburgh. The wooden body of the woman in a glass booth hid mechanisms that allowed her to deal Tarot cards, and a smaller wooden hand wrote several cursive messages once wound.

"I should say I *thought* I knew." He closed his eyes and suddenly looked so much older.

"You were wrong about the mechanism?" She didn't like the look she'd seen in his eyes. *Fear.*

"*How?*" he whispered. "That's three blades now."

"What do you mean *how?* You said it yourself. It's a rigged mechanism. Like the kind in automata."

He shook his head. "I was careful. I *dinnae ken* how I triggered it. It's as if it's *regenerating.* If I didn't know better, I'd say the bloody theater really was haunted."

"It's a good thing you know better." Tempest knew better, too, but there was still something horribly eerie about hearing the mechanical gears spring into action and seeing that blade pop out of the theater's wooden door.

Nicodemus winced. For a moment, Tempest wondered if he was truly considering a supernatural explanation, but his gaze was directed at his hand. He was in pain.

"Should I get a doctor?" she asked.

"Don't be ridiculous. I've had far too much time with doctors today."

Tempest looked around the hospital room more carefully. Small, but private. He looked . . . settled. He'd asked Brodie to bring him a coffee, but surely that was only an excuse to get rid of him. "I can take you home this afternoon, can't I?"

"One of the doctors wasn't pleased with my blood pressure or some such nonsense." He stroked his goatee. It wasn't nearly as scruffy as his hair, which was even more disheveled than usual. "Like the rest of me, my blood is theatrical. Their verdict is daft, but I'm stuck here 'til tomorrow. Then I need to come back for surgery next week—if you'll have me that long."

"Of course. Can I bring you anything from the house for now? Or help with changing the tour arrangements?"

He took her hand. "You're a dear, but it's only 'til tomorrow. Brodie and one of the crew members already in Los Angeles are dealing with the cancellation details."

Tempest remembered what it was like to have a supportive crew. She'd lost the support and friendship of her Las Vegas team when she'd been accused of engineering a reckless stunt that went horribly wrong, not believing her that it was sabotage. Nicodemus and Sanjay were the two people close to her in the magic community who'd stuck by her. But they'd been on their own tours when her world came tumbling down. Even though it was less than a year ago, it felt like another lifetime ago now that she was building a life in Hidden Creek.

"Don't worry about me, Tempest," he added. "Perhaps I'll follow in the footsteps of my fellow Scotsman, the Wizard of the North. A fresh start late in life and all that."

"You mean after he gave up his questionable ways and dedicated himself to exposing fraudulent mediums?"

Scottish magician John Henry Anderson lived in the 1800s and performed magic under the stage name the Wizard of the North. He was a great showman, but most of his successful illusions were ones he'd "borrowed" from other magicians, including those stolen from Jean-Eugène Robert-Houdin. Stealing illusions was a bad look for a magician, but he changed his ways toward the end of his life.

"I suppose it doesn't have the same cachet in this day and age." Nicodemus sighed.

"I could stay a while. I'll—" Tempest broke off as a shadow hovered in the doorway. "Is someone there?"

Detective Rinehart stepped into the room.

He looked older this afternoon. Stress and lack of sleep weren't wearing well on him, and it was only the beginning of the investigation. But his small eyes were still every bit as alert. Tempest was certain he was taking everything in.

Tempest blocked Nicodemus protectively. "You aren't charging him, are you?"

"For disturbing a crime scene? Not at present." He stepped past Tempest to reach Nicodemus's bedside. "I'm told you're here for the time being, but I'm hoping you're up for talking while your memories are fresh. Any details about what you saw of the booby trap would help."

"You believe me now?" Tempest asked.

Rinehart ignored her and kept his attention focused on Nicodemus. "What did you do to trigger the blade?"

Nicodemus shook his head and looked up at the ceiling as he leaned back into the pillow. "Nothing. That's what worries me. I didn't *do anything.*"

"Have you found Paloma Rhodes yet?" Tempest asked.

Rinehart ignored her once more. "You were watching for your opportunity to get inside. *Why?*"

"Police DO NOT CROSS tape is like catnip to an illusionist." Nicodemus forced a lighthearted smile, but his heart wasn't in it.

A nurse came in and told them, in a forceful voice that left no room for argument, that Nicodemus needed to rest.

Tempest gave his uninjured hand a quick squeeze, then left with Rinehart.

"I hate hospitals," the detective mumbled as they made their way down the hallway.

"It's a place where devoted medical professionals take care of people." Tempest gave a fond look at a nurse hurrying down the hallway. She thought of hospitals the way her grandfather did. A decade after retiring, Ash was still in touch with dozens of former patients. To him, hospitals were a place of healing. Even if they couldn't perform miracles—which Tempest wouldn't have been surprised were possible on her grandfather's watch—everyone was doing all that was humanly possible for people who were loved.

She stopped him as soon as they reached the waiting room. "How could your people leave a dangerous booby trap just out there in the open?"

"The trap and its blades were already removed. The mechanism was visible to the naked eye, just hidden by the dim lighting, so there was no reason to believe there was another trap hiding in the door. Besides, the door was blocked off in multiple ways. Mr. Nicodemus already admitted he knew he was breaking in."

"The people who removed the blades," said Tempest. "What did they—"

"Tempest. I've already told you more than I need to. I know my predecessor took liberties in the amount of information he conveyed to you, but that isn't how things work. You answer *my* questions."

She crossed her arms and looked straight into his little bird-like eyes that betrayed nothing. "I'm waiting."

"I didn't come here to talk to you. Unless you have any more to tell me beyond what you shared last night, we're done. Just remember, until we figure out what's going on, that theater is off-limits."

Tempest froze. It should have occurred to her earlier. It had, logically, but not in the way that it hit her right now. Not only was someone she cared about injured and another person dead, for a reason she was sure was connected to her—but now, with Rinehart's words, her own investigation into what happened to her mom in that theater was crashing to a halt.

"A lot of my possessions are inside the theater since I rented it. I have a right to—"

"It's a crime scene."

"At least let me get my notebooks."

"Anything at the theater is part of that crime scene."

"But I need—"

"Crime. Scene."

"Those notebooks are—"

"Crime—" He stopped before adding *scene,* as Tempest gave him a raised-eyebrow scowl that she was fairly confident would have broken a petty criminal. With Rinehart, at least it got him to stop speaking sooner.

"I get it." She heard him loud and clear. That didn't mean she had to listen.

Chapter 9

Tempest had missed several calls while she was at the hospital. Back at her jeep, she texted her dad to let him know Nicky was doing well(-ish), assured Sanjay that he could go on with his show that night knowing nobody else had died and she was safe, and then called Ivy back.

"The reporting online says there was another death—" Ivy began.

"They're wrong," Tempest assured her.

"I was worried he'd taken a turn for the worse. So, he's okay?"

"Depends on your definition of 'okay.'" Tempest rolled her eyes at her own words. "I don't mean to be overly dramatic." Maybe she did. "He'll live, but his career is over."

"Where are you right now?"

"Heading back to you at the Whispering House. No, that doesn't work. My dad is there."

"You don't want to see your dad?" Ivy's voice was hurt on his behalf. In some ways, Ivy was closer to Darius than Tempest. Ivy had lived at Fiddler's Folly for a year during high school when things at her own home were bad and her sister had already gone away to college, and Ivy had been working for Secret Staircase Construction during the years Tempest was in Vegas.

"I love him, but he's not a person I want around when we discuss how to solve the mystery of that booby-trapped door."

"Good point. Except we've already finished up work for the day. We knew he'd been up half the night, so Gideon and I insisted he go home. It's nearly dinnertime."

"It is?" She was usually so good at keeping track of time, but this was twice in the last twenty-four hours that she'd lost her superpower. This day had been too strange to feel like reality.

"Gideon was still finishing a few things at the Whispering House when I left a few minutes ago. I bet he's still there, and I can get back there in a few minutes. I can't believe I'm saying this, since it's nearly dark, but let's meet at the house."

"Right. Since we can't reach Gideon any other way." He was the only guy in his twenties she knew who didn't own a cell phone.

"He's dying to see you." Ivy gulped. "Bad choice of words, but truly, I don't think I've ever seen him so unfocused. He even asked to read more about it on my cell. That's how I know he's worried."

Tempest didn't think she'd ever seen a cell phone in his hand. She couldn't actually imagine it. "Be there in ten minutes."

She made it in eight.

A small wooden box, about the size of a Rubik's Cube, flew through the air as Tempest stepped into the Whispering House. She caught it before it fell to the floor. "Shouldn't you be more careful with this? It looks like a puzzle box."

"I knew you'd catch it," said Gideon. "Besides, it doesn't work. It's going on the scrap pile."

"Really? It's too beautiful for that. Even if it's not a puzzle." She slid open the top panel. The carved, soft wood smelled of pine. "This isn't my dad's woodworking style."

Gideon took the box from her hands, sending a little jolt of electricity through her as he brushed his calloused sculptor's fingertips over hers. "When we first started this job, I thought it would be fun to try something new while you worked on that attic puzzle room. I didn't get it to work, but I found it just now while cleaning up the tool room."

Gideon Torres. She'd known him for nearly a year. The intensity with which he looked at the world—and at her—still excited her and freaked her out a little. He and Tempest weren't exactly more than friends, but it occasionally felt like they were headed in that direction. It wasn't an unpleasant thought. But it was also one she did *not* have time to think about right now.

He took a step back and stood in a domed archway that the Secret Staircase Construction crew had built to recreate what they believed the original house had looked like before drab, standardized doors were added in the 1950s. The carved arch was beautiful, but the real magic was hidden to the left of the open archway, where the secret stairway leading to the attic was hiding in plain sight. That was a detail that architect Chester Hill had envisioned in the partial original blueprints their client had discovered. As they peeled back the layers of the house, the Secret Staircase crew couldn't find any architectural evidence that the secret staircase had ever been realized. But now, with a few modifications to meet modern safety requirements and a couple of magical flourishes in the spirit of the old Gothic bones of the house, the original vision was nearly a reality.

"You doing okay?" Gideon asked. "I didn't even get to see you earlier to ask how you were doing after what happened last night, and now your mentor . . ." His dark eyes were downcast, and there was something different about his face. Stubble. That was it. He was usually clean-shaven, but it looked like he might not have shaved since the last time she'd seen him three days ago. Gideon's dark hair was also more unkempt than usual. He often lost himself in his stone carvings, and he'd been getting thinner and thinner all year.

"He'll be all right."

"What's even going on, Tempest?"

"I wish I knew. A booby trap similar to the one that killed Julian Rhodes got Nicodemus's hand."

Gideon swore. At least Tempest was fairly sure that's what the muttered expression was, though she didn't know the word. Gideon's mom was from France, and his dad was from the Philippines. He'd been raised mostly in California, making him a similar ethnically ambiguous mash-up to her. He joked that the only languages he spoke fluently besides English were Tagalish and Fragalog—English mixed with Tagalog and with French. Tempest didn't come close to speaking another language fluently. A true multicultural mutt, besides English she only spoke rudimentary Tamil, Spanish, Scots, and Scottish Gaelic. Enough Tamil and Spanish to order food, ask for directions, and thank people. And enough Scots and Gaelic to understand simple conversations and late-night singing in pubs across Scotland.

"Ivy's up in the attic." Gideon led the way.

Tempest studied the wooden box as she and Gideon climbed the stairs. Even though it wasn't a puzzle that required you to slide pieces of wood in a certain order to open the box, the lid's delicate carving of an open book surrounded by flowering vines was captivating. She hadn't realized Gideon was experimenting with mediums beyond stone. There was no way she was letting this box go into the recycling bin.

They reached the attic, where Ivy had rolled up the tarps of the previous night and was now scraping a few errant drops of paint from the wainscoting they'd built into puzzle pieces.

Historical documentation on the house showed Chester Hill's sketches for the attic, including sliding wooden panels on the sections of wall beneath its steeply pitched roof and visible beams, so one of the requests from Lenore was to convert this attic into something like a puzzle box. Tempest imagined the mechanisms of a magical puzzle box attic, accessed by a series of sliding movements of pieces of wood that, when moved properly, unlocked a secret door.

Ivy ceased delicately removing paint splatter and threw her arms around Tempest. Ivy was almost a head shorter, so Tempest lifted her off the ground for a moment as she hugged back.

"I couldn't resist fixing that when I saw it," Ivy said. "But let's forget about this job now. Tell us everything that's happened."

Tempest sat down cross-legged on the attic floor, underneath exposed wooden beams and a skylight. "Someone set a fiendish booby trap at my theater—one that seems to be *regenerating*. Why would Paloma Rhodes do that? Who would have done it if it wasn't her? And seriously, *how*? How is it regenerating?"

"Um, isn't that what the police are looking into?" Gideon asked.

Tempest shot a glance at Ivy. "You didn't tell him why we're meeting up?"

"Tempest thinks they're on the wrong track," Ivy said to Gideon.

"Paloma left the hospital just a few hours before Julian was killed," said Tempest. "She wasn't unconscious long enough for her to have trouble walking, so it's technically possible for her to have killed him. But the method doesn't make sense. Why kill him with a complex series of knife booby traps at a theater that has nothing to do with her?"

"She could have set them beforehand," Ivy pointed out. "Maybe she and Julian were attempting to kill each other."

Tempest shook her head. "I've been in that theater countless times since Paloma fell into her coma. I've gone through that door. There was nothing rigged on that door even a few days ago. It can't have been her. Besides, based on everything we know about her from having her as a client and from what we learned later, it just doesn't feel like something she'd do."

As soon as Julian Rhodes filed a suit against Secret Staircase Construction, Tempest's grandfather hired former detective Blackburn, now a private investigator, to dig into Julian's own past. A countermeasure to how Julian was poking into their lives for his lawsuit.

"This is what we know about Julian and Paloma," Tempest began. "Julian sold luxury travel experiences under the company name Bespoke Rhodes. The experiences were aimed at people, especially men in the tech world, who had amassed wealth early in life and were looking for luxury travel beyond the standard high-end tours that skewed older. He founded the company a decade ago, in his late thirties, so he was around fifty years old when he died."

"Fifty-two," said Ivy. "When he questioned my competence when I was welding the floating staircase for their house, he commented that he was exactly twenty-five years older than me."

"Old enough to look respectable with some gray hair at his temples," said Tempest, "but not too old to successfully market to his demographic. When Julian heard about Secret Staircase Construction, he decided to renovate his historic home in a way that would get him featured in *Architectural Digest*. He'd pitched them before—unsuccessfully."

"I'll never understand why people care so much about stuff like that," Gideon murmured. "It felt like he never cared about the beautiful things we were building into his house at all. He only wanted what would get him featured. And how he didn't want Lenore to have what he did? It's like a child who no longer wants a toy when they find out their friend got it too."

It was true. Darius had explained to Julian that there were no cookie-cutter projects, that every home renovation was entirely unique, and that his neighbor's historic home renovation would be nothing like his modern one. Julian's rage was one of the reasons they weren't surprised when something happened to his wife. Nor was it surprising that Julian would look for someone else to blame. They hadn't realized just how treacherous he could be.

The experience made Tempest understand why her dad had fired bad clients in the past, even when they desperately needed the money. Paloma was a pleasure to work with, and she was the one who gave Secret Staircase Construction the details that enabled them to bring their house to life. Julian wanted a renovation that looked expensive and unique; Paloma wanted a home that captured memories from the travels the couple had taken early in their relationship. The circular stairway was inspired by a stairway based on a circular staircase from a German castle that looked straight out of a fairy tale, but Julian had instead decided that a modern staircase that looked as if it floated in the air, unbound, was better for his image.

"Paloma was a decade younger than her husband," Tempest continued, "and it was a first marriage for both of them, so there was no motive involving a previous spouse and no kids in the picture. There was no publicly reported drama in their marriage. Paloma had been a librarian before going to work for Bespoke Rhodes when they married. It was Paloma who had the idea of adding a section to their website that recommended books related to travel."

Paloma had told Tempest she'd wanted to simply call the section of the website "Book Recommendations," but Julian insisted it should be "Curated Literature." Still, Paloma succeeded in recommending books she loved to fellow travelers. Tempest loved the small photo of Paloma on that page of the website, dressed in a bright white dress and surrounded by books. Paloma always dressed in white because she said it was a blank slate, like a blank page in a book ready for words to follow. Tempest wondered if the fact that she liked Paloma so much was pushing her into a misguided belief in Paloma's innocence.

"All of that we knew before the accident," Tempest continued. "When my grandfather hired a private investigator to look more into them after their lawsuit against my dad, he turned to former detective Blackburn because we knew him from my mom's disappearance and considered him trustworthy. Blackburn dug up two facts Julian didn't want known. First, while Julian claimed to be self-made, he'd actually inherited millions from his parents, which gave him ample start-up funds. That was a fact he kept quiet."

"Since it didn't fit with his image of being a self-made entrepreneur," said Gideon.

"And second," said Tempest, "he was a bully way before we met him. He'd threatened a lot of other people with lawsuits. He simply escalated when it came to us—probably because construction comes with risk, so my dad has good insurance."

"That could be a motive for why someone would want to kill him," said Ivy.

"Exactly. We weren't able to get many details though." Tempest wished Blackburn had been more unethical because the public record and voluntary interviews didn't tell them nearly enough. Or maybe she didn't really wish that. This way, she knew they could trust him, even if that didn't get them the answers they wanted as quickly as Tempest wanted them. "Still, the fact that Julian threatened to sue several other people is sketchy. As is the fact that he was trying to dig up dirt on my family so he could bully my dad into a big settlement."

"Everything about that guy was sketchy," said Gideon. "Which is a problem for motives, since guys like that have a lot of people who'd want them dead."

"But to kill him at the Whispering Creek Theater with a set

of booby traps and a page ripped out of my notebook to lure him to his death?" said Tempest.

"Paloma *is* connected to you through hiring your dad's company," said Ivy. "It makes sense the police are focusing on her, especially since she's disappeared."

"She wasn't physically abused by Julian," Gideon said. "At least not on parts of her body that were visible, and she didn't wear clothing like turtleneck sweaters that would cover them up. She didn't wear makeup that would cover up bruises either." He paused. "Why do you two look so shocked?"

"You don't seem like the type of guy to notice a woman's makeup," said Ivy.

"But you would look," Tempest said to him, "if you suspected she might have bruises to cover up."

Gideon shrugged. "Julian was emotionally abusive for sure. That type of abuse can be nearly as bad. She might have snapped. Detective Rinehart might be right about her, Tempest. Whoever set those booby traps set *multiple* traps. They had to know it could be dangerous if not all of them were set off at the same time they killed Julian."

"I know," Tempest admitted. "My gut feeling isn't the same as evidence. I just can't shake the feeling that we're looking at this all wrong." *What were they overlooking?*

"Have you eaten anything since the two bites of lunch you had ages ago?" Ivy asked.

"I'm not wrong just because I'm hungry." Okay, maybe Ivy had a point—she *was* starving. Still, she wasn't wrong.

"Go home, Tempest. Get some food and some rest." Gideon squeezed her hand. His strong hands were warm and comforting. "We'll be here in the morning. Ivy will probably read at least one of her favorite classic mystery novels before bed tonight to get investigative ideas flowing. If you still want to investigate after you sleep on it tonight, we'll help."

"*Harumph*," said Ivy, sounding like her favorite fictional detective, Dr. Fell.

"You don't want to help?" Tempest asked.

"Of course I want to help." Ivy pouted. "I'm upset that Gideon stole my line. I've already got a book in mind I want to reread tonight."

"You do?" Tempest knew that Ivy always thought of classic mystery novels as the answer to anything and everything in life, but she was surprised that her friend already had an idea of a book that might help with such a strange crime.

"*The Reader Is Warned* by John Dickson Carr, under his pseudonym Carter Dickson."

"Why that one?" Tempest couldn't remember if she'd read it. As a teenager, she'd preferred Clayton Rawson's magician character The Great Merlini to Carr's sleuths.

"It's a fair-play mystery with all the clues," said Ivy. "I thought of it because the book isn't exactly a locked-room mystery, just like our real-life booby-trapped door isn't exactly an impossible crime. It's just super creepy because it was made to look like it's regenerating—*to look like it's supernatural*."

"Thanks for the nightmares, Ivy," said Gideon.

"Says the man who carves monsters out of stone." Tempest raised an eyebrow at him.

"In *The Reader Is Warned*," Ivy continued, ignoring both of them, "there's a man who claims he can kill by simply using his mind. Can he precisely predict someone's death and cause it from afar? Or is it a trick?"

"Come on." Gideon pulled Tempest up from the creaking floorboards. "Let's let Ivy get home to her book to see if it gives her ideas about this weird crime."

"It's dark outside," said Tempest. "Nobody is walking out of here alone. We're all leaving together."

Before flicking out the light and following Ivy and Gideon

down the stairs, Tempest took one last look at the construction around her, knowing it would soon be something beautiful. She turned off the light, but dim light from the window still illuminated the room.

She ran to the window. It wasn't a light on at the Rhodeses' house. It was simply a streetlamp near the top-floor window. The Rhodeses' house was dark.

Was the officer who'd been stationed there gone, or was he simply sitting in the dark? *And what had become of Paloma Rhodes?*

Chapter 10

Chester Hill had been dead for a century, and he was driving Tempest crazy.

The architect was, after all, the reason Julian Rhodes had been suing Secret Staircase Construction. No, that wasn't fair. She knew Chester Hill wasn't *personally* responsible, but it was his house that had brought Julian to their renovation company. And it was his theater that had been used to kill the loathsome man.

From the front seat of her jeep, parked in front of the Whispering House, Tempest started the engine, eased away from the curb to turn around, and watched Gideon and Ivy drive away before stopping on the other side of the street. Her dad and grandparents were expecting her home for dinner, but she wasn't ready to leave.

She turned off the engine, but kept the doors firmly locked. After all, she would hate Ivy to accuse her of being TSTL: Too Stupid to Live. If a character in one of Ivy's mystery books was TSTL, by doing something like going alone and unarmed into a dark basement because of the sound of scraping coming from the subterranean room, Ivy would throw the book across the room.

She knew she should go home, but she needed a few more quiet moments with her thoughts. Paloma's connection to the Whispering Creek Theater and the Whispering House was a stretch. But both were linked to *Tempest*.

When Tempest had rented the Whispering Creek Theater earlier that year, a group of local architectural historians had got in touch to make sure she had no intention of tearing down or overhauling the place. Since she was only leasing it, she thought their concern was unfounded. But it turned out to have a positive effect as publicity for Secret Staircase Construction. A Bay Area architecture association newsletter noted that the historic Whispering Creek Theater was back in use thanks to stage illusionist Tempest Raj, who was also now working for Secret Staircase Construction.

Lenore Woods read the article and knew she'd found the perfect company to do the renovations to the house that Chester Hill had built in the 1880s for himself. She was one of Chester's descendants, and an architect herself. The house had gone through various incarnations after Chester's death more than a century ago, so Lenore wanted to renovate it according to Chester's original intent and, in doing so, get a historical home designation from Hidden Creek.

There was nothing sinister about the chain of events that had led Tempest to perform at the Whispering Creek Theater and renovate the Whispering House. With a regenerating booby trap, however, her imagination was in overdrive looking for tenuous connections.

She was about to start the engine once more when a car pulled up in front of the Whispering House. Headlights in the twilight blinded her enough that she couldn't see who it was, only that it wasn't Ivy's pink moped or Gideon's distinctive Renault.

The newcomer turned off their headlights and stepped out

of the car. Tempest let out a breath. It was their client Lenore Woods. She unlocked her car door and stepped onto the road.

"Tempest?" Lenore held a paper grocery bag against her hip. She adjusted her glasses with her free hand and frowned, which wasn't a normal expression on her usually affable face. "Your dad said you'd all wrapped up and gone home for the day."

"I'm the straggler." Tempest crossed the deserted street and reached Lenore's side. "Thanks for continuing to play Santa Claus with the gifts of food you're secretly leaving every couple of days. The mini chocolate cupcakes were an especially big hit."

Lenore wasn't much taller than Tempest's grandmother, who barely came up to her chin. She wore large round glasses with copper frames and a chunky silver and turquoise necklace. Lenore had once told Tempest that all of her jewelry held some meaning for her, be it a necklace she'd bought when she worked in the Southwest or an elastic bracelet made of cheap plastic beads from one of her grandchildren.

"I have an ulterior motive." Lenore grinned and led the way up the path to the house. "I'm well aware that I was overly demanding in the initial phase of the renovation, which is why I'm not on site every day as you finish up the last cosmetic details we agreed on."

Tempest took the bag of groceries as Lenore fumbled for her keys.

"But I'm still particular about my house," Lenore continued, pushing open the door. "The groceries give me an excuse to look things over but also let your dad and his crew do their thing to get back on track and finish soon. I've already told you how much I love your puzzle panels in the attic. They're even better than I imagined."

"Credit goes to my dad for building them." Tempest set the bag on the kitchen island.

Lenore shook her head as she put away the food from the bag Tempest had set on the kitchen island. "You came up with the puzzle box idea as an imaginative explanation for why Chester drew sketches for sliding panels. Then your dad added those dazzling woodworking details. I don't give compliments easily, but you two are a great team."

Tempest agreed, even though the plans for this house had been challenging from the start. Lenore had only a partial set of the original blueprints, and she'd done some initial renovations herself, including removing two odd structures in the backyard that were added in the 1950s: a gazebo and a tiki bar. Though she didn't have the entirety of the original blueprints, she had some of Chester's papers that described what he had envisioned.

As soon as her neighbor Julian heard about Lenore hiring Secret Staircase Construction, he rushed to hire them as well. He was "so close" to having *Architectural Digest* feature his home that he'd be damned if Lenore Woods beat him to it. Never mind the fact that she had no interest in inviting the magazine's cameras into her home. Julian had tried to argue it was a conflict of interest for the crew to work with both of them.

Darius had considered rejecting the Rhodeses as clients even before that ridiculous request; he could tell Julian would be difficult from the start. But they needed the money. Installing the fencing and high-end security system at Fiddler's Folly after the events of earlier that year had been expensive.

After Paloma's "accident," it was clear Julian had an ulterior motive. Perhaps he really had planned to have his home showcased. Now they'd never know. What Tempest did know was that in Lenore Woods, they had an eager client who was a pleasure to work with and didn't believe her unpleasant neighbor's lies, but who was also serious about getting her historical home designation from the city.

Usually, when planning a large job, about half of a client's desires were standard-issue renovations, and the other half were the reason Secret Staircase Construction was selected. Tempest and her dad interviewed clients extensively to find out what was at the heart of each of their requests. There were countless ways to create any bit of architectural magic, so the important thing was how each client wished to interact with their home. A "magical fireplace" for one client could mean that it lit up automatically when they played certain keys on the piano from the first song their child learned to play. For another, it meant a faux fireplace that was actually a door to a secret library. Or perhaps it meant a stone dragon sculpture inside a hearth sleeping with its eyes and mouth closed, which would transform into an open-mouthed, fire-breathing dragon when you pressed certain bricks. Most dreams were possible. It was only a matter of discovering the heart of the dream.

Tempest came up with the idea for the attic's built-in puzzle after interviewing Lenore and looking at the remnants of original blueprints and notes that existed from a century ago. The job of architectural misdirection was much like a magic trick. Misdirection that led you to have one set of expectations, then revealed an enchanting surprise.

Or a horrible surprise, as was the case with the regenerating booby trap.

Tempest couldn't help but feel that the booby traps must have been created by someone who understood the ideas behind magic and the components of construction.

"Tempest?" Lenore asked, craning her neck to look up at her. Tempest got the feeling it wasn't the first time Lenore had just said her name. "Sorry. I'm a bit distracted by everything that's happened."

"What's happened?" Lenore whipped her head around the kitchen and stormed back to the foyer to open the secret door leading to the attic. She pressed a special knot in the wood and the door popped open. "Everything is in working order," she mumbled as she slid her fingers along the inner doorframe and stepped inside.

"Nothing's wrong at the house." Tempest jogged after Lenore, who was charging up the secret staircase. Motion sensor lighting from electric wall sconces clicked on as they wound their way around the stone treads of the castle-like circular staircase. "You haven't read the news today?"

"Why would I read the news?" Lenore pushed open the panel that opened into the attic and smiled as she caught her breath. "I'll be eighty next year. Life's too short to catch up on the news more than once a week. Today isn't my news day."

"It's about Julian Rhodes."

"If you're talking about his gruesome death," said Lenore, "I know all about that. Your dad called earlier. He told me about Julian and your friend. I'm truly sorry to hear that someone you care about was injured. For someone so young, you've lost too many people you care about. But Julian? If you're looking for me to express false niceties about that horrid man, you'll be here until you're as old as I am."

Lenore paused as she ran her fingertips over the intricate rose patterns Darius had carved into the wooden paneling and looked Tempest straight in the eye. "I'm glad the man is dead. It makes all our lives easier. Sometimes the world is better off without a person who's wronged so many people. Don't you agree?"

The thought had crossed Tempest's mind that it was surprising nobody had tried to murder Julian before. For all she knew, maybe they had.

She had also wondered, more times than she cared to admit, what her aunt Elspeth had done to drive someone to murder her on stage. Tempest didn't believe in the supposed "Raj family curse," and she didn't believe in blaming the victim, but Elspeth was no saint. Elspeth and her sister Emma, Tempest's mom, had fought so intensely that they split up their successful Selkie Sisters act and Emma had felt the need to leave Scotland for California. Emma Raj had been looking into her sister's murder. What skeletons had she found in her sister's closet? What would Tempest find in Julian's if she kept looking?

Lenore flipped off the attic light switch, plunging the puzzle room into near darkness. Without a look back at Tempest, she headed back down the secret staircase.

Ten years ago

Before the house lights go dark, the woman in the wings of the stage catches a glimpse of Nicodemus in the front row of the audience. He's home in Edinburgh for a short break during a tour of America. He's made time to see his old protégée. Of course he has. This makes her smile. Her eyes are joyful. She looks as if she's almost forgotten the curse when she flips her dark hair, places a top hat on her head, and takes her first step onto the stage.

Elspeth Raj doesn't know she's stepping onto a stage for the last time in her mortal life. Or that her grave will be desecrated and her hand stolen. As the lights dim, the familiar excitement buzzes through her body, tempered by the weight that accompanies all her performances.

The weight of the Raj family curse.

Nobody knows how it happened that the Raj family curse crossed the sea from the southern tip of India to a cobblestone alley of Edinburgh's Old Town, but it had arrived as if carried by a tempest.

In an ancient city where the modern inhabitants still speak of selkies dripping salt and seaweed as they emerge from the sea, kelpies dragging unsuspecting victims to their watery doom, and ghosts whispering in your ear as you take a shortcut through a dark and narrow lane to reach the Royal Mile, it isn't difficult to believe in curses. Especially with a mentor like Nicodemus the Necromancer. His illusions are all explained rationally, yet Elspeth has always wondered ... Is he so successful because he has a touch of the supernatural?

Emma and Elspeth Raj weren't raised to be superstitious. Their father, Ashok, *half* believes in the Raj family curse. As a medical doctor, he's a rational man of science, yet he also witnessed his eldest brother being killed in an accident on stage. The same fate befell his aunt—also the eldest child of her generation. His great-uncle, who worked for the British during colonial rule, had been the first to die.

The story repeats itself across generations.

The eldest child dies by magic.

Was it a curse or a series of unfortunate accidents? Ashok Raj has a big heart and has never been one to take chances. He left India for the University of Edinburgh, where he met Morag Ferguson, and soon afterward, the happily married couple had two children.

The Raj sisters aren't more superstitious than the average Scot. Still ... tonight's show is listed on the Edinburgh Fringe Festival program as a variety show, filled with stories and songs for all ages. This is not a magic show.

Yet Elspeth knows, deep down, magic is in her heart. Is this what dooms her?

Elspeth is the older of the two sisters. Emma left for California years ago, and Elspeth has performed on her own for more than fifteen years.

Tonight, this night where she is to meet her fate, is her biggest show yet. It's the opening night of her new show at the Edinburgh Fringe Festival. She wishes her niece, Tempest, could be here, but the girl is a teenager and lives across the ocean in California. She's seen her aunt perform many times and doesn't know there's anything special about tonight.

Elspeth is wearing a new costume. A tailored black dress with silver shimmer, and a top hat that not only reminds her of how she got her start thanks to Nicodemus, but also holds much of the magic she plans to perform tonight. The foundations of stage magic were built into the men's suits but not into the women's dresses. Elspeth doesn't especially enjoy performing in a suit, but she likes the pockets of men's dress wear, and a top hat can hide many things.

This night, the hat she loves so much fails her. It offers no protection when a prop that is not part of her act is rolled onto the stage so hastily that she is pressed into the restraints before she can react. It does not shield her confusion as her eyes scan the dark wings of the stage for an explanation that does not come.

As the blade of a guillotine that is more than a prop takes the life of Elspeth Raj, Nicodemus watches in horror from his seat. He realizes, a second too late, that this is not a trick. He has never in his life felt so helpless.

Why is there a real blade at the theater that night? Elspeth would never have agreed to such a dangerous illusion.

Elspeth's top hat rolls away, coming to a stop center stage. Confusion comes first. Then the screams. "A terrible accident," people begin to murmur, once it is clear Elspeth will not be standing up to take a bow ever again.

Whatever really happened, Elspeth Raj takes her secrets to the grave.

Chapter 11

In the morning, Tempest wasn't any less convinced that Julian Rhodes's death was as straightforward as everyone thought. Sleeping eight hours did take the edge off her worry, but only just. She had too many unanswered questions about all three theater deaths that had impacted her life. Elspeth, Emma, and now Julian.

She'd left the Whispering House at the same time as Lenore and gone to bed early after having dinner with her family at Fiddler's Folly. Her dad and grandparents still believed Paloma to be guilty, so dinner had been a somber, but not stressful, affair. Ash cooked what he considered a "simple" dinner. Potato cakes, onion chickpea fritters, and vegetables stir-fried in coconut oil with mustard seeds and curry leaves. He only made one dessert (a delicious mango ice cream), which was the biggest indicator that he wasn't too stressed out. When he stress-baked, he always made at least three desserts.

After taking a quick, cold shower—a trick that was momentarily horrible but really did help activate the brain cells—Tempest fed Abra and then walked with the bunny to the tree house for her own breakfast.

She found her grandfather at the stove. He handed her a mug

of jaggery coffee and told her he'd join her at the deck dining table momentarily.

"Morning, Gran," said Tempest, as she stepped through the tree house kitchen to the deck with a bunny in one arm and warm coffee in the other. But Grannie Mor wasn't alone. She was sitting on the deck with Sanjay. His thick black hair was tousled and far sexier than Tempest wanted to admit. Although he wasn't wearing the tuxedo he performed in, he was wearing a crisp white dress shirt, with his bowler hat resting on his knee. The valuable custom hat was usually filled with dozens, if not hundreds, of items used in his magic. From its presence here at Fiddler's Folly and far from any stage, Tempest was more certain than ever that the hat was his security blanket.

"Check it out!" Sanjay held up an intricately cut pop-up paper theater stage that he'd been showing Grannie Mor. "Nicodemus created this one-handed, using just hospital scratchpads, a newspaper, and dull scissors one of the nurses no doubt scrounged up for him."

"How long have you been here?"

"Only long enough for half a cup of coffee."

"I insisted you needed sleep," said Morag. "Though if you hadn't arrived by the time we finished breakfast, I'm sure he would have woken you anyway."

"Aren't you supposed to be performing in Vancouver?" Tempest asked. "And you've already seen Nicodemus?" She deposited her mug on the table and Abra on the deck floor, then lifted the delicate paper pop-up into her hands. A figure made of multiple layers of newsprint swayed on the paper stage.

"Tuesday night is dark, and that's my only night off this week, so I need to be back in time for tomorrow night's show. I went straight to the hospital from my flight this morning. You aren't even looking at this magical paper pop-up." Sanjay took it back from her. He tugged on a strip of paper, and the bowler hat on the figure's head lifted into the air. The assured pose of the mini-Sanjay was eerily like the real one. It was uncanny how, even with flimsy paper and a single hand, Nicodemus had cut out a figure that was so clearly Sanjay.

Tempest laughed and hugged him.

Sanjay was blushing when she let go. "I have no idea what's so funny, but do I smell death donuts?"

Grandpa Ash chuckled from the kitchen door that led to the deck. "The vada donuts are for Tempest. You should stick to the regular donuts." Ash loved to make mash-ups of traditional dishes, and one of his favorites was adding a combination of both fire and sweetness to traditional South Indian vada. "I'll make more coffee. Didn't you sleep last night, Sanjay?"

"How could I? My show ended close to midnight. Then I had to greet my fans, and I caught the first flight of the morning." He stifled a yawn.

Ash clicked his tongue. "Extra-strong coffee coming up." He retreated to the kitchen.

"I'll help." Morag stood from the table and followed her husband, even though there was no way he needed help. She closed the sliding glass door behind her. Another thing they never did.

"Is anything else on this table spicy?" Sanjay eyed the jar of homemade jam with a skeptical eye.

"It was nice of you to come back to see him. You should probably avoid the jalapeño jam though." She moved the jar out of his reach.

"I came back for you, but I wanted to check on Nic as well. He's dying for some food from the outside world. Aside from that, he was in good spirits."

"Really?"

"He's a hero. He didn't get to see his adoring fans on tour, but he saved the girl."

Tempest groaned. "By braving a booby-trapped door so I wouldn't have to?"

"That's what people are saying."

"They should be saying that both of us are stupid for even considering it."

"Were you really going to break into a booby-trapped theater just to show you're still The Tempest?"

"Not as a magic stunt." Tempest glared at him. "To get my notebooks."

"The ones with ideas for your upcoming show?"

"Including that one."

Sanjay waved a hand over his coffee. Once his fingertips passed over the mug, a thornless rose stem rested on the mug. The red rosebud at its end was pristine, even though it must have been hiding in either his bowler hat or pocket.

"Show-off."

Sanjay handed her the flower and finished the coffee. "Were flowers being delivered to Nic's hospital room when you were there yesterday?"

"Flowers? No, I saw him pretty soon after the accident. Before any of us knew they'd be keeping him overnight."

"His fans have . . . *interesting* taste," Sanjay commented. "I usually get roses. He's received three bouquets of night-blooming flowers and two bundles of dried black roses. I didn't even know black roses were a thing."

"He *is* Nicodemus the Necromancer. Or at least he *was*." Tempest scooped Abra back into her arms.

"This is exactly why I needed to come. To cheer you both up." He yawned. "Do you have any idea how early in the morning flights start?"

"Around the time I used to go to bed."

"Exactly. It's inhumane to get up before sunrise. People didn't evolve to do this. Yet I still got up tragically before sunrise. For you." He gave her a crooked smile that looked both far too practiced and far too sexy.

He and Tempest had once been an item. At the time, Tempest had wondered if it was more than just a fun fling. But that was long ago, way before life got messy and their careers had taken them in different directions and to different parts of the world. Now that they were both based back in the Bay Area, the idea had crossed her mind once more. He was her kind of fun, objectively gorgeous, and perhaps most importantly, she trusted him as if he were her own brother. Which, she observed, might be the problem.

Her first instinct when she thought of Sanjay was that he was a beloved teddy bear. She knew she took him for granted more than she should, but she feared what might happen if she let herself want something more. The only evidence, beyond harmless flirting, that he was interested in Tempest was the jealousy he had shown when she went on a date with Gideon. The enigma that was Gideon Torres was another reason Tempest wasn't sure what exactly she wanted.

But the main reason? Until she figured out what was behind the Raj family curse that had taken both her mom and aunt from her, she couldn't prioritize *any* guy.

"You're saying that having a nightly midnight performance schedule is normal?" she replied, instead of saying any of the many other thoughts in her mind.

He shrugged. "At least it's fun. But forget about me. I really did come home for you."

She melted a little as a lock of unkempt hair fell over his puppy dog eyes.

"Anyway, are you going to show me the scene of the crime?"

"You want to see where Nicky got hurt?"

He blinked at her. "Of course. How else can I help you figure out what's going on with the booby-trapped theater?"

Chapter 12

Hidden Creek was a small town nestled into the hills next
to much larger cities in the East Bay of the San Francisco
Bay Area. Founded shortly after the California Gold
Rush, it never became as populous as neighboring cities because of the unique features of its land. Not only did it sit on a
steep hillside, but a long-ago earthquake split a portion of the
earth underground apart, giving Hidden Creek its name. The
underground stream ran dry during droughts, but otherwise
residents could hear the water flowing from the few places it
appeared aboveground. The land wasn't especially desirable
from a practical point of view, but people who'd come to California for the Gold Rush hadn't been the most practical of
people to begin with. The site and its lush trees were beautiful,
and the land much less sought-after than in nearby areas, so
the impractical dreamers moved in.

Tempest loved the narrow, winding roads surrounded by trees,
which provided a sense of privacy to the residents of Hidden
Creek and belied their proximity to several much larger cities.

When she pulled into Whispering Creek Theater's parking
lot, expecting to see only a bit of crime scene tape marring
the stone theater and its wooden door, Tempest's heart sank.

Dozens of cars filled the parking spaces in the portion of the lot that wasn't roped off by crime scene tape.

Most of the onlookers had their cell phones out, taking selfies with the Gothic theater and wooded hills in the background, or filming the scene while crouched on the ground to frame a shot with the police tape in the foreground. Two people with larger cameras were huddled at the side of the parking lot, which gave more dramatic views of the theater with the steep hillside behind it.

"What the . . . ?" Sanjay murmured. "Is this normal?"

"Who *are* these people?"

"I'll take that as a *no*. My guess is bored people claiming to be fans of Nicodemus, and some paranormal investigators."

"Ghost hunters? But the theater has *always* been supposedly haunted."

"Not by a dangerous ghost who's decided to kill people."

"The third blade," murmured Tempest. "The one that made Nicodemus think it was regenerating."

"If even someone as rational and jaded as Nicodemus is frightened, what hope does everyone else have?"

He was right. Now that *another* blade had sprung from the door and people online were talking about the haunted theater's latest victim, it would become even more crowded as the day progressed. Did the amateur videographers think this would get them their fifteen minutes of fame? She'd already had a lengthy period of moderate fame, and she far preferred relative anonymity.

Tempest tensed as she pulled into one of the few empty parking spots. *Was the killer here?* Wasn't that what they said? That the killer would come back to the scene of the crime? She didn't know who "they" were, but for good measure, as she stepped out of her jeep, she hit "record" on her phone and swept it across the crowd.

Nearby, a woman dressed in black lace insisted to her companion that they call an investigator. Did they know something?

"He never gets up this early," the companion answered. "The paranormal wavelengths aren't strong in the morning. I'm sure he's sleeping."

Ah. They were discussing a *paranormal* investigator. The women put the phone on speaker as they called, but only got the paranormal investigator's voice-mail message.

Tempest continued to scan the mob. A small man bumped her elbow as he walked with purpose through the crowd, holding a floral arrangement unlike any other Tempest had seen. He placed the unusual bouquet next to a pile of equally strange flowers and peculiar stuffed animals, which was when Tempest realized why the flowers struck her as odd. They were artfully arranged dried flowers, like the ones Sanjay had described being delivered to Nicodemus in the hospital. About half of the flowers in the pile were dried, and the other half was an assortment of closed buds Tempest recognized as night-blooming flowers.

The stuffed animals next to the flowers consisted mostly of bats, ravens, and black cats. This wasn't a shrine to honor Julian Rhodes, who'd died there two nights ago, but an altar to Nicodemus the Necromancer.

The sounds and shadows of bats and ravens were often featured in his performances, and his original assistant had been the Cat of Nine Lives, who'd dressed in a black catsuit along with cat ears and a tail. Did these people leaving flowers and plush toys realize he wasn't dead? Or, like Tempest, did they consider this the death of the part of his life that made him who he was?

Wobbly fencing with tarps hung over the sides blocked off the theater's booby-trapped door and prevented people from seeing or reaching the door itself, but it wasn't deterring anyone from hovering nearby. The wind picked up the edge of one of the tarps and gave Tempest a glimpse of the façade before a young woman in uniform ran over to the tarp and quickly tied down the edge that had come loose.

But the tarp had lifted for long enough for Tempest to see that the entire door had been removed. In its place, solid wooden planks covered the entrance to the theater.

"Come on," said Tempest. "I can't get you as close as I wanted to, but let me at least buy you a coffee."

So many people had gathered in the parking lot that an enterprising pop-up coffee shop on wheels was parked in the far corner, with the name Storm Chaser Coffee on the side. Two people were in line in front of the converted van. Maybe the coffee truck was exploiting a tragedy, but more importantly, it was providing caffeine that both Tempest and Sanjay desperately needed.

They reached the front of the line, close enough to read the history of Storm Chaser Coffee printed at the top of the menu, explaining how the van had originally been owned by a group of storm chasers who followed tornadoes. The cute write-up didn't say what had happened to the original storm chasers, and Tempest was afraid to ask.

"I'll take a Storm Warning," Tempest said to the barista. From its description, it was a cappuccino with cinnamon and chocolate shavings on top.

"I'll have the Cyclone," said Sanjay.

"Is that wise?" Tempest raised an eyebrow.

"Two shots of espresso dropped into a dark roast? Hell yes. If you hadn't noticed, I only got a two-hour nap last night."

They took their drinks back across the parking lot to Tempest's jeep. Two officers she didn't recognize were trying to do crowd control on the outside of the fencing. She hoped Officer Quinn had finally gotten some time off to sleep.

"Shouldn't they be calling in a bomb squad at this point?" Sanjay asked. "Since the door was booby-trapped, how do they know what's going on with the rest of the theater?"

"Rinehart doesn't want to share credit with anyone else on solving this case," said Tempest. "He's ambitious. He screwed up a big case earlier this year. He removed the door already, so I doubt he'll ask for more outside help at this point. He thinks all he has to do is find Paloma Rhodes and his case will be solved." She glanced uneasily at the theater.

"I read articles this morning saying the murder suspect, Paloma Rhodes, is still out there," said Sanjay. "That's the story the police department is going with."

"It's too crowded out here for us to be talking about this." She unlocked the car and they got inside. "You don't think they're right, do you?"

Sanjay blinked at her. "I just got here. I have no idea what to believe. You'll need to catch me up so I can come to an informed decision."

Tempest told Sanjay all about what she knew, from Julian's midnight call through to thinking Nicodemus was dead when he cried out as the booby trap sliced through his hand.

"You inspected the booby traps?"

She shook her head. "I didn't see the trap mechanisms, but I was close enough to see the two blades the first night. The long one that killed Julian and the shorter one that hurt the paramedic. The blades came from the space between two slats of the wooden door."

"Then presumably, the traps were hidden on the other side of the door." Sanjay set his coffee in the drink holder and spun a coin between his fingers. "Someone had to know enough about construction to not only rig booby traps but to also alter such a solid door. And break into the theater."

"The last part isn't too difficult. The box office is the only room with a really high-end lock."

"Back to the booby traps, then. Did this Paloma person have the skills to build a booby trap, or would she have needed to hire someone?"

"She used to be a librarian, but I don't know her well enough to know what she's capable of. But that's not the biggest question. Why would Paloma Rhodes kill her husband *here?*" The theater looked so strange, surrounded by white tarps hiding the crimes that had taken place inside, and people milling about like it was a festival rather than a death trap.

"I can think of a dozen reasons." The coin he was spinning disappeared, and he held up his index finger. "One, it would throw suspicion on Secret Staircase Construction instead of herself." He held up a second finger. "Two, it points directly to you since you're the one leasing the theater." He lifted a third finger, then paused. "Actually, that's all I've got. I don't think this coffee is strong enough. I'm too old for all-nighters."

"Two is more than enough reasons if she's trying to frame me."

"Who said anything about framing you? I'm sure she wanted it to look like it was someone else, and you're the ones embroiled in a legal battle with them. But *framing* you?"

"I forgot to mention one thing. There was a note."

"A note?" Sanjay repeated. "What kind of note?"

"A note was found on the door that said, *Come inside, Tempest.* In my handwriting."

Sanjay's face darkened. "Truly in your handwriting?"

"Someone must have ripped it from one of my notebooks I left in the theater locked inside the greenroom. Someone wanted Julian to go inside the theater through that door."

"Triggering the booby trap," he murmured.

"But before he saw the note," said Tempest, "someone made him think I wanted to meet him at the theater at midnight."

"How would they even know you'd be up at midnight? Aren't you on an early schedule these days? Speaking of which, aren't you supposed to be at work? I don't even understand your new job."

"I create architectural misdirection. I do the same kind of thinking about illusions as I used to on stage, only now I do it through architecture. My part of our current big job is nearly wrapped up."

"Did you change your business cards to say 'architectural misdirection' instead of 'stage illusionist'?"

"I don't have any business cards."

"Business cards are classic for a reason. That guy Gideon, who works for your dad, takes his rejection of the modern world too far by shunning cell phones, but he's right that too many aspects of the past have been forgotten. I'll give him that. Hey, I think the officer guarding the tarp is leaving to yell at those guys trying to climb the stone wall. Now's our chance."

Sanjay was out the door before she could stop him.

She was so focused on Sanjay's path that she barely noticed a young woman with dyed black hair, platform boots, and streaked mascara running down her cheeks stomping up to them.

"Get away from here!" the girl cried. "Are you here to help your mom hurt more people?" She held a takeaway cup in clenched fingers, and she flung the contents of the paper cup at Tempest. Cold, light brown liquid splashed over Tempest's hair and T-shirt.

Tempest didn't often find herself too stunned to react, but as the girl's friend dragged her away, Sanjay did the same to Tempest.

The girl had accused her of being there to *help her mom hurt more people*. Who did she think Tempest was?

"Something is very wrong here." Sanjay shoved Tempest into the car and tossed her a towel he found in her back seat so she could mop up her dripping shirt and hair.

"I really hope this is just iced tea."

"I don't see any more crazed Nicodemus fans headed our way." Sanjay reached over her and locked the doors. "You can dry off first, but then I think we need to get out of here. *Quickly.*"

"Who did she think I was?" Tempest sopped up the tea from her dripping hair. A splash of the liquid of unknown origin had gotten onto her face. *Eww.*

"Oh, she knew exactly who you were." Sanjay winced as he scrolled on his phone. "Tempest." Sanjay's phone disappeared— Tempest had no idea where—and he put his hands on her wet shoulders. "All these people . . . I wasn't wrong about who they are, but I was wrong about why it's such a big deal today. They think your mom is the one who rigged these traps."

"They think *my mom* planned this before she vanished?"

"Not exactly." He let go of her and read from his phone. *"Emma Raj sets off booby traps from beyond the grave."*

"That's impossible. Those knives weren't hiding in that door for five years. How could she—"

"Emma Raj worked with Secret Staircase Construction. She was brilliant. Your mom could totally have rigged those booby traps in some secret time-release way if she put her mind to it. But that's not the only thing they're saying."

"But—" The realization dawned on Tempest. "The ghost hunters. They think it's *her ghost?*"

"The paranormal investigators are saying that. Most of these people here are just along for the ride, I expect. What do you want to bet that more than half of those flowers from Nicodemus the Necromancer's supposed fans are from people who'd never heard of him until they caught up on social media posts this morning over breakfast?"

"I'm more worried about what Detective Rinehart will think once he realizes Paloma Rhodes didn't set the booby traps."

"I need to play devil's advocate," Sanjay said softly. "Your mom was behaving oddly before she vanished. All signs pointed to the conclusion that she'd died by suicide in the bay. She might have wanted to leave a legacy . . ."

"A legacy that would *kill* people?"

"You really don't think she could have done it?"

"*Of course not.*" Tempest glared at him. Tempest was only aware of the rage on her face when Sanjay shrank back in his seat.

"I'm not saying it's true," he insisted. "I'm saying how it *looks*. Forget about the ghost hunters. Think about what the more rational haters are thinking. That old wooden door is solid enough to hide a hell of a lot of secrets. Your mom was a brilliant stage illusionist even before she formed a construction company with your dad. She totally could have built booby traps that wouldn't be activated for years."

"She couldn't have lured Julian to the theater."

"Yeah, that bit needs the ghost hunter theory to work . . . Don't blame me! I'm just the messenger. I'm not the one posting these ideas online about the legacy of Emma Raj."

"She wanted to leave a legacy, but *not this*. There's no way my mom set these booby traps."

"The curse," Sanjay murmured.

"The Raj family curse."

It was this family legacy that had dominated Tempest's life for the last decade. Shaped her career—and then destroyed it.

The eldest child dies by magic.

Dangerous magic tricks had killed her great-great-grandfather, followed by the eldest child of the next generation and Grandpa Ash's eldest brother. Three dramatic deaths on stage. The world of stage magic was filled with tragic deaths. The Bullet Catch trick gone wrong when the bullet wasn't switched out, drowning inside a milk can when a safety mechanism was dented, and being buried alive when the weight of dirt was improperly calculated were some of the higher-profile stories that tragically repeated themselves over the years.

The idea of the Raj family curse took hold with three deaths across three generations, but Tempest didn't believe a curse had followed her grandfather to Scotland. When Aunt Elspeth died in a supposed accident on stage, Tempest's mom had discovered that the murderer had taken advantage of the rumors of the eldest child in the Raj family dying by magic. That's what Emma Raj was going to reveal the night she vanished.

Tempest's mom's body had never been found, and despite the suspicious circumstances of her disappearance at the Whispering Creek Theater, the leading theory was that she'd taken her own life. But Tempest had never believed that. Instead, she had thrown herself into magic and written her first headlining stage show based on the story of two sisters who were separated but reunited—it was wish fulfillment, creating a happy ending on stage that didn't exist in real life.

The existing rumors about Emma Raj were bad enough. But for people to think she'd set deadly booby traps before she died that would kill people years later? Or that her *ghost* had set them? It was too much to bear.

As if it wasn't enough that Tempest's notebooks had been used to lure Julian to his death and were now being held captive, now her mom's memory was being dragged into the mess. There was no question she had to figure out who killed Julian Rhodes as quickly as she could to prove it wasn't her mom who had set these booby traps.

EDINBURGH, SCOTLAND

Thirty-five years ago

In a cramped pub with room for only twenty-five members of the audience, sisters Emma and Elspeth Raj make their debut at the Edinburgh Fringe Festival.

During their twenty-five-minute set, they play their fiddles and tell a story that's an imagined version of their own family history.

People have always said the Raj sisters have an otherworldly look about them, with their silky black hair that flows past their waists, dark features, and a haunted look in their eyes. It's easy for members of the audience to believe they are the immortal selkies they pretend to be on stage.

The sisters spin the story that they are the daughters of a selkie from Scottish waters and a sailor from the southern tip of India, always pulled back to the sea. They have not yet invented their biggest illusion, The Tempest, but instead, they accompany each other on the fiddle, each telling a different aspect of the story, while shadows dance behind them in the small theater. The show ends with only the briefest of magic tricks in which their fiddles vanish and their legs are revealed to be the tails of seals.

The audience claps with moderate enthusiasm at the end of the performance, yet nobody stays to talk with them afterward.

Except one person.

The man has a mischievous twinkle in his eye and wears a top hat on his head. Emma vaguely recognizes him, though until he introduces himself, she can't pinpoint why. He isn't yet as famous as he'll become.

"You're the Selkie Sisters," he declares, even though that's not yet what they've named their act. "My name is Nicodemus. Forgive me for taking up your valuable time. You are both talented beyond your years, but would you permit me to give you a few notes?"

The following months are a whirlwind. They have never worked so hard in their lives. Their efforts are rewarded, as the duo become an Edinburgh attraction even more popular than the ghost walks, underground vault explorations, and castle tours. Locals and tourists alike love the Selkie Sisters, the two young women who come from the sea and weave stories together through storytelling and music—with a dash of magic that grows increasingly prominent as the shows progress. Without realizing it, under Nicodemus's guidance and to their father's chagrin, they are full-fledged stage magicians. They can't escape their fate. They are free when they're on the stage telling their magical stories.

The illusion of The Tempest takes shape as they graduate to larger theater bookings. Images from a magic lantern cast shadows across the stage and the audience, replicating the waves from a fierce storm. Emma uses a sailor's knife to break into a mysterious steamer trunk aboard the ship. The sisters step into the trunk for shelter, but it falls overboard and tumbles to the bottom of the sea. The sisters appear moments later, dripping wet, on top of a papier-mâché seaside cliff on the other side of the stage. Most nights, they receive a standing ovation.

Nicodemus is delighted with their success. His own star is rising as well with his act Nicodemus the Necromancer and the Cat of Nine Lives. His audience grows bigger as he adds effects such as blowtorches that cut shadows in half and dried flowers that emerge from Cat's grave before she rises from the opposite side of the stage to which she disappeared. While he thrives on traveling the world as a touring magician, the Selkie Sisters prefer to stay in their hometown of Edinburgh.

Yet one night, something is off. Perhaps it is complacency. Perhaps it is a worn-out prop. Perhaps the sisters had a fight before the curtain rose. Whatever the cause, The Tempest illusion falls flat. There is no standing ovation that night.

Emma and Elspeth Raj never speak of it again, and Emma runs away to California, putting an end to the Selkie Sisters.

Elspeth remains in Scotland and carries on as a stage magician. Her star dims, but shines brightly enough to pay the bills and draw a moderate audience on weekends and at festivals.

Emma finds love in California and never looks back.

Or does she?

Emma Raj is no longer a stage magician like her sister, yet she creates magic for people on a more personal level. Unlike her sister, Emma becomes adept not only at performing but also at building illusions. She plays her fiddle in the hills of California, remembering a time she will not speak of, and she wonders whether she has escaped her fate or if the Raj family curse is real.

can't take you home yet?" Tempest asked.

Standing next to Nicodemus's hospital bed, she felt un-characteristically small in the room that was now crammed full of both dead and night-blooming flowers from old fans and new. There was a pile of stuffed toy black cats as well, with a cute fluffy bat on top. The plan had been for her to pick him up around this time and bring him back to Fiddler's Folly.

"It's all been blown out of proportion," Nicodemus insisted. "The teenage doctor is being overly cautious because he thinks I'm one hundred years old. He wants to monitor me for one more night."

"What's the deal with this terrifying cat?" Sanjay held up a plush black cat with its mouth and eyes sewn shut with red yarn. "Whoever made this monstrosity is clearly the person the police should be looking for."

"It's based on one of my own illusions," said Nicodemus. "In one of my earliest routines with the Cat of Nine Lives, I used to wind red yarn around her until she was a mummy. When I unraveled her, only dust remained—but Cat would appear alive and well in the back row of the seats."

"It's still terrifying." Sanjay held the plush cat at arm's length, before stuffing it underneath the other gifts where they couldn't see it.

"Even more bits and bobs than an hour ago?" a new voice said from just outside the open door, nearly causing Sanjay to knock over the pile. "Glad to see the cat shoved to the bottom. Bats are where you found your stride. You're better off without Cat."

"Sanjay, do you know Brodie Frost?" Tempest asked. "He works with Nicky." She didn't know if he had an actual title, or what he considered himself. He was more than an assistant and stagehand but less than a co-star.

"He hates it when people call him that, you know." Brodie ducked his head to step through the doorway and looked down at Tempest with an expression she couldn't gauge. Maybe it simply felt odd because she didn't usually have to crane her neck upward to look someone in the eye.

"Tempest gets away with calling me Nicky," said Nicodemus. "But don't you get any ideas."

"We met at the Fringe a few years ago." Sanjay extended his hand to shake Brodie's. "Good to see you."

"Wish it was backstage again instead of here." Brodie turned to Nicodemus. "Mary's got paperwork you'll need to sign."

"More?" Nicodemus looked far older than his years as he looked up at the ceiling.

"Different countries, different rules."

Despite his protestations of good health, Nicodemus was clearly tired after talking with them and reading additional forms related to canceling his tour. Brodie had to leave to deal with more tour cancellation details, and Tempest knew it was a good idea for her and Sanjay to depart as well. The doctor was right that Nicodemus needed rest.

Tempest also knew that he'd be bored out of his mind stuck in the room alone, so she offered to stop by the art supply store around the corner to pick up better paper and scissors for him, so at least he wouldn't drive the hospital staff mad.

"I don't want to bother Ash, but perhaps you could also bring me some food from that café near your house that you love?" Nicodemus stroked his devilish goatee and attempted to look as angelic as possible.

"I'll get you an assortment of their best offerings," Tempest agreed.

Sanjay had also been splashed by some of the liquid of unknown origin, so Tempest dropped him off at a BART station so he could take the train to his San Francisco apartment to shower, change, and get his truck. Then she swung by Veggie Magic, to bring Nicodemus a late lunch from the outside world, and the art supply store near the hospital, for paper and art materials. Nicodemus was asleep when she returned, so she left the food and supplies with a note.

Back at Fiddler's Folly, Tempest's plan was to gather her thoughts in the secret turret above her bedroom, where the walls were covered in inspirational magic show posters and she had space to think. By the time Sanjay got back, hopefully she'd have a plan worked out, and they could meet up with Ivy and Gideon.

But as she passed the cedar-clad barn workshop on the way to the main house from the driveway, she heard voices coming from inside. Her dad, and a woman whose voice she didn't recognize. Tempest poked her head inside the airy space of organized chaos. The open-plan workshop retained the feeling of a barn, with its gambrel roof with two different pitches visible both inside and out. A woman with long black hair similar to Tempest's was speaking with Darius at his favorite woodworking table.

Darius spotted Tempest. "Nicky doing okay?"

"Not well enough to check out, but well enough that he's rebelled against hospital food."

The woman turned and Tempest saw she was a teenager, so most likely part of this spring semester's high school student cohort.

For a six-week chunk of each semester, Darius opened the workshop to a different group of high school–age students two weekday afternoons and on Saturdays. It wasn't a formal apprenticeship, but he taught them basic construction skills and mentored them in whatever related profession they were interested in, often bringing in volunteer guest speakers from the community of people he knew. Grandpa Ash provided homemade snacks. And for the last cohort, Grannie Mor had painted a group portrait of the team standing in front of their creation. It had become a full family affair. Darius would often go even further when mentoring a couple of kids with bad home lives. He'd had a rough childhood until he landed with foster mom Mona Mendez when he was a teenager, eventually taking her name because it was the one that was most meaningful to him. Darius had been the one to recognize that Ivy and her sister Dahlia had had a bad home life before Dahlia left for college.

At the end of each semester, the cohort built a structure of their choice that was donated once built. The only parameters were that it be built to code and be small enough to transport out through the oversize barn workshop doors. Previous projects included a walk-in greenhouse for a nearby community garden, a tree house for a park with structures that had burned down but not yet been rebuilt, and a tiny house for the backyard of a local foster parent whose house was full but whose own parents needed a place to live (the tiny house took more than the regular six weeks to complete, with the project lasting the small group closer to a full year).

"This is Florencia," Darius said.

"Just Flo," she corrected him.

"Flo, this is my daughter—"

"Tempest." Flo grinned and extended her hand. "Great to meet you."

"Same."

"You spilled something on your shirt."

The dangers of white T-shirts. And of angry fans of Nicodemus the Necromancer. Tempest never got anything on her costumes on stage, even when working with illusions that involved red wine. But real life was a whole lot messier. "Thanks. I didn't think the spring semester program was getting started for another week."

"It's not," said Darius.

"I had a few questions for your dad," said Flo, "to make sure I'm a good fit."

"It's *you* who's interviewing *me*," said Darius. "I can't blame you if you want to bail."

"Way to sell your training program, Papa," said Tempest.

He ran a large hand across his face. "I've gotta be honest. Two other participants dropped out yesterday."

"You mean their *guardians* pulled them out," said Flo. "My uncle doesn't care what I do, as long as it's legal. Even legal-*ish* is okay. I turned eighteen last month anyway, so I can sign the waiver myself. I just don't know if I'll fit in as a fat girl, you know? Two strikes against me in construction."

"It's true there are fewer women than guys who want to learn about carpentry and construction," said Tempest, "and there will always be guys who'll be jerks about a woman's weight, but I still hear the stories about the ultimate student-led takedown of the one guy who was a total ass."

Tempest's dad wrapped his arm around her and gave her a squeeze. "Word gets around that you don't mess with any women associated with Secret Staircase Construction. The offender was so embarrassed by his peers' reactions to his bullying that he left before I had a chance to kick him out."

Tempest's phone rang. An image of Sanjay wearing his bowler hat on stage showed on the screen so she picked up.

"You wound me, Tempest," he said. "You haven't told me the new security code for the Fiddler's Folly gate."

"So you can sneak up on me? Not likely. Call me when you get here. I'll let you in."

"Why do you think I'm calling?"

"You're *here* already? I saw you like an hour ago."

"You think it takes me more than a few minutes to take a shower and change into clean clothes? I wanted to get back to you as soon as possible. And there was no traffic on the bridge getting back here, for once. Buzz me in already."

"What's that weird noise?" Flo asked.

"Buzzer for our front gate." Darius frowned at the barely audible sound.

"It sounds like a sick frog," Flo commented.

"It broke when a tree branch fell on it during that big rainstorm," Tempest explained while her dad hit the button to open the gate. Nothing happened, so Darius grabbed a toolbox and headed to the gate.

Two minutes later, Sanjay stepped into the workshop spinning his bowler hat on the tip of his left index finger. "I wasn't even apart from you for an hour and the online gossip is even worse. Why am I surprised? I should never be surprised by trolls. Oh." His gaze fell to Flo. The spinning hat faltered, but Sanjay recovered by flipping it onto his head. "Sorry, I didn't realize you had company."

"This is Flo," said Tempest. "She might join this spring's student cohort. Flo, this is my friend Sanjay."

"I've seen videos of you online," Flo said to Sanjay, with a slight blush on her cheeks. "You're good. You slay that tux and old-school hat."

He thanked her and gave her one of his most charming smiles. Her blush deepened, and she buried herself in her phone. His smile had that effect on a lot of people. Unfortunately, Tempest was sometimes one of them.

"Big yikes." Flo looked up from her phone with a horrified

expression on her face. "Have you seen that people are saying it's not that dead guy's wife who killed him but *Tempest's mom?*"

"I know," Tempest and Sanjay said at the same time.

"So messed up," Flo whispered. "Families have enough baggage without internet randos accusing dead relatives of murder. But I've gotta say, it really is creepy how that booby trap is regenerating. What's up with that? You don't think it could really be her ghost, do you?"

"No," Tempest and Sanjay said at the same time once more, sending Flo into a fit of giggles.

"Sorry!" she said, recovering. "That was totally disrespectful, wasn't it? But you two are just so cute together."

"We're not—" Tempest began.

A loud buzz cut her off.

"Your dad fixed it," said Flo, and Tempest hit the button to open the gate. "I'll just see myself out and thank your dad outside. Nice meeting both of you." She gave a little wave as she left the workshop.

"I'd say there's a fifty percent chance that she posts rumors about us online within the hour," said Sanjay once Flo was gone. "Just because two friends are in sync doesn't mean—"

"Forget about that potential rumor. We need to disprove the more important rumors about my mom. The longer it is before the police catch the real killer who also nearly killed Nicky, the more entrenched those rumors will become and the more likely it is they'll focus on me next."

"You make it sound like those two things are equally important."

They were, in a sense. She believed it would eventually be proven that she wasn't the one who'd lured Julian to the theater and killed him, even if the mess with the note in her handwriting muddled the situation initially. But in the meantime, there would be even more damage to the memory of her mom, and that was something she couldn't bear.

The implication that the rumor *could be true* that Tempest's mom had rigged ingenious booby traps that would be set off after she had died was far more serious. Even though it didn't explain the note on the door or the person who'd lured Julian to the theater, the post *Is Emma Raj a murderer from beyond the grave?* got far more views than the videos giving rational explanations that didn't involve Tempest's dead mom.

There was a connection, certainly. Tempest didn't yet know what it was, but it was there. She'd rented the theater precisely because her mom had disappeared there. She had told her manager, Winston, that she rented it to practice for a final performance she'd agreed to film, and while that was true, she hadn't told him what she hoped to do for the performance. What Tempest had wanted, more than anything, was to solve her mom's murder and have that solution be the heart of her story on the stage.

But now, that plan for a happy ending with justice for her mom's murderer was not only falling apart, but the opposite was coming true. Tempest now had to fight the rumors that her mom, Emma Raj, was a killer.

Tempest looked up at the thick wooden beams above as she spoke, so she wouldn't have to face Sanjay's sympathetic gaze. "There are already so many rumors about my family. The Raj family curse. What became of my mom when she vanished. What was behind my sabotaged show last year." She spun into a pirouette. Then another. That always helped her think. When she stopped, she stood in front of Sanjay, close enough to touch him. But she didn't.

Instead, she took a large step back. "Anyone who thinks about the idea of my mom being a murderer from beyond the grave for more than two seconds will know it's ridiculous. I know that. But to have my mom accused of being a murderer, even if it's absurd . . . Is it wrong for that to matter to me?"

"No. I get it."

"Then let's get out of here and get to work."

"What did you have in mind?" Sanjay asked.

"How do you feel about breaking into a crime scene?"

Sanjay grinned at her. "I thought you'd never ask."

Chapter 14

No way," said Ivy.

"Breaking into a crime scene?" added Gideon. "I'm with Ivy on this."

"I knew you shouldn't have brought in the rest of the Scooby gang." Sanjay tugged at his collar and paced the length of the small turret above Tempest's room where the four friends had gathered. "Are you two committed to helping Tempest or not?"

"What can we do to help," asked Gideon, "that *doesn't* involve committing a felony?"

"Do you actually know it's a felony?" Sanjay tapped on the screen of his phone. "You don't even have a cell phone to look it up."

"People got by just fine before cell phones," Gideon said. "I don't care about the level of offense. I don't think it's the best way to help Tempest. If I knew it would sort out this mess, I'd be the first one inside."

He wasn't lying. He'd taken the blame for something she'd foolishly done earlier that year before she could stop him.

Despite the overwhelming task at hand, Tempest was overcome with affection for her friends, as she realized she now had so many people supporting her. It was so different from what her life used to be like.

But she didn't have time for warm and fuzzy feelings. She jumped up, slipped past her friends, and climbed down the steep, secret stairs that were more like a ladder. She jumped down the last two steps, landed on the hardwood floors of her bedroom, and crossed the room to the steamer trunk underneath the window that looked out over the steep hillside.

Ivy's evening reading hadn't given them any answers to their real-life murder, so Tempest knew it was time to act. By the time Ivy, Sanjay, and Gideon reached her side, she'd removed an outfit of chain mail armor.

Sanjay gaped at it. "What illusion did you need medieval chain mail for?"

"A time-travel transposition. The story fell flat so I ditched the idea and didn't end up using it, but it was custom made, so I saved it."

Story was everything in an illusion. It didn't matter how skilled a magician was or how big the mystery of their reveal, if your audience wasn't invested in the story you were telling, any trick would fall flat. That's what people who watch online videos exposing the secrets of magic tricks don't understand. The technical mechanics of a trick are only a small part of the overall effect. The misdirection that makes a trick work is in place from the moment the audience meets the magician.

She donned the body armor and spun into a pirouette. It wasn't as smooth as usual because the outfit was bulky and weighed her down.

Sanjay held out his hands as she peeled it off.

"It's heavy," she warned.

"Oh, please. You just did acrobatics in it. I think I can handle—" He fell to his knees as Tempest placed the chain mail into his hands. "What the hell is this made of?"

"Thousands of little iron rings," Ivy answered. "This suit of armor is amazing."

"Isn't it?" Tempest grinned.

"It's real iron?" Sanjay looked at the chain mail as if it had personally offended him. "That's why it feels like I'm holding a dozen cast-iron skillets. You should have warned me."

"I did," Tempest pointed out.

He stood a little unsteadily and placed the armor on her bed. The mattress sank a couple of inches under its weight.

Tempest scooped it up and put it back into the trunk. "This helps with the potential extra booby-trap issue. I'll be perfectly safe."

"Except for the felony," Gideon said once more. "I could go in your stead."

"This isn't medieval Europe," Sanjay snapped. "She doesn't need a knight in shining—"

"Thanks for the offer, Watson," Tempest said to Gideon, "but if anyone is going somewhere we think this is needed, it should be me."

Tempest and Ivy had dubbed Gideon "Watson" after he inserted himself into an investigation right after Tempest had moved home. But Gideon was far more than that. He was someone who noticed things that others didn't. As annoying as it was sometimes that he didn't have a cell phone, not being attached to the appendage enabled him to truly focus on the things around him. That was how he'd become such a talented sculptor by his midtwenties, and how he picked up on things that a distracted person wouldn't.

Like now.

"Forget about the armor," Gideon said. "And forget about what you're reading online. You're all getting distracted by what people online are saying, but none of them know anything. Have you even stopped to consider the real evidence the police are looking at?"

"That's the problem." Sanjay gave Gideon an exasperated glance. "We're not the police."

"And they're focusing their attention on Paloma," Ivy added, "since she's their main suspect."

"I guarantee they're also examining the booby-trap blades," Gideon said. "The blades that *Tempest saw.*"

Tempest groaned. "He's right. I saw two of the blades up close."

"Have you stopped to think about what you really saw?" Gideon asked.

She closed her eyes and thought back to that night. "The first one. It wasn't a knife. It was a sword." Panic began rising as she remembered the blade that had run through Julian Rhodes. "I thought at first that the hilt of the sword had broken off, before I realized that it had come from the door itself. We didn't yet know it had sprung from the door. Then there was a second blade . . . the smaller one." That's the one that had made her think of her mom.

Tempest's eyes popped open, her heart racing. "I recognized the knife."

"Damn," muttered Sanjay. "This was a good idea after all, Gideon."

Tempest reached for Ivy's hand to steady herself. "It was my mom's knife."

"What?" Ivy whispered.

"It was a sailor's knife," said Tempest. "The knife used in the booby trap was the same kind my mom and her sister used in their illusion, The Tempest."

"I take it back," said Sanjay. "This was a terrible idea."

Chapter 15

Tempest's friends convinced her not to break into the theater, but the argument that won out was the most mundane: none of them had time to stake out the theater and wait for an opportune time. Sanjay had made plans with a local magic builder he thought might have been approached to build a sword-holding booby trap under the pretense of being for a stage show, in case the culprit hadn't built it themselves. Gideon had to prepare for his art show, and Ivy was due at work shortly for her second part-time job. Ivy said she'd have a bit of time to spare before she had to start work, so Tempest went with her to the Locked Room Library.

Located across the bay in San Francisco, the Locked Room Library was a lending library, museum, and meeting space that catered to people who loved classic mystery novels. It was a dream destination for Ivy, and one where she was now working part-time as a library assistant. She hoped to work somewhere like it as a full-time librarian in a few years. Before she could get there, she was taking online classes to complete her previously abandoned undergraduate degree and would soon be applying for a master's in library science.

The library was housed on the first floor of a converted Victorian house in San Francisco's Haight-Ashbury neighborhood, where quirky businesses abounded. Two gargoyles greeted visitors at the front door, and a suit of armor stood at the information desk. The library's curated collection filled 1,500 square feet and specialized in locked-room mysteries, as its name indicated. Roughly half of the space was a traditional library with shelves of physical books that members could check out—which meant that anyone with a local address anywhere in Northern California could sign up for a free membership.

The other half of the first-floor layout was divided between a small "museum," which contained rare books and memorabilia that the public could view but not check out, and a narrow meeting room built in the shape of a vintage train car. Secret Staircase Construction had been hired to design the train car that paid homage to Agatha Christie's *Murder on the Orient Express*. Book clubs were the most common occupants, but today Ivy had booked the room.

"How did you think ahead to book the room for us?" Tempest asked, as she climbed the steps into the faux lounge car.

"I didn't." Ivy locked the door behind them and rolled up the glass window on the top half of the door. "I'm giving my third library talk this afternoon at five o'clock before I work the evening shift. I still get so nervous, so I wanted time to practice beforehand."

"I don't want to take away from your practice time."

"Tempest." Ivy crossed her arms over her pink vest. "This real-life dilemma is way more important than a lecture on classic mysteries. Besides, the last time I gave my talk, only four people showed up."

"Do you know how many people showed up for my second magic show?"

"Three. Which I know because I was one of them."

"I bet you'll have more than that tonight. And even if you don't, it just means you get to practice more."

"Where do you want to begin with research?" Ivy asked.

"Julian and Paloma Rhodes."

"I thought you already knew everything about those two from the lawsuit."

"That was back when we only thought they were suing us. Not when it involved murder. We need to go deeper."

"I have a better idea." Ivy pointed at a towering stack of books on the narrow train car table.

"We run away on a make-believe train and spend the next year reading the enticing novels we never have time to read?" Tempest asked hopefully.

"I wish." Ivy gave a wistful sigh and picked up a skeleton key from the wall. She twisted it into place, and immediately, the sound of a steam engine chugging began. A moment later, the faux scenery behind the train car windows that faced the library wall began to move.

"These are research books?" Tempest picked up a copy of *The Westing Game* by Ellen Raskin. "Not one of your usual selections."

"This mystery we're facing isn't exactly like the impossible crime novels I love. The four impossibilities we encountered earlier this year made sense as a series of impossible puzzles that could be picked apart. But this?"

"It's a puzzle that's part of a bigger game." With the 1970s young adult mystery in her hands, Tempest spotted the book that lay underneath it. The first Three Investigators novel, *The Secret of Terror Castle*, with an early edition cover from the 1960s.

"A trio of friends unmasking a ghost." Ivy smiled as she took the beloved book they'd both loved as kids with teenage sleuths Jupiter Jones, Pete Crenshaw, and Bob Andrews.

"We already know whatever is going on at the theater isn't a ghost," said Tempest. "But I do appreciate the books as inspiration."

"They're more than that," said Ivy. "Books let us see the truth."

"Says the librarian-in-training. I do appreciate it, Ivy." Tempest tossed the book aside and took Ivy's hands in hers. "I really do. But we need to look into Julian Rhodes's life. Not reread books we loved as kids. The longer it takes to solve this, the more people out there who'll think my mom lost it and set a series of macabre booby traps to kill people more than five years after she took her own life—neither of which is true."

"First, it doesn't matter what they think." Ivy held up a preemptive hand. "I know. It hurts."

"I can take what they say about *me*. I've had my own reputation destroyed before. I'll survive. But I don't want this for *her* memory."

"I know. But your family already hired a private investigator to look into Julian Rhodes when he sued your dad. Do you think you're better equipped to dig into things that even a trained professional couldn't find?"

"Well, no." Tempest pulled away and looked out of the train car windows at the false scenery speeding past. "There are those other lawsuits."

"Which you said were sealed for confidentiality. You're not a superspy, Tempest."

"I can't do nothing."

"You're not. We're all doing what we're best at. Even though you're not a spy, you have stage magic superpowers."

"Creating misdirection for a living doesn't seem to be helping me see through this deception right now."

"I've selected a series of relevant books that will give us ideas for how to look at the type of puzzle this is. Those kids' books were for general inspiration, but here are two books that came to mind for their use of architecture and mechanical devices: *Death in the House of Rain* by Szu-Yen Lin, about a house built in the shape of the Chinese character for rain—so it's got architectural misdirection. And *The Crooked Hinge*, a Dr. Fell novel by John Dickson Carr, with an uber creepy automaton that begins to move on its own—like that regenerating booby trap."

They flipped through the books and filled several sheets of paper with notes. A few of them were actually relevant.

Setting—Is the Whispering Creek Theater location relevant?

Three booby traps—someone who likes twisted games, or another purpose?

Motive—a person everyone hated is dead, so motive is less than helpful.

Misdirection—Who started the ghost rumor? Purposeful distraction?

Ivy pushed a book aside and stood up.

"Time for your talk?" Tempest asked.

"Wish me luck."

"Break a leg," said Tempest as Ivy stepped out of the train car meeting room Secret Staircase Construction had built for the library. The train car, like the booby-trapped door, was an illusion. Tempest had spent most of her life watching and creating illusions. She knew she could unravel the multiple illusions the theater was hiding. She only hoped she could do so before the murder of Julian Rhodes became another cold case, like the last murder at the theater.

Chapter 16

T he Locked Room Library," began Ivy, "was created by Enid Maddox, who wished to have a place to celebrate classic mystery novels. Our collection goes back to the mid-1800s, including all of Edgar Allan Poe's works, but the largest section of the catalogue is devoted to locked-room mysteries, thus the name—and the subject of today's talk."

Twelve folding chairs had been set in the space between the main lending library and the museum room where first editions and other rarities of interest could be viewed but not borrowed. Seven seats were filled. *Not bad, Ivy Youngblood.*

Tempest leaned against a tall bookcase behind the chairs, where she could easily slip away in one of many directions if someone recognized her and wished to voice their opinions about her mom that she didn't want to hear. It was better than the alternative. Through a combination of genetics and training, the strength of her legs was phenomenal. In the past, she'd occasionally used that strength when provoked, but she didn't need that kind of trouble right now.

"I'm Ivy Youngblood, a library assistant. I'm studying to become a librarian right now, but really, I've been studying for this my whole life. My best friend and I became best friends because of the mystery books we read and talked about when we were kids. By the time we reached middle school, our local librarians and local secondhand bookshop staff knew us well."

Tempest smiled as she remembered how they'd passed beaten-up books back and forth. Tempest liked to outline things in the books she owned, but Ivy was a purist who didn't believe in defacing books. Their compromise was using only pencil and not dog-earing pages.

"History is messy," Ivy continued. "Scholars disagree about lots of things—including in the mystery fiction world. There are several contenders for who wrote the first locked-room mystery. Personally, I believe it was Edgar Allan Poe's 'Murders in the Rue Morgue,' which he wrote in 1841. But I should back up a moment. What *is* a locked-room mystery?" Ivy looked out at the not-quite-crowd.

The arm of a dark-haired girl who might have been eleven or twelve years old shot up. When Ivy gave her a nod, she lowered her arm and spoke. "A room is locked and there's a mystery inside, because how did the crime happen with the room locked up?"

Ivy smiled. "Exactly. A crime has been committed in a room, or other sealed or isolated location, so it looks like it's impossible for it to have happened. That's why it's known as an 'impossible crime.'"

An elderly woman in the audience opened her mouth and took a breath, but Ivy continued speaking.

"Not everyone agrees that an impossible crime and a locked-room mystery are the exact same thing, because some purists think a locked-room needs a physical room, rather than some other type of contained setting, but that's splitting hairs. I'm not a professor giving a lecture at a university. I'm a librarian-in-training who wants to tell you about the *fun* of classic mysteries with seemingly impossible puzzles. You with me?"

The woman who'd been about to speak pursed her lips, the

girl and her mother smiled and nodded, two middle-aged men clapped politely, and library owner Enid clapped enthusiastically from the front row. Tempest couldn't see the face of the other member of the audience who sat in the front row with one empty chair between himself and Enid.

"A classic example is a dead—" Ivy stumbled, and for a moment Tempest wondered if she'd forgotten what she was going to say, until she realized Ivy was looking at the girl. She must have been wondering if she could talk about a dead body in front of her. Tempest could have reminded her that the two of them read mystery novels featuring dead bodies when they were that age. Ivy's seven-year-old niece, Natalie, might have been a bit young to hear about stabbings and shootings, but this kid was likely reading books far more gruesome than anything Tempest and Ivy had read. Tempest didn't think Ivy would appreciate an interruption to reassure her, and it wasn't needed. Ivy had it covered.

"As I was saying," Ivy continued, "a good example is priceless jewels locked inside the safe of a train car. There's a guard stationed outside the only exit. Even the window is bolted from the inside. Yet when the train comes to a stop and both the train car and the safe are opened, the jewels are gone! How on earth could it have happened? With a classic locked-room mystery, you know there has to be a rational explanation at the end—that's essential. But along the way to get to that point, it *appears* truly impossible. Only a ghost could have walked through the walls undetected, right? Which brings up another aspect of impossible crimes that makes these books and stories so addictive." She paused and looked at each member of the audience in turn, ending with the girl. "If it was impossible to have a person commit the crime, that truly does leave only a supernatural explanation. A mischievous ghost, a curse from a witch, a—"

"Or a ghost who's trapped by a family curse?" The man who interrupted was sitting in the front row. Tempest hadn't gotten a good look at him, but now that he'd spoken, she recognized his voice. It was the voice from the voice-mail greeting when the two women had called a paranormal investigator in the Whispering Creek Theater parking lot.

"Sure," said Ivy with a smile. She didn't know who he was. "Anything that seems impossible. But remember, it has to have a rational explanation in the end. It—"

"Why?"

Ivy blinked a few times, but quickly recovered. "That's the rule because—"

"I'm not talking about rules," said the paranormal investigator. "There's more to the universe than what we understand. That haunted theater across the bay in Hidden Creek. You knew the woman who's haunting it. She's making daggers appear out of nowhere."

Ivy's already pale skin looked even paler. It was all Tempest could do not to do a pirouette and "accidentally" kick that guy in the jaw, but she didn't have to decide. Enid stood in front of Ivy and faced the audience. "Let's save questions until the end."

The ghost hunter didn't protest, but Ivy still looked flustered. She opened her mouth, but closed it again without speaking.

"Sorry to have interrupted." The guy stood up. "I don't want to derail your book talk. I'll catch you later."

Tempest slipped behind the bookcase before he turned around. He didn't spot her as he walked through the library toward the exit. She caught up with him on the front steps, where he was sitting underneath one of the gargoyles.

"I'd say that was a nice thing you did for Ivy," said Tempest, "except that you were the one that threw her off her game in the first place."

He scrambled up. "Tempest Raj."

"That's me. Who are you?"

"Alejandro." He held out his right hand, which had a tattoo of a skull and a deep scar on the back of it. She couldn't remotely guess his age. He could have been anywhere between twenty and forty. His pale olive skin told her he didn't spend a lot of time outside, but feeling the calluses on his hand as she shook it made her wonder how he'd gotten them. "I hear we just missed each other earlier today at that wild cathedral theater. I'm a videographer specializing in the paranormal."

"The Locked Room Library has nothing to do with the Whispering Creek Theater. Why did you come here?"

"Can I interview you?"

"No." Tempest crossed her arms and gave him a look she hoped resembled her fierce on-stage persona of The Tempest.

"Don't you want to tell your side?"

"My side of what?"

"Your mom. Why you think she's back. Why she killed—"

"It's *not* my mom who killed someone."

"You sound just like your friend. There aren't 'rules' that confine the universe."

She blinked at him. "Actually, there are. Didn't you ever take a science class?"

"Don't you ever wonder if there's more than you understand?"

"Of course. That's why ghost stories are so much fun. Because we *do* wonder. But it's also far more likely there's a rational explanation. If an apple falls from a tree and hits you, we assume it is gravity, not that a ghost threw an apple at you."

Alejandro grinned. "I like you, Tempest. I get where you're coming from. But don't you want to see your mom again?"

"More than anything," she snapped. "But do you really think I want to imagine she's an angry spirit who's murdering people? Or even that she was so disturbed before she vanished that she set ingenious booby traps that lay dormant for more than five years?"

"Only to be activated by a man who wanted to harm you and your dad," said Alejandro. "Which still suggests a supernatural expla—"

"All it suggests is that someone knows my family's history. It could be Paloma Rhodes, like the police think. The booby-trapped door isn't even an impossible crime like the ones Ivy is lecturing about inside right now. It's simply a mystery I haven't yet solved."

He perked up. "You're investigating?"

Tempest groaned silently.

"Look," said Alejandro. "I'm really sorry I flustered your friend. I missed out on the news of the paranormal activity at the theater when it happened earlier today. Your online presence ended almost a year ago, but when I looked up people close to you and found out Ivy Youngblood was giving a public lecture, it was perfect. I got here just in time." He shrugged. "I forget that not everyone is good at public speaking. I wanted to catch her off guard with my question so she'd give me an honest answer about what's going on, not make her mess up."

He handed Tempest a postcard with artwork of roses coming out of a skull that looked similar to the tattoo on his hand. She flipped it over with a theatrical flick of her fingertips, a move she made without thinking. The back of the card was filled with four still images of videos of Alejandro speaking to the camera with dark, subterranean-looking settings behind him, along with his name, website, and contact information.

"Let me know if you decide to talk," he said. "I've got a lot of viewers."

"That's not the enticement you think it is." Tempest flicked the card with her finger. At the same time, she swept a lock of hair from her face, splitting Alejandro's attention and causing it to appear as if the card had simply vanished.

It was an unconscious action, not something meant to impress him. When you've practiced enough with cards to do a successful trick, it also activates the part of your brain that performs an action thoughtlessly, like typing or tying your shoes. Tempest wasn't the best at cardistry, but she was practiced enough that palming a card was the natural way to get it into her back pocket.

His eyes widened momentarily with mild amazement, and he chuckled. "If you're trying to prove a point, you didn't. Just because that was a magic trick and not a spirit doesn't prove they don't exist. My audience is interested in this phenomenon, and we might even be able to help you figure out what's going on."

"Thanks. But I don't think so. Someone is using the legend of the Raj family curse for their own purposes."

"Maybe. Maybe not. I've seen some things. I could tell you more about it. I'm heading around the corner for breakfast. Join me?"

"It's after five p.m."

"Why do you think I missed the crowds at the theater this morning? Real paranormal investigators don't keep normal hours. Most activity happens at night."

That explained the pale skin. She wondered how long it had been since he'd seen full sunlight. "Enjoy your breakfast." Tempest took two steps toward the library door.

"Don't you want to know what I've seen that relates to you?"

Tempest froze. He had to be messing with her. She turned back. "What do you know?"

"You're the one who rented the theater, right?"

She nodded.

"Have you gotten inside the Shadow Stage yet?" he asked.

"It's welded shut." The second stage hidden behind the main stage had been shut down long before Tempest's mom vanished, but after being broken down as part of that investigation, it was much more permanently sealed.

"Too bad. That's where the most paranormal activity comes from."

Tempest was losing patience with this ghost hunter. Though his style of teasing just enough to string people along might explain why people watched his videos. She took the bait. "What does that have to do with me?"

"Why do you think I got into this gig in the first place three years ago? I saw the ghost myself. When I was a senior in high school."

Tempest thought back to Officer Quinn's information about the theater break-ins. "You were one of the high school students who broke into the shuttered theater and left a ghost light burning?"

Alejandro shuffled his feet uncomfortably. He was either a good actor or truly shaken by the memory. "That was the first time I saw something. That first night, we broke in as a joke. I saw a woman with long black hair—a woman who vanished."

"Three years ago," Tempest whispered. "After my mom vanished at the theater." Alejandro didn't know Tempest's suspicion that her mom hadn't died by drowning in the San Francisco Bay, as everyone assumed, but she had instead been killed at the theater. Where, if Tempest believed in such things, her ghost would remain.

Chapter 17

Shaken by Alejandro's words, Tempest slipped back inside the library as Ivy was answering questions from the audience. Alejandro believed he'd seen something that night at the theater. But the power of suggestion in a dark, creepy building resembling a miniature Gothic cathedral, with kids scaring each other and possibly even setting out to fool each other, was a far more likely explanation.

The young girl from the audience was speaking as Tempest sat down in the back row of chairs. "You said all the classic locked-room mysteries have a satisfying ending."

"That's right," Ivy said. "The expectation is that the mystery is solved. All the loose ends are tied up. That's how we close the last page with a smile on our faces."

"But you didn't say it was a *happy* ending," the astute girl pointed out.

"It doesn't have to be," Ivy answered. "Have you read any Agatha Christie yet?"

The girl nodded. "I bought way more of them than I was supposed to, which is why my mom brought me here to the library."

"I'm glad you found us." Ivy smiled. "You know that sometimes the guilty person Poirot or Miss Marple reveals isn't always the person you were hoping it would be. But Agatha Christie gave us all the clues we needed for us to see that it was that person, even if it's not exactly a happy ending."

"Yeah, that happened with my detective agency's first case," the girl replied. "It was still fun." The audience chuckled and then broke into a round of applause for Ivy when there were no more questions.

Tempest helped Enid fold chairs while the audience thanked Ivy, and the inquisitive girl asked another few questions of her.

"Sorry I missed most of your talk," Tempest said after the small audience had dispersed and Enid had retreated to the front desk to check out books for several of the attendees.

"I didn't hear any screams coming from the front door, so I take it you managed not to 'accidentally' kick that guy after you finished a round of pirouettes or a backflip?"

Her oldest friend knew her well. "For what it's worth, he felt bad about rattling you." Tempest held up the card he'd given her. "Alejandro Arkady, paranormal investigator. He was still sleeping his vampiric hours when the rumors began about my mom's malicious ghost being at the theater, so when he couldn't find a public presence for me, he tracked down people I know."

"Sometimes I think you're right that it would be nice to go back to a time before creepy stalkers could track people down so easily."

"And sometimes," said Tempest, "I wish I could have one of those satisfying endings like the books surrounding us."

When Tempest got back to Fiddler's Folly, the sun had nearly set. Her dad wasn't in the main house, so she headed for her grandparents' tree house. The front door of the tree house had previously only been locked by a brass gargoyle with a key that turned in its mouth. More whimsical than secure, it had never meant to serve as a true lock. Now they'd had a proper lock and a deadbolt installed by a local locksmith.

Normally, she would have gone straight upstairs to the main floor on the second-story level of the tree house. The stairs led directly into the kitchen, which was the heart of the house. In addition to the cooking area, it held a breakfast nook seating area, and a large sliding glass door that opened up into the outdoor dining area. The covered deck with a massive dining table was the original section of the tree house before it was converted into a functional house. The rest of the top floor contained a cozy bathroom just big enough for a clawfoot tub, Ash and Morag's bedroom, and a private deck for the two of them.

But today, Morag Ferguson-Raj was in the ground-floor art studio with Gideon and two other women. The entire first floor of the tree house in-law unit was dedicated to Grannie Mor's art studio.

Tempest's grandmother introduced her to two artist friends, Tansy and Trina.

"Hello, lass!" said Tansy in a thick Scottish brogue. "We met years ago, but it's been a tick."

"Lovely to meet you," said the more demure Trina, but with an equally Scottish lilt.

Tansy was a large, commanding figure with a look of mild superiority. Trina was so slight she looked as if she could be blown over by a small gust of wind, but she had a friendlier disposition.

"Trina is visiting for an artist residency," said Morag.

"And I," said Tansy, "am looking for art to invest in. I'm sponsoring Gideon's art show. Such a talented young man. I *cannae* wait for the opening."

"You're embarrassing the lad, Tansy," said Trina.

"*Ach,* the boy needs to learn to accept a compliment in this business. He's got the talent, so he'd best get used to it."

Gideon scratched his ear uncomfortably. He did need to get

better at accepting compliments if he was going to be a successful artist.

Everyone besides Tempest seemed to think it was perfectly rational to proceed with normal life. With Paloma Rhodes at large, they weren't entirely comfortable, but there was no reason to think she was a physical threat to any of the family. Only the lawsuit. Besides, after the events of earlier in the year, Fiddler's Folly was now surrounded by a fence, an alarm system, and even a couple of security cameras.

Tempest turned her attention back to her grandmother's friends.

"Your new landscape of the fierce waves crashing against the cliffs is stunning," Trina was saying to Grannie Mor.

"I appreciate that," said Morag, "but I didn't mean to get us distracted by my studio before we have tea upstairs."

"Nonsense!" said Tansy. "I refuse to leave until I've seen these older pieces I've not yet seen."

Tempest left the artists and climbed the stairs to the kitchen, where Ash was happily cooking dinner. He'd put Darius to work chopping vegetables.

In South India, kitchens were an indoor/outdoor combination, and Ash sought to replicate the experience here. It wasn't quite the same, but unless rain was pelting sideways, the sliding door was left open and the kitchen and covered deck felt like part of the same room.

Darius had repeatedly asked Ash to keep the sliding door closed when they weren't home. With his unstable upbringing, Darius never felt truly secure. That's why the lawsuit Julian Rhodes had instigated was especially terrible. Ash had been through a lot as well, but his own reaction to trauma was the opposite. He was adamant about enjoying each moment free from worry, saying, "If someone wants to get inside badly enough, they'll find a way. I'm not going to live in fear."

Morag poked her head into the kitchen a minute later. "I invited Trina and Tansy for tea, but now that it's getting late, what do you think about two more for dinner?"

"Of course," Ash said. "It's no problem to whip up some more." He turned to Tempest. "Any chance Nicodemus will be out by dinnertime?"

"I don't think so, and Brodie is still dealing with the canceled tour."

"I'll tell the group downstairs they should stay for dinner," Morag said.

"Thirty minutes," Ash called after her, then tossed an onion to Darius. "Just a little more food, to be safe."

The "safe" amount of food brought to the table half an hour later was a feast for at least a dozen people, even though there were only seven of them for the sunset meal.

Tempest had called Ivy and Sanjay to see if they could make it. Sanjay was having dinner with the magic builder he'd met with, who hadn't had any booby trap inquiries lately, and Ivy was still at work at the Locked Room Library.

Tempest had fetched Abra from his hutch since he loved dinner parties. She sat at the end of the table between Gideon and Trina, and let Abra hop around underfoot. He was big enough and old enough to fend for himself among so many pairs of feet.

"You're a painter?" Tempest asked Trina.

"Among other things."

"Whereas I," cut in Tansy, "am only a patron of the arts. I don't see how you can all create something out of nothing. I own a small gallery on the water in North Bay." Tansy clapped her hands together. "I love fostering the next generation of artists. I do hope you're working on more creations, Gideon, since the sculptures in this show will disappear quickly."

"Wait, you're *selling* your artwork?" Tempest stared at Gideon.

"Of course," Gideon said. "That's what artists do. We sell our artwork."

"His sculptures will be sure to sell," Tansy said. "Oh!" She chuckled. "Something soft brushed against my foot. I forgot there was a rabbit underfoot."

Tempest was done eating, so she ducked under the table and scooped Abra into her arms. He flopped his large lop-ears before settling into her lap.

"May I hold him?" asked Trina in her quiet voice.

"You'll have to ask him." Tempest didn't want to lift Abra across the table, so she stood and went around to go between Trina and Tansy. "Want to make a new friend?" she asked Abra. Both women reached out to let Abra sniff their hands, Trina timidly, and Tansy more boldly.

"*Aya!*" cried Tansy. "The bunny nicked my finger!"

Ash clicked his tongue. "Abra's overwhelmed by too many people."

Morag leapt up to help her friend. "I'm so sorry. *Doesnae* look like the scratch is bleeding. But Tempest, it's best you put Abra back in his hutch."

"I'll come with you," said Gideon, following Tempest and Abra.

"He doesn't usually act up," Tempest said, as she held onto the bunny on the stairs. "What's the matter, Abra?"

"Let me take him." Gideon lifted the rabbit into his arms. Abra nuzzled his nose into the crook of Gideon's elbow. "Don't worry, little guy," he whispered.

Tempest smiled as she opened the door. "You're good with him."

"I followed for you, not the bunny," Gideon said to Tempest. "You haven't seen my latest sculpture. Would you like to?"

"Tonight?"

"Why not? Give me a five-minute head start. I need to set something up before you arrive."

The dinner group had forgotten all about the rabbit incident when Tempest and Gideon returned a minute later to say their goodbyes. Morag had opened a bottle of Scotch, so they didn't seem bothered about the young people departing early. Only Ash stood, and it was to meet Tempest in the kitchen and press a picnic basket into her hands.

"What's this?" she asked. "We've already eaten."

"Gideon is far too skinny these days. I think the only meals he eats lately are the ones I bring to the job crew on weekdays." Ash lowered his voice. "Tansy is putting too much pressure on him with this gallery show."

"He wants to do it," Tempest said, but she knew her grandfather was right. Gideon was working day and night, pushing himself way too hard. If he kept this up, he'd burn out. She accepted the picnic basket and walked slowly to her car, giving Gideon the head start he'd asked for and wondering what she'd find when she arrived.

Chapter 18

elcome to a theater with no bad memories." Gideon stepped aside, flicked a manual light switch, and the backyard came to life. Spotlights and fairy lights illuminated stone and clay sculptures of animals, both real and imagined. She recognized an owl she'd seen before, with stone eyes that looked as if they were following her every move.

"I can't believe you're going to sell these."

He shrugged. "I don't know if anyone will buy them. Your grandmother, along with Trina and Tansy, helped me set prices, but they're more than I would have charged."

"Whatever you're charging, you should charge more." She walked over and touched the beak of a griffin. She hadn't seen this one before. The creature with the head and wings of an eagle and the body of a lion was crouching with its wings spread as if about to take flight.

Like his other creations, this one had an uncanny ability to look as if it were truly watching you, regardless of where you went.

"An unknown artist can't charge too much," Gideon said. "It's better to set reasonable prices than not sell anything. And I can always make more."

"Didn't you spend ages making these?" Tempest touched the creature's wing. Gideon had made the stone look so much like real feathers.

"I did, but I learn more with each carving I make. I've only done a short apprenticeship, and I'd like to do more, as well as make bigger carvings than these small ones. Tansy is the gallery owner, but I'm pretty sure half the reason Trina recommended me to her was because her own son is a disappointment to her. She likes my work ethic compared to his incompetence."

"That's harsh."

"My parents are still disappointed I'm not pursuing a more stable career, so I feel like it's pretty normal. Depressing, but not surprising."

Tempest looked up from the griffin's smiling beak and playful eyes. "How can you let this go?"

"I could pretend to be wiser than my years and say it's the process I love and that once I've created something, I need to let it go. But it's still hard. I need to be more like the sculptors from the past who inspire me."

"I hate to break it to you, but you're already old-fashioned. I mean, you don't even have a cell phone."

He grinned at that. "How do you think I get so many sculptures done? I don't distract myself."

"So you're saving yourself from yourself."

"Pretty much. Which is also why I need to sell these right away. It's like a painful necessity."

"Like ripping off a Band-Aid?"

"Sort of. I like that analogy of getting it over with quickly instead of tugging slowly and prolonging the pain. But it's more than that. I feel like I want my creations to be enjoyed by others. I don't want to be that guy who's eighty years old sitting alone in a room crammed with my creations."

"You're photographing them though. For yourself."

"Hell yes."

She thought about joking that a 3D printer could have made all of these sculptures based on a computer-generated model, but that would have been both cruel and untrue. There was something magical about these hand-carved works of art. Something that couldn't be replicated by a machine.

It was the same philosophy as Secret Staircase Construction. People could buy a kit to put a bookcase door in a doorframe for the illusion of a secret room, but a kit lacks the personalized details the human touch adds when someone builds something by hand. In her more sentimental moments, Tempest might also have added that the love of creating something by hand somehow came through.

"Come inside for a sec," said Gideon.

"And leave this magical garden? Never."

Gideon grinned as he opened the back door leading into the small house. Tempest followed him into the living room, where he'd replaced the mantel around the fireplace with the open mouth of a dragon. Its teeth dipped over the top of the hearth, with the rest of its head shaped roughly like a high mantelpiece. She'd seen this magical carving before, but Gideon reached onto the top of its head and withdrew a palm-size stone carving of a rabbit.

"I meant to give it to you at my gallery opening, but with everything going on, I thought you might like it now. Especially since I'm not sure if you'll make it—"

"I'll be there." Tempest accepted the small stone bunny. Though it wasn't nearly as soft—or as big—as Abra, the lop-eared rabbit in her hand looked nearly identical to her pet rabbit. "How did you capture Abra so perfectly?"

"Can't you guess?" Gideon took her hand and led her back to the sculpture garden. "It's magic."

"It certainly is." Tempest took a seat on the small bench that was positioned to look out over the lights and sculptures.

"I'll be back with drinks in a sec. You like blackberries, right?"

"And a lot of other things."

Though Gideon joked about his sculptures springing to life, she knew how much work and dedication went into his craft. That was why he'd lost so much weight in the six months she'd known him and was looking disturbingly haggard.

He returned and handed her a red drink on ice that smelled like roses and lemons. "I don't have any real roses to cheer you up, but this is a Black Rose."

"Are you trying to cheer me up?"

"It's not working?"

"It is." Tempest took a sip of the tangy drink and glanced at the gargoyle in the far corner, which—even though she knew it was a trick of the fairy lights—she could have sworn just blinked at her. "I'm sorry I forgot how soon your show was coming up."

"It was originally going to be later, but Tansy had an opening in her gallery, so I wanted to take advantage of the opportunity. Since she usually displays art on the walls, but I don't have any art like that—that's why we're hanging some of Morag's artwork on the walls. I'm glad, because she'll be a bigger draw than me."

"Only until people see these." She left her drink on the small iron table and walked up to the gargoyle. His eyes were stone, but she spotted the tiny light that had made it look like he was blinking. When she turned around, Gideon was at her side.

A lock of Tempest's hair fell across her face in the light breeze. Gideon lifted it with his hand and tucked it behind her ear.

"Go ahead and kiss her already, Gid!" a voice called from over the fence.

They broke apart.

Gideon flushed, but Tempest laughed.

"This backyard makes me forget we're surrounded by other houses," she said through her laughter.

"We'll talk about this later, Reggie," Gideon said toward the fence, then lowered his voice. "Teenage son of my neighbor. Let's go back inside."

But the moment was over, and Tempest didn't need this complication in her life right now. She needed to stay focused.

"Rain check," she said. "And I really do mean that. As soon as all of this has been sorted out."

"I'll walk you to your car."

As they passed through the side gate, a shadow disappeared from the sidewalk, as if a person had shrunk from view. She would have thought it was Reggie, except his voice had come from the opposite side. There was no way he could have gotten to the front of the house so soon.

It was dark outside, so had she imagined it? That must have been it. Still, she was glad Gideon had decided to walk her all the way to her jeep. He only went back inside after she had pulled away from the curb. She had watched him in her rear-view mirror—but now she saw something else. A car from two doors down turned on its headlights and pulled out behind her.

Coincidence? Oakland wasn't a sleepy small town like Hidden Creek. The houses were much closer together here.

She could wonder, or she could act. She twisted the steering wheel to make a tight left turn onto the next street. One that she noticed only too late was a dead end.

The car behind her followed suit.

Calm down, Tempest. There could still be an innocent explanation. Well, not *innocent* exactly, but not dangerous. It was a pickup truck that looked an awful lot like Sanjay's. Could he have driven to Fiddler's Folly after seeing his friend in North Bay and learned from Tempest's dad or grandparents that Tempest was with Gideon? Could he be jealous enough to follow her here? She doubted it, but it wasn't past the realm of possibility. Men were strange creatures. Especially those two.

Which was precisely why she appreciated them both. Gideon and Sanjay weren't typical guys with normal jobs and dreams.

The headlights were too bright for her to identify the driver or the make of the truck. The end of the street was a cul-de-sac with a turning area, so she sped up just enough to spin her jeep around. She pulled up at the side of the truck that had slammed on its brakes.

Moriarty.

Chapter 19

Moriarty wasn't his real name. It was Ivy's idea to call him that because Tempest didn't know his real name. She didn't even know what he looked like. Not really. When she first met him, he dressed so ridiculously that it was all she or anyone else remembered about him. *An easy idea to remember, but a difficult man to recognize.*

Tempest left the car running but jumped out and pulled open his door. The man in the truck was the one she had expected to see but also nothing like the man she thought she knew. She guessed he was a little older than her, in his late twenties or early thirties, which was older than she'd initially thought. His short hair was a more vibrant brown than it had been the last time she'd seen him, with a more expensive cut that matched his tailored shirt.

"Touching, really," he said calmly, "that in his naiveté Gideon thinks he has a chance with you."

"What do you want, Moriarty?"

"I wish it was to show you what a proper date looks like—"

"You can't be serious. You're lucky I'm not calling the police to come and arrest you—"

"For my act of self-defense? That would be a nuisance I'd rather not face but hardly an insurmountable problem."

"What. Do. You. Want?"

"I'm concerned. You've been even more tempestuous than usual lately."

She tensed. "You've been watching me. How long?"

"In town, or here tonight?"

"Both." She hadn't noticed his presence, but she had a feeling she underestimated a lot of things about Moriarty.

"I'm afraid I can't tell you the former. As for the latter, I just got here. I was looking for you at Fiddler's Folly, and when you weren't there, I tried Veggie Magic and the theater before coming here."

He knew Gideon's address. Of course he did.

"Why were you looking for me?"

His face grew serious. "You need to leave this investigation alone, Tempest." He held up a hand. "I'm completely aware I sound like I'm on a cop show. But you really have no idea what you're up against."

"Then why don't you tell me?"

The look he gave her was one that frightened Tempest more than he ever had when she thought he was a physical threat. It was the most genuine expression she'd ever seen on his face. There was sadness, but also something else.

Fear.

"What are you afraid of?" she whispered. She'd never seen him frightened.

Her naming the emotion wiped it off his face. "I'm not afraid." His voice stiffened. "But you should be. I'm telling you the truth. You need to believe me and let this go. She's dangerous and can't be trusted. It will only end badly."

"I'm not doing anything unless you tell me why I should listen to you. *She?* Do you know where Paloma Rhodes is?"

He opened his mouth, but shut it before speaking. He did that once more before settling on what he wanted to say. "If you think about everything you know about me—I mean, *really* know to be true—you'll know I'm only here to help you."

He held her gaze, and she didn't look away. His words were absolutely true, but how could she trust the words of someone who'd killed before? He said he had done it for her, but she'd never really know what happened that night.

"I'm leaving now," she said.

"Please, Tempest. Please listen. You need to—"

Tempest stepped back into her jeep and slammed the door. It took her a few seconds to shake off the unnerving conversation before starting the engine. Moriarty didn't get out of his car and approach her. Instead, he shook his head and drove off first.

Since the street was a cul-de-sac, he had to turn around at the end to get out. As he passed her, he slowed and met her gaze for only a second. But in that brief moment, there was nothing glib or superior in his expression. Instead, only a sincere look of *helplessness*. The vulnerable expression unnerved her and stayed with her after he disappeared from sight. After a few deep breaths, she drove back to Gideon's street.

Gideon was standing on his front porch, holding a mallet and scowling at the road. "I heard tires screech, but I couldn't tell which direction the sound came from."

"So you were going to go all Thor on whoever was after me?"

He smiled sheepishly and spun the mallet. "Glad you're fine."

"You were going to run after me?" Tempest took the mallet from his hands. It really was quite heavy. "I'd rather you get a cell phone."

"I could have called for help from my landline. You going to tell me what's going on?"

"You probably don't want to know."

"Which is why you have to tell me."

Tempest hesitated. She trusted Gideon, and she also cared

about him. Ivy knew about Moriarty, so why was it so difficult to explain the morally questionable man to Gideon? She knew the answer, of course. Moriarty was a fugitive. She should have called the police as soon as she'd seen him.

"At least tell me who that guy was," Gideon prompted when she didn't answer. He sat down on the top step of his porch and motioned for her to join him.

"I would, but I have no idea." She sat down beside Gideon as he opened his mouth to protest, but Tempest continued, "I'm serious. I don't know his real name, but I call him Moriarty."

"As in Sherlock Holmes's nemesis?"

"Ivy, with her love of classic mysteries, picked the name Moriarty so we'd have something memorable to call him. He's been an enthusiastic fan of mine for a long time, and he keeps tabs on me."

Gideon's face grew dark as she spoke. "That's the literal definition of a stalker, Tempest. You need to call the police."

"Not happening."

He looked as if he was going to protest, but instead said, "I should at least see you home."

"I have a killer kick and a three-thousand-pound car. I don't need a knight in shining armor."

"He's just a stone carver with a heart of gold," called the same voice who'd interrupted them before. A scrawny kid with dark skin and burgundy hair appeared a moment later and joined them on the sidewalk.

"Reggie." Gideon sighed. "This is Tempest."

"Pleasure to meet you," Reggie said in a far more formal voice, and he shook her hand as if he was at a job interview.

"I'd say the same," said Tempest, "except you have some serious boundary issues."

Reggie grinned. "So I've been told." He dropped the smile. "I was just coming out here to tell you that I saw the creeper who followed your lady, Gid. He was around here almost as long as you two. I got a good look at him in case you need a witness who can give his physical description."

"The guy in the pickup truck that just drove away?" asked Tempest. That meant Moriarty had lied to her about how long he'd been there. Which didn't surprise her, but why lie about that?

"I don't get all up in everyone's business, but I couldn't help noticing him when he got here. I didn't recognize him. I figured he was here to visit Nida." Reggie indicated the house on the other side of Gideon's with a tilt of his head. "He arrived right after Tempest. What kind of name is Tempest anyway? You named after Shakespeare?"

"Sort of." She held up her charm bracelet so he could see the book charm with *The Tempest* written on the cover. "But the real reason is that I was born during a big storm." She didn't add that it was the name of an illusion her mom and aunt had created with Nicodemus. That was far too much information to share with a nosy teenager.

"Nice." Reggie inspected the silver bracelet. "Reginald means king. Suits me, yeah?"

"Um, I hate to break up you two becoming besties." Gideon looked as if he were about to lose his mind.

"Back to the guy who followed me and went to the house next door," said Tempest.

"Yeah," said Reggie. "He pulled up right after you and then went over there. But I don't think Nida's home. I didn't go over there or anything. Like I said, I'm not in everyone's business. I go to school, and I have an after-school job selling cell phones. Minding my own business, saving for my future. You need a phone upgrade?" He turned to Gideon when she shook her head. "I'm sure he was following your lady. He was here the whole time she was. That dude, he's bad news."

He certainly was. But why was Moriarty back *now*?

Chapter 20

Shortly before the sun rose the next morning, Tempest and her dad climbed the hill behind their house to watch the sunrise.

They walked out the back gate of the house, along the overgrown path that wasn't a proper trail, and toward the wishing well, with the crest of the hill in sight through the trees. At this time of day, it was silent enough that you could hear the soft lapping of the hidden creek that gave Tempest's hometown its name.

This had become a new tradition, the two of them climbing the hill at sunrise whenever they knew there were things unsaid between them. They'd both woken up early and exchanged a look of understanding in the kitchen. *Time for a sunrise walk.* It was another thing that made Tempest both love and hate having moved home.

The earth beneath her feet was damp with morning dew, and they walked in silence, as twigs crunched underfoot on the unpaved section of the hillside. In the crisp morning air, Tempest was bundled in her white peacoat and red beanie, which Ivy's sister Dahlia had knitted for her, but Darius wore a black T-shirt and nothing on his shaved head. He wasn't naturally bald like his father-in-law but had enjoyed the look and feel of a smooth head for as long as Tempest could remember. It suited him.

Pausing at the wishing well, Tempest closed her eyes and felt the cool, moss-covered stones under her palms. Before meeting Gideon, she never gave the texture of stone a second thought. Now, she thought of varieties of stone having their own unique personalities, and as a living thing shaped by both nature and human hands. When she opened her eyes, her dad was smiling at her.

"Here." He handed her a shiny penny.

"Thanks, Papa." She made a silent wish as she tossed a penny into the well. She wished for the piece of the puzzle that would connect the murders at the theater. Her mom vanishing on stage more than five years ago, and Julian being stabbed via a booby trap at the door. There was a connection, she was sure. She just couldn't see it yet.

Darius tossed in a penny of his own, and they continued on their way. She breathed in the fresh air and stood with her hands on her hips, feeling the warm energy of the sun. Looking behind her, the water of the San Francisco Bay was gray with fog, but facing the eastern sunrise high atop the Hidden Creek hillside, Tempest knew she would get through this. But only with her family and friends at her side.

"Caffeine?" Darius handed her a thermos of coffee from the full-size backpack that looked like a kindergartener's accessory on his back.

"Always."

Darius removed a plaid blanket from his backpack and spread it over the dew-covered bench at the crest of the hill. A Ferguson tartan from Grannie Mor. Tempest doubted she knew Darius was using it as a picnic blanket. Still, she accepted a seat.

"Thanks for that extra work you and Ivy did at the Whispering House, painting late into the night while your old papa was asleep. Now we'll be able to wrap up the Lenore Woods project and get everything cleared out and cleaned within the week."

Tempest shrugged off the compliment. "We would've just been up watching an old movie anyway. You think the city will give her the historical home designation even with our puzzle room imaginings in the attic?"

"We were true to everything in the historical records about Chester Hill's vision. The way the wood panels form a puzzle is all you, but that guy was a trip. The Gothic cathedral façade and pivoting Shadow Stage in his theater? And the way he built a whispering hallway into the house he had built to be his home in his old age? When he wrote about a puzzle for the attic, reached by a secret passageway, I have no doubt it either once existed and was torn down by more 'proper' occupants or that he died before he could see his vision through." Darius paused long enough to take a long drink of coffee as he looked out at the sunrise. "You ready to tell me what you and Ivy are up to?"

"It's not just me and Ivy," she admitted. "Sanjay and Gideon are helping."

"You roped the guys into being part of your mystery-solving gang?" He shifted his attention to Tempest and flexed his biceps. Not that he'd ever use his strength to harm the guys, but it was a reflexive instinct when it came to his baby girl. "I thought it was only you and Ivy that liked those old novels where amateurs solve crimes. What can you all do to find Paloma Rhodes that the police aren't doing?" He paused and squinted at her. "Ah. I see. You don't think she's guilty."

"I didn't say anything."

"Your poker face is useless with me."

"Is it? What am I thinking right now?"

"That your papa knows how to make a damn good cup of coffee." He grinned.

She stuck out her tongue at him. "You get up this early every day of the year, so you better have learned how to make a good cup of coffee in your fifty years on the planet."

"That's as far as my mind-reading skills go, so you've gotta help me out." He was smiling, but there were visible dark circles under his eyes.

"You don't need to worry. We're only armchair detectives."

"Since when?"

"They're a good influence on me. I promise. We're not up to anything dangerous."

Tempest's phone buzzed in her coat pocket. "It's Sanjay," she told her dad. "I'd better take it. He's never up this early. Something is wrong."

"Are you seeing this?" Sanjay asked, when Tempest picked up.

"Seeing what?"

"At the theater. The ghost was spotted at the theater during the night by one of those ghost hunters. He broke inside and is trapped inside by the ghost."

☠ ☠ ☠

Wind rustled the trees that loomed in the hills above the Gothic Whispering Creek Theater. The pointed spires looked menacing in the hillside shadows as Tempest pulled into the parking lot.

Sanjay was on his way from San Francisco so he wasn't there yet, but her dad was. He'd gone on ahead in his truck while she grabbed something from home. Tempest spotted him speaking to a uniformed officer who was guarding the perimeter that had been set up a distance from the theater. The new barricade was necessary because, despite the early hour, a crowd was forming. It was nothing like it had been the day before, but it would be soon.

"What's going on?" she asked her dad as she reached his side.

Darius walked them away from the scowling officer as muffled shouts came from inside the theater. He ran a hand across his face and shook his head. "It's worse than Sanjay told you."

"Worse than someone being trapped inside?"

"It's two of them." He swallowed hard. "And they're just kids."

"That's not the full story," an eavesdropper cut in with a smirk.

If the last couple of days had taught Tempest anything, it was not to stereotype. It wasn't all Goth ghost hunters and macabre magic show devotees who were curious. This guy was her dad's age and dressed in tan slacks and a white dress shirt. His cross-body bag looked like it cost far more than a functional bag should have.

"You know the full story?" Darius loomed over the man. Tempest knew him well enough to know he didn't mean to look threatening. It was the stress of having been told it was kids inside.

"Well, um," the man stammered, his smug expression gone.

"Whatever you can tell us," Tempest added, "would be helpful."

He smiled weakly. "It's not little kids. It's a couple of teenagers. One of them is being held captive by what they think is the ghost of the woman who disappeared here five years ago, and his friend won't leave him alone. That's why the officers inside haven't been able to get them out."

"The ghost of Emma Raj?" Tempest whispered.

"Yeah, you've heard of her?"

"How do you know this?" Darius asked the man, his rage barely under control.

Tempest knew her dad would keep it together, or at least not physically harm the poor man who'd interrupted the wrong conversation, so her attention was already back on the theater. What was going on here? The sun was barely up, and the stone theater nestled at the base of the hillside was still covered in shadow. Dozens of people were gathered around the perimeter barricade that circled the theater. There was no longer a tarp covering the façade, since the original booby-trapped vaulted door had been replaced by a new, utilitarian one with multiple locks. The door was locked and shut, and nobody was stationed outside it. The kids hadn't gotten into the theater through the main door.

"I was driving to work just now," the man was saying, "listening to the radio . . . It was a caller to the radio show. She saw a social media post with a video of the ghost."

Tempest's attention snapped back to the eavesdropper. This was bad. "How long ago?"

"Four, maybe five minutes? I just got here. I—"

"Papa." Tempest grabbed her dad's arm. "This isn't what it appears to be."

"Obviously." Darius tensed his jaw, and the man slunk away from him. "This isn't the ghost of—"

"I know," said Tempest. "This is a trap."

Chapter 21

You're not calling in the bomb squad for whatever new booby traps have been placed inside?" Tempest had found Detective Rinehart near the back door, speaking with Officer Quinn, and was trying to explain to them that this had to be a trap. A distraction from the killer.

"We have no reason to believe there are any traps in the theater." Rinehart glared at her, clearly regretting his decision to let Tempest and her dad through the barricade. "Just a couple of stupid kids playing a prank."

"Hidden Creek isn't big enough for our own bomb squad," Officer Quinn said.

"Isn't that what bigger county and state agencies help small towns with?"

"Well, yes," Quinn said, "but—"

"Quinn," snapped Rinehart. "Do shut up." He turned to Tempest. "Ms. Raj, I have things under control."

"Then where are the kids?" Darius asked.

Rinehart and Quinn exchanged a look.

In spite of the situation, Tempest laughed. She had a guess. A good one. Because she knew the theater. "You can't find them, can you?"

Quinn's eyes grew wide, and Rinehart reddened.

"Out," growled Rinehart. "Go back to your vehicles. Better yet, go home. We can take care of this. Your presence is a distraction."

"This whole thing is a distraction," Tempest said, as the officer from the barricade led them away from the building.

"That man," said Darius, shaking his head. "He'd be more than competent if he could just get over his ego."

"At least it looks like they're going back inside to search."

They sat on the tailgate of the pickup truck Darius had driven over, Tempest's anxiety rising each minute the kids didn't appear. It obviously wasn't a ghost holding the teenagers captive, but was it a person? Or more booby traps left behind?

There wouldn't be any more knives or swords. There had already been three blades. Like a magician's trick, this successful booby trap was all about expectations. Nicodemus had been caught off guard because a backup blade had already been triggered. But after the third time something happens, a feeling of familiarity sets in, meaning the magician would switch gears to defy expectations.

A magician. Tempest had instinctively thought of the person who set these traps as a magician, not as a murderer. Brodie? Moriarty?

Clouds were sweeping in overhead, and the wind whipped up Tempest's hair. She was reaching for a band to tie her hair back when a scream sounded from inside the theater. Then another.

"What the—" Darius began.

Tempest jumped down from the bumper.

"Let me out!" It was Officer Quinn's voice. Banging followed. Not ghostly thumping like fake spiritualist mediums use to suggest spirits are communicating, but the pounding of fists on the new front door of the theater.

The officer who'd been guarding the barricade scrambled

to open the multiple locks as several members of the crowd filmed the scene.

As soon as the door was unlocked, Quinn flew from the theater, nearly stumbling over his feet. Nobody else was with him. He hadn't found the kids.

Tempest ran to her jeep and grabbed the chain mail she'd brought from the house. She slipped the main piece of the hefty armor on, feeling its weight slump her shoulders, then hopped the barricade and ran into the theater. There was so much confusion that nobody stopped her.

She stepped through the vaulted entryway and into the lobby. The lights were off, but from the light of the open door, the hazy impression of burgundy velvet wallpaper and decorative crown molding made it feel like she was stepping back in time.

"Don't go any farther." Rinehart held out his arm protectively, like parents do for their kids in a car when they brake too quickly. It does nothing in that situation, just as his arm did nothing now, except to convince her he wasn't a bad guy. Narrow in his thinking, certainly, but not a bad guy. "Something really strange is going on. Something frightened Quinn as he explored the stage. And now there's this." He looked up, and Tempest followed his gaze.

Above them, a gleaming metal axe hovered in the air. Tempest had donned the chain mail that covered her chest, not her head.

"Get out of here, Tempest." Rinehart was frightened, but he wanted to make sure nobody else got hurt.

Tempest looked from him back to the axe. It wasn't hovering. It was *dangling*. By a fishing wire. Barely visible in the dim light but easy to see when you knew what you were looking for. Amateurish. This wasn't meant to hold up to scrutiny.

"This is what I do," she replied. "I think you were right this time. This isn't a booby trap. It's a performance." She jumped up, hoping she was right. Her thighs and calves protested under the additional weight of the chain mail, but her leap was as high as ever. Her hand made contact with the hilt of the axe—it was plastic. She jumped once more, this time wrapping her hand around it.

This was performance art, not unlike what she had done with her stage persona. As The Tempest, her tagline was *Destruction follows in my wake.*

"It's harmless," Tempest said. "I thought it was the killer who was creating a distraction, but it's attention seekers."

"Where are you going?"

She carried the axe past the Gothic sconces on the wall and stepped out of the lobby into the theater seating area. Like a cathedral, pews filled the space leading to the stage. The Whispering Creek Theater had never been a church, but architect Chester Hill had gone all out to make it look like a miniature cathedral not only in its exterior but also its interior. Red cushions lined the original hardwood oak pews, but they were faded and sagging.

Tempest strode confidently through the aisle toward the stage, using her phone as a flashlight. "I see you up on the catwalk," she called out. They were dressed in black, so she wouldn't have seen them if her light hadn't reflected off a lens in one of their hands. "I'm not a ghost, and I don't consent to being filmed, so you'd better stop filming too."

The sound of whispers carried down to her.

"They're up there." Tempest pointed to the catwalk above the stage as Rinehart reached her side.

"You're not going to arrest us, are you?" a youthful voice called from the catwalk.

"Are you?" Tempest asked Rinehart.

"Assaulting an officer is an offense," he said.

"We didn't touch him!" a second young voice from above

the stage blurted out. "We just dropped a piece of gauze and he freaked out."

"It wasn't even our idea," the first voice said. "She told us how to get inside without breaking anything and where the best spot was to see the ghost."

"*She?*" Tempest jumped onto the stage and shone her light straight up. The pair above her couldn't have been more than fifteen, but they looked even younger.

"Paloma Rhodes," Rinehart muttered. "She's got all my attention focused here and away from her." He joined Tempest on the stage and shouted upward, "I'm losing my patience."

"We didn't really even do any breaking and entering," a nervous voice answered, "since we didn't break anything."

"Who was she?" Tempest asked again. "This woman who told you about the ghost?"

"She didn't give a name when she called us." The young voice was desperate now.

"If I have to come up there and get you, things will be a lot worse for you." Rinehart looked around for how to get up to the catwalk, but it wasn't necessary. The two teenagers climbed down on their own.

Tempest wasn't concerned about two kids wanting to get attention by posting videos of fake ghosts. They were only puppets. She was more concerned with who had created this distraction.

Chapter 22

Tempest ran her fingers across the smooth silver of her charm bracelet. She was now behind the theater in an area roped off from the public to stay out of sight as much as possible. But it was too late. There was no way to keep what was happening from becoming the talk of the town.

She dreaded the footage and comments that would show up online. Especially because she remembered the wind whipping up her hair as she'd stepped out of the theater.

"How did you know that axe wasn't dangerous?" Sanjay scowled at her. He'd arrived shortly after Tempest's idea had been proven right. "Or do you have a death wish I don't know about?"

Tempest had been asking herself that question ever since she'd leapt into action. "I'm not holding back on you. It was a gut reaction. Something about this whole situation screamed that it was a performance. As soon as I saw the fishing wire, I knew I was right." Her dad was talking to Rinehart now, trying to get more information about what they knew as of this morning.

"Do you want to hear something horrible?" Sanjay asked. "One of the people in the crowd out there claimed to be a fan of mine, but she kept calling me Hindu Houdini instead of The Hindi Houdini."

"Shocking."

"I'm not even Hindu."

"You don't speak Hindi either," Tempest pointed out.

"It's a wonderfully alliterative stage name though. Plus I get to pay homage to Houdini. And I'll have you know I speak at least two dozen words of Hindi, a few hundred words of Punjabi, and not nearly enough Latin to finish law school." He gave her a charming smile that told her he'd used that line before.

Sanjay's Punjabi grandparents had converted to Catholicism during the British rule of India. His immigrant parents had followed suit. Their biggest disappointment in their son had nothing to do with religion. It was the fact that he hadn't finished law school, leaving instead to become a stage magician.

"Seriously, Tempest. You shouldn't have gone inside." The levity from Sanjay's voice was gone. "You're truly not shaken?"

"By the blade of a fake axe hanging over my head? I'm not shaken. I'm *angry*." She glared at the back of the theater, which was nearly as dramatic and ornate as the front, except for the modern fire door.

Sanjay didn't reply immediately, and in the silence, voices from a few yards away carried over.

"Their tricks on that stage looked so real," Officer Quinn was saying to one of his colleagues.

"I don't think that guy is cut out for police work," Sanjay commented quietly, then swore loudly in Punjabi.

"Your concern for Officer Quinn is commendable—"

"Not that." Sanjay thrust his phone into Tempest's face. "*This*."

He showed her a video of Quinn running from the theater, followed by Tempest running in before striding confidently out the same door, carrying an axe held high over her head like the victor of a battle. Smoke surrounded the edges of the frame, making it look as if she was a superhero emerging from a burning building.

"I don't really look like that." Tempest grabbed the phone from his hands. "Do I really look like that? This has to be doctored."

"The smoke around the edges is a filter they added, but that's exactly what you looked like. With the officer running out of the theater, followed by you running inside in your chain mail and emerging looking hella fierce."

Tempest groaned. This was not the kind of publicity she wanted. Her manager, Winnie, was going to love this. But personally? She wanted anything but attention. This would only make it more difficult to find out what was really going on at the theater.

Sanjay plucked the phone from her fingers. "The comments say it was your mom who put the axe there . . ."

"That doesn't make any sense!" cried Tempest. "Everyone should have seen those two fakers being led out of the theater."

"Some people are still saying they were trapped by Emma Raj."

"Her ghost, or booby traps being triggered after all this time?" Tempest growled at him.

"Both?" Sanjay frowned as he scrolled on his phone.

"If she had rigged booby traps before she died and they only got triggered now for some reason, then how did she hang an axe from the ceiling with fishing wire without anyone seeing it for more than five years?"

Sanjay shrugged. "Since when do people on the internet make any sense?" He swept his bowler hat off his head and shook out his thick mane of hair. "You could use one of these video stills as a poster for a show. The chain mail is a fierce touch, especially since you didn't put on the headgear so you can still see your face and hair. The added smoke even makes it look like one of your shows."

Tempest ignored him. "The axe was a childish prop." She led them around to the side of the theater, where they could see the parking lot. The crowd was even bigger now.

"That's not what it'll look like in the photos." Sanjay jogged after her. "People want their supernatural explanation."

"I know."

"Oh, goodie," Sanjay deadpanned, followed by a sigh. "Here's the cavalry."

Gideon's blue Renault was being waved through the police line at the back of the theater. He stopped a few feet from Sanjay's truck and pulled Tempest into his arms. Sanjay stood at the side, glaring.

"You're okay?" Gideon let go of the embrace but kept his hands gently on her shoulders.

"One of us," Sanjay cut in, "was here to make sure nothing worse happened to her."

Gideon noticed Sanjay for the first time. "Thank you," he said, sincerely. He released Tempest and looked as if he was going to formally shake Sanjay's hand, but then pulled him into a bear hug. "Thank you," Gideon repeated.

Sanjay squirmed uncomfortably, but Tempest's attention was drawn elsewhere. Ivy was driving up on her pink moped.

"This is a weird combo of hugs." Ivy pointed at Gideon and Sanjay. "But I'll take my opening." She gave Tempest a hug. "Since you had chain mail on, I guess I can't accuse you of being Too Stupid to Live."

Sanjay's phone buzzed. "Damn. My alarm. I've got to catch my flight to Vancouver to finish out my week of shows."

Darius snuck up behind Sanjay and put a large hand on his shoulder. Sanjay's eyes flickered, but the rest of his body didn't react. He'd been a performer long enough to control his reaction to being surprised. "You in the business of scaring young men out of their wits now?"

Darius chuckled. "You're not so young anymore. I think I see a couple of gray hairs on your temples."

Sanjay gasped in horror as his hands flew to the sides of his head.

Tempest threw him a bone. "Gray hair isn't a bad thing. It's dignified."

"And sexy," Ivy added. "Very sexy. But . . . I don't see a single gray hair on Sanjay's head."

"Unless you all want to stay here discussing Sanjay's hair," said Darius, "Rinehart said we're free to leave." He pulled his daughter toward him and kissed the top of her head. He was one of the few men tall enough to do that, and it always made her feel like a kid again. "I see you've got your car, so I'll follow you back to the house."

"I'm fine," Tempest insisted.

Darius crossed his arms and raised an eyebrow. If he wasn't her papa, it would have been an incredibly intimidating gesture. His raised eyebrow might have been even better than her own. And hers was damn good.

"Fine," she consented. "Let's get back to the house." There was just one thing she needed to do first.

Chapter 23

Before leaving the theater for the drive back to Fiddler's Folly, Tempest started a call and tossed her phone onto the passenger seat while it rang. She drove out of the parking lot.

"I want to hire you," she said to the man who answered.

Blackburn grunted. "You can't."

Even though she couldn't see him, his grunt reminded her of how much he'd aged in the five years she'd known him. The case of Emma Raj was one of the few he'd never solved, and it wore him down. His once brown hair was replaced by a full head of bright white, and he'd retired far younger than he'd intended to. He was now lying to everyone in his life—including himself—by pretending that he enjoyed gardening in his early retirement.

"I know I don't have my formerly large salary, but I've still got credit cards." That wasn't actually true. After her Vegas house was foreclosed, all she had was a debit card. And she was pretty sure the balance had shrunk to barely enough to buy two tickets to a show like the one she used to headline in Las Vegas. She'd paid for her jeep in cash years ago when she was flush, so it hadn't been repossessed with most of the rest of her belongings from her old life in Las Vegas.

She'd rented the theater with the meager advance funds from the TV deal. The rental wasn't an extravagance, though, because the theater had been shuttered for several years, so the rent was cheaper than any alternatives. She had needed somewhere to practice her farewell show to dedicate to her mom, and the Whispering Creek Theater helped with inspiration.

"I'm not getting involved in an active police investigation," Blackburn said.

"Then what do you do as a PI?" Tempest glowered at the phone resting on her passenger seat, even though he couldn't see her. "And don't tell me it's looking into unfaithful spouses."

"I haven't done much of *anything* yet. I just got the license. Your grandfather was my first client."

"When he asked you to look into Julian Rhodes because of the lawsuit?"

"That's right. Your grandfather was right—Rhodes was a sleazy guy—and Ash was right about something else. I've been bored in retirement. Gardening isn't what I thought it would be. Do you realize how slowly plants grow?"

Tempest held her tongue. Did he really think this was news to her? "I'm sorry to hear that. But that sounds like you want to help."

"Shouldn't you be off investigating with your Scooby gang?"

"Ivy is working three jobs, if you count studying to finish her degree in the evenings. Gideon is getting ready for his first gallery show. And Sanjay is at the airport on his way back to Vancouver for a few more nights of sold-out performances."

"You mean I'm your backup plan."

"I wouldn't put it like that. I'm asking you to do something none of us can do."

He groaned. "Just because I'm not in law enforcement any longer doesn't mean I'm going to break the law."

"Who said anything about breaking the law? I'm talking about what I want to know about two old investigations."

"You're not talking about more intel on Julian Rhodes and his missing wife?"

"No. The police have that angle covered. Paloma Rhodes's phone pinged in Michigan, and they still seem sure she's the killer. I'm not, though, so what I need is someone who can track down information at two police departments." Officer Quinn had been the one to let that slip to her, which she was sure Rinehart wouldn't appreciate.

"I'm no longer—"

"You're still the best person to reach out to the police. It's nothing confidential. Really. Old case files and evidence that should already have been released from two former cases that were already closed."

"This really isn't related to Julian Rhodes?"

"It is and it isn't. The cases are connected. I just don't know how yet."

"What cases?"

"First, my aunt's 'accidental' death in Edinburgh ten years ago. My grandmother asked about the cold case files when she was in Edinburgh earlier this year, but she couldn't find anyone who could help her. But if someone like you contacts them—"

"I see your point. So the other case is your mom's disappearance in Hidden Creek five years ago?"

"No. I already know all about that one. But it's something related to her. A book that the author Corbin Colt was writing. His manuscript that was seized as part of the séance-gone-wrong investigation. I have permission from the owner to have it, but Rinehart is giving me the runaround. The case is closed, so I should have been able to get it, but I was told I couldn't have it yet."

"Huh." Blackburn paused. Tempest didn't mind the silence.

She just hoped he hadn't hung up. "This is the manuscript you think has information about your mom's disappearance?"

"Corbin Colt lived in Hidden Creek and knew my mom. He knew more about her and my aunt than we thought. Rinehart's ego is bruised because I'm the one who solved the Colt case. I don't know if that's why he's stalling on the manuscript, but he can't say no to you." She waited for a reply, and when he didn't say no, she knew he couldn't refuse in spite of himself. "So, are you in?"

Chapter 24

She pulled into the driveway with a smile on her face, which got even bigger when she stepped out of her jeep and made her way up the path to the tree house. Nicodemus was sitting on the deck with her grandparents.

"We were worried sick." Morag leaned against the railing.

"I didn't think it would be good for me to make an appearance at the theater." Grandpa Ash rocked back and forth on the balls of his feet. "Detective Rinehart is still sore at me after his number one suspect didn't turn out to be guilty. But I would have faced his wrath if you hadn't gotten back shortly."

Nicodemus disappeared from the deck as Ash spoke, and reappeared through the tree house front door before Tempest could turn the key. He gave her a warm, though lopsided, hug with his good hand.

Tempest stepped back and looked at him. "You smell like coconut and ginger."

"It's good to see you too. Though I heard about what you were up to this morning, and I can't say I'm pleased about it."

They climbed the stairs back to the dining room deck, arm in arm, with Darius behind them.

Ash smiled at them from the open sliding door leading from

the kitchen to the deck. "I picked him up at the hospital and didn't tell him what you were up to until he'd already eaten. He's skin and bones. He requested a full South Indian breakfast. I couldn't make dosa without advance notice, but I fixed him upma and puttu."

"After eating upma for the first time decades ago," said Nicodemus, "I've never been able to imagine why most people prefer sweet porridge."

The savory wheat porridge cooked with cashews, onion, ginger, lentils, and various spices was one of Tempest's favorites as well. Her favorite was dosas though. The flat crepe-like pancakes had a batter that normally had to ferment overnight, but even her grandfather's quick-batter recipes, made with rice flour instead of whole grain rice, were spectacular.

While Ash served her breakfast, Darius walked the perimeter of Fiddler's Folly, checking the fences, gate, and security system to make sure they would be safe while he was at work. Tempest knew he would have stayed home if he thought it would help anything, but they were behind on the Whispering House job. Keeping income coming in was the best way he could protect his family.

"Three unwelcome visitors at the gate," he reported, when he got back to the deck. "They weren't there when we got home, so they must have followed us from the theater."

"Reporters?" Morag asked.

"I don't know what I'm supposed to call them."

"Ghost hunter influencers?" Tempest suggested.

Nicodemus and her grandparents chuckled. She hadn't been joking.

"Don't worry about finishing your work at the Whispering House today," Darius said to Tempest.

"We've talked about this. I don't want special treatment."

"For being my daughter?" Darius shook his head. "Ivy gets

special treatment so she can get her master's. Gideon gets special treatment so he can prepare for his art show. Victor gets special treatment so he can have as much time off as he wants in between the structural planning part of projects." He smiled. "Then there's you and me. That's all I've got. So don't say you get special treatment. You get the same Darius Mendez treatment as everyone else on the team."

"You haven't taken a day off in five years. You barely made it to Christmas."

"Owner's prerogative."

"If you were hoping to stay here to keep me company," Nicodemus cut in, "I'm going to disappoint you. I gave in and took some painkillers with breakfast. I need to sleep for the next few hours."

While Ash fixed Darius a tiffin box of breakfast to go, Tempest walked Nicodemus over to the guest room to make sure he had everything he needed.

"Where's Brodie?" she asked.

Nicodemus yawned. "I spoke to him this morning. He's off dealing with the logistics of my canceled tour."

"Nicky." Tempest spoke his name slowly as she opened a paper pop-up of Nicodemus and Brodie on the stage together, an idea forming in her mind.

"Has anyone ever told you how marvelously devious your voice can sound? You should use it more on stage. That's not a critique of your physical performances. Only a compliment that—"

"Nicky," she repeated, this time more forcefully. "Why did you call Ash to come and get you from the hospital instead of calling me?" She hadn't seen any missed calls.

"I spoke with Brodie first. He mentioned that you were busy this morning. I knew Ash would be happy to fetch me."

So Brodie had been keeping tabs on her.

Tempest got Nicodemus settled back in the guest room bed, and he was asleep before she reached the door. Daylight streamed into the room, so she retraced her steps to close the curtains. Being one of the highest rooms at Fiddler's Folly, she caught a glimpse of some movement at the far end of the property.

A figure was standing at the back gate, *on the inside.*

She steadied her breathing. Four people lived at Fiddler's Folly, and Brodie and Nicodemus were staying there as their guests. There was nothing worrisome about the fact that someone was at the gate, but it wasn't someone she immediately recognized. She knew the shapes and mannerisms of her dad and grandparents well enough that she expected she'd recognize even their shadows. She knew Nicodemus almost as well. But there was one person staying at Fiddler's Folly for whom that wasn't true. The one person who matched the lanky body type of the faraway figure.

Brodie.

And he wasn't alone.

Chapter 25

Tempest slipped down the secret staircase and out the door, and headed up the hill toward the two figures. It was definitely Brodie at the gate. His lean, towering frame and spiky hair gave him away.

Brodie was speaking softly with someone on the outside of the gate. This side of the property had a chain-link fence and gate, so Tempest could see through it. But not well enough. Brodie's towering figure blocked her view of the smaller person outside the gate.

Before she could decide whether to give up stealth to get closer, the figure hastily departed. But as soon as Brodie turned, Tempest stepped into the path.

"What were you doing?"

"I'm the one who has to deal with the canceled tour."

"What does that mean?"

"That you should leave things alone you don't understand, Tempest."

She raised an eyebrow and directed her fiercest scowl at him. A weaker man would have shrunk back, or at least laughed nervously. But Brodie, as Tempest was coming to realize, was far more devious than she'd suspected. It was a mistake to underestimate someone simply because they were an assistant.

"Fine," she said. "I'll wake Nicky and see what he thinks."

Brodie was at her side before she realized he'd moved. He grabbed her elbow with greater strength than his knobby limbs suggested they had in them. His breath smelled of whisky and decay, as if Nicodemus had truly raised him from the dead.

"You'll do no such thing," he hissed in her ear.

"Are you seriously threatening me?" Tempest easily twisted out of his grip. It had been more of a scare tactic than something meant to constrain her.

He looked up at the trees above them. "You have to understand. I've never been the one in the spotlight. I like it like that, but I would've liked the paycheck that came with it." He returned his gaze to Tempest. "He's been more than fair with my pay, but I hadn't planned on his forced retirement coming so soon. He has no use for the magical apparatus I've lugged around for him all these years."

"You were *selling* his props?"

"They're not just his," Brodie snapped. "I helped him more than he ever gave me credit for. But I couldn't go through with it. I'd like the money, but not that badly."

"You want me to believe you backed out at the last moment?"

He lifted a puppet on strings from an inner pocket of his jacket. "The first shadow puppet Nicodemus used on stage for his Nicodemus the Necromancer act. Worth a lot." He paused and ran his fingers over the strings. "I was angry. I *am* angry about that damn booby trap that's wrecked our lives."

"But not angry enough to sell that out from under him."

Brodie nodded. "It'll kill him if he finds out I was thinking about it, you know. You'll shove another dagger into him if you tell him. Only this one'll be in his heart, and you'll be the one to have done it."

"I don't like being manipulated."

"And I don't like being out of a job. We both have to make decisions from this point forward."

Tempest glared at him. "I'll check, you know. I'll make sure his props are all where they're supposed to be."

"Have at it." He strode back toward his room without waiting for a reply.

Tempest hated to admit it, but he was right. It would crush Nicodemus to know what Brodie was doing. She wouldn't tell him if she didn't have to. The security system her dad had installed included video, but only of the front gate, not the back one. No wonder he'd chosen the back gate as a rendezvous. It wasn't marked as an official address, and was only met by a path up the hillside to the old wishing well.

Several curious onlookers were still hovering outside the front gate as Brodie disappeared back into his room in the guest wing. Most of the items for their planned tour had been shipped directly to Los Angeles, where their tour was supposed to begin, but the items that had traveled with them on their flight were locked in the Fiddler's Folly workshop.

She waited a few more minutes to make sure Brodie wasn't leaving his room and unlocked the workshop door.

Tempest smiled to herself at the steamer trunk, wondering if they really were better than regular suitcases, or if only stage magicians with a fondness for the past thought so. She told herself it wasn't an invasion of privacy to look through their props. She only wanted to see if it appeared as if Brodie had removed anything. How would she tell?

Damn. She couldn't even get inside.

If Sanjay had been there, he'd have been able to pick the lock, but that was a skill she'd never taken the time to master.

She sat down with her back against the trunk and looked across the workshop. She thought about her life that was nearly ready to begin. She had told herself that she'd fully embraced her role as creator of architectural misdirection for Secret Staircase Construction, but it wasn't exactly true. She was still waiting to move on from her past life. To fully understand what had happened to her family.

Screw this. She needed to get inside the trunk for Nicky's own good. She stood up, grabbed a hammer, and smashed the lock.

Chapter 26

When Tempest returned to the tree house after searching through the steamer trunk, her gran was leaning against a kitchen countertop holding a cinnamon stick like a cigarette, watching Ash rinse a bowl of short-grain rice.

There hadn't been anything out of the ordinary in Nicky's trunk. Nor did it look like Brodie had stolen anything. Smashing the lock had been a bust.

"Tempest!" Ash turned without splashing a single drop of water. "I knew you didn't get enough breakfast. What can I get you? I'm afraid I gave your father the last of the puttu."

"One of the people at the gate has already given up and departed, and the other two are buried in their phones. I'm hoping they'll go away soon so I can leave the house in peace." She didn't need any more photos or videos of her showing up online. It was probably a losing battle, but she always felt so cozy and loved in this kitchen. It was nice to hide out here for a little time before she stepped back into real life.

"Can't that detective make them go away?" Morag asked.

"Technically, they're in the street." Tempest's gaze fell to the nervous grip her grandmother had on the stick of cinnamon between her fingers. "Is cinnamon smoking a new fad I missed?"

Morag raised an eyebrow and grinned. "I nearly choked to death when I forgot it was a stick of cinnamon and inhaled."

"Even after more than forty years, she misses smoking." Ash finished rinsing the rice and moved to lentils.

"I don't miss the smoking itself," Morag clarified. "I miss having something that helps me relax when there's an unknown stress weighing me down."

"I wasn't in danger—"

"It's not that. It's *everything*. I don't know why it's taking the authorities so long to find Paloma Rhodes." Morag jumped as the front gate buzzer sounded.

Tempest went to the monitor her dad had installed by the kitchen entrance. "Looks like they got tired of waiting for me to leave and are trying a more straightforward approach."

"I'll take care of it." Ash dried his hands and scooped up a small cardboard box sitting on the counter. He kissed both Tempest and Morag on the cheek and disappeared down the stairs.

"Dare I speculate what he's up to?" Tempest asked her grandmother.

"I'm sure you can guess."

Two minutes later, her suspicions were confirmed. "You bribed them with cookies?" she asked her empty-handed grandfather when he appeared on the stairs.

"Why must you use such an unpleasant word for an act of generosity? I regretfully informed them that you'd departed with your father. I had some extra cardamom shortbread cookies, so it would have been a shame for them to go to waste."

"Do you want me to wait for you to finish the lunch boxes so I can deliver lunches to the crew?" Tempest asked.

Ash shook his head. "I need my daily exercise."

☠ ☠ ☠

Tempest arrived at the Whispering House and found Ivy and Lenore standing in front of a computer tablet on the kitchen island.

"Please don't tell me you've decided you want to paint the walls a different color," said Tempest.

"Remember that rat's nest your dad found when he opened up the wall for the secret staircase?" Lenore asked. "The architectural historians' results just arrived. It's a gold mine. Let me tell you, if you ever want to make dignified architectural historians squeal like schoolchildren, tell them you've found a rat's nest in your wall. They've pieced together even more than they initially thought they'd find."

Tempest had been horrified when the old rat's nest had been discovered, but it turned out that rat's nests are essentially perfectly preserved time capsules. Rats are hoarders who gather items for their nests within a fifty-foot radius. Not only that, but rat urine acts as a preservative. Tiny fragments of paper preserved in rat's nests could reveal handwritten details from centuries past. The Whispering House was nearly 150 years old, so it was entirely possible Lenore's rat's nests could shine a light on more of the history of the house.

"What did they discover?" Tempest asked.

"The future librarian in me is giddy with anticipation." Ivy quiet-clapped and did a little dance in her rubber-soled work boots. Today's boots weren't pink, but her pink overalls covered most of them.

"Nineteen oh-one," read Lenore. "That's the only writing I see so far. Just lines . . . maybe damage?"

"This preserved snippet is from more than a century ago," said Tempest, "so that's not surprising."

"Let me see if I can magnify the image." Lenore cleaned her glasses on the fabric of her dress, zoomed in, and leaned closer. She leaned back abruptly and closed the tablet.

"What did you see?" Tempest asked.

She shook her head. "The screen is giving me a headache. I'll print out all the images and look at them later, on paper."

A bicycle bell sounded before Tempest could ask to see the rest of the images. "My grandfather is here with lunch."

"Perfect timing," said Lenore. "I couldn't sleep last night and woke up far too early, so I'm famished."

It was only 11:30, but Tempest had learned that it was a pretty common lunchtime for a business that was at work by seven o'clock.

"It's lovely of him to always include me in his cooking for the crew," Lenore said, "though it doesn't seem very efficient for your grandfather to cook and then travel so far to bring the crew lunch. There are great restaurants down the street. Plus good pop-ups, but those are only twice a week."

"Why does everything have to be efficient?" The *dabbawalla* meal delivery system was incredibly efficient, but that was because of its scale. Grandpa Ash's system was admittedly anything but efficient. "My grandfather loves cooking, and it gives him something satisfying to do in his retirement. Riding his bike helps him stay fit, and the crew, who are always working in a different location, get the comfort of a home-cooked meal prepared with love. As for patronizing local businesses, Gideon will often do that for dinner, and Ivy will pick something up between her two jobs."

The sweet scent of coconut milk filled the air as Lenore opened the door for Ash.

Lenore said her headache was getting worse, so she took her lunch upstairs, but she told Ivy and Tempest to make themselves at home in the kitchen. Ash dropped off lunches for everyone, including Darius and Gideon who were in the back, but then departed, saying he had his own lunch date with Morag and a friend of theirs.

"I'm envious of your family, you know," Ivy said to Tempest as she watched Ash ride his bike down the long driveway.

"Remember it comes with a curse."

"But also a family who loves you more than anything."

"I can't get the curse out of my head though. Not right now. Not when I'm so close to figuring out what happened to my aunt and mom. And I know it's related to what happened this week. If there's no supernatural curse—"

"Which there's not," said Ivy.

"Agreed. Someone mortal killed my aunt in Scotland. But what if it goes back even further? What if it's related to the original curse from India?"

"How?"

"Let me start at the beginning. I mean, *my* beginning, when I first realized the curse might have come for my mom."

"I'm in," said Ivy, "as long as I can start eating your grandfather's coconut milk curry while you talk."

Tempest couldn't think about food, even food as good as her grandfather's.

"My mom vanished—presumably murdered—because she was going to reveal the truth about her sister's death in Edinburgh ten years ago. Nobody realized at the time that Elspeth's death on stage was more than an accident. It was the convenient answer because the festival was starting and a murder would have been worse than a tragic accident. Even when her grave was disturbed, it was part of a larger pattern of grave robberies, so nobody connected it. Elspeth hadn't told people much about the illusion she was working on. She was secretive and only told her stagehands what they needed to know. That was dangerous, but then again, she was always the reckless one.

"And why nobody could say for sure whether the guillotine was part of Elspeth's act. My mom suspected it wasn't, because they didn't believe in acts that showed violence against women.

The illusion of sawing a woman in half became popular right around the time women were fighting for the right to vote. The first time the illusion was done, it was a guy who was put in a box and sawn in half, but the illusion never really took off until suffragists were fighting for the right to vote. Then, when women became the ones on stage being sawn in half, the trick became huge. It was what people wanted to see."

There was nuance to the story, of course. P. T. Selbit, a master showman, was one of the first magicians to popularize the illusion. He hired a controversial suffragist for his act "Sawing Through a Woman," used a copious amount of fake blood on the stage, and hired ambulances as show promotion. But it was the right act for the right time. He tapped into the spirit of the time, and the paying public ate it up.

"If the guillotine hadn't killed her, what do you think Elspeth was going to perform that night?" Ivy asked.

"I wish I knew. It could have been anything. Having Nicodemus in town this week reminded me of how many magicians in the past borrowed each other's illusions. What if my aunt was going to use an illusion from the Raj family curse?"

"But why does that matter?" Ivy asked.

"I don't know . . ."

"I'll help you figure it out. But right now, lunch is over. I need to put on my protective gear and finish the attic wall. You can help."

"I thought the attic was finished."

"Lenore had one more minor request," Ivy said. "Keeping clients happy is key to us all having jobs. And Lenore is lovely to work with most of the time. Like Paloma was."

"You make it sound like she's dead." Goose bumps formed on Tempest's arms.

"Why hasn't she turned up? She's either dead or she killed Julian, which means she's not lovely after all. I mean, I know she had good reason and all, if she did it . . . but still."

"Did you not listen to anything I said about the Raj family curse?"

"I know there are so many things that overlap, but it just doesn't make sense. Paloma running makes sense. Except for the fact that she was a school librarian before she married Julian. That makes her far less likely to be a killer."

"That's why she wanted the secret library in their house."

"Which Julian vetoed. I know it's terrible to say, but I'm really not sorry he's dead."

"I had a great trick for her secret library," said Tempest, remembering the nixed plans. "It wasn't just going to be one book that slid open the secret door, but three books placed in the spots of 7–1–4, the area code where she had her first library job."

"Maybe we can still build it for her once a jury finds her Not Guilty."

Tempest scrunched up her face at her friend. "You're a bit obsessed with her getting away with murder."

"I'm the worst," Ivy agreed. "Okay, I should get to work. I'll see if Lenore's door is open when I pass by on my way up to the attic. If it is, I'll let her know you're eager to see the rat's nest findings."

But Ivy ran downstairs thirty-five seconds later. "Lenore's gone."

"What do you mean she's gone?"

"She's not in her room. Her food is untouched. Maybe she fell. Oh no . . ."

Ivy ran back up the stairs, but Tempest had a better idea. She opened the front door of the house. Lenore's car was gone.

It was one thing for Lenore to secretly leave food for them at night, but she'd never before disappeared without saying goodbye. What had Lenore seen in the rat's nest findings?

Chapter 27

The long afternoon push to finish up at the Whispering House was briefly interrupted by news that a disruption had taken place outside the theater. An onlooker in the crowd had scaled one of the theater's stone walls and climbed onto a spire. Though it didn't look high from the ground, he'd needed the help of a firefighter's ladder to get down. Several videos of the ordeal had been posted online, so Tempest and Ivy were able to watch from afar without stopping work.

"An attention seeker," Ivy reminded her. "That's all he is."

"He's a grown man who should know better." At least this guy wasn't a ghost hunter, just someone who showed videos of himself online pulling pranks.

Tempest's phone rang as she was driving home. Night was falling, and her headlights bounced off the remnants of a fallen tree along the side of the road. She expected it would be more news of the theater, but it wasn't.

"I wanted to keep you posted about what I found," Blackburn said. The private investigator's voice crackled over the phone line. "HCPD wasn't turning you away for no reason. They've misplaced Corbin Colt's manuscript."

"What do you mean *misplaced?*"

"There's been some turnover lately. Things aren't as organized as I'd have hoped."

"But those pages were evidence that was supposed to be released after the investigation was over." Tempest hadn't even had time to take photographs of those pages before they were seized.

"I know."

"I need those pages." She'd had her hopes set on Corbin Colt's hidden manuscript pages. Even though it was only a fictionalized version of her mom's disappearance, he'd known things that nobody else had known.

"There's no need to worry," Blackburn insisted. "I'm concerned about the state of affairs, but it doesn't mean it's related to this case in particular."

Tempest wasn't so sure.

She clicked the button to open the gate and pulled into her driveway. She hated that they had to be fenced off from the world, but with everything that had happened, on balance, she was glad that her dad had insisted on the security, even if it *was* making her paranoid. She watched the gate close in her rearview mirror before stepping out of the car.

Tempest checked on Abra first. The bunny seemed restless, even after he was fed, so Tempest scooped him up in her arms and took him with her to the tree house. She knocked on the tree house door, and immediately heard her grandfather's footsteps.

He kissed her cheeks, displacing his fedora as he did so. "I'm glad I'll have company for dinner."

"No Grannie Mor?"

"Tansy and Trina invited Morag, Gideon, and a couple of other artists out to dinner."

"They didn't invite you to come along?"

He chuckled. "*All* artists, Tempest. I'd have been a fish out of water. I'd rather commune with my kitchen and the oak tree.

And now you." He turned and walked up the stairs. "I wish the police had located Paloma Rhodes already so we could finally close this chapter in our lives."

"You really think she did it?"

"Abused women must sometimes take drastic measures."

"At my theater? The one I rented. The one where my mom vanished?"

Ash sighed and turned around. "I know what you're thinking, but it can't be our curse."

"I didn't say that, but I do think it's related to us."

Ash wiped his forehead with a handkerchief. "Come. Let's get to the kitchen. Everything is better there." He fixed them both a cup of tea and took homemade shortbread cookies from a jar before continuing. "You have to understand," Ash said, after taking a long swig. "I know, rationally, that it was a dangerous trick that killed my brother. It's all in the past. It's not related to what happened to your mother. Let's leave it in the past, eh?"

Ash was such a jovial man that Tempest sometimes forgot how much heartbreak he'd suffered. Her aunt's death, thought to be accidental at the time, was what had brought Tempest and her grandparents closer.

Ash had always said that even though he'd suffered the horrific loss of his two beloved daughters, he had gained a son and granddaughter in return. He never would have wished for it, but he had accepted the life he'd been given.

"Your phone is buzzing," said Ash.

It was a text from Ivy. *I have an idea about what happened. My house in 10 minutes? Dinner on me.*

☠ ☠ ☠

Ivy lived in the top half of a duplex, which was smaller than the lower unit, where her older sister Dahlia lived with her family. Tempest walked past the three custom-made garden gnomes in the garden that represented her sister's family: a plump, redheaded gnome with a magnifying glass for true crime writer Dahlia; a dark-haired gnome holding a gavel for her attorney wife, Vanessa; and a giggling baby gnome for their daughter, Natalie, even though Natalie was now seven years old. She continued around to the side of the house, where a circular staircase led to Ivy's unit.

A locked gate blocked off the start of the stairs, but this was no ordinary lock. A comically oversize lock that looked like it was straight out of a cartoon left room for you to slip your hand inside the keyhole and act as the key yourself. Tempest did so, and the gate swung open.

When Tempest told her grandfather about the invitation, he insisted he'd be fine on his own that evening, and he also insisted on whipping up dessert for her to take, so she carried a container of quick-cook coconut ladoo up the stairs with her.

"Coconut and cardamom?" Dahlia sniffed the round cookies before sweeping Tempest into a hug. Dahlia's bright yellow glasses Tempest remembered had been replaced by sparkling purple ones.

"Good sniffer."

"Natalie is in a stage where she refuses to eat certain foods and instead sneakily hides food deemed unworthy in potted plants around the house. My nose is all about detecting specific scents these days."

"I'm happy to see you," said Tempest, "but I didn't realize this was a family gathering. Are Natalie and Vanessa inside too?"

Dahlia looked at her sister. "You didn't tell her?"

"Tell me what?" Tempest looked back and forth from one sister to the other.

You could tell the two women were related, but aside from their auburn hair, they were gentle opposites in most realms.

Dahlia was a nonfiction writer, true crime whenever possible, and had been obsessed with dark crime stories ever since learning about the Black Dahlia unsolved murder of the 1940s when she was a kid, though she hadn't actually been named after the case, but the flower. Ivy couldn't stand anything as grim as true crime but thrived on classic mystery novels where you always knew you'd get a happy ending, or at least a satisfying resolution. Even physically, where Ivy's hair was straight, Dahlia's was curly. And while Ivy lacked curves of any kind, Dahlia had enough to spare, and she wasn't shy about wearing bold clothes that showed off her round figure. They never had to worry about dressing alike when they went out in public together, since most of Ivy's clothes were pink or other light colors, but Dahlia's closet was filled with purples and reds. And right now, yellow go-go boots with two-inch heels that still left her half a head shorter than Tempest.

"Ivy caught me up on what's been happening this week," said Dahlia, "and how you're investigating. Nat and Van are at a playdate with some other kids and parents tonight. Ivy thought it was the perfect time for me to walk you through my methods to see if that jars anything loose for you."

"Your methods?" Tempest asked.

Dahlia lifted a corkboard from Ivy's coffee table. A stack of notecards, pens, and thumbtacks were on top. "Ivy informed me that you two don't even have a murder board."

Ivy groaned. "I asked you not to call it that."

Dahlia cracked open the pack of multicolored pens. "But that's what it is. A man was murdered this week. I'm so sorry you're involved in this, Tempest. But if Ivy wasn't lying about you looking into it, you two need to step up your murder game."

Ivy groaned again.

"It's okay," said Tempest. "It's true. Euphemisms won't help us. Aren't you missing some red string to connect to some note-cards?"

Dahlia plopped the stack of materials back onto the coffee table and waved her hand through the air dismissively. "I've never understood those. If you're doing your investigative job right, the connections can be brought together in a much more organized manner. Now—" She paused and gave them a diabolical grin. "It's time for our council of war."

"Let's call Gideon," said Tempest. "Maybe he'll even answer his landline, if he's back home after his dinner with the artists."

Tempest tried calling his house. He sometimes was so caught up in his stone carving that he didn't answer the phone, even if he heard it. As expected, the call went to his answering machine. "Gideon Torres here," the message began. "I could lie and say I'll call you back shortly, but that's probably not the case. I'm not a phone person, but please do leave me a message, and I'll respond in due time. Maybe." That was just like Gideon. He appeared formal and old-fashioned on the surface, but then he surprised you.

She spoke a few words to the answering machine just in case he was already home but screening calls, but he wasn't. Before putting her phone away, her finger hovered over Sanjay's number. It was right before the time he'd be going on stage this evening, nearly a thousand miles away. He'd probably pick up his phone, but she didn't want to distract him. She slipped the phone into her pocket.

While Dahlia placed an order for dinner from a Thai restaurant down the street and Ivy found a stand for the corkboard, Tempest began writing out a list of suspects. By the time the order was delivered and they'd dished out plates of food, they'd filled the corkboard with notecards of suspects, facts about them, and locations. Ivy had even printed out photos of Julian Rhodes and each of the suspects from what was available online.

Julian Rhodes's photo was on top. It was his headshot from the Bespoke Rhodes website. Underneath were the suspects.

"Brodie Frost," said Tempest. Ivy had found his most reposted photo on the internet, an old one from when he'd played Ichabod Crane from *The Legend of Sleepy Hollow*. "Suspect number one. He might be selling off Nicky's props now that he's out of a job, and he's been tracking my movements. He's up to something."

"But not necessarily murder," Dahlia pointed out. "Save your theories for after we lay out the facts."

"Isn't she great?" said Ivy. "This is why I didn't think you'd object."

"Paloma Rhodes," continued Tempest. Ivy's own biases came through in the photo she'd selected of Paloma. Rather than use her headshot from the Bespoke Rhodes luxury travel website, she'd selected a candid shot from more than a decade ago when Paloma was a librarian. "The main suspect of the police, because she ran away. Her phone pinged from Michigan, but that doesn't mean she's with it. Her husband tried to kill her, so she has the strongest motive to have wanted Julian dead. But she has no connection to the Whispering Creek Theater."

"That you know of," noted Dahlia.

"Point taken," said Tempest. "Next, Moriarty. Real name unknown." There was no photograph of Moriarty. He'd avoided cameras to a creepily precise degree. "He's fixated on me, but he says he's my guardian angel, not a stalker or nemesis."

"Why does the notecard say he's in town?" Ivy asked. "You said he hadn't made contact in months."

Tempest took a deep breath. "Until last night."

Dahlia stood up. "I need wine. I'm opening a bottle. Who else wants in?"

Tempest and Ivy both raised their hands but didn't look away from each other.

"I'm sorry I didn't tell you when I saw you earlier today," said Tempest. "I didn't mean to keep it from you. It was late last night, and he came to Gideon's house while I was there. It was so surreal, it didn't even register as real when I woke up today. But it was."

"Drink up, ladies." Dahlia set two glasses of red wine in front of them and raised her own glass. "To surreal experiences and getting to the bottom of this mystery."

Tempest took a big gulp and told Ivy and Dahlia about Moriarty's strange visit.

"He said, '*She's dangerous*,'" Tempest concluded. "I thought he meant Paloma Rhodes, that he believed she was guilty like everyone else seems to think and that he was just worried about me in general."

"Since he's a creepy stalker fan," Dahlia murmured.

"But what if Moriarty is actually involved in some way? He knows the world of magic and is equipped to create an ingenious booby trap. But I don't see Paloma teaming up with him. What if he was talking about *another* woman? Moriarty, or he and his partner, could have killed Julian Rhodes because Julian was trying to destroy my dad's business. We know he's capable of killing when he believes it's justified."

"Hold on," said Ivy. "What other woman would he be involved with?"

"Lenore Woods," said Tempest.

Ivy choked on a bite of rice noodles. "I need more wine." She held out her glass to her sister, who obliged.

"Lenore snuck out of her house this afternoon without telling us," said Tempest.

"That's right," Ivy whispered.

"Was it really sneaking out?" asked Dahlia. "This is a woman whose house your crew has basically taken over. Plus she's not living there. She might have just needed some peace and quiet."

"She's also the architect descendant of Chester Hill," Tempest said. "That's the same man who built the Whispering Creek Theater. *That* could be our connection. The Whispering Creek Theater is involved."

"You're getting distracted by a location because of its striking appearance and history," said Dahlia. "I'm not disagreeing that it's relevant. It's where the booby traps were set. But people are more important than places. Is that all your suspects? Brodie Frost, Paloma Rhodes, Lenore Woods, and Moriarty?"

"One more," said Tempest. She'd debated whether to put it on the murder board. She doubted he was a real suspect, but after what Blackburn had told her . . . she tacked one more notecard onto the corkboard. "Detective Rinehart."

Ivy hid her face behind her hands. "Please tell me you're joking, that you're just upset he once thought your grandfather was a murderer, so you want to put him on the board out of spite."

"Some evidence from his last case has gone missing at HCPD," Tempest explained. "Corbin Colt's manuscript that I was supposed to have after the case was over, which it is. That manuscript is related to my mom vanishing. But they 'misplaced' it."

"As much as I love a good conspiracy," said Dahlia, "it's upsetting how frequently files really do get misplaced."

"I liked it better when we were investigating an impossible crime earlier this year." Ivy speared a spring roll with her fork. "Then I didn't have to think about the horrid person who'd kill someone. We could simply focus on the puzzle."

"The puzzle is still key," said Tempest. "Because there's got to be a reason the killer—Paloma or whoever it is—chose this devious method. It's still a puzzle—just not an impossible one."

"The booby-trap blade might have hit the wrong victim," Ivy suggested.

"The trap delayed me from getting inside," said Tempest. "Maybe *that* was the plan. To keep me from discovering something inside the theater. Because something we haven't talked about yet is the Raj family curse." Tempest pointed to the corkboard's family curse column. "Whatever is happening this week has to be related to me and my family's past. It's too big a coincidence that booby traps like a magician would build are shooting out of a theater that I happen to be renting and where my mom disappeared, and that the man who was murdered was suing my dad. Even people on the internet are saying my mom is responsible for the booby traps from beyond the grave."

"I hope you're not being influenced by the internet mob," said Dahlia. "Listening to those voices never did anyone any good."

"They're wrong about my mom, but they're right to point out the obvious connection. Someone is hiding behind the Raj family curse."

"Which brings up the biggest omission on the board," said Dahlia.

"My grandparents aren't involved," said Tempest. "I'd bet my life on—"

"Not them," said Dahlia. "*Nicodemus.*"

Tempest felt her hand go numb as she gripped her fork so tightly it nearly snapped.

"You didn't put him on the board," Dahlia continued, "and I'm in favor of loyalty, but if you think this is truly related to your family curse, Nicodemus has been there the whole time. And he's here this week."

"No." Tempest's voice was louder and angrier than she meant it to be. "He was nearly killed by the booby trap. And it ruined his career."

"Dahl has a point," Ivy said gently. "He might have been

accidentally hurt by the knife. Maybe he screwed up when trying to remove the booby-trap evidence, or setting up another one. He builds illusions. He collects automata."

"He's also not a woman," said Tempest. "Moriarty said—"

"Moriarty," Dahlia cut in, "might be the killer. You're not thinking dispassionately enough about the facts."

"Of course I'm not thinking dispassionately. But beyond my biases, Nicodemus was on the other side of the world when my mom vanished. And I was with him when Julian Rhodes was killed."

"By a booby trap. That means the killer didn't have to be there."

"There's something that feels wrong about the booby-trapped door." Tempest thought again about what she'd seen that morning. She'd seen something that mattered. She knew it. But she couldn't quite place what it was that felt wrong.

"Of course something feels wrong," said Ivy. "It's super creepy that it's regenerating. Way creepier than a supposed ghost from a classic impossible crime novel. It's like it's from a horror movie. And I don't want to be in a horror movie."

"I give up," said Dahlia. "I was trying to keep us on track with known facts to start, but you two are right. There's a lot more going on here than a simple murder board will tell us."

"No." Tempest pushed aside her plate and stood up to look more closely at the board. "You're the one who's right. I'm too close to this. I need to look at the facts on the board, not go with a gut feeling. I know the facts are all here. I just haven't put the pieces of the puzzle together yet. Brodie Frost, Paloma Rhodes, Moriarty, Lenore Woods, Detective Rinehart, and Nicodemus the Necromancer. Looking at all of them, Nicodemus alibis out for my mom vanishing; hopefully we can trust a detective, so I'm ruling out Rinehart for my sanity; Lenore Woods has an interest in architectural history, so her connection is innocently explained; Moriarty is a wild card, so we don't know enough to pass judgment on him; Paloma Rhodes could reasonably have wanted her husband dead, so I'll grant that the police are right about her being a person of interest who needs to be found so she can share what she knows. That leaves Brodie Frost."

Tempest lifted his creepy photograph from the corkboard and turned it over. She didn't want to be biased by his stage costume. She was looking only at facts. "Brodie has been around since before my Aunt Elspeth was killed in a supposed accident on stage. *He was in Scotland when she died there.* As far as I know, his alibi was never checked for when my mom vanished. He's been here in Hidden Creek this week. He's been sneaking around. And he's willing to go behind his boss's back to sell off valuable props."

"Oh no!" Ivy squealed, causing Dahlia to knock over her wineglass. "This really is a horror movie."

Tempest and Dahlia blinked at Ivy as red wine spread across the table like blood.

"Don't you see?" said Ivy. *"The killer is in your house."*

Ivy was right. The prime suspect was at Fiddler's Folly with her family.

Chapter 28

Tempest called her grandfather, who assured her that he and Morag were safe and sound in their tree house, as was her father in the main house. Morag had gotten back from her dinner out, and she and Ash had locked up the tree house and were enjoying mugs of warm turmeric milk before bed.

"Of course the doors are locked," Ash said. Tempest imagined him frowning and rocking back and forth on his heels as he spoke to her. "Why are you asking?"

"Brodie has been acting strangely. I just want to make sure everyone is safe."

"Brodie?" Ash clicked his tongue. "He's been misunderstood the entire time I've known him. He was typecast because of his features. You know better than to judge someone based on their physical appearance."

"But you don't know him well."

"I suppose not." Ash paused. "But he's not related to . . . what you asked about earlier this evening." He must have been with Grannie Mor, and he didn't want to upset her.

"I'm not sure of anything," Tempest admitted.

"You're still at Ivy's?"

"I'll be home soon."

"Good. Your father is waiting up for you."

Tempest sighed. Of course he was. He was normally an early-to-bed kind of guy, with the hours he kept for Secret Staircase Construction, but anything involving his family took precedence over sleep.

"Even if you're right," Ash continued, "you don't need to worry. I've been here all day, and Brodie hasn't come back to Fiddler's Folly yet."

"He has the code to get through the security gate, so you might have missed him."

"You know the system alerts us when anyone comes or goes."

She did know. It wasn't something she liked, but she appreciated it based on everything that had happened that year.

"I had dinner with Nicodemus," Ash continued, "and Brodie wasn't back when I helped Nicodemus back to his guest room with a basket of midnight snacks."

She called her dad as soon as she hung up with her grandfather. She didn't ask if he'd locked up because that would only worry him. She was sure he would have, plus she'd bet on her dad winning a fight with anyone who wasn't a superhero. But she wanted to hear his voice and let him know she'd be back soon.

☠ ☠ ☠

Nicodemus's light was on when Tempest got back from Ivy's house, so she rang the buzzer to the secret entrance that led to the guest wing. She could have just pulled on the arrow held by the cupid statue that activated the secret staircase, but she liked to give guests their privacy.

The secret stairs opened up three seconds later. Nicodemus

was grinning when she reached the top of the stairs. "Between that nap and jet lag, I couldn't sleep. Not to steal your grand-father's line, but have you eaten?"

"Extremely well." Tempest patted her stomach and avoided his gaze. Dahlia couldn't be right about Nicodemus.

"Your grandfather sent me back from dinner at the tree house with a midnight-snack basket."

"What did he give you?"

"Enough to feed an entire theatrical troupe."

"How's the hand?"

"In a strange way, the pain reminds me of when I was young, when I took terrible risks on stage and got injured all the time. But I never risked the safety of anyone else besides myself."

Tempest pointed at the poster of Nicodemus and the Cat of Nine Lives on the wall. "I remember it took me years before I earned your trust and you'd tell me how you accomplished your illusions bringing Cat back to life."

"You weren't a particularly trustworthy teenager."

Tempest winced. "Is *anyone* trustworthy at that age?"

"Your grandfather was entrusted with a lot of Raj family illusion secrets even before he was a teenager."

"Not all of them. Plus that was a different time."

"Ha! Every generation thinks they're unique and that life was *so different* before them. I refuse to be provoked into gen-erational warfare. Why don't you tell me what you think of my latest pop-up. And are you sure I can't tempt you with some idli? There's a bit of everything left, except for his guacamole. I finished that jar. I think he has a secret ingredient."

"Maybe you'll earn his trust one day."

He chuckled and tossed her a folded card with his good hand. This one wasn't made only of paper, but also string. The cuts of the black paper weren't especially crisp, as if he'd been in a hurry, but it was still easy to recognize the shape of Brodie's tall figure and the puppet strings that pulled the figure left and right.

"Where's Brodie?" Tempest shut the card.

Nicodemus pressed his lips together. "Haven't seen him since this morning. He's cross with me."

"Why?"

Nicodemus took the card back and opened it up. He tugged on the string. Unlike when Tempest had pulled it, this time the string twisted the figure around, revealing not a black shadow nearly hidden by the black stage but a light gray figure that shone brightly compared to the darker paper. "He always said he was happiest being in the shadows, but I don't think he's pleased that in all the support pouring in from my fans, nobody is mentioning his contribution. A few people have mentioned the puppet, but they don't know his name."

Tempest's phone rang before she could decide whether to tell him her suspicions about Brodie.

"I'm sorry to wake you," former detective Blackburn said, "but it's important."

"I'm not asleep. What's so important—Oh! They found Paloma?"

"They found Paloma?" Nicodemus whispered.

"Where are you?" Blackburn's voice hardened.

"At home, why?"

"I heard another voice."

"I'm having a drink with Nicodemus."

"Your phone isn't on speaker, is it?"

"No, why?" She scowled at the phone, even though she knew he couldn't see her. "Stop being so cryptic."

"I need you to meet me at the police station."

"The police station? Is Paloma there? Is that why—"

"Tempest. This is a situation where I need you to trust me. Have you had too much to drink to drive?"

She looked at her barely touched glass. "No."

"Good. Stay on the phone with me, and come to the police station. Don't wake your dad or your grandparents. Don't bring your guests. Come alone."

"But—"

"Tempest. Please."

She wasn't afraid of Blackburn, but he was definitely freaking her out right now.

"I have to head to the police station," she said to Nicodemus.

"What's happened? Let me find my shoes—"

"No." She put her hand on his. "I'm fine. I don't know what's going on yet. I'll be fine on my own."

"You're sure?"

"Of course. I'll be perfectly safe at the police station." Tempest gave him her best stage smile. One she was so good at, she almost believed it herself.

"Tempest," Blackburn said softly into the phone. "Pull your car out of the gate and go the direction you'd head if you were going to the police station—then take the back way to the hill. You're meeting me at the Whispering Creek Theater."

Chapter 29

Tempest arrived at the Whispering Creek Theater seven minutes later. It was twelve minutes to midnight.

It wasn't an ambush. Blackburn hadn't been held at gunpoint and forced to lure her there. The theater parking lot was dark and empty, except for Blackburn and his old sedan. Underneath the light of the repaired streetlamp, Blackburn's prematurely white hair made him stand out like a beacon in the deserted lot.

The tarp around the theater's door was back in place, this time tightened so it wouldn't blow away, and copious amounts of police tape made sure nobody would accidentally cross it. The outdoor lighting had been fixed, and three large security cameras had been mounted high up on the Gothic building, pointing to the areas immediately surrounding the theater and discouraging anyone trespassing. Dozens of bouquets of dried or dying flowers and a pile of creepy stuffed animals remained off to one side, but there was nothing to see here tonight, so the crowds had dispersed.

"Why the clandestine meeting?" Tempest stepped out of her jeep and wrapped her white peacoat around herself.

Blackburn didn't wait for her to reach him. "That missing

manuscript bothered me a lot. It got me thinking. As did the fact that I have a nagging feeling that Rinehart is on a wild-goose chase looking for Paloma Rhodes. Her cell phone sporadically turns on, out in Michigan, but the woman herself can't be located."

"You think she's dead?"

"I don't know. But there's too much else that doesn't sit right."

"What happened to thinking those files I asked about were 'misplaced'?"

"I dug deeper, looking for the file from your mom's disappearance from the Whispering Creek Theater."

"I didn't ask for—"

"I know. You were there for the investigation, so you already had those details. But it's a good thing I checked." Blackburn paused, a look of fatherly concern crossing his face, as if he wasn't sure how to tell her whatever he wanted to say.

"Go on, tell me."

"Tempest." He spoke softly. "The original file is gone."

"Like someone else was looking at it?"

He shook his head. "The physical evidence should be there, but it's not. It vanished."

Vanished? Tempest stared at the former detective she'd known for so many years. He'd aged so much since her mom had vanished, but his kind eyes remained the same, filled with so much concern.

"Like my mom," Tempest whispered. "And you thought it would be fun to have a midnight chat to tell me this disturbing news?"

"It's even worse. That's why I needed to see you right away. I reached Edinburgh right before I called you. It's already morning there. The report from your aunt Elspeth's accident ten years ago is missing too."

She'd been right. Someone was covering up the Raj family curse.

Two old murders intimately connected to Tempest that occurred in theaters, and now a third this week. Julian Rhodes's death was bigger than the murder of an unlikable man. Something bigger than Julian—bigger than Tempest—was happening right now.

Her knees didn't buckle, and she didn't sink to the ground. Instead, she felt oddly calm.

Even though she wished Blackburn had found something different, the weight of uncertainty was now lifted from her shoulders. It was one thing to have a theory but another to be proven right. The police records from both her mom's disappearance in Hidden Creek and her aunt's supposedly accidental death in Edinburgh were gone. There was no more ambiguity. But another piece of the puzzle was waiting to be assembled.

She couldn't help but think that somewhere in her mind she already had the answer. That the puzzle pieces were nearly all there, if only she could see how they fit together. Some of the pieces were shrouded in shadows, making it difficult to see the true picture. But it was there, waiting for the light that would cut through the shadows.

PART II

Shadows

The truth had always been there in the shadows. Emma Raj could have seen it sooner if only she'd looked in the right place.

She knows it's not the smartest idea to reveal the truth live on stage. Still, she also knows that the person she believes can hurt her won't be there. The danger will come later if she's unable to prove her case.

She should be putting the last pieces in place, but she thinks of her beloved daughter. Emma has commissioned a custom charm bracelet for Tempest's twenty-first birthday and set things up so Tempest will find out what Emma wants her to know if the worst happens. She hopes it doesn't come to that, but she knows none of them will be free until the truth about Elspeth is revealed.

The Whispering Creek Theater is the perfect place for her show. She doesn't tell the audience what's in store for them that night. Instead, she makes an event of it. A one-time show at midnight in Hidden Creek by a briefly famous stage illusionist. Normally, residents would need to travel to a nearby town or across the bay to San Francisco to find this type of entertainment, so she thinks she'll draw a crowd.

She's right. The performance sells out.

Emma Raj doesn't employ an assistant. It's a risk to be on her own, but she doesn't trust anyone with what she's about to do. Not even her husband, which she regrets. But her darling Darius would never let her go through with it.

She thinks she knows what to expect at the theater—until she finds the Shadow Stage. A mirror of the main stage that facilitates elaborate set changes. It's boarded up, but when has that ever stopped her?

Emma plays the fiddle from the wings as the audience files in. The houselights fade to black. She steps onto the stage.

Chapter 30

Blackburn waited silently for Tempest to respond to his news that police records of the cold cases of Emma and Elspeth Raj were missing from both Hidden Creek and Edinburgh.

"Are you okay, Tempest?"

"I am," she said. "It's weird. It's like I've been holding my breath, but I always knew that was the answer. I'm glad that I finally know." Uncertainty had brought with it a weight that made everything worse. A weight that had now shifted. Vague discomfort transformed into frightening freedom.

"I told you earlier today I wasn't worried. That was when just one item was misplaced." Blackburn spoke softly now. "But *now* I'm worried. More worried than I think I've ever been."

"You know what I am?" Tempest asked. "I'm *angry*. Someone is deliberately erasing all the facts gathered about those crimes."

Someone wanted to cover up what happened to Elspeth and Emma Raj. Tempest ran her fingers across her silver charm bracelet as everything sank in. Julian Rhodes's murder *was* connected to the Raj family curse.

An owl hooted, causing Blackburn to move protectively in front of Tempest.

"I don't like it here," he said.

"You're the one who suggested meeting here." She shivered as she looked at the police tape crisscrossing the front of the theater.

"I wanted to come by here tonight to make sure nothing odd was going on, so I thought I'd kill two birds with one stone."

"You couldn't do that first?"

"I needed to get you out of the house."

She gaped at him.

"I drove to your house," he continued. "When the only light I saw came from the guest wing, I drove past and pulled over at the side of the road before calling you."

"If I hadn't been with Nicodemus, you would have asked me to simply open the front gate to meet you?"

He nodded.

"The missing files," she said. "That's why you didn't like that I was with Nicodemus."

"Only Nicodemus? You weren't with his assistant as well?"

"No," Tempest said slowly. "Brodie hasn't come back for the night yet."

"Do you know where he is?"

"You suspect him too?"

"Too?" Blackburn snapped. "Do you know something? You should have told me—"

"I don't really know anything. Only that Brodie was thinking about selling props to get money, now that their tour is canceled. But I don't think he went through with it. So yes, I know how weak that sounds. He's probably drowning his sorrows from his lost job, or maybe something related to the nightmare of canceling their tour."

"Aren't there people who deal with that stuff?"

Tempest raised an eyebrow at him. "Yes. He's that person." But as she said it, she didn't really know if it was true. He was handling a lot of logistics, but would he be dealing with a canceled tour at midnight? It was more likely he was in a bar drinking his troubles away. "But how would Brodie have stolen secure files in two countries?"

"I didn't say they were stolen."

"Then what do you think happened to them?"

"I wish I knew. Mistakes happen. Old files are lost. But *everything* related to the cases of your aunt and mom in two different cities across the world from each other? It's too much of a coincidence."

"Aren't you supposed to end a speech like that by telling me to stay out of it?"

"It's far too late to ask you to do that." He ran a hand through his prematurely white hair, perhaps remembering the case that had been partly responsible. "Both because I know you won't listen to me—and because I think you need a miracle."

"You're not doing a very good job of being reassuring."

"I'm not here to be reassuring. I care about you and your family. Even that weirdo mentor of yours."

"I'm surprised you only suspect Brodie, not Nicodemus."

"If Nicodemus had been in the country when your mom vanished, I'd be a hell of a lot more suspicious of him. But I checked. He wasn't."

She stared at him in the dim light of the parking lot. "We need to find Brodie."

"I thought you said you didn't know where he was."

She held up her phone. "I know it's not much bigger than a pack of cards, but I bet this little computer can tell me." She tapped Brodie's number and waited for it to ring.

She heard it begin to ring on her phone, but with an odd echo.

"What the . . ." Blackburn began.

Tempest muted her phone. The soft ringing continued. *Brodie's phone was ringing from inside the theater.*

Tempest's heart sped up. "He's inside the theater," she whispered.

"I need to call this in."

"You're not a cop."

"I'm a concerned citizen. Tempest! Hey, where are you going?"

"Where do you think?"

Ivy would have said she was Too Stupid to Live, but she had Blackburn. So it was only slightly foolhardy.

Since the lighting had been fixed, there was plenty of light. She pulled back the tarp that had been reinstated and examined the replacement door. It wasn't a perfect fit, which made sense, since the original door had been custom built. Two hefty padlocks held the ill-fitting door shut.

She suspected that they were more for show than anything else, to deter paranormal investigators and other curious people. It wouldn't keep out anyone serious about getting inside. It hadn't even kept those teenagers from finding another way in, although they had had help.

Anyone who knew how to pick a lock could have opened them within minutes. Blackburn must have known how to do so, but he was pulling out his phone, not looking at the locks. Tempest knelt at the door. That's when she saw it. The door itself was solid, but the steel hasps and staple locks were affixed with simple screws.

"Don't call whoever you're calling," she said. "Give me your Swiss Army knife."

"What makes you think I have a Swiss Army knife?" He pocketed his phone.

"Don't you know that all magicians read minds?" She didn't look up at him as he grumbled and placed it in her hand, but she decided to come clean. "I've seen you use it at least three times in the five-plus years I've known you."

"You've been holding back on me. You told me it wasn't true that all magicians knew how to pick locks."

"I don't. I'm doing something far easier." She stood up and held up the hasps and staples—with the locked padlocks intact. "You have more pockets than me. Hold onto these, along with the screws."

He grunted, but obliged. Tempest swung open the door, which slid silently on its new hinges. The lobby lights weren't on, but lights mounted in sconces on the wall along the hallway-to-nowhere cast a dim light into the lobby.

The red velvet sash that normally blocked off the hallway was no longer pulled across the opening. That was probably from when they'd searched the theater for the teenagers. Still, Tempest had a strong sensation that something was different from when she'd last been inside.

"There." Blackburn spoke in a barely audible whisper as he pointed at the shadow of a figure creeping down the hallway-to-nowhere.

"Brodie," Tempest whispered. His recognizable spiky hair—as if he'd just rolled out of bed—stood on end in the shadow. "He must've gotten in through one of the other doors."

"Stay here." Blackburn spoke so softly she could barely hear him. "I'll follow him."

"Wait," she whispered back, scanning the area. She felt certain this wasn't as simple as Brodie having a clandestine meeting in the theater at midnight. Something was wrong with the way Brodie was walking. *As if he'd been injured.*

Before she could call out to him, another thought struck her: Maybe he was walking oddly because he was carrying something heavy. Something he didn't want them to see.

It wasn't only his gait but the direction he was walking. The hallway-to-nowhere was given that name because it was exactly that. There was no destination at the end. Or at least, there shouldn't have been. The only thing at the end of that hallway was a spot that had been sealed shut years ago: the entrance to the Shadow Stage.

Blackburn didn't wait. He took two steps—before Tempest tackled him. They crashed to the ground, her elbow burning from skidding across the threadbare red carpet.

But they'd gone an inch too far. Just an inch, but an inch that meant everything. An inch that meant they'd touched the object Tempest had spotted just a moment too late.

"Get back." Tempest rolled Blackburn away from the taut thread that would have been invisible if Tempest hadn't been looking for it. Thread that shouldn't have been there—inches off the ground, waiting to be triggered.

"Another booby trap!" she yelled, giving up the pretense of quiet.

Blackburn didn't need another nudge. They both scrambled backward as a loud, crackling sound began.

Tempest braced herself for a dagger flying out from some unknown location, but instead, what hit her didn't land on her skin. She breathed in the scent of smoke. *The theater was burning.*

The smoke in the hallway-to-nowhere, where Brodie had gone, grew thicker. Tempest paused several steps from the exit, wondering why she didn't see Brodie running back their way. Perhaps he really was injured.

Blackburn pulled Tempest toward the door with one arm while calling 9-1-1 with the other. He let go of her in the doorway as the operator answered. She was so focused on looking behind her that she barely heard what he said. *Where was Brodie?*

"Tempest." Blackburn glared at her as she lingered in the doorway. "Get out of here."

"Brodie is still inside." She stepped from the theater's lobby to the paved stones outside.

"With a fire. Tempest, please. They'll be here in a couple of minutes."

"You want his death on your conscience?"

"*I'm* going back inside. You're not."

Tempest opened her mouth, but closed it before speaking. Time was of the essence. She gave a nod as Blackburn stepped back into the burning building.

Since she hadn't spoken, she hadn't actually *agreed* to stay behind. She waited three seconds before following Blackburn into the depths of the burning theater.

Chapter 31

With the thick smoke and stark shadows, Tempest feared that even though the Whispering Creek Theater had plenty of stonework, the fire would still take hold and consume the structure.

The exterior stone was primarily for show. The small fairy-tale towers and spires presented the image of a stone structure, but the building wasn't even large enough for a faux flying buttress. And inside? There was wood everywhere, from the box office and detailed molding of the lobby to the rows of pews and the stage.

Tempest followed the hallway-to-nowhere, wondering once again why Brodie wasn't rushing past her to get out. Surely, they'd hear him choking on the smoke, even if he was trying to hide from them.

Huh. That was odd.

The smoke hadn't gotten thicker. In fact, most had already dispersed, though the scent of charred wood lingered. Or perhaps it was charred thread? The booby-trap wire was gone. Was that what had gone up in smoke?

The bright light of Blackburn's phone's flashlight lit up the twisting hallway and cast a far starker shadow of the former detective against the wall. Tempest followed him toward the Shadow Stage.

"I thought I told you to wait outside." Blackburn was kneeling on a charred section of carpet.

"You did." She stopped and knelt beside him.

"Paper ashes." He looked up at her and showed her the soot between his thumb and index finger, with the curled remnants of paper below it.

"Brodie was trying to burn something so we wouldn't find it. We need to find him." She stepped over the charred paper remains.

"Tempest." The quiet dread in Blackburn's voice made her freeze. "Was that door to the Shadow Stage open when you were here with Rinehart?"

"No. They didn't open it up. The Shadow Stage has been sealed up since the end of the investigation into my mother's disappearance. It's still welded shut."

"But it *isn't*."

At first glance, the door that was once hidden still looked impregnable, with the welding the police had used to seal up the fire trap they'd unearthed five years ago. But Blackburn was right. The welded metal seal had been ripped apart jaggedly, as if a huge beast had run its claws around the door, and the door was cracked open an inch.

Five years ago, after they had discovered that the Shadow Stage had been opened and was most likely where Tempest's mom had hidden—or was hidden against her will—for a brief interval after she vanished, Blackburn's team had resealed the hidden stage so it could never facilitate another death. What secrets beyond the Shadow Stage was it hiding now?

Tempest rushed forward before Blackburn could stop her. She pushed open the door and stopped so abruptly she nearly fell forward. Not from another booby trap, but from the stale, musty air that hit her. There was no question that the Shadow Stage hadn't been opened in years. But where was Brodie? It was so dark she could hardly see a thing.

This was a stage, so there was no light switch inside the door like a normal room. Blackburn came up behind her, holding a proper, yet small, flashlight in his hand. In the snatches of light, the Shadow Stage looked exactly as it had the last time she saw it—except for a coating of dust that covered the exposed surfaces of the stage and the cobwebs that hung from above, now swaying slightly in the disturbed air.

Tempest stifled the urge to sneeze from the thick dust she'd stirred up on entering the room. As Blackburn shone his flashlight onto the stage, the sensation of stale air overwhelmed her. She could barely breathe. It wasn't the air that had changed. It was what she could now see clearly on the stage.

Brodie lay in the center of the dusty stage. It almost looked as if he was sleeping—except his unblinking eyes were open, and shining under the light was a dark pool of blood.

Aside from his body, nothing had disturbed the dust that covered the stage and everything surrounding it. Yet there he was, in an impossible position in the middle of the stage.

Tempest's gaze snapped to the space above the stage where a catwalk once stretched and lights once hung. Both had been removed and disassembled five years ago during the search, so Brodie couldn't have climbed up from the wings and fallen to his death in the center of the stage. Nor could he have jumped from where they stood at the edge of the stage or fallen through the solid ceiling.

There was no way for Brodie to have gotten onto that stage that was preserved as it had been five years ago, let alone died there. But that's exactly what Tempest was looking at.

Chapter 32

'm so sorry," Tempest said to Nicodemus. "There was nothing we could do."

Upon returning home after more than an hour of questioning, she woke up her dad and grandparents to give them the news of Brodie's death and was now sitting with Nicodemus in the lounge of his guest room.

She stared into the crackling fire in the hearth. The flames were low and the wood noisy. It wasn't chilly, the wood was damp, and the flue wasn't cleaned as much as it should have been, but having a cozy fire going helped ease the shock. She *knew* Brodie had been up to something. Was there anything she could have done to prevent this?

Nicodemus joined her in front of the fire. "What you described sounds just like an illusion you'd create on the stage. Did Rinehart suspect you'd had a hand in Brodie's death?" His voice tightened as he spoke Brodie's name.

"I think it helped that I was with a former detective he respects. Detective Rinehart might not like either me or Blackburn right now, but I don't think he questions our credibility. At least not Blackburn's."

"You were released, which is a good sign."

"He's more confused and angry than I've ever seen him. But

I'm pretty sure that's because we found Brodie on the Shadow Stage."

"But you didn't disturb anything."

"That only makes it worse in his eyes. He can't blame me and Blackburn for messing up the evidence. We didn't go any farther than the doorway Blackburn sealed up five years ago, and it looked exactly the same inside. Exactly as you'd imagine it would after five years. Only spiders and dust mites in residence."

"And Brodie's body," Nicodemus murmured.

Not only was Brodie dead, but *how* could Tempest have seen what she did? He'd been found on the stage, but the dust was unbroken.

How had he been dropped onto the stage dead?

There was no way from above, was there? How had someone managed to kill him like this—and *why*?

"I do know," said Tempest, "that Rinehart has no choice but to look into other suspects besides Paloma Rhodes. If she's really on the run, it's not because she was guilty but because she was frightened."

Unless Paloma was dead as well, and someone had taken her phone to confuse things. Not that Tempest shared that idea. She'd told Rinehart everything she'd seen when she found Brodie, but she didn't trust him with her theories.

"What I like least about where this leaves us," said Nicodemus, "is that you lied to me, and that you went into the theater at midnight. It's like you to be headstrong, but not stupid."

"I didn't lie to you. *I* was the one who was lied to. Blackburn kept me in the dark until I met up with him. And I had him with me the whole time. I wasn't alone."

Nicodemus scoffed. "The murderer has killed two people already. Do you think that would stop them?"

"How could I do anything less? They nearly killed you too."

He attempted a smile. "This scratch?" He sighed. "Well, at

least it enabled me to hear the nice things people would have said about me upon my death. Haven't you seen? The well-wishers have come out of the woodwork. Apparently, I'm one of the grandest performers of our time."

Tempest kissed his forehead. "That's no surprise to me."

"How did they get him onto that blasted stage?" Nicodemus whispered.

"I've been thinking about how I'd do it if it had been a trick," said Tempest. "And everything comes down to that catwalk above the stage."

"A catwalk that doesn't exist over the Shadow Stage."

"But the walkway for lighting the stage used to be there. Blackburn wondered if the outer bracing might still be there. I think that's what the police are looking into."

Nicodemus shook his head. "Then you're looking at a whole team of people to get it into place and remove it. This isn't a grand conspiracy."

Tempest sighed. He was right. She closed her eyes for only five seconds, and when she opened them, Nicodemus held a handmade book in his hands and unshed tears in his eyes. She took the book and pretended to give all her attention to it while he composed himself. That wasn't quite true. She didn't need to pretend. The slim book contained multiple pages of his paper pop-ups, and it was perhaps the most beautiful book she'd ever seen.

The first page opened with an empty theater stage. She tugged a tab on the left curtain, and a woman in a catsuit and cat ears appeared on the stage. A tug on the right curtain brought a man in a top hat to her side. On the next page, the strings of a puppet dangled over a similar stage, with only a shadow underneath. Brodie Frost's shadow.

"Brodie," said Nicodemus, "was the one who got me out of my aimlessness after Cat left."

"I wish I could have seen your act with the Cat of Nine Lives."

"You would have hated it."

"I seriously doubt that."

"Oh, our illusions were good, but our shows were incredibly misogynistic. Not that we ever thought about it like that at the time. But the whole story was incredibly violent. All against Cat, of course. I was merely the benevolent savior who brought her back to life each time. I brought her back to life after she was buried alive, shot in the heart with an arrow, and sliced in half."

"Don't forget falling to the bottom of the ocean after going overboard," added Tempest. "I know that one inspired my mom and aunt's Selkie Sisters show."

Nicodemus gave her an odd look. "Your mom told you about that?"

"She left me all her journals."

"She gave those to you? All of them?"

"Only a partial set. Why do you look so surprised?"

"Your mother was a very private person, even before she left Scotland for California."

"She had a set of journals dedicated to magic. I think this was the set she always planned for me to have, just not under those particular circumstances."

"So you know what I was like as a young man." His voice wasn't exactly wistful, but something Tempest couldn't place.

"I don't have to stretch my imagination much. I expect you never grew up."

"Why do you think I chose this profession?" He smiled, but the grin became a grimace, and two tears escaped his eyes. He covered it up as best he could with a swipe of his good hand, but she saw it.

"I should go."

"Don't go." His eyes were wild as he grabbed her hand. His grip was strong but shaky.

"You're scaring me, Nicky."

"I hope so. Because I don't want anything to happen to you. I know you're a capable woman. But Brodie is—*was*—incredibly strong, and smarter than he let on. And he was killed. I don't want that to happen to you."

Tempest couldn't decide if she was touched or annoyed by the patronizing concern. "Brodie was arrogant and alone. I'm humble and have my friends." All right. Perhaps she wasn't exactly humble. But she'd definitely lost the Sanjay-level ego she'd had before her spectacularly public fall from grace last year.

"Tempest, you're splitting hairs. Please. I don't know how much more I can take of any of this. Brodie wasn't killed randomly."

"I know. I wonder if he was looking into Julian Rhodes's murder."

Nicodemus narrowed his eyes. "Why do you say that?"

"I caught him talking to someone at the back gate before dawn, the day he was killed. He said he was looking to sell off some of your more expensive props, since you didn't need them anymore and he was going to be out of a job."

"You didn't tell me."

"He still had the prop with him after talking to the person. Said he'd had second thoughts—and he also tried to convince me that you'd be crushed if you found out the truth. Since he didn't go through with it, I went ahead and kept it to myself. But now I think I didn't actually get a confession out of him. What if that's not what he was doing at all? What if he was asking questions about Julian's death?"

Nicodemus barked out a harsh laugh. "You had it right the first time. It would be far more like Brodie to sell expensive props he knew would be useless in the future than to try to solve a murder."

"Maybe to avenge your ruined career?" Tempest nodded toward his hand.

"Even less likely. Do you know why I've kept Brodie on for all these years?"

"As you said, because he was strong and smart. Plus he fit your creepy vibe."

"Also a smidge of blackmail."

Tempest gaped at him. "Brodie was blackmailing you?"

Nicodemus waved away the comment with his uninjured hand. "A *grain* of blackmail. A pinch. No, I'd say it's as small as a molecule. That's all."

"For what?"

Nicodemus didn't respond for a moment. "Someone accused me once, long ago, of stealing one of their illusions."

"That's a serious accusation."

Stage performers and magic builders weren't necessarily the same person, though they often were. In close-up magic like cardistry, they were often one and the same, with practitioners learning the classics then branching out with their own adaptations and routines. But with larger stage illusions, it wasn't always the case. The creator of an illusion could choose to patent their invention to protect their intellectual property in court, but then the secret would be public record, available to unscrupulous people.

It was a dilemma. Keep your secret but fear imitation you can't defend against, or legally protect it by letting go of the secret. Most magicians Tempest had met were honest and respected both the magician's code of not revealing secrets and the expectation that they would not steal from each other, only using illusions they'd purchased, invented, or that were now in the public domain. But like any profession, it included a handful of malicious people.

"The accusation wasn't founded." Nicodemus's voice was raw with indignation. "But I was young and I simply wanted the accusation to go away so I could get on with my life. So I made up a rumor about the accuser in return. It wasn't true, but neither was theirs. An eye for an eye."

"Brodie knew."

"As I said, it wasn't anything illegal. But it would have damaged my reputation if it got out that I was the person who discredited my accuser. I was still growing my career at the time. Brodie gets—got—a salary from me, with bonuses when a tour went well, rather than simply a share of the profits. I had enough to pay him well, so it was a good agreement for both of us. Perhaps I was being overly dramatic when I said blackmail was why we continued to work together. But it was how our payment arrangement began. He's always good at hiding in the shadows and picking things up. One sees a lot from the wings of a theater."

Nicodemus opened one more page of the pop-up book. In this one, a tall figure helped a figure meant to be Nicodemus back onto the stage, with an even taller and ganglier figure in the wings.

"He was always watching," he whispered.

"He could have seen something that spooked the murderer."

"Why didn't the fool say something?"

"Maybe he did."

"He's not especially fond of the police. I doubt he would have—"

"That's not what I mean. You just admitted he was a blackmailer. Being out of a job, would he try another spot of blackmail?"

"If he saw the killer up to something . . ."

"Instead of telling the police what he knew," said Tempest, "Brodie might have tried to blackmail the killer."

"Bloody fool," Nicodemus murmured.

Tempest added another log to the fire and adjusted their feeble fire with a poker.

"You need to stop investigating," Nicodemus said to her

back. "I know you've been looking into not only the murder of Julian Rhodes but also that of your mother."

Tempest spun around. "You knew?"

"I might be old, injured, busy sorting out my canceled tour, fighting with insurance companies, and now also mourning the loss of someone I considered a friend, in spite of our complicated relationship. But I am *not* daft."

"I wanted to tell you, but there was never a good time since you arrived. I wanted to catch up with you at first, and then—"

"And then we walked into that murder scene."

"Nicky." Tempest took his uninjured hand between her hands as another piece of the puzzle fell into place. Nicodemus had been with her when they found Julian, but they hadn't been together all night. He was used to adjusting to different time zones, so there was no good reason for him to have had jet lag. "Do you know anything that could tell me what's happening? Anything at all? If you were protecting Brodie, now's the time to tell me—"

"I wasn't. And I'm not." He squeezed her hand and looked into her eyes. "I swear to you I have no idea who lured Julian Rhodes to that theater or how he was killed by that blade. You don't think I—"

"No. I know you didn't kill him." She wasn't lying to him, and she hoped more than anything that she wasn't lying to herself.

Chapter 33

Tempest let herself out of the guest wing secret staircase as the moon rose, casting an eerie glow over the old-growth trees. As she crossed the living room of the main house, past the faux fireplace leading to the secret library, her dad appeared from the bedroom hallway.

"Glad I didn't have to wake you," he said.

"When do I ever get any sleep these days?" She attempted a wry smile and nearly succeeded. "Where are you headed?"

Darius pulled a light sweater over his T-shirt and headed to the front door. As soon as it was open, he pointed at the closed front gate. Detective Rinehart was on the other side, leaning against the door of his police car.

"You didn't buzz open the gate," Tempest whispered to her dad.

"Hell no."

They met Rinehart at the gate.

"No sleep for the wicked?" Tempest asked.

"Where were you both between noon and two o'clock yesterday afternoon?" Rinehart asked through the bars of the gate.

"Don't answer him," Darius said to Tempest before turning to Rinehart. "Do we need our lawyer?"

The detective rolled his eyes and let out an exasperated sigh.

"It's fine, Papa. Remember, that's when we were eating lunch together at Lenore Woods's jobsite."

"She's right," Darius added. "The whole Secret Staircase Construction crew was there. Except for Victor, our architect, who's not working on this phase of the project. I'm sure you can confirm that if you need to."

"Wait," said Tempest. "What happened yesterday at lunchtime?"

Rinehart's scowl deepened. It was directed at Tempest. "You told me you'd seen Brodie Frost walking into the theater minutes before his death late last night."

"I did—" Tempest began.

"No," Rinehart growled. "You didn't. You couldn't have."

"Blackburn saw him too. Inside the theater. We saw—" She broke off. He couldn't possibly mean what she thought he did. Rinehart was asking about a specific time of importance. A window of opportunity . . . "Do you mean Brodie was killed earlier, between noon and two o'clock?"

Rinehart's face reddened. That man was going to have an early heart attack. Tempest would have felt bad for him if he hadn't done it to himself with his ego. "That's correct. It couldn't have been Mr. Frost you saw last night. He'd already been dead for several hours by the time you got there. Do you want to explain to me how you saw a dead man walking down the hallway-to-nowhere?"

How *had* she seen a dead man? And if it truly wasn't Brodie, *who* had Tempest and Blackburn seen at the theater?

Chapter 34

With Abra at her feet, Tempest lifted the dragon's wing, which activated the secret staircase leading to her bedroom. It was nearly three a.m. Her feet dragged as she climbed the steps. Her rabbit hopped to the top step before Tempest reached it.

"What do you think, Abra?" Tempest sat cross-legged on the floor next to the bunny. "Is it a good idea to go to bed?"

Abra wriggled his nose and bumped up against Tempest's hand.

"I agree. There's way too much to do. That's what caffeine is for." Tempest texted Ivy: *I need your help.*

Twenty minutes later, she and Ivy were in the secret turret above her bedroom.

"Are you okay?" Ivy scooped Abra into her arms and curled up on a bean bag underneath the Hindi Houdini magic show poster. "And Nicodemus?"

Tempest shrugged. "He's as good as can be expected. He's devastated that someone he's so close to was killed. He said he was going to take a sleeping pill to get some sleep. I'm sorry if my text pinging woke you up."

"It didn't. Rinehart woke me. He questioned me about the

alibi you gave him for all of us for lunchtime. At first I thought he was just checking up on you, but it sounds like he suspects us all. I guess I'm flattered to be a suspect."

"You should be worried. He's not stupid, but he's also not going to let this case go unsolved for too much longer."

Ivy gaped at her. "You don't think he . . . What *do* you think he's up to?"

"He's no longer considering Paloma Rhodes the main suspect."

"That's good, right?"

Tempest considered the question. "Yesterday, I would have said yes, but now . . ."

"Why did you say it like that? Wait, back up. What exactly *did you* see last night? Brodie, I mean. Are the details true about how you found Brodie?"

"Rinehart told you?"

"Not exactly. Just enough to gauge if I knew anything. Was it horrible?"

"Yes and no. It wasn't gruesome. It looked rather like he was sleeping on the stage. Except for the fact that his eyes were open."

Ivy shivered.

"Did Rinehart tell you," Tempest continued, "that not only did I see him walking on the hallway-to-nowhere hours after Brodie was dead, but he was in the middle of a stage that hadn't been disturbed in years? The layer of dust was still there, exactly as it was before, but there were no footprints."

"Our earlier discussion is out the window," said Ivy. "This murder *is* an impossible crime."

"I know. There's no catwalk. No way for him to have climbed there or been dumped there. What disturbs me most is that there's no question it was staged to look impossible."

"Why would someone do that?"

"To confuse me?" Tempest closed her eyes. So many scenes, both real and imagined, flashed through her mind. It was as if her brain was spinning faster and faster. She opened her eyes, stepped into the center of the small turret room, and spun into three pirouettes. She came to a stop in front of the poster for her show, The Tempest.

On paper, in an illustrated poster, The Tempest was bold, strong, and fearless. Someone who couldn't be rattled by creepy, impossible situations. In real life, who was Tempest Raj? Right now, it felt like the closest she came to her stage persona was her incredible hair. Which admittedly looked great on a poster and on stage if the wind machines were positioned just right, but in real life did her little good beyond giving her a boost of confidence she could have found elsewhere.

That stage persona was a vehicle, not an end goal. Whatever Tempest did with her life, she wanted to bring magic into people's lives, give them a sense of wonder. When her dad hired her after her career in Vegas fell apart, Tempest worried he was doing it out of pity. But it turned out he'd been right. Her brand of architectural misdirection, which was accompanied by the stories she wrote for each client to accompany their unique renovations, was helping turn the business around. After her mom vanished five years ago, the business suffered, but it was finally getting back on track—or at least it was before Julian Rhodes's lawsuit and now these murders.

"It's all falling apart," said Tempest. "All of it. Why is someone doing this to me?"

"The killer couldn't have known you and Blackburn would hear Brodie's cell phone and follow him—or rather, the killer—into the theater right then."

"You don't think this is all related to me?"

"I didn't say that. I said Brodie's death wasn't staged for you in particular. It definitely confuses everything, but what do you want to bet it mainly just adds fuel to the fire of online social media rumors about the theater being haunted?"

"Great," Tempest grumbled. "A new round of people throwing iced tea at me."

"Who's throwing iced tea at you?" Abra wriggled his nose as Ivy's arms tightened around him.

"See? I can't even keep you caught up with everything that's going on. At least there isn't a video of that fan of Nicky's throwing her drink all over me."

"I think we've gotten way off track from why you invited me over here. You said you need my help."

"Right. It's about Paloma, who clearly isn't the killer. I think."

"So you think she's dead?"

"I hope not. And I don't think she is. I have a suspicion I want to test. And I need your help to do it."

Ivy zipped up her pink vest until the collar hid half her face. Only her eyes peeked out over the top. "What do you need?" Her voice was muffled through the fabric, and Abra squirmed in her arms, sensing her unease.

"Help me think through the best platform to reach Paloma."

"Platform?"

Abra hopped off Ivy's lap, and Tempest made sure the door was closed so the curious bunny wouldn't tumble down the steep stairs. Sometimes Tempest felt like the rabbit had nine lives, like a cat, but she didn't want to test that theory.

"Paloma's phone is part of this game." Tempest twirled her own phone in her hand after securing the turret's narrow door. "It's been off but pinged a few times in the Midwest. I don't think she's the one with her phone."

"But you said you didn't think she was dead."

"She could be in hiding. If she's nearby, she'd want people to think she's elsewhere. Her phone could do that. We already talked about how, if she believed Julian tried to kill her, she might leave the hospital without contacting him. That's much less suspicious than everyone made it out to be."

"Then why not come out as soon as she heard he was dead?" Ivy asked. "She has to be following the news somehow."

"Enough to know she's the main suspect. Would you come out of hiding under those circumstances?"

"What are you proposing?" Ivy asked.

"If I were her, I'd be obsessively following the news, as well as any online discussions about Julian's murder. I hate that it's come to this, but I want to do an interview or something else public that Paloma will see, so I can get her a coded message that I want to meet with her."

"It's not like you're practicing a magic show with her and can tell her your secret code words in advance."

"No, but I talked with Paloma during the construction project about the sliding bookcase she would have loved. The one Julian vetoed."

"How did we put up with that guy for so long?" Ivy's hands flew to her mouth. "I'm sorry. I shouldn't be happy he's dead."

"You didn't kill him, so you have no reason to feel bad."

"You were talking about Paloma's dream bookcase."

"If I reference her favorite book that she wanted to use as the lever to her secret library, which I told her I'd never read, hopefully she'll understand I'm talking to her. If she's in hiding, and she sees me reference that—"

"She might understand that it's a secret message for her."

"That's my hope." Tempest scooped Abra into her arms. "Abra thought it was a good idea."

"Abra is your subconscious."

"Obvs."

"Wherever she is, she's gotta be monitoring everything that's happening here. But you can't post a cryptic social media message since you deleted all your accounts last year, and it's not like she'd see a post from me."

"I was thinking of messaging one of the paranormal investigators who was hanging around the theater."

"The ghost hunters?"

"One in particular." She lifted the card with roses coming out of a skull that she'd been given two nights ago. "Alejandro Arkady gets hundreds of thousands of views for everything he posts."

"You hate doing media. Especially that kind."

"This is worth it."

Chapter 35

Alejandro, the paranormal investigator with more than a hundred thousand social media followers who had heckled Ivy at her classic mystery lecture, was awake when Tempest messaged him at nearly three o'clock in the morning. He wasn't kidding about keeping late hours.

He agreed to her terms, and they met at the Whispering Creek Theater parking lot at 3:30 a.m. Tempest didn't know whether to call that desolate hour night or morning.

"To be honest," Alejandro said, as he extricated himself from an ancient VW Bug his long limbs barely fit into, "I didn't expect to hear from you."

"I didn't expect to be getting in touch either."

He turned to Ivy at Tempest's side. "Sorry about throwing you off your game at your library talk. No hard feelings?"

"It's already forgotten." Ivy pulled her pink coat around her. "As long as you get this done quickly, so we can get out of this place."

Tempest's gaze fell to the huge camera in his hand with the skull tattoo.

"Top of the line," Alejandro said. "It's good for shooting at night and in other dark places. We filming in the theater?

We're not getting in through that door, even if you have a key, but we could break in through one of the windows."

Tempest shook her head. "Out here in front is best."

The tarp was gone, but both crime scene tape and extra boards across the door made it clear this was not a door to be messed with ever again.

They were the only ones at the theater at 3:37 a.m., and it felt even more desolate because the bouquets of nocturnal flowers placed among the stuffed animal bats and cats were beginning to decompose. The only living thing in the parking lot was a potted flower that caught the light of the streetlamp above. The delicate white petals of the night-blooming cereus had come to life in the dead of night.

Alejandro positioned Tempest so the spires of the theater were behind her and an overhead light would illuminate half her face, clipped a microphone to her peacoat collar, and set his camera on a tripod. He did a sound check and grinned as Tempest explained to him what she was about to do.

"I'm Tempest Raj," she said into the camera. She'd practiced the first several sentences she had to say. The ones that were clues for Paloma that she hoped she'd understand without the rest of the world thinking she had lost her mind.

"I've been silent until now," she continued as Alejandro gave her a thumbs-up, "but it's the middle of the night and I can't sleep yet again, so I'm filming this short vlog. It's true I found the body of Julian Rhodes here at the Whispering Creek Theater. I'm not allowed to say more about an ongoing investigation, but I can share what I *feel*. I checked out one of my favorite novels, *Possession*, from a sliding bookcase at my best friend's library, but it didn't work to help me get to sleep. I've never been much of a philosopher, but the idea of teleology has always fascinated me. Especially *today*. But I'm guessing most of you aren't watching to hear me talk about philosophy, or how I wish I could get the answers about who killed Julian Rhodes. Instead, I'll do what you expect me to do. A magic trick."

She performed a simple card trick that would have been forgettable, except she added a story to it. The story is what makes a trick memorable. She told the story of her mom and aunt— Emma Raj, the Queen of Hearts, and Aunt Elspeth, the Queen of Diamonds. She ripped the two cards into pieces, but the two queens were restored at the end.

While Tempest filmed the video, Ivy texted Enid, her boss and the owner of the Locked Room Library, about what they needed from her the following day. Enid loved mysteries so they knew she'd be up for it.

Alejandro posted the video just a few minutes after four a.m. Now they just had to wait and see if the hidden message reached Paloma.

It didn't take long. When Tempest got up at six a.m. after a short nap, the video had been viewed more than 50,000 times.

At 7:10 a.m., Ivy received an email from Enid that someone had requested booking the train car meeting room for 1:24 p.m., just as Tempest had cryptically conveyed in the video. Tempest was certain this was Paloma. *Possession* by A. S. Byatt was the novel that former librarian Paloma wanted to use as the trigger to enter her secret library. Paloma also knew that Tempest's best friend, Ivy, worked at the Locked Room Library. And the last piece of the clue was that teleology was number 124 in the Dewey Decimal System.

That afternoon, Tempest would be meeting with missing murder suspect Paloma Rhodes.

Chapter 36

Tempest didn't want to worry her family, so she headed to the tree house to let them know not to pay attention to anything they saw online and that she'd be with Ivy that day.

When she got there, she saw someone she hadn't been expecting to see. Flo, the teenager who was considering joining her dad's mentorship program, was having breakfast with her dad and grandparents.

"Things are rough at home right now," said Flo, who must have registered the look of confusion on Tempest's face, "so your grandpa insisted I come over for a good breakfast before heading to school."

"One more idli?" Ash asked Flo.

She grinned at him. "I don't need another of those fluffy rice pancakes, but I have the strongest desire to call you Grandpa."

He beamed back at her. "Nothing would make me more delighted." And Tempest knew he meant it.

The front gate buzzed faintly in the distance, then more loudly on both the tree house console and a second later on Darius's cell phone. His eyes grew wide as he looked at the video feed on his phone screen. "Rinehart?"

Oh no . . .

"Yo," Darius said into the phone, tensing his jaw as he spoke. "Has something happened?"

"I'd like to talk with Tempest." Through the phone's speaker, Rinehart's muffled voice filled the deck.

All eyes turned to Tempest.

"Let me see if she's here," Darius said with his eyes on his daughter.

She gestured for her dad to mute his phone. He nodded and did so.

Tempest didn't think Rinehart wanted to arrest her, but she didn't have time to become embroiled in their investigation. "I can't talk with him right now. I—"

"Are you in trouble?" Ash asked.

"No," she said honestly. "But I think I've just about solved this."

"You should tell the detective," Ash said, but the words lacked conviction. He sighed. "You can't trust him to do the right thing with the information you give him, can you?"

Tempest shook her head. "I'm meeting Ivy right now. Not to do anything dangerous. I promise. We're going to the Locked Room Library. If I can figure out how to get there."

"You mean to get away from that detective?" Flo asked. A wicked smile formed on her lips as she pulled her hair out of a ponytail. Hair that so resembled Tempest's. "I bet I can help you fool him." She flipped her hair over her shoulder and fluffed it just a little, making it look more like Tempest's wave.

"You'd help me mislead the police?" Tempest asked.

"I'll do better than that." Flo dangled her car keys from her index finger. A red Matchbox car keychain bounced against a car key. "I've been fixing up a 1967 Impala. It's parked outside the gate, so you can take it once that cop walks over to the workshop."

"I can't ask you to do that," Tempest said.

Flo shrugged. "But you're not asking. I'm offering. Big difference. You look like someone who can handle a big car."

Tempest grinned and accepted the key.

Darius unmuted the phone. "I found her. She's in the barn workshop. I'll come open the gate, and you can meet us there."

"Why don't you just buzz me—"

Darius hung up before Rinehart was done speaking.

Tempest got Flo set up in the workshop, where Rinehart would see her from behind when he came in. Just as Tempest was slipping out the door, her grandfather met her with a picnic basket.

"I don't know what you have in mind," he said, "but whatever it is, you'll need sustenance." He kissed her forehead. "Be safe."

"I will, Grandpa." She gave him a squeeze, took the picnic basket, and slipped around the back of the workshop and out the gate.

Chapter 37

Tempest arrived outside the Locked Room Library in Flo's classic car at 10:05 a.m.

Driving the half-century-old car that had been fixed up was a much different experience from driving her four-year-old jeep. She rather liked it. It felt real in a way that so many things these days didn't.

After parking the behemoth car, Tempest saw that she'd missed a call from Flo, so she listened to the voice-mail message.

"That was like the most amazing thing *ever*, Tempest," Flo gushed. "The look on his face when I stood up from a chair, turned around, and he saw I wasn't you! Is this what it feels like to be an illusionist on stage? So. Feking. Amazing."

Ivy was already at the library when Tempest stepped inside. The library had opened at ten, and Ivy wasn't working that day, but a man Tempest had met before was at the front desk. Tempest felt a twinge of regret as he said hello. His gangly appearance reminded her of Brodie. She knew it wasn't her fault that the killer had struck again, but she couldn't help but wonder whether she could have prevented it.

Tempest hid out in the train car meeting room while they waited for Paloma to show up. Though it would be at least three hours, it was a safe place to lay low. They reserved the meeting room under the name of a fictional book club, Tempest kept the curtains of the train car drawn, and Ivy picked up takeout Thai food at noon.

At 1:32, their takeout long since devoured, Ivy paced the narrow length of the train car meeting room. "She's not going to come."

"Or she's being cautious to make sure it's not a trap from the police."

At 1:42, an elderly woman stepped into the train car.

The person in front of them didn't look anything like the woman they had worked with earlier that year. The stooped figure sported white hair hidden under a scarf, thick glasses that obscured her eyes, and a dull gray sweater and slacks.

"It's only you two?" The voice was one Tempest recognized. Paloma Rhodes's.

"I'm so glad you're safe." Tempest bolted the door and pulled the curtains over the windows facing the main library.

Paloma straightened and pulled off the wig and glasses. "My sister didn't want me to come. But I can't keep living like this." She pulled a much smaller pair of glasses from her purse and ran a hand through her dark brown hair, which had only a few strands of gray.

"You didn't kill your husband," Ivy said, "did you?"

"Ivy." Tempest glared at her friend.

"It's all right," said Paloma. "That's what everyone reasonably thinks, isn't it?" She shook her head sadly. "He tried to kill me. You know that, right? My sister lives in the Midwest and she's been helping me hide from afar. She told me about that lawsuit against Secret Staircase Construction. I'm so sorry. I should have known that would happen."

"You couldn't have known," said Tempest. She was glad she also now knew why Paloma's phone had pinged in Michigan.

Misdirection from an abused woman whose sister was helping her hide.

Paloma began coughing. For a moment Tempest thought she might have been ill from the effects of being in a coma. But a moment later, it became clear she was stifling sobs. "I *should* have seen it. And his brother will still pursue it. And he'll press charges against me if I say anything more. I don't know why I even came here."

"We're not recording anything." Tempest placed her phone on the table in front of them. Ivy followed suit.

"It doesn't matter," Paloma said. "You don't understand."

Ivy opened her mouth, but Tempest gave her a small shake of her head. Paloma was there. She *wanted* to talk. She just needed time.

"Coffee?" Ivy pointed at the coffee maker at the back of the meeting room. "We already brewed some."

"There's whisky in the cabinet below it," Tempest added, "if you need a shot added to the coffee. You look like you could use it."

Paloma smiled, and Tempest was reminded of the woman she'd laughed with on the jobsite. "I'll take it."

Two minutes later, the three of them were seated around the meeting table.

"I didn't know he'd try to kill me that day," Paloma said. "But I knew he might try after he found out I was going to leave him. That's why I was *already* prepared to disappear. And I should have thought it was a risk he'd sue your dad's company. I'm so sorry."

"Why did you think he'd use us to kill you?"

She shook her head. "You misunderstand me. I didn't think he'd combine murder *and* fraud. Do you want to know how he made most of his money?"

"He inherited millions."

"Only a couple million. Not nearly enough for someone of his tastes. And that business of his looks glamorous, but it barely breaks even these days. He made his money by suing people."

"I know." Tempest felt anger rising through her body, but forced herself to stay calm.

"What you don't know," said Paloma, "are his methods. None of his lawsuits would have held up in court. He'd *threaten* to sue people. And then offer to settle for an amount of money that was large but only a fraction of what he'd get if he won. And probably less than the legal fees that the person would have to pay after Julian was done with them."

"I know that as well. He tried to dig up dirt on my family so that my dad would settle. It was getting so bad that my dad was considering a settlement."

"He didn't only dig up dirt," said Paloma. "He *created* it. Nothing that would stand up in court, but for people who have reputations . . ."

Tempest didn't think Julian could get any more despicable. "Like a small family business."

"He used that threat to get them to pay a huge settlement," said Paloma, "*and* he always settled cases with an NDA—a nondisclosure agreement that guaranteed none of his bullying would come to light."

"That's awful," Ivy whispered.

And even worse than Tempest had thought. Julian Rhodes had followed the same pattern with Secret Staircase Construction, threatening Darius with a lawsuit, then supposedly calming down the next day and saying he was simply upset about his wife, but he'd be reasonable and accept a settlement—but if it also went with an NDA, Darius wouldn't have been able to speak about the case at all, even to say they were innocent of negligence. Darius must have known it would ruin the business if he couldn't publicly defend himself. It wasn't only the money. Had Julian also told her papa the lies he'd make up if Darius didn't cooperate?

"I'm probably in breach of everything by even telling you about this in the abstract," said Paloma. "He can no longer hurt me—but his brother still can."

"You mean you won't go to the police?" asked Ivy.

Paloma shrank back. "I can't. And I really can't tell you any more. I've already said too much."

"About that," said Tempest. "I have an idea."

Chapter 38

As early morning sunlight hit the asphalt parking lot of the Hidden Creek main square the next morning, Tempest stepped onto the platform for the press conference she'd called.

Several dozen people had crowded into the space, with more filing in. It didn't approach the size of the huge crowds Tempest used to command, but hey, she'd called it a "press conference," put the word out less than twelve hours ago, and said the time would be posted at dawn.

Most of the people in attendance were only curious members of the public, not reporters, but that would serve her purpose just fine. Many of them held their cell phones high, recording her. Which was exactly what she wanted. There would be no way to silence the message she revealed. She may have exaggerated just a little bit to get them here. But not much.

"You may have heard a story about a woman who suffered a grave injury falling down a flight of stairs," Tempest began, "and her husband who was murdered shortly after she woke up. It's true that Julian Rhodes was murdered at the Whispering Creek Theater. But he wasn't murdered by his wife. And he wasn't murdered by my mother, Emma Raj, either, by a booby trap she set before she died or by her ghost. What you read is only a tiny snippet of the truth. Today, I'm going to tell you the rest.

"Julian Rhodes tried to kill his wife, Paloma, and he tried to blame it on Secret Staircase Construction. Even though he tried to cover it up with nondisclosure agreements, I've discovered he had a pattern of suing people and bullying them into paying a settlement that included not only money, but also their silence.

"After Julian tried to kill his wife and blame it on my father's company, Paloma lay in a coma from the injuries she sustained by the hand of her abusive husband. You don't have to take my word for it. This isn't my story. This is Paloma's. I found a way to reach out to her. She's still frightened. But thanks to the strength in numbers, she's willing to talk to you. And she's here to tell you her story." Tempest turned to the side of the stage. "Paloma, would you join me on stage?"

Paloma stepped onto the stage. Her stance conveyed confidence, but up close, Tempest could see the dark circles under her eyes and the quiver in her hands.

"Thank you all for coming," said Paloma. "I didn't kill my husband. I wasn't hiding because I've done anything wrong. I was in hiding because I was afraid. Afraid of being blamed for a murder I didn't commit. And afraid of Julian's older brother."

"She's bound by legalities to stop there," said Tempest. "*But I'm not.* What I'm telling you now isn't anything I learned from Paloma. It's information I learned because of what Julian tried to do to my dad: *extortion.* But we didn't accept his terms. We didn't bend to pressure to make his nuisance lawsuit go away. So we didn't sign a nondisclosure agreement. I can tell you that the way Julian Rhodes won lawsuits wasn't by being in the right. Nor was it by telling the truth. It was through intimidation. He threatened to destroy Secret Staircase Construction by tying us up in legal battles until we were broke.

Even though we knew we were in the right, it would have been the smart thing to pay him off. Especially after he threatened to make up lies. But still, we didn't pay. I expect that a lot of other people—maybe even people who are watching the videos that members of this audience are livestreaming now—were also defrauded."

"Before we leave you," said Paloma, "I'd like to prove that my fall wasn't due to shoddy work. I know it's my word against my husband's that he pushed me down the stairs. So there will always be some people who won't believe me without proof. But before my fall, I took a video of all of the wonderful work Secret Staircase Construction did. I wanted to remember it. Julian didn't know I'd made the video. I haven't shared it with anyone. Until now."

Tempest pushed a button and the screen on the back of the stage was filled with a video showing the staircase, including the fateful second step. It was fully welded into place, unlike the so-called evidence Julian had created after the fact to claim that it had been done improperly. Tempest stopped the video.

"I'm sorry, that's all I can say," Paloma concluded.

"But that's enough," Tempest picked up. "Far more than enough to prove what really happened with her attempted murder. Her husband was not a good man. I'm sorry to have misled you today. I don't have the identity of a killer—only an *attempted* killer. Julian Rhodes tried to kill his wife, but someone else killed both Julian and another man, Brodie Frost, at the Whispering Creek Theater. This is the first step toward getting justice."

Tempest couldn't resist ending with a theatrical flourish. She launched into her signature twirl, and the music of a fiddle filled the air. She spun and spun like a tornado until she finished in both a cloud of quickly improvised smoke and a black cloak.

When the police lifted the cloak twenty seconds later, Tempest was already winding her way through the crowd. It was Flo they found underneath the cloak.

"Not again," Tempest heard Rinehart groan as she slipped away.

She was well on her way to solving the greatest mystery of her life.

Chapter 39

T hat was phenomenal," said Tempest's manager, Winston Kapoor. "You could have saved that for our televised show."

"It *was* televised," Tempest pointed out.

"By a crowd of amateurs with cell phones."

"But Winnie, doesn't that make it more *authentic?*"

"Touché. But seriously, Tempest. This is great stuff. Can you recreate it for my cameras? You'll have to write a different script—"

"That wasn't scripted." She switched the phone from one hand to the other as she walked calmly down the street. No. It wasn't exactly calmly. She walked at a forced pace to imitate a calm demeanor. She had also pulled her black hair into a bun, thrown an oversize white sweatshirt over her clothes, and donned a baseball cap to create the illusion of a person who hadn't been on a stage moments before and who most certainly wasn't running away.

A pause. "Wait. That was *real?*"

"You didn't know?" She glanced over her shoulder. Nobody was behind her. Yet.

Winston swore. Then his face lit up on the screen. "But that's even better! You seriously just saved your dad's company?"

"You saw the videos. Aren't you reading the accompanying comments and stories?"

"Who *reads* these days? That's why we need you back on the stage."

"Once. One more performance. I love my life here." She surprised herself by meaning it.

"I know I tried to fight you on that last year, after you cleared your name and the funders wanted you back, but now I see your point. A couple of those videos already have a hundred thousand views. Oh . . ."

"What?"

"Does that mean it's real, not scripted, that you're a 'person of interest' in Brodie Frost's death?"

Tempest swore. It was worse than she thought. She hadn't wanted to stick around to answer questions because she had something else to look into. But if she was truly a "person of interest," she might be detained for twenty-four hours, or more. She'd told her dad what she was up to, so he was on hand to wrap up questions for the civil case against Secret Staircase Construction. Her time was best spent elsewhere.

"I don't have time to be a person of interest. I'm so close to figuring out what really happened to both Julian Rhodes and my mom." That's why she was kinda sorta fleeing.

"Really?" He perked up. "For the stage show you're going to film? I mean," he added hastily, "of course, that's not the important reason for you to figure out what really happened. But . . . really? You're close?"

"I am." And she *was*. She'd forgotten about something important. Moriarty had said "she's" dangerous. Tempest had assumed at the time that he meant Paloma. Even after Tempest no longer believed it was Paloma, others still did. She also believed that Moriarty didn't want to hurt her. Others, yes. And he might mislead her, certainly, if he thought it was for her own good. Which was horrible on so many levels.

"Then I think you'd better ditch this phone," Winnie said, "and that bright red jeep."

"I'm already one step ahead of you."

Tempest thought of Flo's beautiful car that nobody knew about.

She hung up with Winston. Did one merely have to turn off one's cell phone to make it untraceable? She thought there was probably more to it, but she hadn't ever had the need to do so. She had no idea how to take out the battery. But she didn't especially want to destroy such an expensive phone. She was no longer made of money like she once was.

Tempest couldn't turn herself in yet. She had ignored one very important "she." Someone she'd taken for granted, but it all made sense—*if* she was right about her.

She spotted the fender of Flo's car, which she'd hidden three blocks away. A moment of unease crept over her before she reached the car. Was she wrong that nobody was following her?

She paused, just for three seconds. The street wasn't silent. It was even more crowded than usual. Cars and pedestrians were headed toward the pop-up stage.

She proceeded to the car—and smiled when she saw who was already there.

Ivy was leaning against the passenger side door. "You didn't think I'd let you take off alone, did you?"

"Your obligation ended at helping me set this up. You don't have to go on the run with me."

"Is that what's happening? You don't want to talk to Rinehart?"

Tempest manually unlocked the doors. "If you're coming, get in."

"Where are we going?"

"First stop, anywhere away from here. Put on your seat belt."

"This thing *has* a seat belt?" Ivy looked around the edges of the wide seat.

"Hmm. Maybe just hold on."

Ivy gripped the dashboard as Tempest peeled out of the parking spot.

While Tempest drove, Ivy texted Tempest's family and Nicodemus to let them know they were together and fine. They dropped Tempest's phone at Ivy's house. She doubted they'd find her through tracking her phone and were now triangulating to get her position as she drove, but she couldn't be certain.

"You going to tell me where we're going?" Ivy asked.

"If your phone has enough battery, all we need to do is put a little distance between us and Hidden Creek, and then I need to look up what we can find."

"Which is *what*?"

"Moriarty said 'she' was dangerous. He wasn't talking about Paloma. But there's one other woman who had good reason to hate Julian Rhodes, who has an active interest in Secret Staircase Construction, and, if I'm right, also the theater."

"What are you talking about?"

"Lenore Woods," said Tempest.

"Lenore? Our *client* Lenore?" Ivy loosened her grip on the dashboard for a moment as she gaped at Tempest.

"The rat's nest discovery of something in the walls from the house Chester Hill built. She was so excited about the historical discovery at first, but as soon as she saw it, there was something in there she didn't want us to see. And she knows all about the weird architecture of her house." Tempest pressed her foot more firmly on the accelerator as the words flowed out of her. "Don't you see? Chester Hill built the theater as well. She must know about it. All its secrets."

"Tempest, I—"

"She's lived here for ages. Meaning she knew about the secret Shadow Stage before my mom vanished from the theater."

"But—"

"I don't know what her connection to my mom is yet, but it's got to be there. We can look into—"

"Tempest!" Ivy shouted.

Tempest stole a glance at Ivy. "You don't have to yell."

"You wouldn't let me get a word in. Listen to me. We don't have time to figure out if your hunch is right."

"We don't? Why not?"

"Gideon," said Ivy, "is at the Whispering House right now. And so is Lenore. She wanted to do one last walk-through today."

Tempest gripped the steering wheel. "He wasn't in the press conference crowd? My dad was supposed to tell him." She'd been so focused on her performance that she hadn't looked for Gideon in the audience. Since he didn't have a cell phone, they hadn't been able to reach him to let him know about their last-minute change of plans to move up the timing from midday to dawn.

"Your dad couldn't reach him this morning on the landline of his house because he'd already gone to the jobsite."

"Meaning that while I was on stage, Gideon arrived at the house of the killer."

Tempest writes her breakout show in lieu of therapy. She has now lost both her mom and aunt. *The Tempest and the Sea* is the show that gets her funding as a headliner.

The signature illusion is superficially the key to it being a success, but she knows the heart of the show and the secret to why it is such a success is because of the story.

She begins with the basic premise of her mom and aunt's original Selkie Sisters act. A story from the sea, told in the universal language of music, illusions, and movement. Unlike Emma and Elspeth's original show, there are no spoken words.

Only music.

Two fiddles, to be precise—a Scottish fiddle and a sarangi, the Indian fiddle. Her mentor Nicodemus, who plays the fiddle nearly as well as Emma, writes the score with an Indian fiddle player. The idea of dueling fiddles is nothing new. The Indian fiddler is stage right, the Scottish fiddler is stage left. East and West.

Two sisters are caught on rough seas in a storm, and

they lose each other. Tempest's character searches for her beloved sister through a series of water/sea-themed illusions. After her sister is pulled away to sea at the end of the opening sequence, Tempest's unnamed character wakes up alone on a Scottish island and has many adventures, illusion after illusion, always trying to find her way back to her sister.

The push and pull of the two fiddles sends her in both directions of the stage. Finally, she sees she doesn't need to pick. Instead, she embraces her true self, dives into the ocean in the center of the stage, and emerges above the waves in an illusion that takes her high above the sea—and the audience. The top half of her body is the one from the beginning, but her legs are those of a seal. A selkie. There in the ocean, she finds her selkie sister.

It's a happy ending. The one Tempest, and her mom and aunt, never got in real life. A new beginning in which they are free. Not the truth in which *the eldest child dies by magic.*

Tempest is safe, as long as her show is only a fairy tale. What will become of her if she seeks to use her platform to reveal the truth?

Chapter 40

Y ou might be wrong," Ivy said, on their frantic drive to the Whispering House.

"I could be," Tempest admitted. "But let's make sure Gideon is safe first. Then we'll figure that out."

"Why would Lenore want to kill Julian?"

"If you had a neighbor like Julian," said Tempest, "wouldn't you want to kill him?"

"Good point."

"We already know he tried to bully Lenore so she wouldn't work with Secret Staircase Construction, because he didn't want competition for having a unique house. I can imagine him doing any number of other things that would have made her hate him even before that."

"What about Brodie's death?"

"Brodie figured it out." The tires shrieked as she rounded a corner. "Nicodemus told me about Brodie's history with black-mail."

"Really? Nicodemus knew that about him but kept working with him?"

"It's complicated. But what I can't figure out is why she framed Paloma, and why the files are missing that relate to both my

258 ※ Gigi Pandian

aunt's death and mom's disappearance. I really thought everything was connected. Lenore *is* connected to the theater, so she could have been involved in my mom's disappearance. But my aunt's supposedly accidental death in Edinburgh more than ten years ago? *That's* the piece that doesn't fit."

"In other words, you're not certain enough about Lenore to let me call the police."

Tempest stole a glance at Ivy, who was pouting. "Partly. But mainly it's because I don't want anything to happen to Gideon." She gripped the steering wheel more tightly. If anything happened to him . . . She didn't want to lose him. Not like this. "No police sirens. You and I are simply coming to work. If the police show up with their sirens . . ." She didn't want to think about what might happen to Gideon.

"So we'll show up acting normal," said Ivy.

"Exactly. Then we'll make an excuse, and the three of us will leave together. *Then* we'll call the police."

Ivy's eyes went wide, but not in response to Tempest's words. She was looking at her phone.

"What's gone wrong now?" Tempest asked.

"Sanjay has sent me at least ten text messages in the last five minutes."

"That man has no patience."

"He's worried about you."

"Can you text him back to let him know I'm okay?" Tempest felt marginally bad she hadn't thought to get in touch. But he was busy with his shows.

"Already done. He wants to know where you are. He just landed at SFO. He's done with his shows for the week."

"Tell him I'm on my way to catch a killer. No, on second thought, you'd better not."

☠ ☠ ☠

When they reached the Whispering House, Tempest had to use all her self-control to drive slowly enough on the street so the tires didn't screech as she came to a stop and arouse suspicion.

Inside, they found three people sitting around a laptop, their eyes transfixed by the screen. They were all watching a replay of a shaky cell phone video of Tempest's pop-up. Lenore, Gideon—and Officer Quinn. The three of them turned when Tempest and Ivy entered.

Surely Lenore wouldn't do anything rash with Officer Quinn there, but Tempest's relief was tempered by the fact that he might be there looking for her.

"You here for me?" Tempest asked him.

"You're not under arrest, but we do have some questions. If you could come with me—"

"Do you need a lawyer?" Lenore asked. "I can recommend someone. She's not cheap, but if you're in trouble—"

"I have someone. And I do want to talk to Rinehart. But first, could you indulge me for just a couple of minutes? I need to ask Lenore something."

Quinn hesitated, then gave a nod.

"Thank you." Tempest extended her right hand to shake his hand.

The handshake was, of course, only to disguise the note that she had slipped him. She hoped he'd understand he should read it out of sight of the others. His eyes narrowed in confusion as he felt the folded paper she had pressed into his palm.

"I really do appreciate it," Tempest added, her hand still in his. She tapped her middle finger against the note, then folded his hand as she let go. It could have been an awkward gesture, and indeed it should have been, but she'd practiced enough with members of her audience that it now worked smoothly. The whole exchange took less than five seconds.

"What did you want to ask me?" Lenore closed the laptop screen and faced Tempest.

"What was in the rat's nest findings that you wanted to keep from us?"

Lenore pursed her lips. "This whole mess with Julian Rhodes made me realize that private things are best kept private. Things can be taken out of context and used against people."

"But he's dead," said Tempest. "And you admitted to me that the world was better off without him."

She shrugged. "Don't tell me you don't feel the same way. And I didn't say it had to do with Julian. Only that everything going on has made me realize I'm far too open a person. I simply thought better of sharing personal things publicly."

"So you'll show us the findings if it doesn't go beyond this room?"

Lenore blinked at Tempest. "Why would I do that?"

"Because this is a murder investigation," Officer Quinn said.

Lenore gaped at him. "Which has nothing to do with me!"

"Then why don't you show us whatever was found inside the wall?"

"You have to understand what this house means to me," said Lenore. "After my husband, Frank, died, I realized how important family history was. I needed something to throw myself into. I wanted this house to be both a legacy to my family history and to be filled with happy memories from my life with Frank. Like the safe you're building, Tempest. That's for me to look at one of the things my Frank gave me. I got the house into the shape it was when I first met you, and then I decided it needed help with the magical touches that Chester originally intended."

"Why didn't you tell us you own the theater as well?" Tempest asked. She was guessing, but Lenore had held information back from them, so it wasn't a stretch.

Lenore's mouth dropped open. "Because I don't. This house is the only thing of Chester's I own. My brother and his family own another of the houses he built, but my family sold off the theater generations ago."

"But you know about the Shadow Stage."

"Of course. Because of my connection to it, I followed its journey—including the rumors. But after it was rediscovered more publicly five years ago, I doubt I know more about it than you do at this point."

"What do you know about my mom's disappearance?" Tempest tried to speak the question forcefully, but it came out as barely more than a whisper.

"Nothing! Why would I know anything about that?"

"How did you manage Brodie's body?" Ivy asked. "That's the one that's the most baffling. I mean, it's like he materialized onto that old stage. There was no way for him to have gotten there."

"You've all lost your minds," said Lenore. "How would I know that? Officer, are you going to let them get away with this abuse?"

"Lenore Woods. Maybe it's best if you were to come with me to the station."

She blinked at him from behind her round glasses. "You can't be serious."

He looked like a frightened deer caught in headlights. "Um, please?"

Tempest leaned in. "I think you'd rather go with him than that Rinehart guy."

Lenore glared at Tempest. "Don't pretend to have my best interests in mind. You're the one who brought this to his attention."

"It's only the truth," said Gideon. "Why are you afraid of that?"

"Ivy," Lenore seethed, "just accused me of murder."

Ivy zipped her pink vest over half her face as she reddened. "I only asked a scientific question. Brodie's body was found in an impossible situation on the Shadow Stage. I'm truly curious about how it was done."

"Ms. Woods." Officer Quinn spoke more forcefully this time, and Lenore must have noticed the change.

She grabbed her purse. "I'm calling my lawyer to meet us there."

Quinn swallowed hard and nodded.

"He's definitely not cut out for this line of work," Tempest murmured as she, Ivy, and Gideon watched from the driveway as Lenore and Officer Quinn drove away. "He didn't remember he was here to bring *me* in."

"He never believed you were guilty," Gideon said.

Tempest kept watch on the patrol car until it turned a corner, then sat down on the porch steps. "I was so sure of my theory in the abstract, since she's a woman, she hated Julian, and she has the skills to make the booby traps and the opportunity to have set them. But she doesn't have as strong a connection to the theater as I thought, and she didn't tell us what was in the rat's nest."

"So we don't know if it was something worth killing over," said Ivy.

"I don't understand why she wouldn't tell us what was in there," Tempest grumbled.

"You two came to rescue me," said Gideon, "but now you don't think I needed rescuing?"

"If Julian was the only person killed, it would make more sense for her to have done it. Even Brodie as well, since he could have known something. There has to be a reason for the strange setup of their deaths. As an architect, she absolutely would understand how to build a spring-loaded booby trap into a wooden door, but why would she kill them at the theater?"

"Nobody knew she was connected to it," Ivy pointed out.

"It's not really hidden. She's not living under a false identity, and we already knew about her connection to Chester Hill."

"Maybe it's the opposite." Gideon picked up a small, smooth rock from the yard. "Maybe she picked the theater because she knew it so well. She could get in and out in ways that allowed her to kill people with booby traps, which she couldn't do in some other random location."

Tempest shook her head. "But that doesn't tell us why she killed my mom."

Ivy and Gideon exchanged a glance.

"What?" Tempest asked. "Why are you two looking at each other like that?"

"It might not be connected," said Ivy.

"Of course it's—" She broke off as Ivy and Gideon exchanged another glance. This one was one of pity. "You don't believe me. I'm finally putting together the connections."

"It's not that we don't believe you," said Gideon. "But you might be too close to it to see clearly what's really going on."

"Fine." Tempest jumped up from the porch step. "Ivy, you can get a ride from Gideon. I need some space to think."

If even her friends didn't believe her, where did that leave her? Were they right? Was she trying to force puzzle pieces together that didn't fit?

Chapter 41

I can't believe you didn't wait for me to be there for your performance." Sanjay paced the length of the outdoor dining room of the tree house, twirling his bowler hat in his hands. "And now you confronted a murderer without me? I'm wounded. Truly wounded."

"You're supposed to be in Canada. I didn't want to distract you. And it wasn't a performance. It was a press conference."

"My Vancouver shows ended last night. I was only booked for a week. I have a few days off before Montreal. And it was totally a performance."

"You said you'd be in Vancouver through the weekend."

"Of course. It's rude to bail the moment a performance ends." Without breaking eye contact, he deftly flipped his hat onto the one empty corner of the table. "I had plans to meet up with people this weekend. See some other shows. You put me in a very awkward position—"

"*I* did? I didn't ask you to do anything."

Sanjay leaned back against the oak tree and blinked at her, as if the idea had never occurred to him that she didn't need him.

In truth, Tempest would have loved to have had him by her

side helping, but with that ego, she definitely wasn't going to tell him that now.

The two of them were alone on the tree house deck. Ash and Darius had discreetly departed, leaving her and Sanjay with snacks that constituted a feast and enough coffee to keep them up for a week. Tempest's dad and grandfather were now downstairs helping Morag move her paintings that would be hung in the background of Gideon's sculptures at the gallery exhibit.

"Am I supposed to thank you for dropping everything to come back and save little old me?" She batted her eyelashes in an attempt to look demure—a state that was most likely impossible for her to ever achieve.

He reddened. "Fine. If you don't want me here—" He broke off, snatched his bowler hat from the table, and strode toward the kitchen.

"Don't go." She caught him and grabbed his hand. His skin was soft. Even though he used his hands in his work and should have had hundreds of healed paper cuts and thousands of splinters, he took good care of them since they were so important to his career. She thought of Nicodemus, who would never again be able to perform sleight of hand.

"Really?" Both his voice and his big brown eyes held a question that was deeper than the single word.

"Really. Now sit down and have a dosa."

He tossed his hat aside and sat, but he eyed the flat pancake suspiciously. "There's nothing spicy in it?"

Sanjay thrived when performing outdoor acts under the hottest conditions in India, but the man couldn't eat anything with the tiniest hint of spice.

"Ash even made both savory and sweet fillings for them, so you don't have to eat a single chili seed."

"Dosas aren't supposed to have a chocolate almond filling option. That's crepes."

Tempest grinned. "Ash whipped it up just for you."

Sanjay returned the smile and slathered the chocolate spread onto a rice and lentil dosa. "This is so good. Why doesn't everyone do this?"

"You can give him your appreciation later."

"Do you want my notes now?"

"Notes?"

"From your performance. I watched several of the videos, and I have notes on what you can do better next time."

Tempest gaped at him. "Seriously? You're giving me *notes* on my show that just proved a woman innocent of murder?"

"Of course. You're a professional. Since when do you *not* want notes?"

He was right, not that she'd admit it.

"Am I interrupting?" Nicodemus stepped onto the deck. He was still looking weak, but he attempted a smile.

"Try a dessert dosa." Sanjay set the platter in front of an empty seat for Nicodemus. "Ash is a genius."

"I know. I already ate three of them earlier this morning before taking a nap." He lifted a coffee mug, but as voices drifted up from the art studio below, the mug shook in his hand, sloshing sweet jaggery coffee onto the wooden table.

"Are you all right?" Tempest took the mug and took his unbandaged hand in hers.

"It's strange. My hand injury and now Brodie's death . . . they've stirred up so many memories for me. I'm imagining things from long ago."

"That's to be expected. You were already reminiscing about the past while getting ready for your farewell tour."

"It feels like another lifetime ago when I was creating illusions with my Cat of Nine Lives, when I met your mom and aunt performing as the Selkie Sisters, and when Brodie gave up character acting for a life in the shadows of the stage."

"I've got something to bring you back to the present," said Sanjay. "Tempest just caught the killer."

Instead of helping, that caused Nicodemus to knock over the mug on the table. As Tempest explained what had happened in the hours following her pop-up performance to clear Paloma and Secret Staircase Construction, Sanjay grabbed a tea towel from the kitchen and mopped up the spilled coffee. Nicodemus was even more furious than her family about her reckless behavior.

"The most reckless thing about what I did," said Tempest, "was acting too quickly. I needed to get Gideon away from Lenore, but when I saw Officer Quinn there, I went ahead and asked my questions. She answered most of them like I expected she would, which gave her the means and motive, but . . . I don't know if I was right."

Ash stepped onto the deck. "Sanjay, I hate to pull you away, but could I trouble you to help with one piece of installation art? It's a bit heavier than we thought."

"I can help." Tempest stood.

"You two can reminisce." Sanjay tossed his bowler hat onto his head. "I'm happy to help. Lead the way, Ash."

Tempest and Nicodemus sat in silence for sixteen seconds. She watched his face, which, without his stage makeup and stage persona affectation and with the added sadness of loss, looked like it had been stripped of its soul. "There's something more than reminiscing on your mind."

"I fear I share your opinion that there's more going on than can be explained by Lenore Woods. The past keeps rearing its head."

"About Brodie?"

"Earlier than that . . ." He shook his head. "I can't be right."

"Tempest?" Sanjay called up to the deck.

She leaned over the railing. "What's up?"

"I'm going with them to the gallery. Back soon. Don't eat all the dosas without me." He grinned.

On the ground below, Ash put a hand on Sanjay's shoulder. "I'll make fresh ones when we're back. You don't need to eat stale dosas. Trina, my apologies, I didn't offer you any refreshments. How about a snack before we head off?"

Trina must've been standing directly underneath the deck because Tempest couldn't see her from where she stood.

"Better hurry," Tempest whispered to Nicodemus as she stepped back from the railing. "Take your pick of your favorites before we're descended upon."

She knew he wasn't hungry, so she meant it as a joke, but the words didn't seem to register with him. None of the group from below headed upstairs for snacks, so they must have been eager to get to the gallery.

"Earth to Nicky." Tempest flipped into a headstand next to the table. She wobbled more than she should have. She wasn't nearly as in shape as she had been when performing. She still got a fair amount of exercise working for Secret Staircase Construction compared with sitting at a desk, but it wasn't the same.

When she got no reaction and Nicodemus seemed more fascinated with a branch of the old oak tree, she flipped right side up. She landed with a louder thud than she would have liked and nearly crashed into the table, but at least it got his attention.

"This can't be happening." He nearly toppled the wooden bench as he stood. "I need to go."

"What's going on, Nic—"

"Tempest." He took her shoulders in his hands and cried out in pain. Whatever was bothering him was so overwhelming that he'd forgotten about his injury. He cradled his bandaged hand.

"Let me call Ash to come back and look at your hand."

"No," he snapped. "I just need a moment."

He rushed through the sliding door and down the stairs so quickly that Tempest half expected him to tumble down the steps. He wasn't as nimble as he used to be, so he faltered but caught himself with the railing. Tempest caught up with him when he was only a few feet past the door.

"Where are you going?" she asked.

"I—" He broke off and cleared his throat. The mask of Nicodemus the Necromancer, the consummate performer, was back in place. "Nothing. It must have been the painkillers."

But Tempest had seen it in his eyes before his mask was back in place. She froze for a fraction of a single second, and then she ran.

Chapter 42

Running from Nicodemus was an instinct, but what she really wanted to do was confront him.

She hadn't known where she was running to when she started, but after her brain caught up with her legs, she turned toward the main house she shared with her dad. Crashing through the front door, she sped past the faux fireplace and into the kitchen they barely used. The soles of her sneakers squealed as she came to an abrupt stop in front of the cherrywood grandfather clock that led to the secret garden. The eight-foot clock was nestled into a nook the perfect size for the antique clock that would have been at home in a Victorian mansion, except for the wooden griffin that clung to its side.

Tempest pushed on the lion body of the griffin more forcefully than usual, but the eagle head and wings took their time climbing up the side of the clock. As soon as the climbing creature unlocked the pendulum door, Tempest yanked hard on the pendulum. Although the clock above was real, it didn't need this faux pendulum to function. It was merely decorative, to disguise the door behind it. Tempest's arm brushed against the side of the smooth wood as she stepped through the narrow door to the secret garden, leaving the door of the grandfather clock open behind her.

The spot was secluded, but it also gave her escape routes. She desperately hoped she didn't need them, but she was taking no chances. If she was right, her whole life had just turned upside down.

Her inelegant entrance scared away two hummingbirds, reminding her of the benefits of entering a difficult situation with a calm disposition. She spun on her heel to face the open doorway, then took a moment to steady her breathing. She didn't close her eyes, but she took deep breaths of the fragrant air from the blooming snapdragons and red hummingbird sage.

One of her grandmother's easels was set up in a corner of the small enclosed garden. A large canvas rested on the wooden frame, and a thick background of acrylic paint was built up on the canvas—an abstract assortment of greens and blues that could have been sky or sea.

Eleven seconds after she'd entered the secret garden, Nicodemus stepped through the grandfather clock. He was breathing hard, and he rested his good hand against the frame of the secret door.

Tempest took four steps to cross the small garden to face him without the sun in her eyes. "You planted the theater's booby trap."

"Tempest, there's more going on than you understand."

"Then why don't you tell me?"

"I'm trying to protect you. I've *always* been trying to protect you."

"Don't patronize me," Tempest snapped. "You at least owe me that much."

Nicodemus remained silent as he sat on the wooden bench with wrought iron legs.

"Fine," said Tempest. "Then I'll tell you what I know. The

great Nicodemus the Necromancer, who commanded stages across the world and was used to rousing applause and standing ovations, found his health fading more quickly than he would have liked. He wanted to go out with a bang, not a whimper. At first, he thought of a farewell tour. He spent the better part of a year arranging it, with dozens of locations around the world, where he'd take a last bow in front of his adoring fans and retire as a beloved semi-famous figure. The Elder Statesman of Scottish Magic would be enshrined in the history of magic."

He gave her a barely perceptible nod.

"But in the course of the year," Tempest continued, "his health deteriorated more than he admitted to anyone. The thought of a three-month tour went from exciting to frightening. What if he couldn't pull off his previous level of illusion?

"But among his many talents as an illusionist, this magician had always loved mechanical automata. He didn't only collect them, he built them. What we thought of as a 'booby trap' at the theater could also be thought of as a mechanical apparatus—otherwise known as the mechanics behind an automaton.

"The magician never set out to kill Julian Rhodes, but he wanted to go out with a bang instead of a whimper. So instead of embarrassing himself in his farewell tour, what if he was injured saving his protégée, The Tempest? The pair were planning on visiting the Whispering Creek Theater together. A theater that was long suspected of being haunted and that was tied to the infamous Raj family curse. A theater that Emma Raj's daughter had rented out and was using. If the nearly retired magician could convince the world that a malicious prankster was trying to harm Tempest Raj, but that he, Nicodemus the Necromancer, could jump into action to save her, sacrificing himself for his beloved mentee . . . that would be even better.

"He would have known exactly how the mechanism was

triggered. His protégée would never be in any danger. He could trigger the blade to spring from the door, injure his hand, and force the cancellation of the farewell tour he knew he could never successfully perform."

She should have seen it sooner. Since arriving, Nicodemus hadn't been practicing his routine. Instead, he had been visiting friends in the area, keeping his unsteady hands busy making paper pop-ups, and reminiscing with her. None of those things were individually suspicious, but any performer about to go on a farewell tour would have been far more concerned with practicing their act and getting the logistics right. In magic, you have to be precise. But Nicodemus was already in retirement mode. *Because he already knew he wouldn't be going on tour.*

The biggest clue of all? His shaking hands. It wasn't that he was shaken by witnessing the aftermath of a murder. His hands were no longer steady enough to perform sleight of hand.

"I don't think you meant to kill anyone with that hidden knife, Nicky." Tempest's voice was more gentle as she addressed him personally. "But I've got it right, haven't I?"

"Almost," Nicodemus said, with a sad smile. "You *almost* have it right. I should have known you'd see through me."

"I was about to say I can't believe it took me so long to see it, but no. It never even crossed my mind because *I trusted you.* I never imagined you'd betray me and use the theater I'd rented to stage a dangerous booby trap."

But he had. It was small comfort that Nicodemus never set out to kill anyone. One of the few people who'd stood by her when her career fell apart, and one of the few people she trusted, had used her. He had ensnarled her in his trap, which he created to make *himself* look good, not bothering to think about how dangerous it truly was. *And* he'd set it at the theater where Emma Raj had vanished and that Tempest had rented. Not bothering to think how the fallout would hurt her, even if it had gone according to plan. No matter how he tried to spin it, it was a betrayal.

"You betrayed me." Tempest felt her voice shaking as she spoke. She'd been so calm as she relayed what she'd figured out, but now that Nicodemus had admitted she was right, she felt her resolve crumbling. She'd hoped beyond hope that she'd been wrong.

"It's not what you think," he pleaded. "Julian shouldn't have been there. I didn't—"

"Oh, I know," said Tempest. "That's the key, isn't it? Because even though you were the one who set things in motion, Julian Rhodes was lured to the theater that night. Someone else taped a note onto the door, knowing *Julian* would be stabbed by the dagger instead of what was supposed to happen the next morning with your carefully controlled hand injury."

"It's far more than that." Nicodemus's eyes were pleading. "I only placed *one small dagger* in the door. I had to set it once more the following day. The trap I set that night *wasnae* the one that killed Julian Rhodes. Julian was killed with a far bigger sword than would fit in my wee booby trap. It *wasnae* me or my booby trap that killed him."

"But you set two traps."

"I did. I set the trap that nicked the paramedic and the one I used to end my own career. Only those. Not the sword. I wanted to go out with a heroic bang rather than a pathetic whimper. I might be a vain coward, but I'm not a killer."

The name on the UK passport reads Gareth Nicodemus. He hasn't used his given name in decades, and few people know it. He has always been careful in this regard. Even when referred to by the press by his given name instead of his stage name, they simply call him Nicodemus. Like Cher or Beyoncé. Gareth Nicodemus no longer exists. It's the name of a man who ceased existing after he stepped onto the stage more than forty years ago.

It's nearly two years until the document expires. If things were different, he would be renewing it soon. But he doubts he'll have need of it after what's to come.

With a shaking hand, he closes the soft cover. Next, he closes his eyes. He wishes things were different. He wishes he didn't have to go through with his plan. Yet he knows there's no other choice. Not for him. Nicodemus the Necromancer cannot stand the idea of failure. He's worked too hard for it to end like this.

When the tour planning began more than a year ago, he thought he'd have more time. But life is unpredictable, as he knows all too well.

As soon as Tempest told him that she had rented the

Whispering Creek Theater, his plan began to take shape. It's a risk, but what in life isn't? He only hopes he'll be well enough for the dagger to work properly. If he gets it wrong, the consequences could be fatal. Even if he gets it right, he risks losing Tempest's love.

Nicodemus has never known the love of a child of his own, but Tempest fills the role more than anyone else. She doesn't lack a strong father figure, so he knows she doesn't think of him as more than a mentor. Perhaps a beloved mentor, but not as much as he cares for her. He loves Tempest as if she were his own flesh and blood. He hopes she won't see through this deception. But it's worth the risk. He knows he could stage the trick in a location that doesn't involve Tempest, but the payoff won't be nearly as great. He needs her involved for him to become a martyr and end his career in a manner worthy of the image he's built.

Because at the end of the day, as much as Nicodemus loves Tempest, he thinks he loves himself more.

Chapter 43

Tempest wanted to believe Nicodemus, but could she?

"The sword!" she cried, realizing Nicky was telling the truth. "There was no booby-trap mechanism visible for the sword because it wasn't a trap. The killer was there at the theater. The killer *wasn't* someone who understood booby traps but someone who used an opportunity to break into the theater and stab a man they wanted dead. That's why Rinehart told me they found the *trap and its blades*—one mechanical trap and multiple blades. We could have put that together a lot sooner if you'd been honest with me."

"I'm sorry, Tempest. I know I kept things from you, but I never meant for any of this to happen. All I wanted was to save myself from a fate of embarrassment. Nobody was supposed to get hurt. Only me. I swear it. I set up the single knife mechanism that evening while you were with Ivy. I pretended I was tired from jet lag and needed to sleep. You were going to take me to the theater the next morning, and that's why I hired a car to take me to the Whispering House to be with you that night. To be sure you wouldn't be in any danger."

"But somebody else could have been."

He shook his head. "The knife I used was placed in a position that shouldn't have done much damage. Which it didn't. Even if someone *happened* to come by and try to break into the theater, they'd only get a scratch. But nobody should have been there."

"But Julian Rhodes was. With a note from me left on the door."

"I *dinnae ken* who did that. The only thing I know is that ever since we arrived, I've had the strangest sensation that someone is following me."

Tempest glared at him. "Which you didn't think to mention, because it would have ruined your plan to pretend-rescue me from a booby trap that everyone now thinks my dead mother set."

"I *never* meant for that to happen. There's a world of mystery associated with that theater that goes far beyond what happened to Emma. I had half a dozen ideas for how to spin the story of the knife, depending on how people began talking about it, but everything got out of hand."

"Always go with what your audience believes," Tempest murmured. That was one of the lessons she'd learned from Nicodemus. "Did you even think how that would affect me?"

"You're resilient."

"You don't know anything about me at all, do you? You pretend to care, but you don't. Not really."

Of all her accusations, that was the one that Nicodemus didn't have a comeback for. He shrank back, as if she'd physically struck him.

"Wait," Tempest said slowly, studying his face. He was hurt, yes, but there was something else. "You're keeping something else from me."

The hint of a devilish smile appeared on his lips as he spoke. "Perhaps. If I am, it's only to protect you."

"You know who the killer is."

He didn't answer. He didn't even change his expression, but she saw it in his eyes.

"You're not leaving this garden," she said, "until you tell me."

He gave a slow nod as he gripped the edge of the bench to stand. His movements were slow, as if he still hadn't recovered from sprinting to follow her. She should have known better. It was a misdirect. Less than a second later, he was at the easel. He lifted the canvas and smashed it over Tempest's head.

The soft canvas split easily, not injuring her in the slightest, but the wooden frame kept her arms trapped for a few key seconds as Nicodemus ran through the grandfather clock. She was so flustered, she wasn't even sure how many seconds had passed.

Tossing the broken frame aside, Tempest followed—or at least she tried to. When the handle didn't give way, she slammed her shoulder into the wood. It didn't budge. He'd jammed something in the door to stop her from following him.

Why was he running away?

She knew the answer. He knew who the killer was, and for some reason he didn't want to tell her.

Her mentor had betrayed her, but if he wasn't the killer . . .
Then who was?

Chapter 44

Tempest dragged a wrought iron chair next to the fence to jump over the side.

Who was the real killer? Nicodemus was involved, but she didn't believe he was a murderer.

Moriarty had warned her that "she" couldn't be trusted. He hadn't been referring to Paloma. Could he have meant Lenore? Even though she'd been acting suspiciously, was she really the killer? Moriarty couldn't have meant Grannie Mor. For all she knew, he might have been misleading her altogether.

Or maybe she'd been wrong about Moriarty's warning. Maybe the woman he'd mentioned was involved, but wasn't the killer. It was a clue, but it didn't necessarily tell her who the killer was. Only that Tempest shouldn't trust someone. If she should even believe a word he said, which was debatable.

The door at the front gate was closing just as she reached it, but knowing Nicodemus, that could easily have been a misdirect.

Tempest dialed her grandmother's number. "Grannie Mor, I'm going to tell you something confusing, but I need you to trust me."

"What's going on? Are you all right?"

"I'm fine, but I don't believe the police have the killer in custody."

"Lenore escaped?"

"I don't think Lenore is the killer."

"Then who—"

"I don't know that yet, but something very strange is going on, and I'm calling to tell you that you need to stay in a group of people right now. Don't go off on your own at all. Don't be by yourself with anyone. You're with Ash, Sanjay, and my dad now?"

"Aye, but—"

"Gran, please. I promise I'll explain everything as soon as I can. I'm probably overreacting, but please just stick with them."

"*Dinnae* you remember who you're talking to? I can take care of myself. You think I'm less capable than three strong men?"

"How do you know I'm not asking you to protect *them*? I have to go, Gran, but please just do as I ask." She clicked off before her grandmother could say another word and silenced her phone.

She'd taken too long on the phone already. She had to search Fiddler's Folly for the man she'd thought of as both a trusted friend and mentor.

Where to begin? She knew him well. Or at least she *thought* she did. She began with the guest wing. She pulled the wooden arrow resting in the arms of a cupid statue that stood a few feet away from the fireplace. The mechanism clicked, releasing a door hidden by a shallow bookcase of paperback books. The door hid a secret staircase leading to the guest rooms. An earlier attempt than her own bedroom, this staircase was steeper than ideal, plus the top steps didn't stretch completely across the width of the space.

The bookcase slid open, and she conducted a quick search of

the two guest bedrooms, two small bathrooms, and the central sitting room. Empty.

Before descending the stairs, she stood in the sloping doorway of Nicodemus's room. She picked up a folded paper pop-up that had fallen to the floor and opened it up. The cardstock paper was folded into crisp corners, with jagged edges so sharp the paper sliced through Tempest's fingertip as she examined the card. A single drop of blood formed on the paper cut.

She nearly dropped the pop-up card. Not from pain, but because she didn't want to taint the intricate design with her blood. Each of the intertwined sheets of paper was bright white. The tableau was so thick with overlapping cutouts that she couldn't make out what this one represented. Trees in a forest? She knew she should get back to searching the rest of the house, but an idea was hovering at the periphery of her mind. She could almost see it, just like she could almost see what this card was meant to represent.

Unlike the cards Nicodemus had cut that included a folded backdrop behind the main attraction, this one was layers of delicate cuts that fit together whether the card was open or closed. Tempest set it on the side table in its open state, then turned on the flashlight of her cell phone. Shining the light through the pop-up, the paper cast shadows on the wall. *This* was the story the pop-up told. It was hidden before she shone a light through it because the shadows told the story.

The shadows were indeed a forest of trees. The barren, gnarled branches cast eerie shadows on the wall. Hidden in the depth of the forest was a man in a top hat. Nicodemus. Tempest never would have seen the figure without looking at the pop-up card as a shadow box. He wasn't standing on a stage pulling the strings of puppets or taking a bow. Instead, he was cowering underneath a barren oak tree. She felt as if she could see the anguish on the face of the paper man, even though no features were visible. He'd hidden his truth in plain sight. He must have felt guilty, but she didn't care in that moment.

"What are you up to, Nicky?" she whispered to herself as she ran down the secret staircase.

It was Nicodemus's paper hobby that gave Tempest the idea that was now forming in her mind. Whenever she created a new illusion, she had to ask herself if she was inspired by an idea or stealing it. It was a fine line, but one she and other magicians took seriously. Nicodemus had admitted he'd once been accused of stealing an illusion, and that's why Brodie had been able to blackmail him. At the time, Tempest assumed Nicodemus hadn't crossed that line, but now that she saw what he was capable of, what if he had? Had his whole career been built on lies?

She knelt at the unlit logs in the hearth. It wasn't a working fireplace. The logs were real wood, but they were treated so they'd never light even if a well-meaning guest attempted it. She lifted the log in the back. The lever activated the faux-brick panel behind the logs, which slid open and led to the secret library.

Far taller than wide, the narrow library stretched up two floors, with a skylight providing the only natural light. Two walls were lined with built-in bookcases and a built-in ladder that facilitated climbing to any shelf in search of a book. The books themselves weren't organized nearly as well as they could have been, but Tempest wasn't here for a book. She grabbed the side of the ladder and climbed the rungs. She doubted he was in here for a book, but there was a recess at the top of the bookcases that was large enough for a person to hide. Again, she doubted he was hiding at Fiddler's Folly, but she had to check. She couldn't afford to make assumptions. Not anymore.

Stepping on a high rung, the nook came into view—and it was completely empty. It was also coated in dust.

She hurried down the ladder, slamming to a halt a few rungs from the ground.

"The dust," she murmured.

It was a magician who pulled off the illusion of Brodie's impossible death.

Tempest now knew how Brodie had been killed on the Shadow Stage. And who did it. It was the same person who'd killed Julian—and the person who'd also killed her aunt and mom.

After all these years, the answer was so simple. There was no grand conspiracy. No convoluted web of people working to perpetuate the Raj family curse. It was simply a single person who'd been hurt and lashed out ten years ago when Aunt Elspeth was killed. Things snowballed from there.

Tempest knew why Nicodemus had fled. He had figured out who the killer was. *And he knew it was all his fault.*

She feared Nicodemus was going to go after the killer himself. She had to act quickly.

And she knew exactly what she would do. Sanjay and her manager Winnie were both right: it *was* a performance. She now knew what her farewell performance would be.

Tempest was going to perform a show unlike any other. She was going to use a magical performance to reveal the truth. To get justice after all these years. She couldn't plan a normal show on a stage where she'd sell tickets in advance. This would spring up as a surprise. As a pop-up show.

Pop-up justice.

PART III

☠☠☠

Justice

Chapter 45

By the time her friends arrived at Fiddler's Folly, Tempest's plan was in place. Now she just had to convince them to help her.

"You seriously want us to help you catch a cold-blooded killer?" asked Gideon.

"Without the police?" Ivy nervously scraped the last of her pink nail polish off her index finger.

Sanjay gripped his bowler hat so tightly a silver coin came loose and clattered to the floor of Tempest's secret turret. "Even for me, that sounds like a risky idea."

"Don't worry," Tempest assured them. "I have a plan."

She closed her eyes and took a deep breath. As she breathed in the scents of old and new wood that Secret Staircase Construction had used to build this home, she was no longer in the real world of the rambling home where ghost hunters waited outside, where Julian's lawsuit still threatened to destroy the family business, or where random people on the internet dictated the story about Emma Raj. In the reality she saw for herself in the future, Tempest took charge and solved her mom's disappearance and her aunt's supposedly accidental death, proving it so dramatically that everyone in the world would pay attention and know the truth.

She opened her eyes. Ivy, Sanjay, and Gideon stood before her in the small octagonal room.

"This," she said to her friends, who were as dear to her as anyone she'd ever known, "is the story of Pop-Up Justice. My show that I've been searching for."

"The final performance?" Sanjay asked.

Tempest nodded. "*The* show. And the anticipation leading up to it. Posters that aren't just shared online, but physical ones that blanket the city. And artwork that tells more than one story. Front and center is a woman with raven black hair whose face is half hidden in shadow. If anyone observes her carefully, they'll see a vengeance on her face that will send a shiver down their spine. She carries the scales of justice. A date is etched onto one scale: that day. Carved onto the second scale is the time. Twelve o'clock. The stroke of—"

"Midnight," Gideon whispered.

"Exactly. And if you look closely, you can see curious creatures—half woman and half seal—swimming in the cool waters behind her."

"Selkies," said Ivy.

"Now people will notice her shadow: a swirl of black that looks like the waves of a violent sea. Her shadow balances on a twisted wave of coil, as if a tidal wave has pushed her out from the top hat like a jack-in-the-box. But that's not what draws people to this poster." Tempest paused and held up her arm. "In her hands, she holds a sailor's knife—dripping with blood."

They all shivered.

"It's this realization," said Tempest, "that will make people stop and pay attention. Words are written in the wavelike folds of fabric that swirl around the woman:

I am The Tempest.

Destruction follows in my wake.

Justice will be served.

Pop-Up Justice begins tonight.

Midnight.

"At one minute after midnight that night, the audience—those lucky enough to get a ticket—will be startled when a spotlight bursts into life and the glistening skin of a selkie falls from nowhere onto the stage. The skin of the mythical seal that has been shed. The stage lights will shift. The backdrop will no longer be black folds of curtain but a giant playing card. It's a Janus-faced jester, presented as a joker from a deck of cards. The two figures are one and the same. The card that can be anything it wants to be. The card that can perform magic.

"The lights will flicker. The illustration will become real and step out of the card and onto the stage, leaving only a blank card behind her. She will kneel on stage at the spot where the seal skin lies, but when she moves to lift the selkie skin she has shed, it vanishes. The selkie skin will now be a flat image trapped on the playing card.

"Her face will be hidden, but her voice will be true. She will reveal, through the illusion she presents, the evidence of both Elspeth's and Emma Raj's murders that the authorities either suppressed or didn't have legal authority to use. The woman who stepped out of the playing card has no such constraints. She will see justice served. The finale is the best part. The killer is arrested.

"Then, the encore. Will the woman delivering Pop-Up Justice on stage be able to swap her human skin for her selkie seal skin and slip away into the ocean, or will the authorities take her away too?

"It no longer matters to her because she will have set out

what she went there to do. See justice for her aunt and her mom.

"And that," Tempest concluded, "is how I imagine Pop-Up Justice."

"That," said Ivy, "is the most kick-ass thing I've ever heard in my life."

"That's the fantasy version," Tempest admitted. "It's a culmination of the ideas that have been swirling around for years about the story I've always needed to tell. My subconscious always knew all the elements—which is why they were always part of my story. But real life isn't a fantasy. Not exactly. I can't stage a full theatrical production in a day—but I can come close. I know who can illustrate the posters I imagine as well. Posters that can be shared both here in Hidden Creek and online with a message that will get everyone to be there for my midnight show. The most important show of my life."

Chapter 46

For the plan to work, Tempest couldn't do it alone. They *all* had to play a part. Not only her friends, but also her family: Darius, Morag, and Ashok.

Her family were the ones who needed convincing, which is why she got her friends on board first. But soon, it was decided.

Darius would make sure Fiddler's Folly was secure, and then run interference with Detective Rinehart.

Grannie Mor would illustrate the posters.

Ash would visit the local printer he'd met on one of his *dabbawalla* bike rides and print hundreds of posters and thousands of smaller flyers.

Gideon would blanket the town with the posters and flyers.

Ivy would use social media to get the word out digitally.

As for Sanjay, he had a secret mission for the show itself.

Tempest would reveal all at midnight. *This* was the story she had always wanted to tell, but didn't know how to. And now, through Pop-Up Justice, she could finally pull it off.

☠☠☠

It was all coming together, and fast. It had to be tonight.

Morag sketched the image slightly differently from Tempest's vision, but she made it even better. The Tempest in Grannie Mor's poster was a powerful shadow with long hair swirling around her, peeking out from behind a gnarled oak tree on the Hidden Creek hillside. The woman's shadow held an open book. A handful of words emerged from the pages, shaped as if they were carried by the wind, a winding river, or perhaps followed the path of the musical notes of a score.

The Tempest invites you to Pop-Up Justice.

Four murders across ten years.

Solved tonight.

This story begins at midnight in the Hidden Creek town square.

At the local copy shop, Ash photocopied the black-and-white flyer, as Tempest had requested, but went a step further. He stopped by each of the local businesses to get their support by leaving a stack of flyers at their front counters and a poster in their windows. This was Ash, who knew everyone's life story and dreams within minutes of meeting them, so not a single proprietor turned him away.

Ivy photographed the artwork, and stayed hunched over her laptop posting it on every social media platform she could think of, hoping it would go viral. Gideon had an idea that would spread the word even further: After borrowing Ivy's projector she used to watch movies on a white wall of her home, he asked Lavinia Kingsley, owner of café Veggie Magic, if he could project a huge image of the artwork onto the brick wall siding of the café that had a prominent spot on Hidden Creek's main street. Lavinia owed a great debt to Tempest, so she quickly agreed.

Darius made sure that Rinehart knew that Tempest wouldn't be breaking any laws with the brief performance and that she wasn't going to reveal anything confidential from the investigation, such as what she'd been able to do at the theater that Rinehart hadn't. His words and his physique might have held a hint of coercion, but Tempest didn't think her papa had crossed a line. She also knew he wouldn't reveal to the detective what she really had in store. It was better to seek forgiveness than to ask permission for something he never would have agreed to.

Everyone in her circle had gone above and beyond what she'd asked of them.

With their help, she was ready.

Chapter 47

Before the show could begin, there was one unanswered question Tempest had to make sure she was right about. Because for an illusion to work, you have to know all the angles. You can leave nothing to chance.

She had the address she was after in the Secret Staircase Construction files. The house wasn't far.

"I know you don't want to see me," Tempest said to Lenore as the front door swung open, "but I need to ask you one more thing."

"I knew I shouldn't have opened the door." Lenore didn't welcome Tempest inside, but she didn't slam the door in her face either. Unlike the architecture of the Whispering House, Lenore's main residence was a midcentury ranch-style home, with a low-pitched roof over its single sprawling story. Asymmetrical picture windows with neat shutters flanked the front door. Where the Whispering House was imposing, this house was cozy, giving Tempest the push she needed to confront Lenore. Again.

"I think I know why you let yourself be questioned at the police station."

"That was your doing, if you recall." Lenore's words were

clipped and her expression hard. She didn't stand aside. But then again, she still hadn't slammed the door.

"You could have easily set the record straight about what was preserved in the rat's nest," said Tempest. "But you didn't want to for some reason. You didn't want to let us know that it was a piece of Chester Hill's original missing blueprints."

In her shock, Lenore's anger fell away. She gave Tempest a wry smile. "Floor plans, technically. But they serve the same function here. How did you know?"

"There were multiple clues. First, the fact that the section of the paper I saw was covered with lines, not writing. Then, as soon as you zoomed in closer and we saw the one bit of text that wasn't just lines, you closed the screen. You didn't want us to see what you did."

"No," she murmured. "I didn't."

"And then there was the date. The only word on the page: 1901. A date when Chester was already living at the house but *before* the additional exterior buildings were completed. That's what you didn't want me to see."

"You could tell that my headache was faked?"

"You're not a good liar, Lenore. Officer Quinn and the rest of us could tell you were hiding something, which is why he took you in for questioning. But why would you keep an old floor plan secret, even if it meant you'd be accused of murder?"

"I knew I'd get released since I wasn't involved."

"You must have paid a fortune to get your lawyer to meet you there."

Lenore shrugged. "Some things are worth spending money on. As well as a few hours of inconvenience. It was better than the alternative."

"But *why*?"

"Can't you guess?"

"The only thing that makes sense is if the floor plans were

Chester Hill's and they showed different ideas about his intent for the house from what we're doing. I can understand you being upset if you miss your early window for a historical home designation if it takes us longer to complete renovations. But is the timing that big a deal?" Tempest studied the dignified woman. Unlike Julian, Lenore wasn't fixing up her house to impress other people. She believed in architectural history and wanted to celebrate both the first architect in her family and her own contributions.

"It's worse than that, Tempest." Lenore sighed and wiped her glasses on her blouse. "*I got it wrong.* That gazebo I tore down in the back because I thought it was a 1950s addition done along with the tiki bar and the tacky renovations done inside the house? I was wrong." She pursed her lips. "The gazebo was original. Conceived of and built by Chester Hill. *And I tore it down.*"

"And you don't want that to come to light because you want that historical designation for the house." She'd done so much work to restore it with all the original elements along with her own touches that her research showed were part of Chester Hill's original intent.

Lenore sighed. "You're too young to understand this, but I don't want my legacy to be undone by a stupid mistake. I admit I'm being selfish by covering up the findings. I worked so hard to get taken seriously in a man's profession. Things aren't perfect now, but they were even harder forty years ago. I'm proud that I'll be a minor footnote in architectural history. I don't want to be a footnote because I ruined one of Chester Hill's last standing creations."

"I understand," said Tempest. Because she did.

Chapter 48

At midnight, Tempest's words rang out across the stage, but she was nowhere to be seen.

I am The Tempest.

Destruction follows in my wake.

Tonight, justice will be served.

The clock is striking midnight.

Pop-Up Justice begins . . . NOW.

The words echoed through the night. Smoke filled the stage. Still, Tempest was nowhere in sight.

Ten years ago, my aunt, Elspeth Raj,
was murdered live on stage in Edinburgh.

Five years ago, my mom, Emma Raj, learned who had killed her sister. She was silenced here in Hidden Creek before she could reveal the truth.

This week, two men were killed at the Whispering Creek Theater, one on its Shadow Stage.

Some of you believe Emma Raj came back from the grave to kill these men. Some of you believe she set devious booby traps before she took her own life.

None of this is true. But I know the truth.

Tonight, you are all part of the history of justice being served.

Join me in making history.

A single spotlight illuminated the stage. It pierced the smoke but lit only an empty spot on the stage.

From the wings, Tempest began to spin into a pirouette. Her hair whipped through the air around her. She spun onto the stage and came to a stop in the spotlight.

But she *wasn't* in the spotlight on the pop-up stage in downtown Hidden Creek as her pop-up flyers had claimed. Instead, this performance was being broadcast live on a large monitor set up on that outdoor stage. Her grandmother and Alejandro were both on site in the town square to make sure the video was being broadcast as Tempest intended. Alejandro would make sure the technical details worked, and her small-but-mighty grandmother would make sure nobody shut down the show.

"I'm filming live from the Shadow Stage." Tempest looked at the phone in Ivy's hand as she spoke. "I'm sorry for the deception about my location, but you can all see me live, so it's the next best thing—and the thing that's safest for everyone involved. I've locked myself in here with only my trusted friends."

She paused and waited for confirmation from Ivy that the recording was being broadcast properly to the monitor at her pop-up stage. Three seconds later, Ivy grinned and gave her a thumbs-up with her free hand.

"Tonight," Tempest continued, her heart beating furiously, "from this secure location, I'm going to reveal to you the identity of the murderer who killed two men at the Whispering Creek Theater this week. If you're watching this, I'm assuming you already know about the deadly, regenerating booby trap, and the rumors that the woman who vanished from the theater five years ago set the booby traps from beyond the grave—either her ghost, if you're inclined to believe such things, or that she set the ingenious traps before she died by her own hand. I'm also assuming you know about this Shadow Stage behind the main stage, where a man was killed in a seemingly impossible way, looking like his murder on the stage untouched by time could only have been committed by a supernatural entity.

"None of that is true. Yes, two men died this week. But they were killed by a mortal hand. By the same person who killed my aunt Elspeth Raj *and* my mom, Emma Raj. Because the murderer is one and the same. Four murders, one killer."

Gideon, who stood next to Ivy, was scribbling on a notepad of paper. He held it up. *Introduce yourself. Not "The Tempest," but YOU.*

She'd gotten carried away and forgotten that part. He had her back, as she knew he would. He'd barely made it there in time for the performance to begin, but she was grateful he was there. Grateful they were *all* there.

"For those of you who don't know me, I should introduce myself. I'm Tempest Raj, formerly known as The Tempest on the Las Vegas stage." She flipped into a backbend kick over. When she came to a stop on her feet, she held one of her old posters in her hand. She held it up toward Ivy's phone. "My show, *The Tempest and the Sea*, had a good run for a few years. But the first night of my new show that debuted last year ended with sabotage that nearly burned the theater down, almost killed me, and did kill my career."

She glanced up at the A/V box where Sanjay was controlling the lights they'd set up. The old panel was gone, along with the original lighting, but his local magic producer friends had come through with loaned equipment. Though Sanjay wasn't the star tonight, this was still a performance, so he'd dressed in his signature tuxedo and bowler hat. She melted a little as he smiled at her, remembering how he'd stood by her side when she was unjustly accused of reckless negligence.

"But that's nothing," she continued, "compared to the reason I created my show in the first place. I come from a long line of Indian stage magicians who've been plagued by a supposed curse. *The eldest child dies by magic.* The Raj family curse began simply as an accident from a dangerous illusion—but curses have a way of spinning out of control."

Tempest opened her palm. A wisp of smoke curled around her fingertips. The curl of smoke grew bigger until she was almost obscured. She dropped to the stage floor. Not that anyone watching would have seen her if she'd done it right. She hadn't had much time to practice, so she hoped it worked with Gideon using the dry ice procured by Sanjay, and Ivy as the videographer. When the smoke cleared seconds later, only a skeleton remained on stage.

People could be cruel, but they could also be magnificent. With Ivy, Gideon, and Sanjay at her side, and her family members playing their roles nearby, she knew she could do this.

"The idea of a curse can be manipulated by people for any number of reasons," Tempest said from off camera. "*Like a person using a rumored curse to cover up a crime.*"

Tempest spun around in a pirouette, and when she came

to a stop, the skeleton was gone and Tempest was back. Ivy kept her phone pointed at the stage, and gave Tempest a big thumbs-up.

"This story really begins thirty-five years ago, nearly a decade before I was born. But you're all here tonight because of the seemingly impossible murders that happened *this week* in Hidden Creek at the Whispering Creek Theater and its hidden Shadow Stage, so let's start there.

"We have a theater that looks like a Gothic church, with a high wooden door fitted with booby traps that kept regenerating. The first blade killed a man, Julian Rhodes, who was lured to the theater. A second smaller blade wounded a paramedic who was attempting to help Julian. A third blade wounded stage magician Nicodemus the Necromancer.

"Baffling, yes. But not impossible. There are mechanisms that can cause a deadly trap to spring. Was Julian an accidental victim? That didn't appear to be the case because someone had lured him to the theater. The authorities thought at first that his wife, Paloma, had killed him because he had attempted to kill her already. But why use this theater? Surely there are much simpler ways to kill someone.

"The answer lies in the fact that there was no mechanism that caused the largest blade to spring. *Because that one was never a trap.* The person who lured Julian to the theater stabbed him themselves through the door. There *was* a booby trap already in place. But it was a distraction. One to make sure the killer wouldn't be discovered, and as a bonus, might also shut down the theater.

"Why would they want the theater shut down? Because they were worried. Worried that their long-ago crimes were about to be discovered. But the location was secondary. Julian Rhodes had to die because *he also had information that was dangerous to the killer.*

"You see, Julian Rhodes was suing my dad's company. Julian Rhodes was a man who bullied people into getting his way. He knew he couldn't win a lawsuit against us because it had no merit. But what he *could* do was send his lawyers and investigators after us in a way that made our lives miserable. Including requesting all the paperwork potentially connected to the designs of Secret Staircase Construction's work, supposedly as possible evidence of our shoddy work. *But that discovery would also reveal additional information.* The killer knew I was investigating who killed my aunt and mom. The killer also knew I kept paper notebooks filled with my ideas, like my mom before me, since I've talked about that publicly. A man like Julian Rhodes would most certainly use that information for his own gain. Had Julian already read my notebooks? The killer couldn't be sure. Therefore, the killer could do away with Julian Rhodes to make sure he wouldn't use the information.

"The killer was both meticulous and desperate. They were careful not to be seen by people who would realize who they really were. But the killer slipped up. Brodie Frost identified them. Instead of going to the authorities, he tried a spot of blackmail. So Brodie had to die. He was killed here on the Shadow Stage—only that was *impossible*, wasn't it?"

Tempest closed her eyes and imagined the untouched stage and that horrible vision. She opened her eyes and looked back at the camera. How many people were watching? She couldn't worry about that now.

"Until the crime scene crews entered the sealed room," she said, "the Shadow Stage hadn't been touched in more than five years. Dust covered every surface. Cobwebs dangled from the ceiling. The air was stale.

"I saw Brodie Frost's shadow in the hallway leading to the Shadow Stage shortly before I found his body lying in the center of the stage, and yet nothing in that room had been disturbed. Not only that—but I soon learned that Brodie had been killed at least ten hours before I saw him creeping down the hallway. Which is, of course, impossible.

"The internet had a field day with the two seemingly impossible crimes. *Emma Raj killing from beyond the grave* with the booby traps. And *a ghostly killing* for the Shadow Stage's eerie crime scene.

"But both are easily explained if we consider that the killer is a *stage magician.*

"Stage magicians know all about automata and other mechanical devices that aid us with our acts. It was no problem for our killer to rig booby traps, but you never know exactly where a person will be standing, to know if the booby trap will do what it's supposed to. The traps set the stage, but the killer simply cut a small sliver out of the wooden plank door, stabbed Julian, and then left the confusing mess that would baffle the authorities.

"As for the Shadow Stage? That was the trick that was the most baffling. I was so sure I knew what I was seeing when I opened the door and my companion shined his light onto the stage. In the dark, with dust that made me sneeze, my senses were in overdrive and I thought I could trust them.

"But I was wrong. The scene was *too perfect.* Why did I sneeze if the dust hadn't been disturbed? Because the dust *had already* been disturbed. That was the secret to their trick. Cleaning first, then replacing the dust evenly so it wouldn't look disturbed.

"They put their plan into effect earlier that day, creating a distraction outside the theater by having an unwitting member of the public scale the theater walls. The murderer wanted to kill Brodie in this symbolic location, creating even more misdirection.

"Knowing how to create things like falling snow and the scent of a beach for a stage show, a magician could easily create a fake coating of dust and the scent of stale air. Our magician killer simply reversed the airflow of a dust-filled vacuum and covered the stage. It wouldn't stand up to chemical analysis, but it didn't need to. It was that initial effect that was important. We weren't thinking about it because they misdirected our attention away from an imperfect recreation. Brodie's body was meant to shock us, and it did.

"As for how we were lured to his body in the first place, that was another magician's trick. We saw a distinctive shadow, followed by a very small fire. The fire went out by itself, but we found a piece of thread and burnt paper ashes.

"That trick was in the shadow—it was merely a paper cutout being controlled by threads, all of which burned up. Again, it wasn't perfect, and analysis would have eventually revealed the truth, but it did the job in that moment. It accomplished what it needed to. If I hadn't shown up when I did, I have no doubt the killer would have found a way to lure me there soon enough. The killer has been great at manipulating us.

"By now, I know you're wondering *who* this killer is. *Who is the magician* I'm talking about?"

Sanjay hit a button, and white smoke filled the base of the stage at Tempest's feet, setting the stage for a story that began more than thirty-five years ago.

Chapter 49

T his story begins," said Tempest, "when Nicodemus the Necromancer, the Scottish stage magician who was gravely wounded by the theater booby trap that killed Julian Rhodes, was getting his start on the stage in Edinburgh, Scotland. Nicodemus and his assistant, the Cat of Nine Lives, developed a series of intriguing illusions involving a cat character dying strange deaths and being resurrected by a necromancer who controlled the dead like a puppeteer.

"Nicodemus was the headliner, but Cat was far more than just an assistant. She was an equal partner in creating those illusions. *At least* an equal partner, maybe more. But she never got any credit."

Tempest was standing still at this point, but her heart was racing faster than it had all night. She was nearly there. Nearly to the point of revealing the truth she'd been searching for all these years. A truth that only Julian Rhodes's seemingly unrelated death had allowed her to discover.

"My mom and her older sister grew up in Edinburgh, and they created an act that had potential but wasn't yet developed. Nicodemus discovered and mentored the sisters. He renamed their act the Selkie Sisters, playing up the Scottish lore of half-seal, half-human creatures, which was already in their story of being from the sea.

"Nicodemus and his stage partner Cat split up around this time, so he hired Brodie Frost as his stagehand and on-stage assistant. With Cat out of the picture, and never again appearing on the magic scene, Nicodemus was free to do what he wanted with their illusions. Which is exactly what he did. He grew his own career spectacularly, and he continued to mentor my aunt Elspeth after her falling out with my mom—*including giving her one of his illusions*. This is the key to all these deaths. Nicodemus, with his big ego, believed he'd created the illusions he was sharing. *But they weren't his to give away.*"

Tempest brought her seemingly empty hand in front of her face and blew. Small specks of light, like fireflies, filled the air.

"You need to understand something about stage magicians. We have a code. One we take seriously. We don't reveal secrets. And we don't steal each other's tricks. Magicians can sell their tricks to other magicians, and we can adapt basic concepts to make them our own, but we do not steal."

The last of the pinpricks of light disappeared.

"But the Cat of Nine Lives, who'd been used up and thrown away, discovered that rising star Elspeth Raj was going to debut with one of *Cat's* tricks. So she made sure Elspeth was caught in another illusion—one that killed Elspeth but looked like an accident. So yes, that means the killer is—" Tempest broke off as Sanjay jumped up from his seat in the A/V booth, holding his cell phone to his ear.

Ivy spun around to record Sanjay, whose face lit up with a grin. "They've got her!" he shouted from the booth, then tipped his bowler hat toward the camera.

"My team have done their job," said Tempest, "and you're about to meet the killer. She raided the Shadow Stage, where she *thought* I was filming. I'm sorry to have deceived you yet again. I'm not actually on that stage. The Shadow Stage is the one with too much history of curses and shadows. Whereas I believe in truth and justice. I'm standing on the Whispering Creek Theater's *main* stage. And if I'm not mistaken, I hear my dad and a trusted friend bringing the killer to us in hand-cuffs."

Ivy pivoted once more as Darius and Blackburn burst through the side door, the killer between them. Her hands were cuffed behind her back. The two men brought her to the stage.

"I'd like to introduce you to the Cat of Nine Lives," Tempest said to the camera, her heart thudding furiously behind her well-practiced cool exterior. "This is the person who killed El-speth Raj ten years ago, Emma Raj five years ago, and Julian Rhodes and Brodie Frost this week."

This was real.

The moment she'd been trying to achieve for more than five years.

Breathe, Tempest. Breathe.

She turned from the camera to face the Cat of Nine Lives. The killer. "Hello, Catriona. Or would you prefer I call you the name my grandmother knows you as, Trina?"

"You've got this," Gideon whispered, just loudly enough for her to hear. Had he heard the ever-so-slight falter in her voice?

"The best illusions," said Tempest to the camera, her voice and pose confident, "are like the best lies. Only altering the fewest necessary elements. A Scottish woman who couldn't do a perfect American accent simply ingratiated herself with a circle of artist friends, many of whom were Scottish. A woman who'd killed multiple times before wouldn't want to be too far away when I began looking into her murders."

And a woman who went by variations of her given name, Catriona, pronounced *Katrina*, wouldn't want to go by a name that she wouldn't respond to. Cat, Catriona, Trina. They're the *same person.*

FIDDLER'S FOLLY

Five and a half years ago

Astoryteller is the ultimate escape artist, Emma Raj has always told her daughter. If you use your imagination properly, you can find a path out of any situation.

Harry Houdini, Emma's favorite magician, was a key who could open any lock. Born Erik Weisz in Hungary, he was a self-made man—and a natural showman. Tempest, as a woman of color in a man's profession, doesn't share some of the benefits Houdini had, but she shares some of his characteristics. She's physically powerful and has a family who loves her more than anything. She has also grown up the child and grandchild of people who think creatively.

When Tempest comes home to Fiddler's Folly for a visit a few weeks before her twenty-first birthday, Emma hands her a box covered in silver wrapping paper decorated with a pattern of gold keys. Thick red ribbon loops across the mug-size box, and tied to the bow on top is a Houdini bobblehead toy. Emma had looped the red ribbon through the spot where the plastic toy's wrists were handcuffed. A folded piece of notepaper on top of the bracelet inside reads, *Happy 21st! A magical inheritance for my magical daughter. Love love love xxx Mom.*

Emma Raj writes those words to her beloved daughter the night before she vanishes. Inside the box are the keys to her daughter's past and future. The charm bracelet representing their shared love of magic. The top hat, selkie, lightning bolt, book, a fiddle, jester, handcuffs, and a key.

"You don't need a special key to unlock handcuffs, or the world," says Emma. "You are the key."

Chapter 50

This," Tempest said, "is the Cat of Nine Lives. I've put all the pieces together that prove she killed four people. I'm hoping she'll enlighten us as to how exactly she committed each of her murders. I know the basics, but the devil is in the details, don't you agree?"

"I *dinnae ken* what on earth you mean," said Catriona in the most endearingly shy Scottish lilt. Darius sat her down on a chair on the stage, and Blackburn made sure she was handcuffed to it. Catriona stretched her neck and squirmed, as if the handcuffs were hurting her.

Blackburn leaned close to Tempest and whispered in her ear. She nodded. It was as she suspected. She took a moment to compose herself and turned back to Catriona and the camera.

"You deny that you once played the Cat of Nine Lives on stage?" Tempest asked.

"I'm an artist who's friends with your grandmother. I understand that fame has a deleterious impact on the minds of the younger generation. You wish for a lot of people to view your video. I'm sure you'll succeed on that front. Please let me go, lass. I'm a victim of circumstance."

Tempest knelt in front of Catriona's chair to speak to her up close. "You just happened to be breaking into the off-limits Shadow Stage at midnight?"

Catriona looked past Tempest and straight ahead at the camera. "I'm a great admirer of Nicodemus the Necromancer. I had the pleasure of seeing him perform on stage when we were both young. It was a beautiful memory. If I'm guilty of anything, it's ignoring some flimsy police tape. I'll gladly pay the fine for trespassing. Now if you'll kindly remove these cuffs . . ."

"You were careful not to let Nicodemus or Brodie see you." Tempest stood. "A name might be a coincidence. I'm sure there are thousands of Scottish women with the name Catriona, many of whom go by Trina. That was only the first clue that gave you away. But when Nicodemus heard your voice earlier today, he *knew*."

Catriona looked around. "I don't see that lovely man anywhere. I wonder if he's gotten into a spot of trouble and fled the country."

"You also made the mistake of removing items from police custody in both Edinburgh and Hidden Creek," said Tempest. "That proved to me that I was right about the connection between the crimes. There was probably nothing in those records that could have been of use to me in those cold cases anyway. You weren't taking any chances though. You acted out of fear, and in doing so, you revealed your hand."

"I think you're in over your head, dear. I've never entered a police station in either town you mentioned." Catriona clicked her tongue and shook her head. "I'm so sorry you're disappointing your audience with these flimsy lies. I understand you're under a lot of pressure, lass. I *willnae* press charges for kidnapping. *Yet*."

"Oh, I know you didn't break into police stations yourself. In Edinburgh, you asked for the assistance of an older officer, a man who'd been one of your fans thirty years ago. He removed

Elspeth Raj's file for you. It was ruled an accidental death, so I'm sure the officer barely felt he was doing anything wrong. Did you say you were looking into how to avoid repeating future stage accidents? Maybe you even made him feel heroic for helping you with your noble quest."

Catriona's neutral gaze faltered. She quickly regained her composure, but it was enough for Tempest to know her theory was right.

"And here in Hidden Creek," Tempest continued, "I know you paid Officer Quinn to get them. He's drowning in debt due to his poor choice of girlfriends, so he couldn't resist the seemingly harmless offer."

Catriona's nostrils flared. Tempest had only been 90 percent sure about Quinn. But now that Catriona was rattled, she knew she was right.

Catriona was probably smart enough to approach him anonymously, so Tempest doubted Officer Quinn would be able to point a finger at Catriona. Still, Tempest was exposing Catriona's weak spots.

"I should have guessed earlier," Tempest continued. "Abracadabra is a fantastic judge of character. He bites people he doesn't trust. When he scratched Tansy, it was because I was lifting him closer to you because you'd asked to hold him."

Catriona began squirming again. Only this time, it wasn't her torso, but her feet.

"This isn't fun anymore." Catriona flung her left foot forward, flipping her left boot into the air—right at Ivy. Ivy dodged, but she lost her grip on her phone. Taking her chance while Ivy was no longer filming the stage, Catriona pulled her arms out from behind her back. She was a magician. She'd broken free of her handcuffs.

"What are you waiting for?" Catriona yelled.

That's when a figure Tempest hadn't seen stepped out of

the shadows. He kicked Ivy's cell phone into the wings and smashed it with his shoe. The recording was over.

"I'll take the rest of your phones," said Catriona, pulling a knife out of her right boot and holding it to Tempest's neck.

"There's no need for—" Darius began, but Catriona cut him off.

"All your phones," hissed Catriona. "Toss them onto the stage, *now*, or I stab your beloved Tempest."

Darius, Blackburn, and Sanjay complied with Catriona's demand to drop their cell phones onto the stage.

"I don't have a cell phone," Gideon said. "You can search me."

"Oh, I know, dear," said Catriona. "I know all about you. I was the one who convinced Tansy to fund your overwrought sculptures. You want to go back in time and live in a Charles Dickens novel, when women like me were even more oppressed."

Catriona's compatriot stepped out of the shadows. "That's enough, Mother."

Mother?

"Moriarty," Tempest whispered.

That was a twist she hadn't seen coming.

Chapter 51

Tempest tried to focus. They were so close to getting a confession. She had to stick to the plan, but Moriarty wasn't part of the plan.

It all made sense now. The timing of when the man she thought of as Moriarty entered her life, the way he'd only helped her in circuitous ways, and how he'd been so secretive but at the same time wanted Tempest to know about a woman she needed to be worried about.

"I believe you know my useless son," said Catriona. "He should be the one standing here holding a knife to your throat. When you began looking into your mother's disappearance five years ago, he was supposed to keep an eye on you to see if you'd make the connection to me. But the damn fool fell in love with you instead."

"Mother, you don't need to do this. There's no more live camera feed. They don't know anything about us, so they won't be able to find us. Let's just get out of here. The police will be here soon."

"The police are arresting Officer Quinn at that pop-up stage right about now, I expect. He'll be telling them about Tansy—that's who he thinks contacted him—so they'll be after her, and they'll be thinking that Tempest detained an innocent woman and wondering how hard they should prosecute her. They'll clean up this mess later."

"Since it's just us," said Tempest, "why don't you tell us what really happened?"

"Right," Catriona scoffed. "My son is right about one thing. We don't know how soon they'll be here."

"If you hurt her," Darius growled, "I will hunt you down."

"Oh, please," said Catriona. "You're a teddy bear. All of you are. Except for former detective Blackburn. Son, keep an eye on that one. I know he doesn't have a gun—I was searching him when I was pretending to squirm as he handcuffed me. But I don't trust him. Use the duct tape on him."

Moriarty grimaced.

"What are you *waiting* for?" Catriona pressed the knife more tightly against Tempest's neck.

"You'll never get out of here if you hurt her," Moriarty said. "Please, Mother. Let her go."

Catriona snorted. "Not likely. You're pathetic. Show some backbone and help your mum."

"You can't do this anymore," Moriarty said softly.

"Where was your conscience when I killed those two horrid men last week?" Catriona shrieked.

Tempest smiled. "We got it. That's the confession we needed." She gripped the blade of the knife—the *fake* knife—and pushed it away from her neck.

"I guess I should tell you," Tempest said to Catriona, "that I swapped your knife for this fake one. When I knelt down at your chair, I substituted it with the closest match among Sanjay's collection of fake knives. Did you really think Blackburn had missed that when he searched you? *Tsk, tsk.*"

Catriona gaped at the plastic knife in her hand, then dropped it as a sick smile formed on her lips.

Why was she so pleased with herself?

"Search her more carefully," Tempest blurted out. "Make sure she's not hiding any weapons you missed."

"No matter," Catriona said, as Darius yanked her away from Tempest and patted her down. "*Och*, you don't have to be so rough with me. I'm not hiding anything else. I'm simply pleased with your incompetence. You *dinnae* have anything recorded! You have *nothing*." She spat out the last word. "My son broke your camera. You didn't get a confession on tape."

"We have a backup." Sanjay smirked.

"You mean this one?" Moriarty held up the broken fragments of the video camera Sanjay had hidden in the A/V booth.

Sanjay's eyes bulged and he choked out a strangled "*No!*" Ivy gasped. Blackburn groaned. Darius growled. It was a veritable cacophony of frustration, but none of their sounds made any difference. *Neither* recording had captured Catriona's confession. Their carefully constructed plan was falling apart.

Darius wound duct tape around Catriona's wrists more tightly than was necessary for security. Unlike her handcuff confinement, this time she squirmed like she meant it. "This is all your fault!" she screamed at Moriarty.

"You see what I have to put up with?" Moriarty said to Tempest. He slipped into the shadows as Darius moved to duct-tape his wrists as well.

Darius grasped the curtains Moriarty had stepped behind. "Where the hell did he go?"

"Don't worry about him," said Tempest.

"I hope you're right." Blackburn stepped onto the stage from the wings. "He took our phones, and it looks like he slipped out the greenroom window."

"Dammit," Sanjay murmured. "My lucky illustration from a fan is on that phone case."

"More importantly," Tempest said as she rolled her eyes at

Sanjay, "we can still prove our case against Catriona, even without things being broadcast." Her voice conveyed a confidence she didn't feel.

"Um, you guys?" said Gideon. "I didn't have time to tell you this before we got started, but my neighbor Reggie helped me buy a cell phone this afternoon." He held up a slim phone that looked so out of place in his calloused stonemason's hands. "I started recording as soon as everyone else tossed their phones aside. Nobody was looking my way. Everyone knows I don't own a cell phone, so she overlooked me. I started a livestream as soon as Ivy's phone was smashed. Reggie showed me how to do that too."

Tempest blinked at him—and, as she now knew, at the camera. "Everything was recorded after all?"

"No," Catriona murmured. "No!"

"There are hundreds of comments popping up." Gideon held the edge of the phone like it was dipped in poison. "I think that means it's working? They keep coming. Um, how do you deal with this?"

"This is not happening," Catriona howled.

"Gideon," said Tempest, "I could kiss you."

Sanjay scowled. "Let's not." He gestured toward Gideon's phone. "You can't leave our viewers waiting. Our audience needs the final wrap-up."

"I believe that's my cue," said a newcomer. Nicodemus stepped onto the stage.

Chapter 52

ello, Cat," said Nicodemus, as he walked to center stage. He was dressed in a white tuxedo, which matched his white hair and goatee, and black-and-white wing-tip shoes.

Catriona's face was crimson with anger. She didn't speak, but if her glare could have killed, Nicodemus would have gone up in a puff of smoke.

It hadn't been a conscious decision for Tempest to leave Nicodemus out of the story she spun for the audience. She told herself it was because it was too complicated to introduce a second booby-trap maker into the equation. Catriona was the main culprit, so it was simplest to explain it to her audience that way. But now that he was here, what was he going to reveal?

Gideon handed his phone to Ivy so she could keep recording and actually get the right people in the frame.

Nicodemus glanced at the camera as it changed hands, then looked to Tempest. "It's time for the truth to come out. You have no idea how sorry I am that I didn't have the strength to tell you this earlier, but it's time." He spun on his heel toward the camera and gave a slight bow. "Good evening. I'm Nicodemus. Just Nicodemus. I was watching this evening's entertainment, so I know you've heard about me. But Tempest's neutral words were far more than I deserve. I'd like to fill in the gaps in Tempest's true story. She figured it out. I'm simply here to tell you the last few details."

Gideon had been scribbling a few words in his notebook and held it up for Tempest to see. *Did you know he was coming?* She gave a small shake of her head in response. *What was he planning?*

"You'll never see him," Catriona blurted out to Nicodemus. "If you say one more word, I'll hide him away so you'll never get to meet him."

Nicodemus shook his head sadly. "Cat. It's been thirty years. I'm an old fool in many ways, but I'm not *that* daft. You've been stringing me along this whole time with the threat of never letting me meet my son. But he's a grown man now. Whether he chooses to introduce himself to his father or not is his choice. Whatever you do, it won't affect that."

"Son?" Sanjay repeated. "I didn't know you—ohhhh . . ."

Tempest's whole body buzzed. She had never even considered the possibility. "Moriarty," Tempest said. Moriarty was Nicodemus and Cat's son. And she still didn't know his real name.

Ivy's eyes grew wide, and her unsteady hands shook Gideon's phone, but she kept recording.

"Moriarty?" Nicodemus squinted at Tempest.

"You missed the last part of the recording before you got here?" she asked him.

"I did." He frowned. "My son is *here*? And his name is *Moriarty*?"

"He was here a few minutes ago," said Tempest. "And that's not exactly his name . . . He slipped out through the greenroom window." She realized that even though Moriarty had spoken when he showed them the smashed backup video camera, he hadn't ever stepped onto the stage. So Gideon's clandestine recording wouldn't have captured anything besides his voice anyway.

Nicodemus laughed without humor. "I suppose this is the part of the performance in which I say I have nothing left to lose. So I should tell you—"

"Don't!" screamed Catriona. "I was tricked into confessing, but it was a lie. I was trying to escape. Nobody will believe the words of a kidnap victim. I said what I had to so they'd let me escape! They don't know anything."

"It's over, Cat," Nicodemus said calmly. "I'm sorry I didn't put an end to your deviousness long ago, before you killed more people."

"Deviousness?" Catriona's face twisted in anger. "You're calling *me* devious? You're the one who stole my ideas and handed them to those dull Raj sisters."

"They were *our* ideas," said Nicodemus, "but you're right. I should have asked your permission or changed the illusions enough to make them mine. I understand why you wrecked their show thirty years ago."

Tempest gasped. "It was *you*," she said to Cat. "The Selkie Sisters show that went wrong and caused a rift between my mom and aunt. Long before you killed anyone, you made my mom believe in the Raj family curse. That's why she stopped performing magic and ran away to California."

All the little things that had never made sense. All the questions her family had deflected because they either didn't know or had wanted to put behind them.

"You should be thanking me," said Cat. "You would never have been born without me."

"If it had stopped there," said Nicodemus, "we would all have understood. You were wronged. By me. You lashed out. You frightened two young women, but nobody got hurt. But you couldn't stop there. You left for Canada with our son, whom I didn't yet know existed. Elspeth Raj became successful in Scotland, which made you angry. And when the largest show to date was debuting ten years ago, you read that she would be performing an illusion similar to the one you and I created together. Why couldn't you let it go? Did you do it to hurt me most of all?"

Cat glared at him but didn't speak.

"Did you know I was in the audience that night you killed Elspeth?" Nicodemus asked. "Like everyone else, I believed it was an accident until you asked for my help to cover it up—telling me, for the first time, about our son. It was smart of you to bring a copy of the birth certificate with the date of birth, but with his name blacked out and no father listed. I wouldn't have believed you otherwise. You promised you'd introduce us if I helped you cover up your crime. I did so, but you never followed through. I was now complicit, so you had me trapped.

"Then a little over five years ago," Nicodemus continued, "Elspeth's sister Emma figured out her sister's death wasn't an accident. She was going to reveal the identity of her sister's killer. But you killed her first."

"You didn't have to do it," Tempest cut in. "I don't believe my mom ever realized that the Cat of Nine Lives was the killer. She believed it was Nicodemus. And she thought she was safe because he was on tour, performing in northern Scotland when she staged her midnight performance. She knew there was no way Nicodemus could get to Hidden Creek to stop her or hurt her. But she was wrong about him. Nicodemus isn't a murderer. But you, Cat? All you had to do was get in a car and drive down from Canada. You thought you were about to be revealed as a killer, but you never were. You didn't have to kill her."

Sirens sounded in the distance.

"But you were afraid," Tempest continued. "Afraid, just like you were this year, when I was investigating what happened to both my mom and my aunt. You were afraid I'd do the exact same thing my mom set out to do. If I was the person who was killed, the investigation would point to the fact that I was looking into their deaths, which could lead back to you. You must've been even more worried when you learned Secret Staircase Construction was being sued by a devious man who liked to leverage information. He had access to my research. He could have figured out the truth too. But he was only tangentially related to me. If he were to die, you could kill two birds with one stone. One—" She held up her index finger. "Remove a person who had access to my research. Two—" She held up a second finger. "Shut down the theater that might still have evidence of your past crime. Did you kill her on the Shadow Stage? Is there still evidence there?"

"It was *underneath* the stage," Nicodemus said softly. "The same way the stagehand was killed all those years ago. From what Cat told me afterward, that was the safest place. Where they wouldn't know to look."

The sirens grew louder.

"Did you think I'd give up?" Tempest stared at Catriona, barely able to speak. "It wasn't a very well-thought-out plan. Unless you think I'm that stupid."

A smile curled on Cat's lips. "Oh, you are."

A shadow shifted behind Cat. The shadow of a man who wasn't supposed to be there.

Moriarty sliced through the duct tape on her wrists. He was careful to keep his face hidden from the camera, but Tempest knew him well enough at this point to identify him. He hadn't left through the greenroom window. That was misdirection.

"Come on," Moriarty whispered to his mom, grabbing her wrist. "We need to go."

"I don't think so." Cat grabbed the knife in Moriarty's hand that he'd used to cut her free. He didn't want to let go, but she twisted his little finger backward until it cracked and he gasped in pain, loosening his grip.

Cat grasped the knife and flew at Nicodemus. Tempest reacted before her brain could catch up with what she was doing. She crashed into Catriona and, taking hold of her arm, flipped her onto her back. But Cat didn't fight clean. Keeping hold of the knife in one hand, she grabbed hold of Tempest's hair and wrapped it around her fist.

Darius and Blackburn ran forward, but the two women flipped over once more, landing several feet from where the two men had pounced. This time, it was Tempest who landed on her back. In the moment Tempest had her breath knocked out of her, Catriona released Tempest's hair and raised the knife over her head.

Tempest's dad pulled Tempest backward to safety as Blackburn lunged for Cat, but Cat spun on her heel, out of his grasp—and closer to Tempest. A third man stepped in front of Tempest, shielding her, and Cat plunged the knife into Nicodemus's chest.

As Nicodemus collapsed onto the stage floor, Cat backed off stage, keeping hold of the knife. "I won't hesitate to use this again."

Tempest saw both her dad and Blackburn flexing to charge Cat, but she knew if they did that one of them was going to get stabbed. She couldn't look at Nicodemus or she'd fall apart. She could help him in a moment. She had to stop Cat first.

Tempest launched into a flip that ended with a kick to Cat's nose. Cat cried out in pain and dropped the knife. Darius tackled her, and Blackburn wrapped her entire body in duct tape.

Tempest turned around to see Nicodemus in Moriarty's arms on the floor of the stage.

"She never told me it was you." Moriarty wiped Nicodemus's brow. "I would have reached out to you if I'd known."

Tempest knelt and took Nicodemus's hand.

"I never meant—" Nicodemus paused to cough up blood as he laughed weakly. "I never meant to be this heroic." Blood was spreading across his chest. "I'm sorry. Both of you. I'm so sorry." He looked from Moriarty to Tempest with the hint of a serene smile on his lips, then closed his eyes.

Blackburn finished securing the screaming Catriona and rushed to inspect Nicodemus's stab wound. He shook his head as a swarm of police and paramedics rushed into the theater.

Nicodemus isn't able to write the truth in the first person. His first-person identity is Nicodemus the Necromancer, the performer. He is comfortable saying "I" when it comes to his stage persona. But he cannot bring himself to write the truth as if he's the one confessing.

He wishes he felt more of a sense of relief now that Tempest knows the truth about him. But he is not that brave. He is a coward, if he is honest with himself. He has stolen ideas. He has enabled the stealing of lives. His misdeeds have enabled him to remain close to Tempest, whom he loves, and to her mother and aunt, whom he loved as well.

He helped Cat cover up her crimes in hopes he would have a relationship with his son. But now he no longer believes the young man exists. He thinks it is possible that Cat faked the boy's birth certificate and baby photos. He would be happy to meet the lad, even once, before he dies. But even that is a fanciful dream. One he knows he does not deserve.

Nicodemus never knew how to dispose of Elspeth's

hand. Cat was convinced there were scrapings of her own skin under Elspeth's fingernails, or on Emma's body that she had hidden. So he did the only thing he could think to do. When you're a stage magician who goes by the name of Nicodemus the Necromancer, nobody questions the use of skeletons in your collection. Of course they are fake. Only Nicodemus's aren't. He has kept Elspeth's hand bones and Emma's skeleton as his beloved automata in his magic workshop in Leith. Elspeth's hand writes messages, and Emma tells fortunes.

He cannot verbalize the words to explain this to Tempest, how he believes he kept Emma and Elspeth as safe as he could, and that in his magic workshop, they are loved. But he can write these words. Writing the words in the third person, in his journal, in the shadow pages where he writes the truth, separate from the first-person narration he collects in his journal for his memoir.

He hasn't yet decided which version of his memoir will be published. Now he knows how to decide—by giving the choice to someone else. Perhaps the one person in the world he truly trusts. Once he's finished writing these words, he will pack his leather-bound journals into a package and mail them all to Tempest. She can decide which truth the world will hear.

Nicodemus sets down his pen and smiles. Perhaps he is happy with this turn of events after all. Not his mistakes of the past, but that Tempest finally knows the truth. He hopes it will set her free.

He imagines what her final show will look like. Tempest will take a bow as the audience rises to a standing ovation. The spotlight half blinds her, as it always does.

She can't see her dad, her grandparents, or her friends, but she knows they are there. He imagines that one of them has snuck in Abracadabra for the event. That animal is smarter than any rabbit he's ever encountered, and it's a shame Tempest doesn't believe in using animals in her performances.

In the spotlight, Tempest spins and spins. She has always loved the physicality of performance. She has told the world what happened to Emma and Elspeth, and laid the Raj family curse to rest for good. She is ready to create her own story. The eldest child *is freed* by magic.

Chapter 53

The package arrived at Fiddler's Folly the next morning, when Tempest was sitting on the tree house deck, still feeling numb after hearing that Nicodemus didn't pull through. He died as he lived, in the spotlight.

Abra hopped from Tempest's lap to the floor as her dad handed her the heavy package. Before she could open it, her phone rang. No image appeared on the screen, but since Ivy's phone had been broken beyond repair, Tempest expected it was Ivy calling from a different phone.

"I'm so sorry," a sad, deep voice said.

Moriarty.

Tempest left the package on the floor of the deck, scooped Abra into her arm, and slipped down the stairs. "I'm putting Abra back in his hutch," she called over her shoulder. "Back in a minute."

Moriarty, whose real name she still didn't know, had slipped away last night while all the attention was focused on attempting to save Nicodemus and arresting Catriona. His mother.

"I didn't think she'd hurt anyone else," he continued. "I was only trying to free her so we could get away."

"I wish I could believe you." Tempest trudged up the sloping hillside to the unfinished Secret Fort, which housed Abra's hutch and would one day be the start of Tempest's own small home.

"I swear it, Tempest. I know this will be hard for you to understand because you have such a loving, functional family, who you can count on in spite of their quirks. But even after I found out what my mother had done, I couldn't turn her in."

"You might not believe this," said Tempest, "but I understand more than you could possibly know."

Tempest still hadn't told anyone that Nicodemus had been the one to booby-trap the theater door to injure himself just enough to get his tour canceled. She couldn't articulate why, even to herself, but perhaps she was speaking to the one person who would understand her complicated feelings about her former mentor.

"I tried to help him in those last moments," said Moriarty. "I really did. She never told me he was my . . . She never even hinted at it. And I never knew what she'd done to your mom and aunt until afterward when she needed my help. She confessed, then, that she'd been forced to kill two people who'd stolen her illusions."

"You knew she was a magician?"

"She was still working as a magic builder when I grew up. Never on the stage, only behind the scenes. She made it sound like your mom and aunt had wanted to destroy her, that they were both responsible for ruining her stage career and that they were about to claim my mother's latest inventions as their own. I didn't condone what she'd done, but she'd already done it. She made it sound like if I didn't help her keep an eye on you, she'd have no choice but to kill again."

"You could have turned her in. But no, that's not your style. You're your mother's son. You're not above killing either."

He paused for so long that she wondered if he'd hung up.

"That," he said, "was self-defense. Or a defense of you, however you'd like to think of it. But you know it's true that I acted in your best interest. And I couldn't have turned in my mother when she told me only the basic facts. I didn't really know anything. Not until I started looking into it more this year."

He'd even told her what he was doing at the time. Before she knew his connection to any of this.

"I can work remotely from anywhere," he said, "so when my mother asked me to keep an eye on you, it was easy."

"You don't sound too broken up over her arrest. She's never getting out of jail. Though she's probably attempting to get a plea deal by giving you up."

"I doubt that. But even if she does, she doesn't know where I live. She considered it a betrayal that I protected you instead of killing you when I had the chance. At that point, I thought it better to make sure she didn't know how to find me if I didn't want her to. Still, I thought it was better for me if she wasn't caught and didn't have an incentive to turn me in. Last night, I only wanted to help her get away."

"But your heart wasn't in it. You knew neither of us would be safe if she was free. That's why your main objective was to stop the filming. You didn't want to be on camera."

Moriarty chuckled. "I never guessed that Gideon would have gotten himself a cell phone. You got your recording after all."

"There are no images of you. You stayed in the shadows."

"Until I went to help Nicodemus." His voice broke. Was it an act, or was he truly choked up?

"The new phone had fallen to the floor at that point."

"I wasn't even thinking of that. I was only thinking of saving him. But I failed."

"I'm not so sure. I don't think I've ever seen him look so peaceful as when the two of us were there at his side at the end. His health was already failing. He knew it. He wasn't sure he'd be able to go through with his farewell tour even before his injury."

"Why, Tempest, I do believe you're trying to cheer me up."

By the time Tempest returned to the tree house deck, Ash had laid out a full brunch spread, and the first of her friends had arrived.

Sanjay pulled her into a bear hug. "What's with the big box?"

"I don't know," she said. "Let's find out."

She opened it up and found Nicodemus's journals. "His memoirs. I never knew if he was really working on them or if it was just talk."

"He wanted you to have them." Morag squeezed Tempest's waist and rested her head on Tempest's shoulder. "He died saving you."

"To Nicodemus," said Ash, raising a mug.

Tempest found her mug on the table and raised it high. "To Nicodemus."

Chapter 54

What do you mean you're not going through with your art show?" Tempest stood in front of Gideon's dragon-mouth mantel carving with her hands on her hips. She raised an eyebrow at him.

"It wasn't my art that caused Trina to recommend me to Tansy's gallery." Gideon looked into the unlit hearth, avoiding her gaze. "She only did it to ingratiate herself with Morag and me, since we're in your inner circle."

"Your art is truly magical, Gideon. It wasn't only Trina. My grandmother was also showing photos of your sculptures to gallery owners."

"But Trina was the one who really pushed the idea on Tansy," Gideon insisted.

"Gideon. Sometimes you just have to accept a bit of luck. Hold the show. See where it goes from there."

He looked up from the fireplace and finally met her gaze. His eyes were still tired, and his face thinner than it should have been, but his smile was genuine. "I'm starving. How about we get out of here and grab some food at Veggie Magic?"

"As long as we can slip out without seeing Reggie."

"He's a good guy, you know."

"That's exactly why I don't want to see him right now. Because I'm starving too."

Gideon's neighbor Reggie, who Gideon publicly acknowledged had taught a luddite how to use a cell phone for their streaming video, was getting a big bonus at work because of how many new customers he was bringing into the cell phone store.

"He wouldn't stop thanking you when I came over," Tempest said. "I'd like to leave before we die of hunger."

After lunch, Gideon left for the gallery to see through the finishing touches of his show, which he agreed not to cancel, and Tempest headed across the Bay Bridge to meet Sanjay for coffee before seeing Ivy's lecture that night.

"This one might be my favorite." Sanjay held up a beautifully illustrated sticker of a man with olive skin and big brown eyes wearing a bowler hat with flowers of all kinds springing from its band. "At least it's my favorite of the ones that arrived today."

Now that Sanjay's fans knew how much he appreciated fan artwork, he was receiving dozens of beautiful pieces of fan art. He was making a collage with the art, which he planned to make as the backdrop of his upcoming stage shows so that audiences would see it as they filed into the theater.

After drinking exquisite, if overpriced, coffee in Sanjay's neighborhood, they headed to the Locked Room Library together.

"Standing room only." Sanjay let out a low whistle. "Nicely done, Ivy Youngblood."

He and Tempest stood in the back and listened as Ivy delivered an expert talk on classic detective fiction.

After the lecture, the enthusiastic audience had so many questions that the trio had to eat a late dinner, but none of them minded. Ivy shared that she'd just heard that an essay she wrote on impossible crimes would be published in a student publication. She only had a few more classes to take to finish her bachelor's degree, and she was excited to be applying to master's programs in library and information science.

When Tempest got home that night, she went to the tree house and accepted a warm mug of turmeric milk from her grandfather, while her dad filled her in on what was happening with the mentorship program. Darius's high school student mentorship program, which had been in danger of fizzling due to the bad press surrounding Secret Staircase Construction, was back on track and had more students applying than it could handle, so he'd added a second cohort. To keep it manageable, he decided that the students would focus on building various magical cabinets and booths for a summer festival coming up in Hidden Creek.

Secret Staircase Construction also had more job inquiries than they could handle, so they were able to take jobs where they could add the most value for clients who wouldn't mistreat or sue them. Even after making referrals to local contractors they trusted, they still had a waiting list that filled at least the next year.

The following week, they got news that Detective Rinehart had resigned. It was embarrassing that Officer Quinn had taken a bribe to make evidence disappear on his watch and that he hadn't seen fit to call in a larger team of law enforcement when he should have.

Former detective Blackburn was asked if he'd be willing to come out of retirement. He'd retired early, disappointed that he'd never solved the case of Emma Raj. But now that he'd learned he hated retirement and he and Tempest had worked together to solve the case that had plagued him, he accepted the offer to be a detective once more.

Moriarty hadn't been seen since that night at the theater. Tempest hadn't heard from him since that phone call, and the number he called from had been disconnected. Catriona was remanded to await trial without bail, and between her confession, the live stabbing of Nicodemus, and all the witnesses, there was no chance she'd ever get out of prison.

The only thing that hadn't been explained was who had left the fake axe hanging in the theater. The two teenagers swore they had only dropped ghostly pieces of gauze from the catwalk for their filming; Catriona had admitted to thrusting a sword through the door to kill Julian, killing Brodie when he tried to blackmail her, and fueling rumors at the theater to confuse things; and Nicodemus's explanation of the two booby traps he set made sense for his goal of having his career go out with a sympathetic bang. There couldn't really be a mischievous theater ghost, could there? Perhaps there were some things she'd never know, and that was okay.

Tempest's manager, Winston Kapoor, was fielding dozens of requests for her to return to the stage, but she'd found her new stage creating architectural misdirection. She'd still perform a farewell show, as promised, which would be a version of the true story she'd told, but with illusions she'd been working on in her notebooks. Her identity wasn't tied to her career, plus she could be more than one thing. The most important thing was that she finally knew what had happened. Her mom and aunt could be laid to rest, and her family could put the Raj family curse behind them.

Chapter 55

One month after the murders at the Whispering Creek Theater, the family gathered at a small service in Edinburgh. Afterward, Morag Ferguson-Raj's musician friends played music at a *ceilidh*, her husband, Ashok, cooked a feast, and hundreds of friends gathered to celebrate the lives of Elspeth and Emma Raj.

Six weeks later, pop-up magic show flyers blanketed Hidden Creek and the details were shared online. Tempest took to the stage of a sold-out performance at the Whispering Creek Theater, this time with multiple professional videographers recording the show. Her dad, Ivy, and Gideon had built the set, her grandmother was accompanying her on the fiddle, and Sanjay filled the role of Tempest's assistant on the stage. With lifelike shadows from paper cutouts dancing across the background, Tempest told the story of the Raj family curse as it began on the southern tip of India, across the ocean to Scottish lochs, and to Hidden Creek's mysterious underground creek, where it was finally laid to rest. Tempest hadn't yet figured out which of Nicodemus's stories she'd reveal, but she felt his influence in her own work as she carried on the tradition of bringing pop-ups and shadows to life.

One of the people in attendance at her show was Lenore

Woods, who'd forgiven Tempest for her accusation, and had come to thank Tempest for her vision for the puzzle room at the Whispering House. Along with Lenore's own renovations to restore the home to its original beauty, Tempest's architectural sleight of hand had won over the local architectural society.

In addition to her role in creating architectural misdirection for Secret Staircase Construction, Tempest was working on plans to build her own house on the site of the Secret Fort at the edge of Fiddler's Folly. The mystery that had dominated her life for years hadn't turned out the way she thought it would, but she was now ready for whatever came next.

Well, *almost* ready. Someone was walking up to the tree house deck where she was enjoying a cup of jaggery coffee with Ivy.

"Enid?" Tempest stood and leaned on the railing. What was the owner of the Locked Room Library doing at Fiddler's Folly?

"Your dad buzzed me in." Enid shielded her eyes from the sun as she looked up at Ivy and Tempest. Dressed in a polka-dot swing dress and peep-toe pumps, Enid was decked out in her usual 1940s-style attire.

"I'm so sorry, Enid." Ivy joined Tempest at the edge of the deck. "Did I miss a shift? I haven't been looking at my phone since I thought I had the day off."

"You didn't miss anything." Enid bit her lip and turned her contorted face to Tempest. "I'm no good at asking for help. I thought it would be easier to explain in person."

"Do you want to come up?" Tempest asked.

"I'd rather you come with me, Tempest. If you can. Something really strange has happened at the library, and it looks impossible . . . I know you've been through a lot, but you're the only one who can help."

Tempest took a deep breath. She hadn't even had time to strike the set of her show, but that could wait. "I'll be right down."

RECIPES

Quick-Cook Dosa

A dosa is a South Indian pancake. This version isn't a traditional dosa, which needs to ferment and can't be enjoyed the same day. This version is a quick variation that approximates the dosa experience when you want to enjoy it at home in just over thirty minutes.

INGREDIENTS

2 Tbsp shredded coconut
2 Tbsp roasted cashews
½ cup rice flour
½ cup semolina
¼ tsp sea salt
2½ cups water
Neutral oil (e.g., canola)

DIRECTIONS

In a spice grinder or small blender, pulverize the coconut and cashews into a fine powder. Mix in a large bowl with the rice flour, semolina flour, and salt. Mix the water in slowly until the batter is smooth. It will be thin, which is perfect. Set aside for 30 minutes.

After 30 minutes, stir the batter and heat a large nonstick skillet on medium heat. Add 2 tsp oil to the pan. Ladle a ½-cup scoop of the thin batter onto the pan, forming a thin crepe-like pancake that nearly fills the pan. Cook for approx. 4–5 minutes until it crisps on the bottom. Flip and cook for another 3 minutes. Repeat with the remainder of the batter.

SERVING SUGGESTION

Dosas are traditionally made with a rice and lentil base and are served with savory fillings. However, with this non-fermented version, which uses rice flour and no added savory spices in the batter, it works well with savory or sweet fillings, much like a crepe.

Below is a chocolate spread that's a great topping for this dosa.

Chocolate Almond Spread

INGREDIENTS

2 cups raw, unsalted almonds
¾ cup dates, pitted
¾ cup almond milk
3 Tbsp cacao powder
1 Tbsp maple syrup

DIRECTIONS

Soak the dates in ½ cup boiling water for 10 minutes. Blend all the ingredients together in a blender (including the water used for soaking the dates). It will take a few minutes, and you might need to scrape the sides of the blender a few times. Blend until smooth. Spread on the dosas above, or onto toasted bread. Enjoy!

Mango Ice Cream

(NO ICE CREAM MAKER REQUIRED)

No ice cream maker? No problem! This dairy-free ice cream is every bit as tasty as fruit-flavored ice creams and much easier to make.

INGREDIENTS

4 cups frozen mango
1 14 oz. can full fat coconut milk, refrigerated
¼ cup maple syrup
1 Tbsp tapioca flour
½ Tbsp vanilla extract
¼ tsp ground cardamom
¼ tsp ground turmeric
Dash of ground pepper

DIRECTIONS

Blend all the ingredients together in a food processor until well blended. Transfer to a freezer-safe container and chill in the freezer for at least six to eight hours. Remove the container from the freezer half an hour before serving to make it easier to scoop.

Find more plant-based recipes on Gigi's website: www.gigipandian .com/recipes.

Acknowledgments

I'm so grateful to so many people who helped with this book!

Thank you to my publishing team at Minotaur Books and the St. Martin's Publishing Group, including Madeline Houpt, Kayla Janas Sarah Melnyk, Mac Nicolas, Gabriel Guma, Benjamin Allen, Ken Silver, and Cathy Turiano, who all do so much behind the scenes. At Macmillan Audio, I'm lucky to have phenomenal audiobook narrator Soneela Nankani as the voice of the Secret Staircase Mysteries, and audiobook producer Elishia Merricks making each book even better than the last. And my brilliant agent Jill Marsal, who's been with me from the start.

I don't know where I'd be without my critique readers, brainstorm partners, and writer pals. There are too many folks to name here (the list would fill a book on its own), but special thanks to Nancy Adams, Juliet Blackwell, Ellen Byron, Shelly Dickson Carr, Kellye Garrett, Jeff Marks, Sujata Massey, Lisa Q. Mathews, Emberly Nesbitt, Brian Selfon, and Diane Vallere. And the mystery writers groups where I find so much camaraderie and learn so much: Crime Writers of Color, Mystery Writers of America, and Sisters in Crime.

Thank you to architectural historian and museum curator Lauren Northup and Cloverdale police chief Jason Ferguson, who generously answered my research questions but also told me not to let how they'd do things get in the way of a good story! And thank you to Catriona McPherson, who set me straight when I misused Scottish expressions. Any liberties and mistakes in these pages are my own.

To the booksellers, librarians, reviewers, podcasters, and bloggers who tell readers about my books, I can't thank you enough.

My family, you're truly the best. Thank you for putting up with me as I disappear into my writing cave for long stretches of time—which I'm doing once more as I work on the *next* Secret Staircase Mystery. Tempest and her Scooby gang have many more mysteries to solve, and I've got so many more stories to tell, so you're in it with me for the long haul.

And last, but far from least, my wonderful readers! It's because of you that I'm lucky enough to be a mystery novelist. Thank you for your continued enthusiasm for my books. I love hearing from you. You can contact me and sign up for my email newsletter at www.gigipandian.com.